AN ORIGINAL GRAPHIC NOVEL

THE DRAGON PRINCE

Bloodmoon HUNT

Story by **AARON EHASZ**
and **JUSTIN RICHMOND**

Written by **NICOLE ANDELFINGER**

Illustrated by **FELIA HANAKATA**

graphix
An Imprint of
SCHOLASTIC

wonderstorm

All rights reserved. Published by Graphix, an imprint of Scholastic Inc.,
Publishers since 1920. SCHOLASTIC, GRAPHIX, and associated logos are
trademarks and/or registered trademarks of Scholastic Inc.

The publisher does not have any control over and does not assume any responsibility
for author or third-party websites or their content.

ISBN 978-1-338-76995-1

10 9 8 7 6 5 4 3 2 1   22 23 24 25 26

Printed in the U.S.A.   40

First edition, July 2022

Edited by Katie Woehr

Book design by Jessica Meltzer

Colors by Arley Nopra

Letters by Olga Andreyeva

Creative director: Yaffa Jaskoll

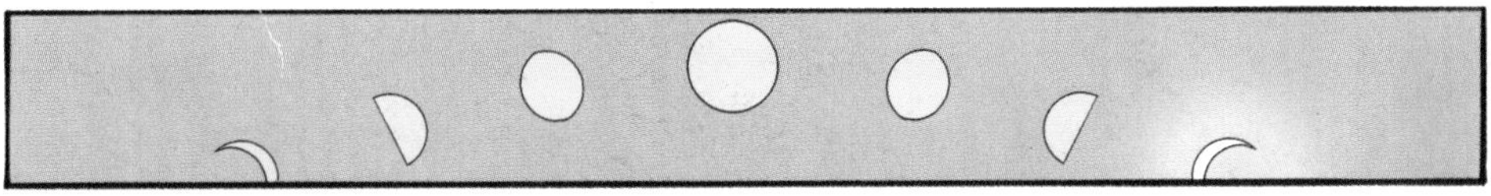

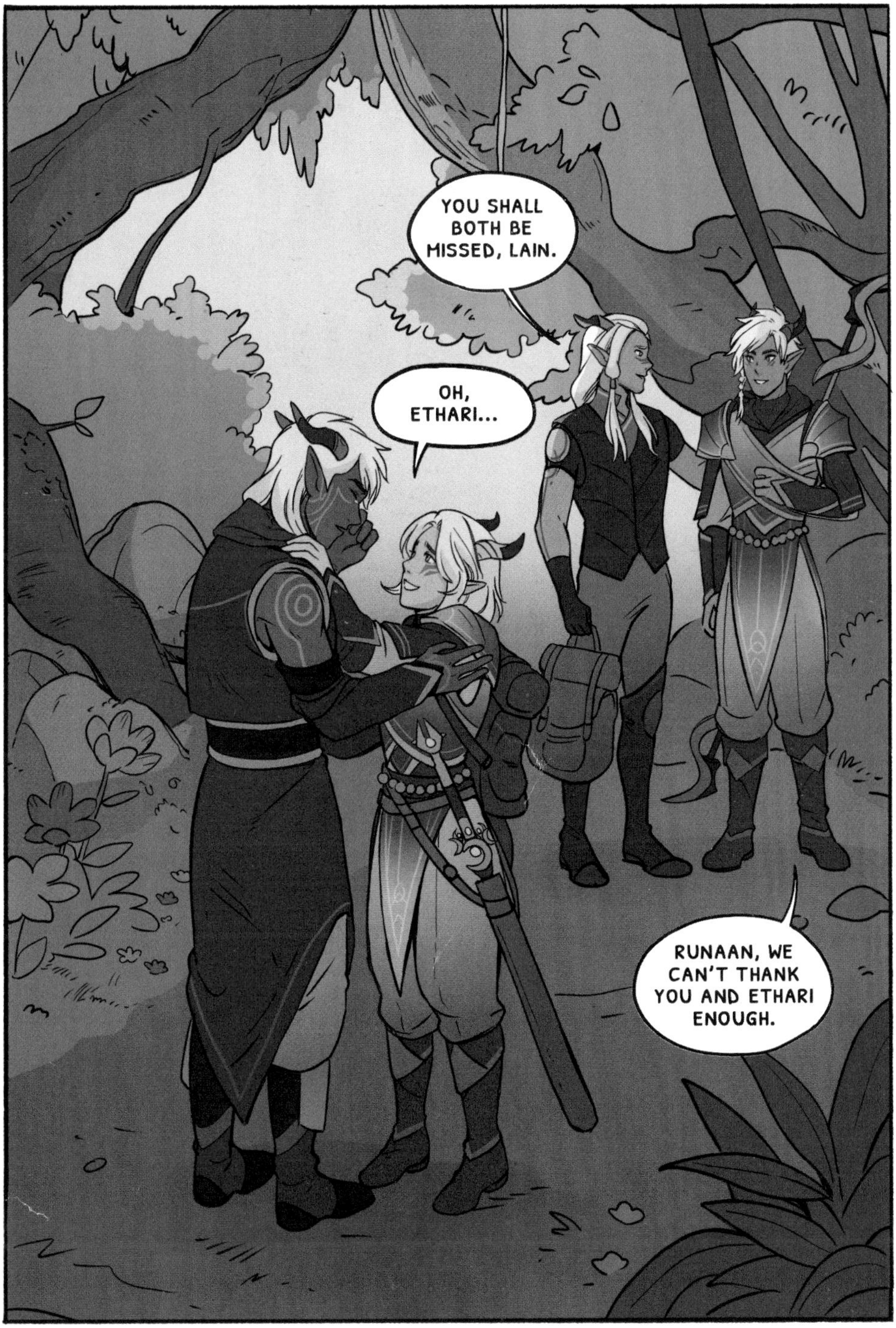
YOU SHALL BOTH BE MISSED, LAIN.
OH, ETHARI...
RUNAAN, WE CAN'T THANK YOU AND ETHARI ENOUGH.

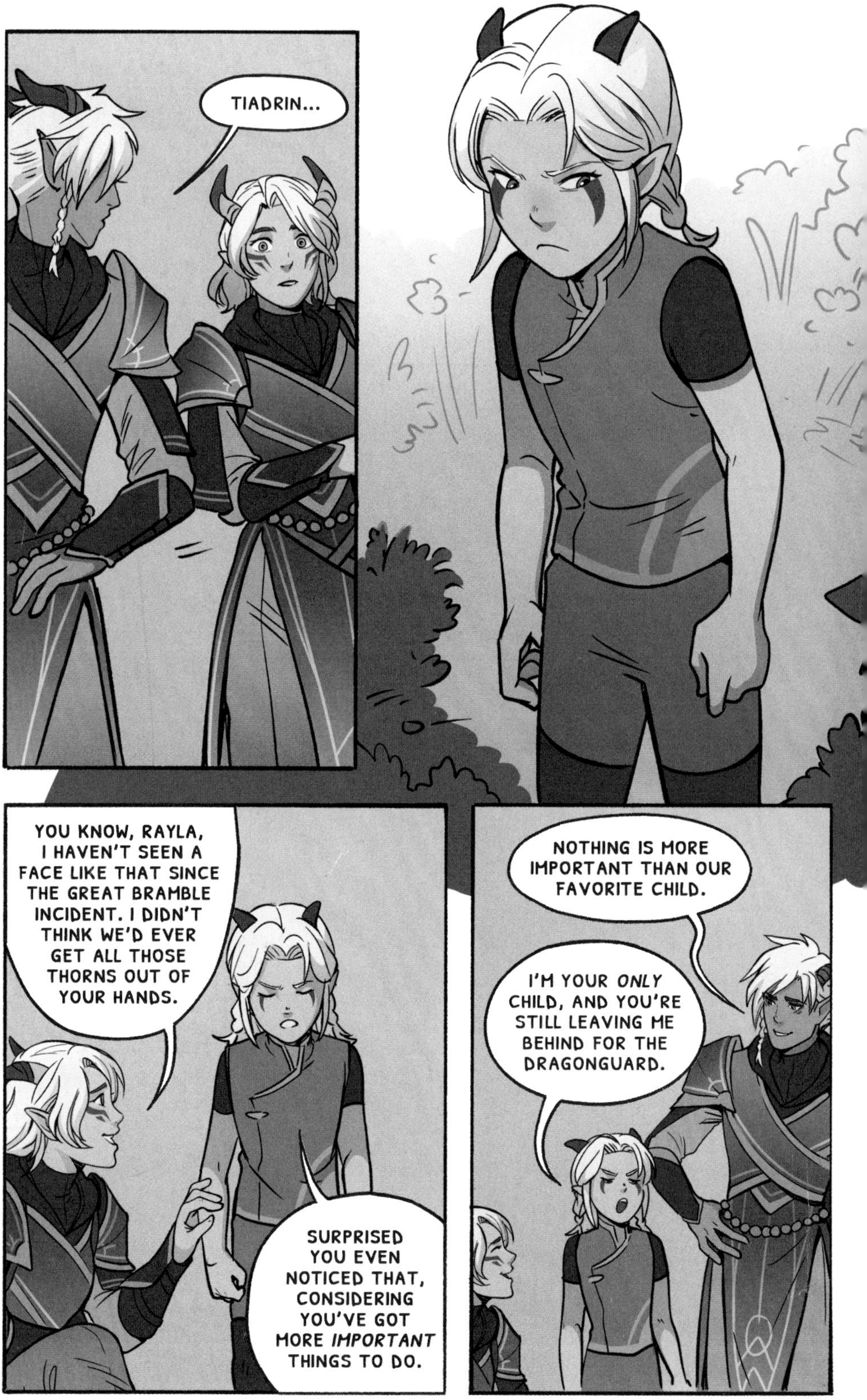
TIADRIN...
YOU KNOW, RAYLA, I HAVEN'T SEEN A FACE LIKE THAT SINCE THE GREAT BRAMBLE INCIDENT. I DIDN'T THINK WE'D EVER GET ALL THOSE THORNS OUT OF YOUR HANDS.
SURPRISED YOU EVEN NOTICED THAT, CONSIDERING YOU'VE GOT MORE *IMPORTANT* THINGS TO DO.
NOTHING IS MORE IMPORTANT THAN OUR FAVORITE CHILD.
I'M YOUR *ONLY* CHILD, AND YOU'RE STILL LEAVING ME BEHIND FOR THE DRAGONGUARD.

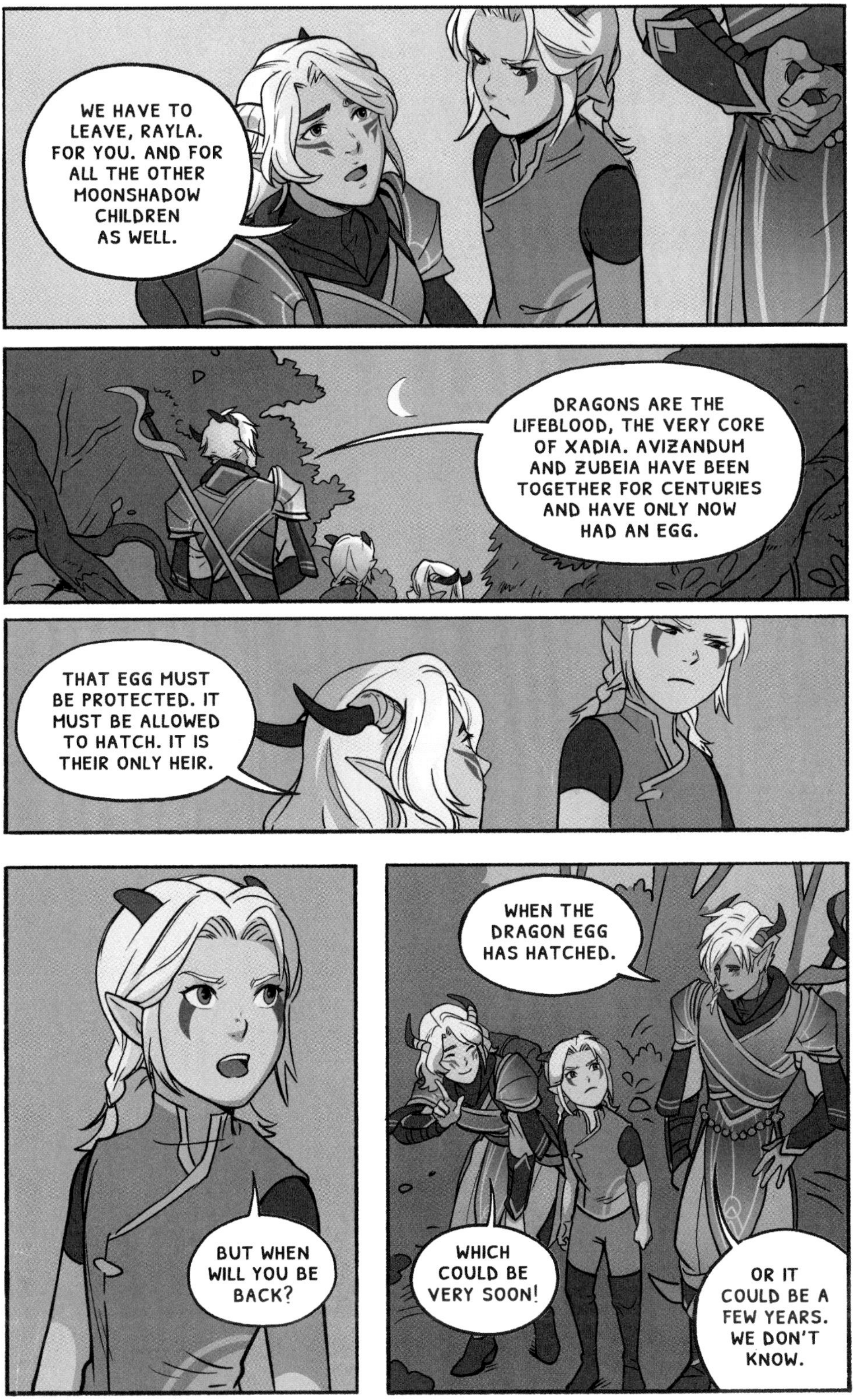
WE HAVE TO LEAVE, RAYLA. FOR YOU. AND FOR ALL THE OTHER MOONSHADOW CHILDREN AS WELL.
DRAGONS ARE THE LIFEBLOOD, THE VERY CORE OF XADIA. AVIZANDUM AND ZUBEIA HAVE BEEN TOGETHER FOR CENTURIES AND HAVE ONLY NOW HAD AN EGG.
THAT EGG MUST BE PROTECTED. IT MUST BE ALLOWED TO HATCH. IT IS THEIR ONLY HEIR.
BUT WHEN WILL YOU BE BACK?
WHEN THE DRAGON EGG HAS HATCHED.
WHICH COULD BE VERY SOON!
OR IT COULD BE A FEW YEARS. WE DON'T KNOW.

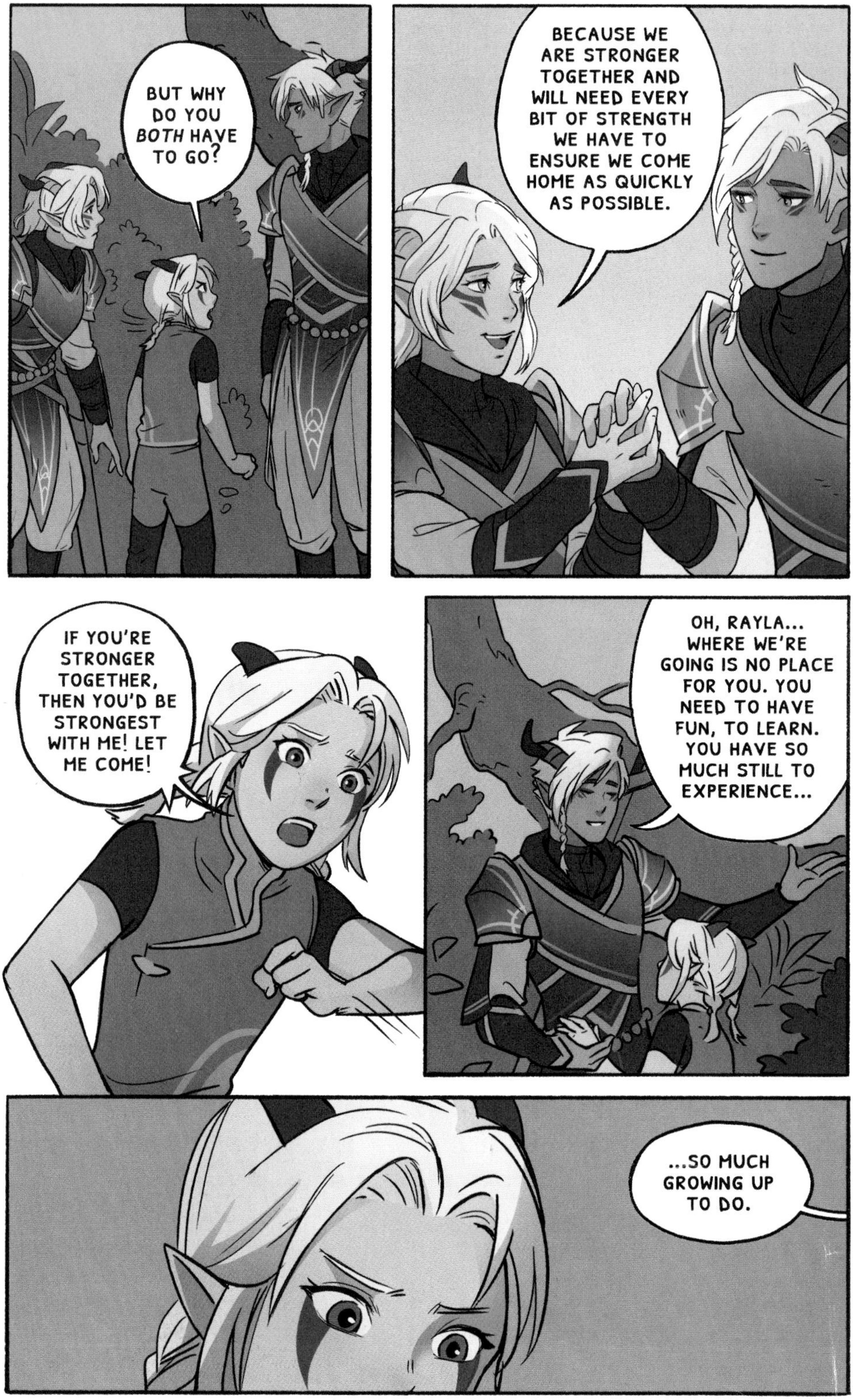
BUT WHY DO YOU *BOTH* HAVE TO GO?
BECAUSE WE ARE STRONGER TOGETHER AND WILL NEED EVERY BIT OF STRENGTH WE HAVE TO ENSURE WE COME HOME AS QUICKLY AS POSSIBLE.
IF YOU'RE STRONGER TOGETHER, THEN YOU'D BE STRONGEST WITH ME! LET ME COME!
OH, RAYLA... WHERE WE'RE GOING IS NO PLACE FOR YOU. YOU NEED TO HAVE FUN, TO LEARN. YOU HAVE SO MUCH STILL TO EXPERIENCE...
...SO MUCH GROWING UP TO DO.

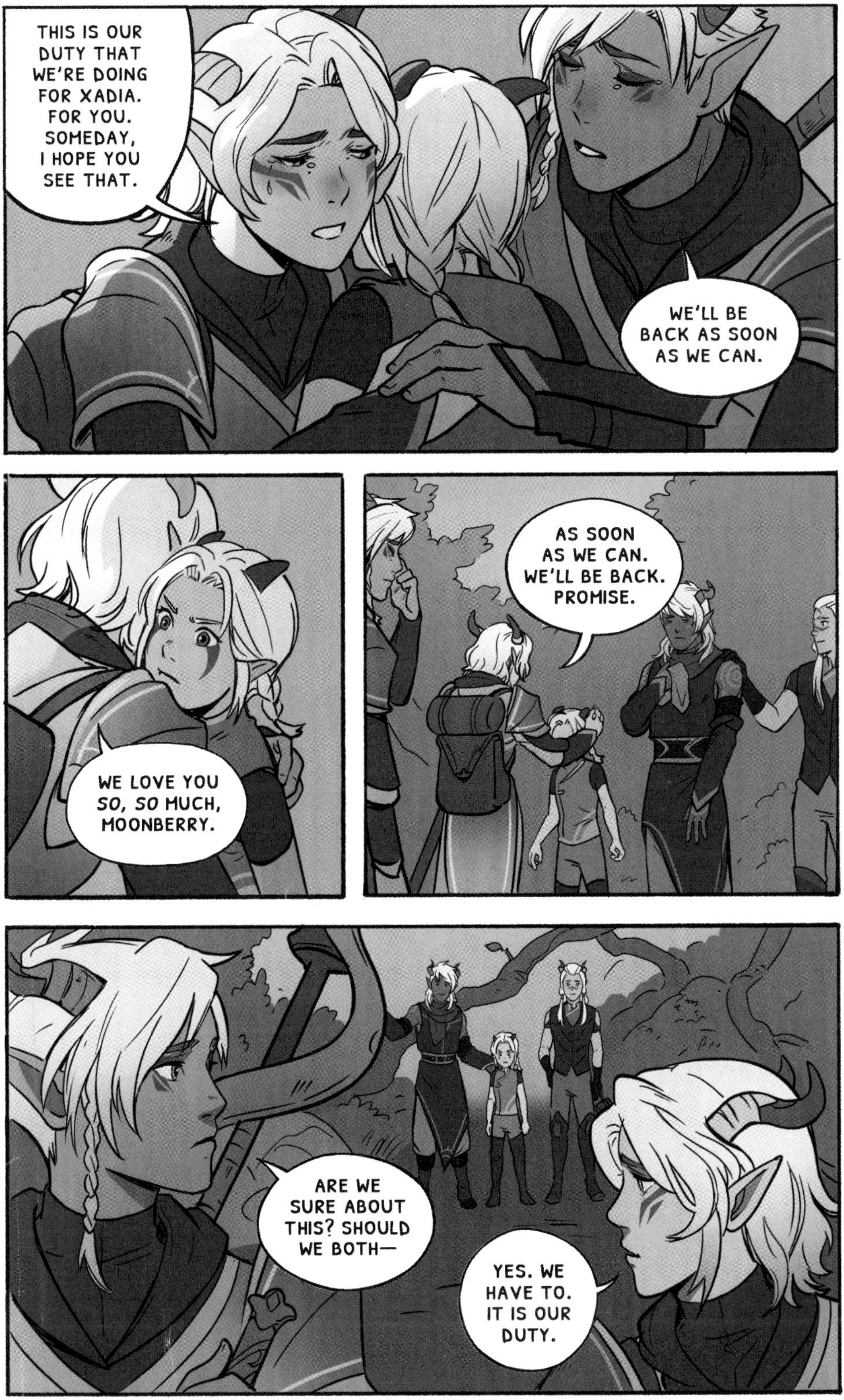
THIS IS OUR DUTY THAT WE'RE DOING FOR XADIA. FOR YOU. SOMEDAY, I HOPE YOU SEE THAT.
WE'LL BE BACK AS SOON AS WE CAN.
WE LOVE YOU *SO, SO* MUCH, MOONBERRY.
AS SOON AS WE CAN. WE'LL BE BACK. PROMISE.
ARE WE SURE ABOUT THIS? SHOULD WE BOTH—
YES. WE HAVE TO. IT IS OUR DUTY.

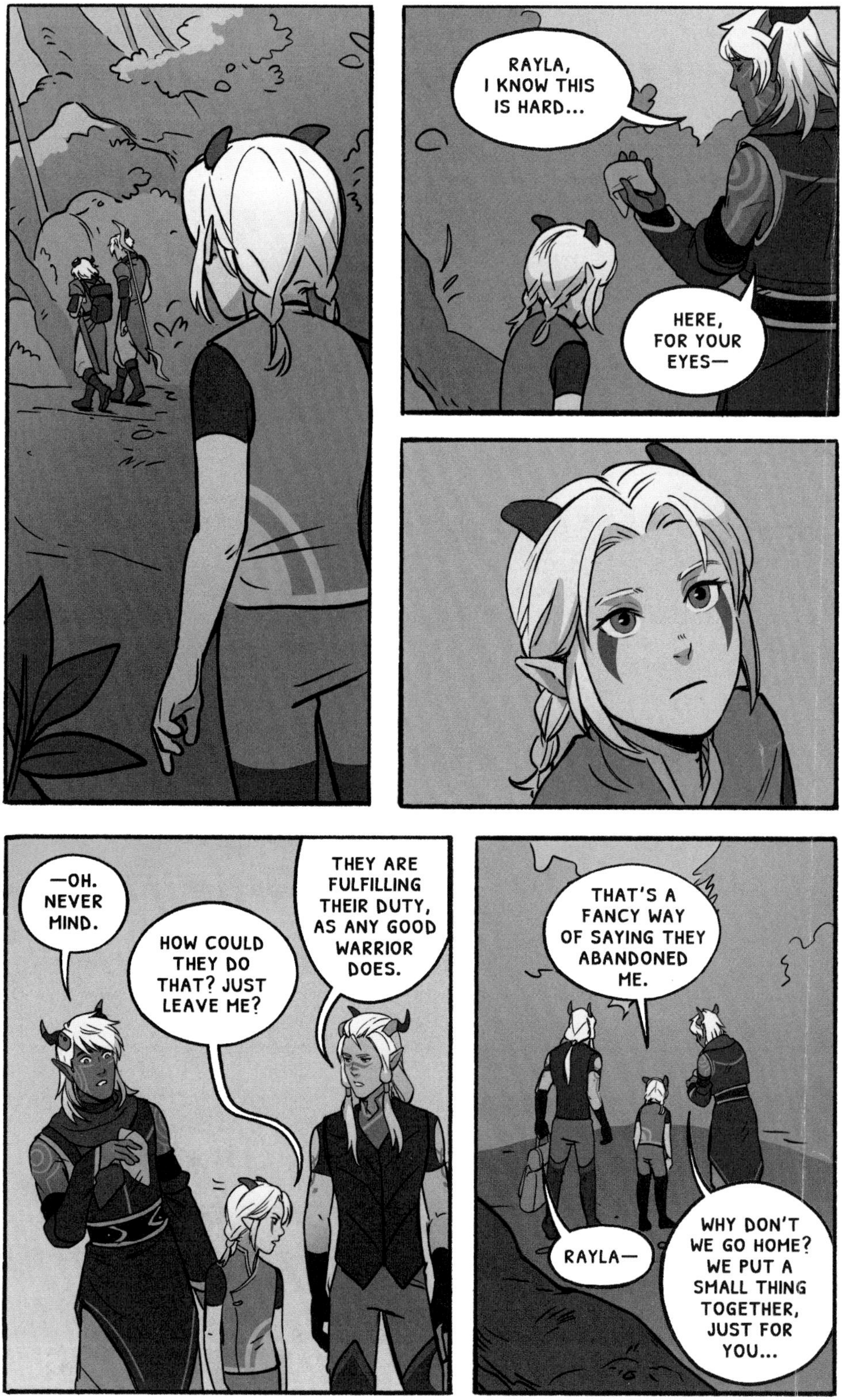
RAYLA, I KNOW THIS IS HARD...
HERE, FOR YOUR EYES—
—OH. NEVER MIND.
HOW COULD THEY DO THAT? JUST LEAVE ME?
THEY ARE FULFILLING THEIR DUTY, AS ANY GOOD WARRIOR DOES.
THAT'S A FANCY WAY OF SAYING THEY ABANDONED ME.
RAYLA—
WHY DON'T WE GO HOME? WE PUT A SMALL THING TOGETHER, JUST FOR YOU...

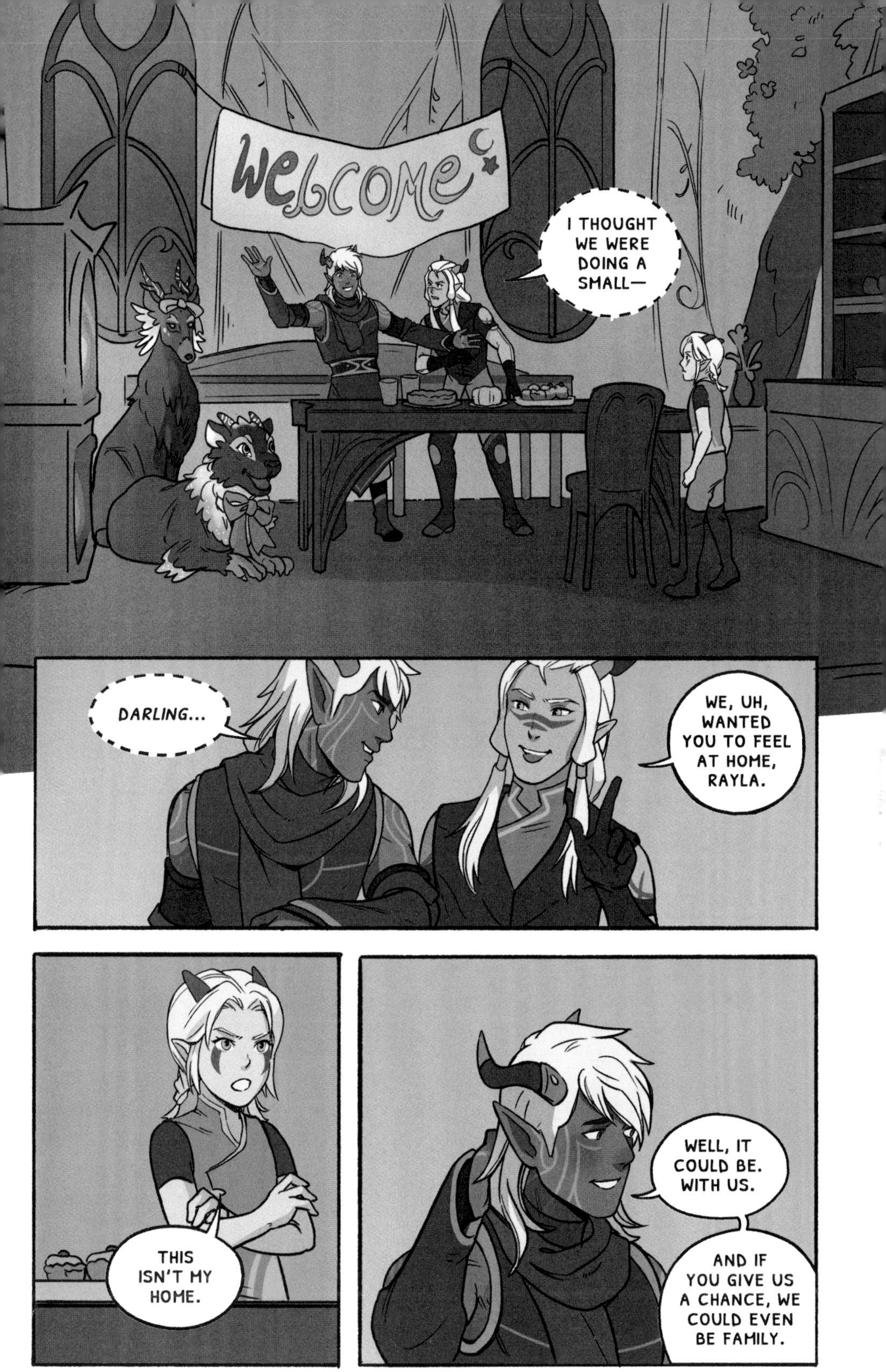
WELCOME
I THOUGHT WE WERE DOING A SMALL—
DARLING...
WE, UH, WANTED YOU TO FEEL AT HOME, RAYLA.
THIS ISN'T MY HOME.
WELL, IT COULD BE. WITH US.
AND IF YOU GIVE US A CHANCE, WE COULD EVEN BE FAMILY.

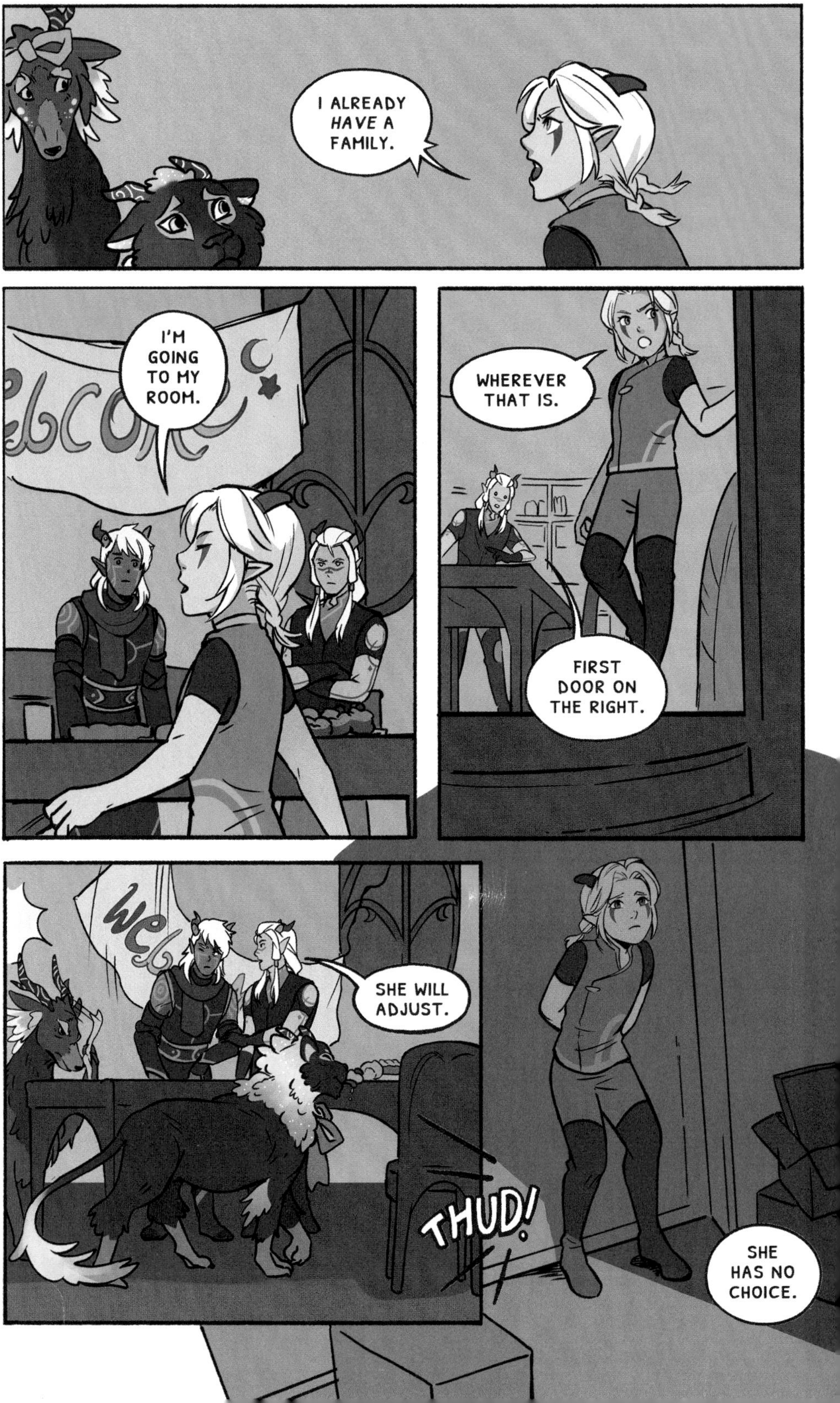
I ALREADY HAVE A FAMILY.
I'M GOING TO MY ROOM.
WHEREVER THAT IS.
FIRST DOOR ON THE RIGHT.
SHE WILL ADJUST.
THUD!
SHE HAS NO CHOICE.

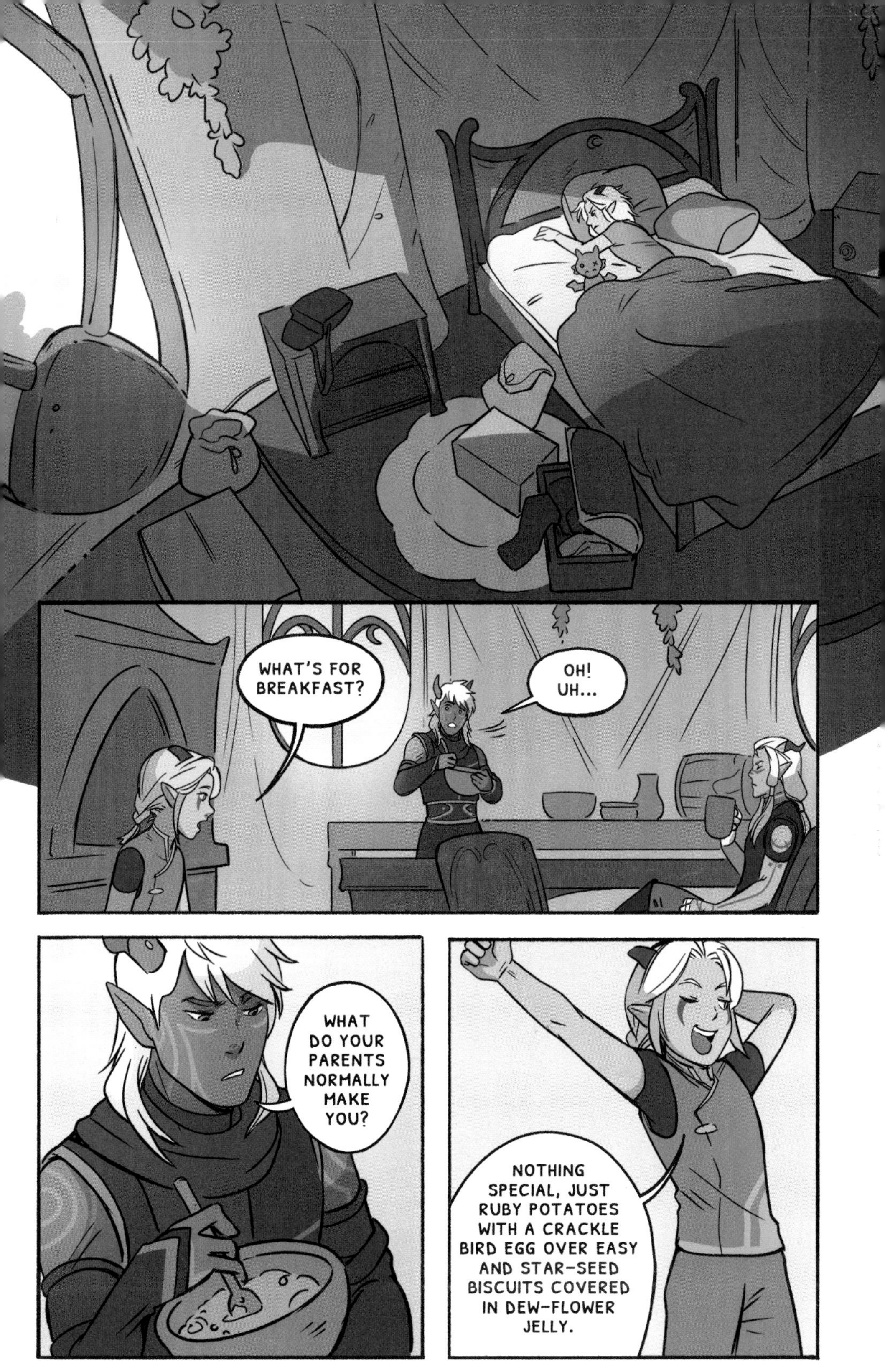
WHAT'S FOR BREAKFAST?
OH! UH...
WHAT DO YOUR PARENTS NORMALLY MAKE YOU?
NOTHING SPECIAL, JUST RUBY POTATOES WITH A CRACKLE BIRD EGG OVER EASY AND STAR-SEED BISCUITS COVERED IN DEW-FLOWER JELLY.

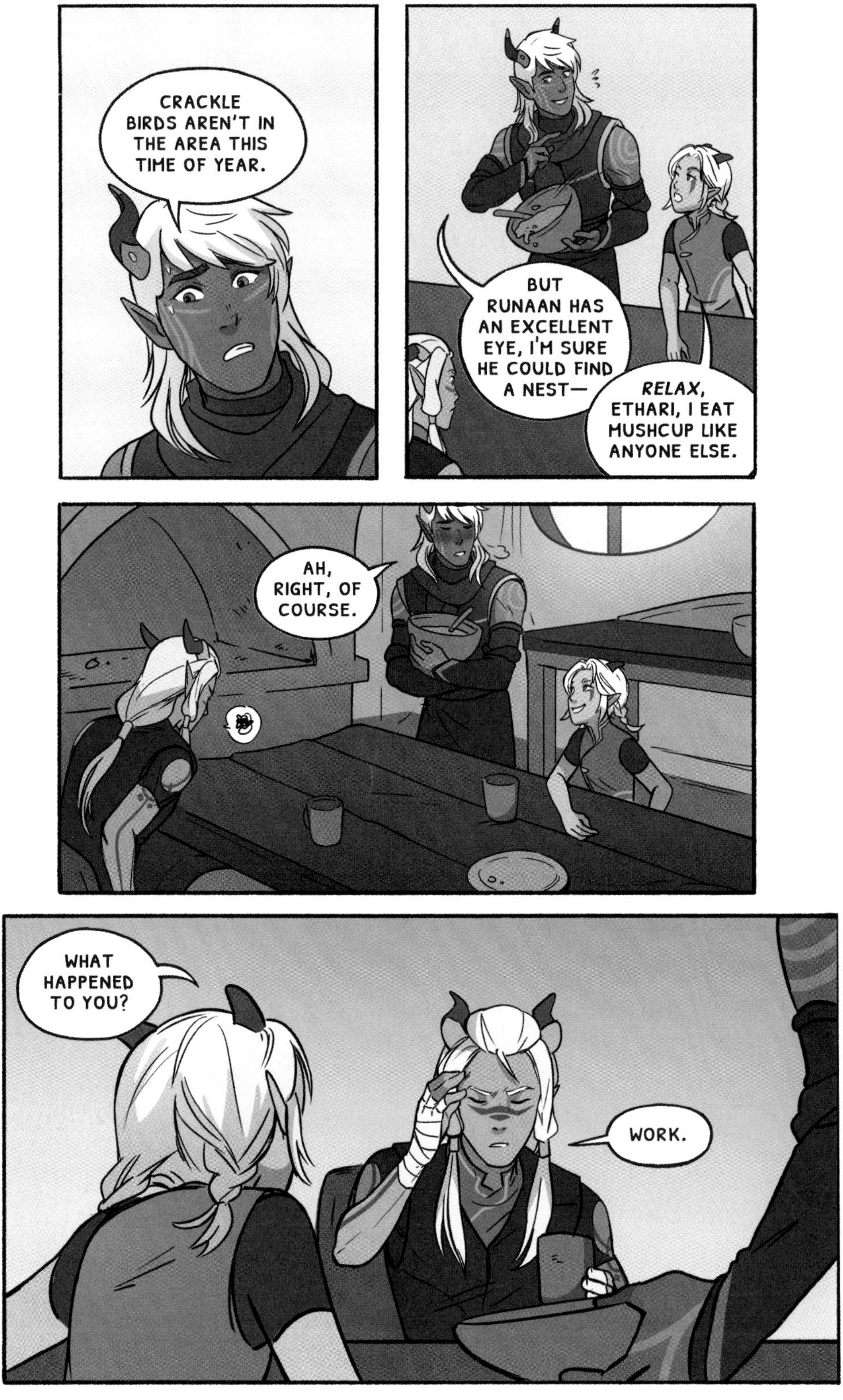
CRACKLE BIRDS AREN'T IN THE AREA THIS TIME OF YEAR.
BUT RUNAAN HAS AN EXCELLENT EYE, I'M SURE HE COULD FIND A NEST—
RELAX, ETHARI, I EAT MUSHCUP LIKE ANYONE ELSE.
AH, RIGHT, OF COURSE.
WHAT HAPPENED TO YOU?
WORK.

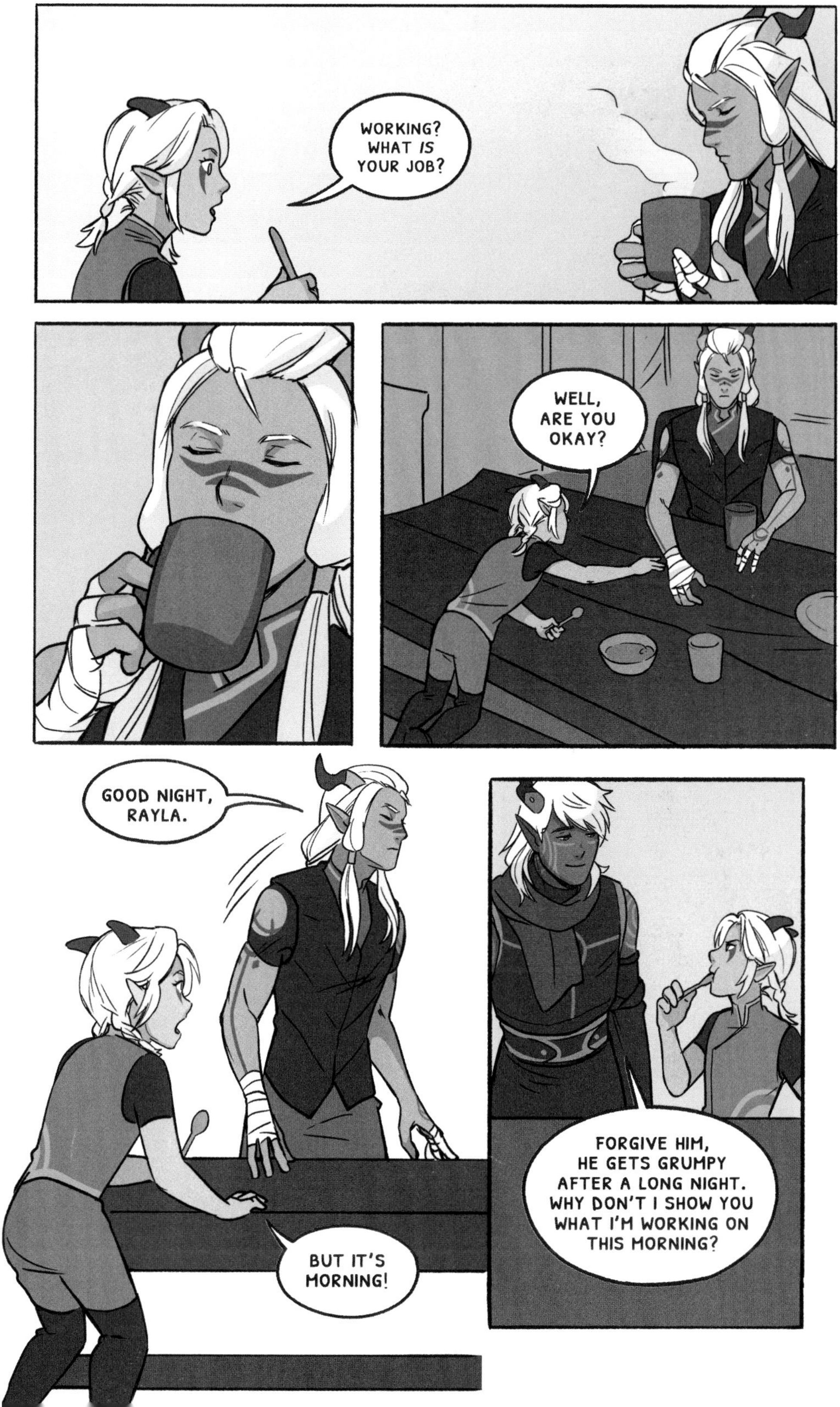
WORKING? WHAT *IS* YOUR JOB?
WELL, ARE YOU OKAY?
GOOD NIGHT, RAYLA.
BUT IT'S MORNING!
FORGIVE HIM, HE GETS GRUMPY AFTER A LONG NIGHT. WHY DON'T I SHOW YOU WHAT I'M WORKING ON THIS MORNING?

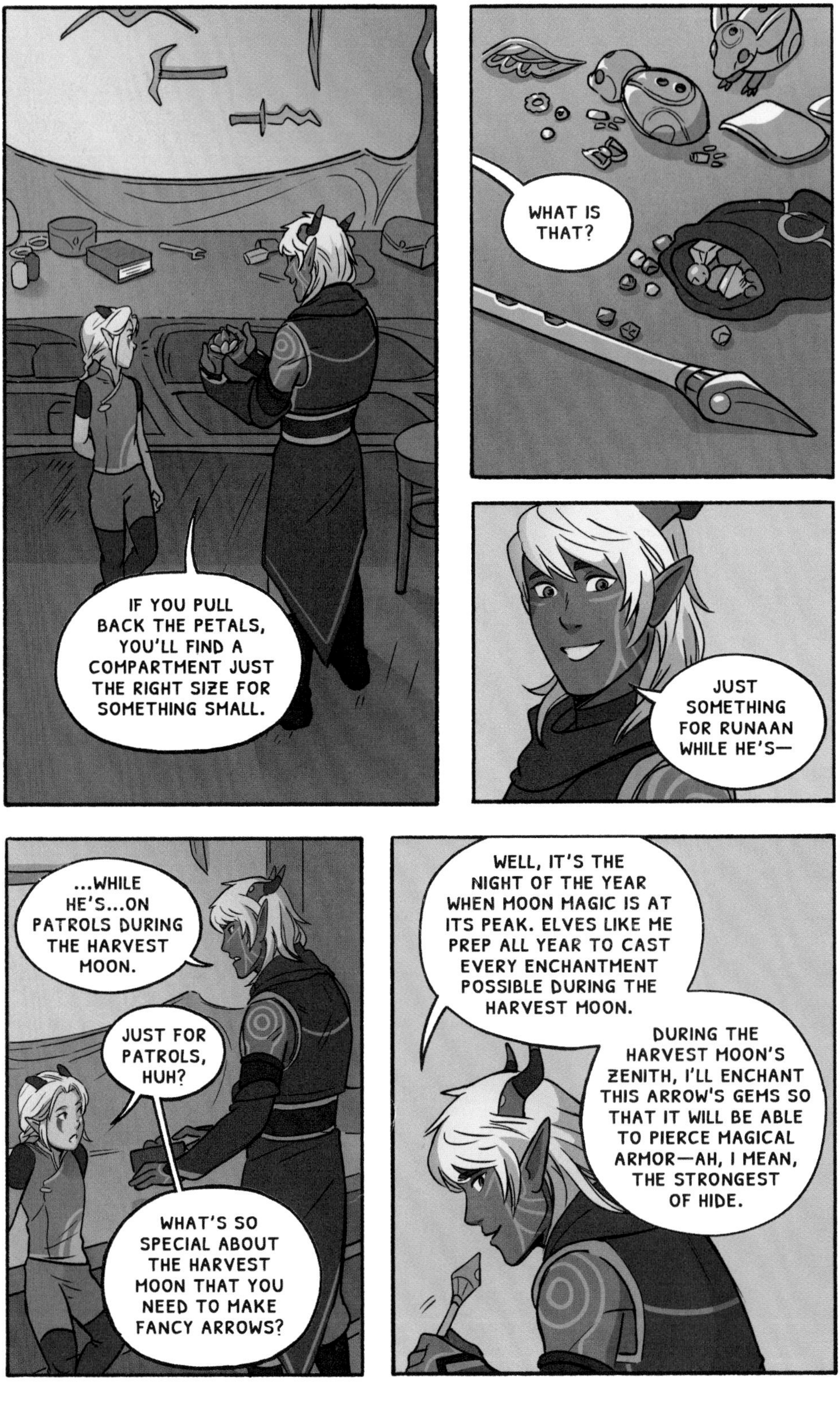
IF YOU PULL BACK THE PETALS, YOU'LL FIND A COMPARTMENT JUST THE RIGHT SIZE FOR SOMETHING SMALL.
WHAT IS THAT?
JUST SOMETHING FOR RUNAAN WHILE HE'S—
...WHILE HE'S...ON PATROLS DURING THE HARVEST MOON.
JUST FOR PATROLS, HUH?
WHAT'S SO SPECIAL ABOUT THE HARVEST MOON THAT YOU NEED TO MAKE FANCY ARROWS?
WELL, IT'S THE NIGHT OF THE YEAR WHEN MOON MAGIC IS AT ITS PEAK. ELVES LIKE ME PREP ALL YEAR TO CAST EVERY ENCHANTMENT POSSIBLE DURING THE HARVEST MOON.
DURING THE HARVEST MOON'S ZENITH, I'LL ENCHANT THIS ARROW'S GEMS SO THAT IT WILL BE ABLE TO PIERCE MAGICAL ARMOR—AH, I MEAN, THE STRONGEST OF HIDE.

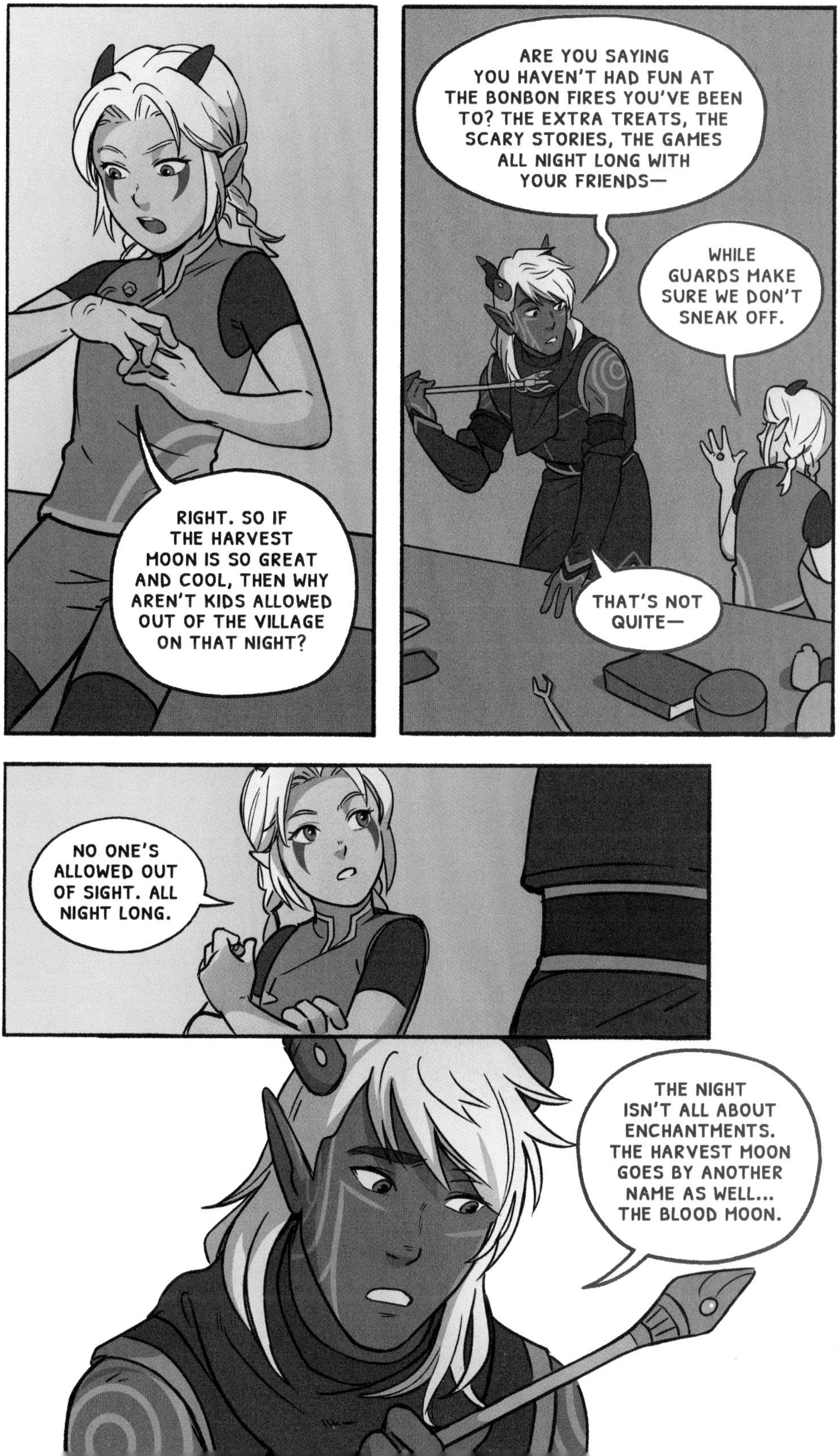
RIGHT. SO IF THE HARVEST MOON IS SO GREAT AND COOL, THEN WHY AREN'T KIDS ALLOWED OUT OF THE VILLAGE ON THAT NIGHT?
ARE YOU SAYING YOU HAVEN'T HAD FUN AT THE BONBON FIRES YOU'VE BEEN TO? THE EXTRA TREATS, THE SCARY STORIES, THE GAMES ALL NIGHT LONG WITH YOUR FRIENDS—
WHILE GUARDS MAKE SURE WE DON'T SNEAK OFF.
THAT'S NOT QUITE—
NO ONE'S ALLOWED OUT OF SIGHT. ALL NIGHT LONG.
THE NIGHT ISN'T ALL ABOUT ENCHANTMENTS. THE HARVEST MOON GOES BY ANOTHER NAME AS WELL... THE BLOOD MOON.

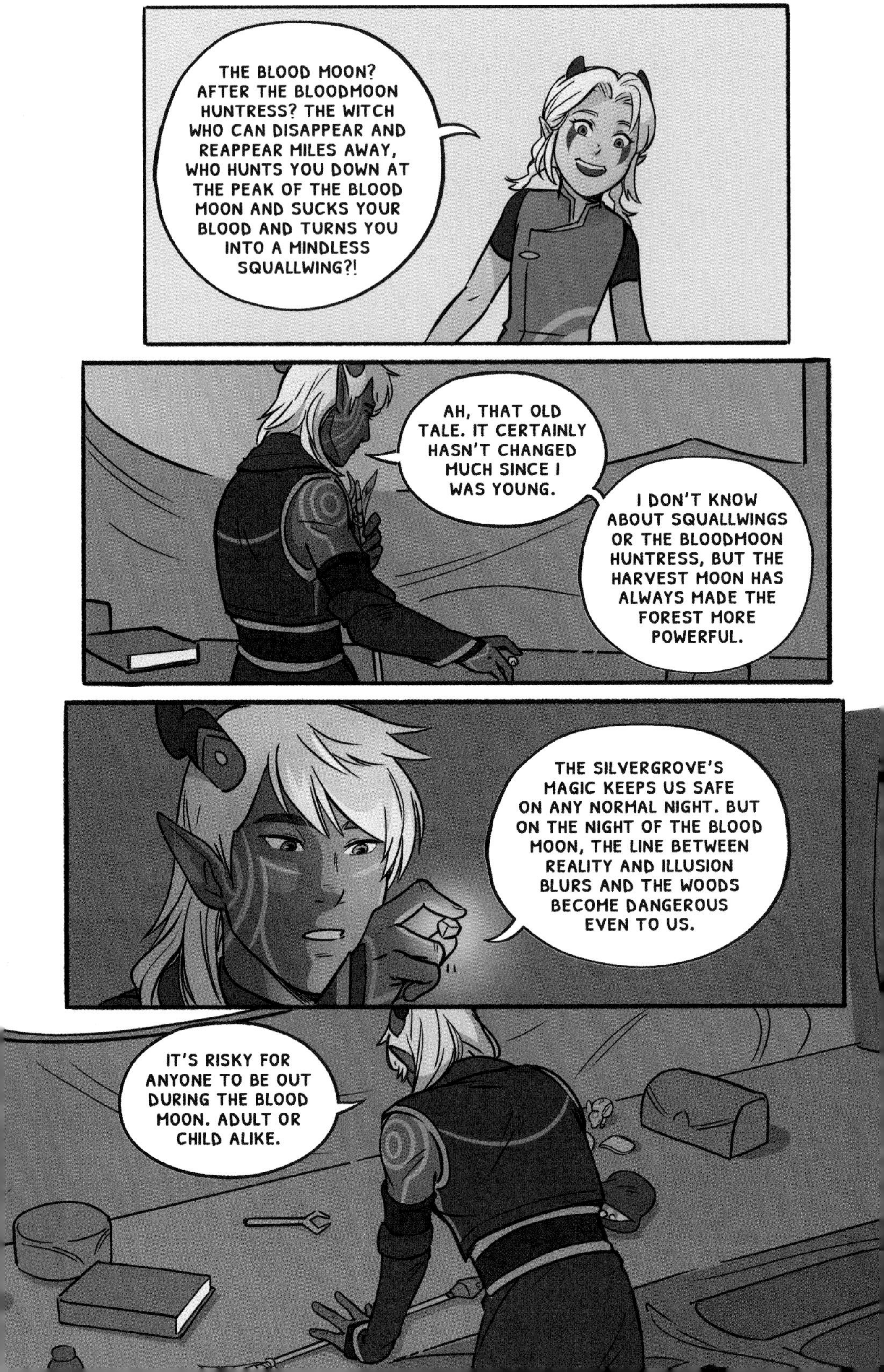
THE BLOOD MOON? AFTER THE BLOODMOON HUNTRESS? THE WITCH WHO CAN DISAPPEAR AND REAPPEAR MILES AWAY, WHO HUNTS YOU DOWN AT THE PEAK OF THE BLOOD MOON AND SUCKS YOUR BLOOD AND TURNS YOU INTO A MINDLESS SQUALLWING?!
AH, THAT OLD TALE. IT CERTAINLY HASN'T CHANGED MUCH SINCE I WAS YOUNG.
I DON'T KNOW ABOUT SQUALLWINGS OR THE BLOODMOON HUNTRESS, BUT THE HARVEST MOON HAS ALWAYS MADE THE FOREST MORE POWERFUL.
THE SILVERGROVE'S MAGIC KEEPS US SAFE ON ANY NORMAL NIGHT. BUT ON THE NIGHT OF THE BLOOD MOON, THE LINE BETWEEN REALITY AND ILLUSION BLURS AND THE WOODS BECOME DANGEROUS EVEN TO US.
IT'S RISKY FOR ANYONE TO BE OUT DURING THE BLOOD MOON. ADULT OR CHILD ALIKE.

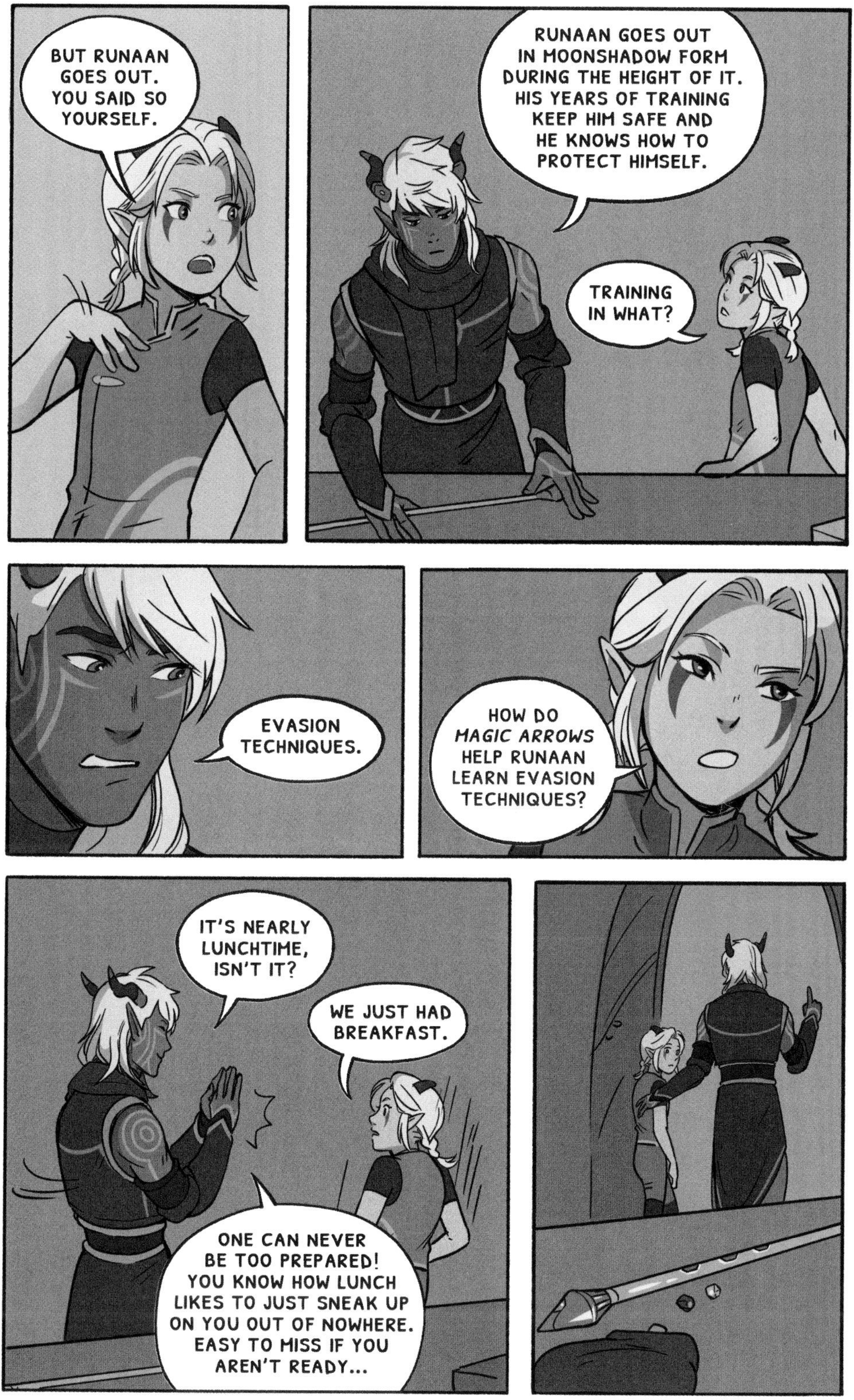
BUT RUNAAN GOES OUT. YOU SAID SO YOURSELF.
RUNAAN GOES OUT IN MOONSHADOW FORM DURING THE HEIGHT OF IT. HIS YEARS OF TRAINING KEEP HIM SAFE AND HE KNOWS HOW TO PROTECT HIMSELF.
TRAINING IN WHAT?
EVASION TECHNIQUES.
HOW DO *MAGIC ARROWS* HELP RUNAAN LEARN EVASION TECHNIQUES?
IT'S NEARLY LUNCHTIME, ISN'T IT?
WE JUST HAD BREAKFAST.
ONE CAN NEVER BE TOO PREPARED! YOU KNOW HOW LUNCH LIKES TO JUST SNEAK UP ON YOU OUT OF NOWHERE. EASY TO MISS IF YOU AREN'T READY...

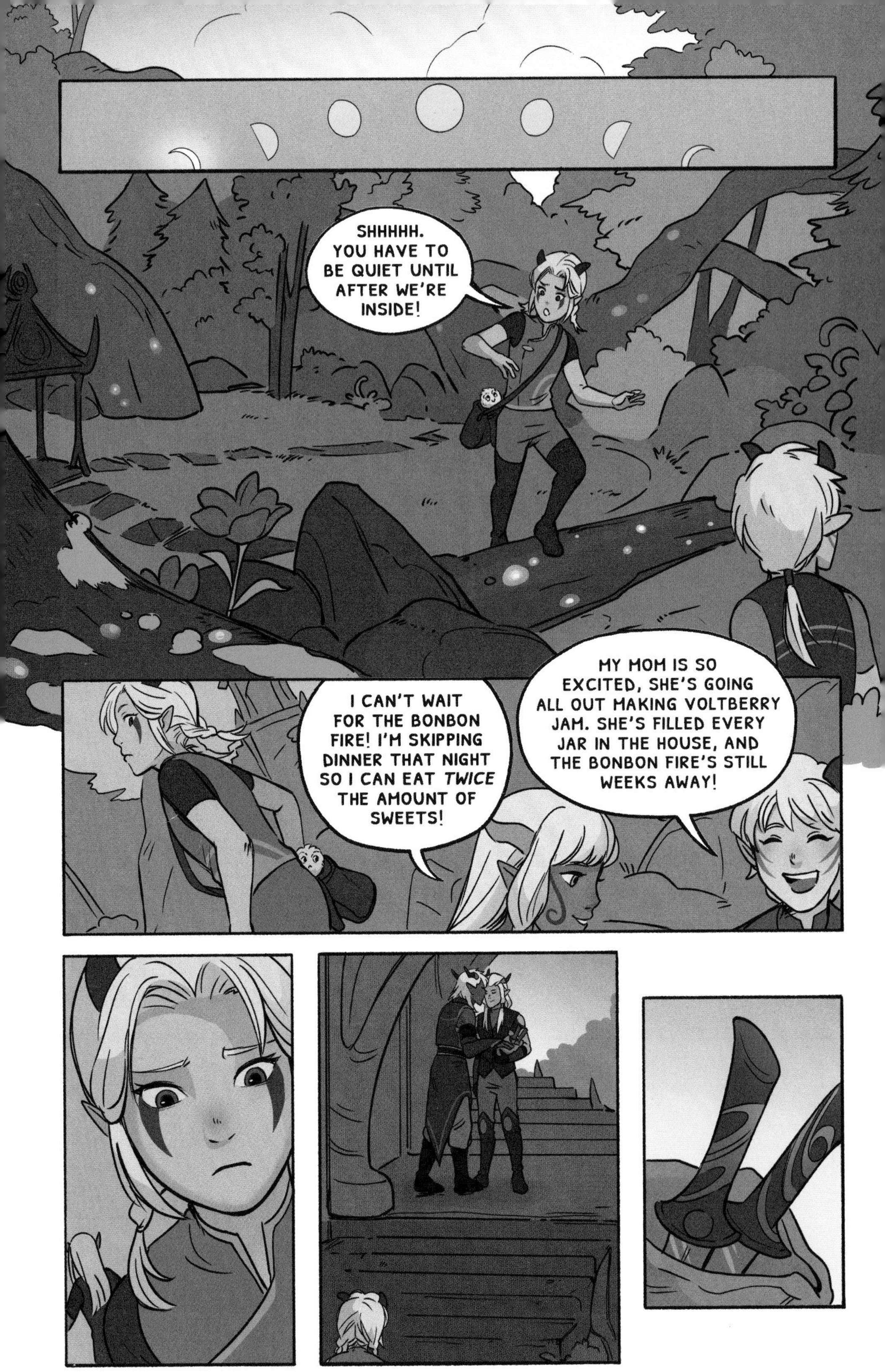
SHHHHH. YOU HAVE TO BE QUIET UNTIL AFTER WE'RE INSIDE!
I CAN'T WAIT FOR THE BONBON FIRE! I'M SKIPPING DINNER THAT NIGHT SO I CAN EAT *TWICE* THE AMOUNT OF SWEETS!
MY MOM IS SO EXCITED, SHE'S GOING ALL OUT MAKING VOLTBERRY JAM. SHE'S FILLED EVERY JAR IN THE HOUSE, AND THE BONBON FIRE'S STILL WEEKS AWAY!

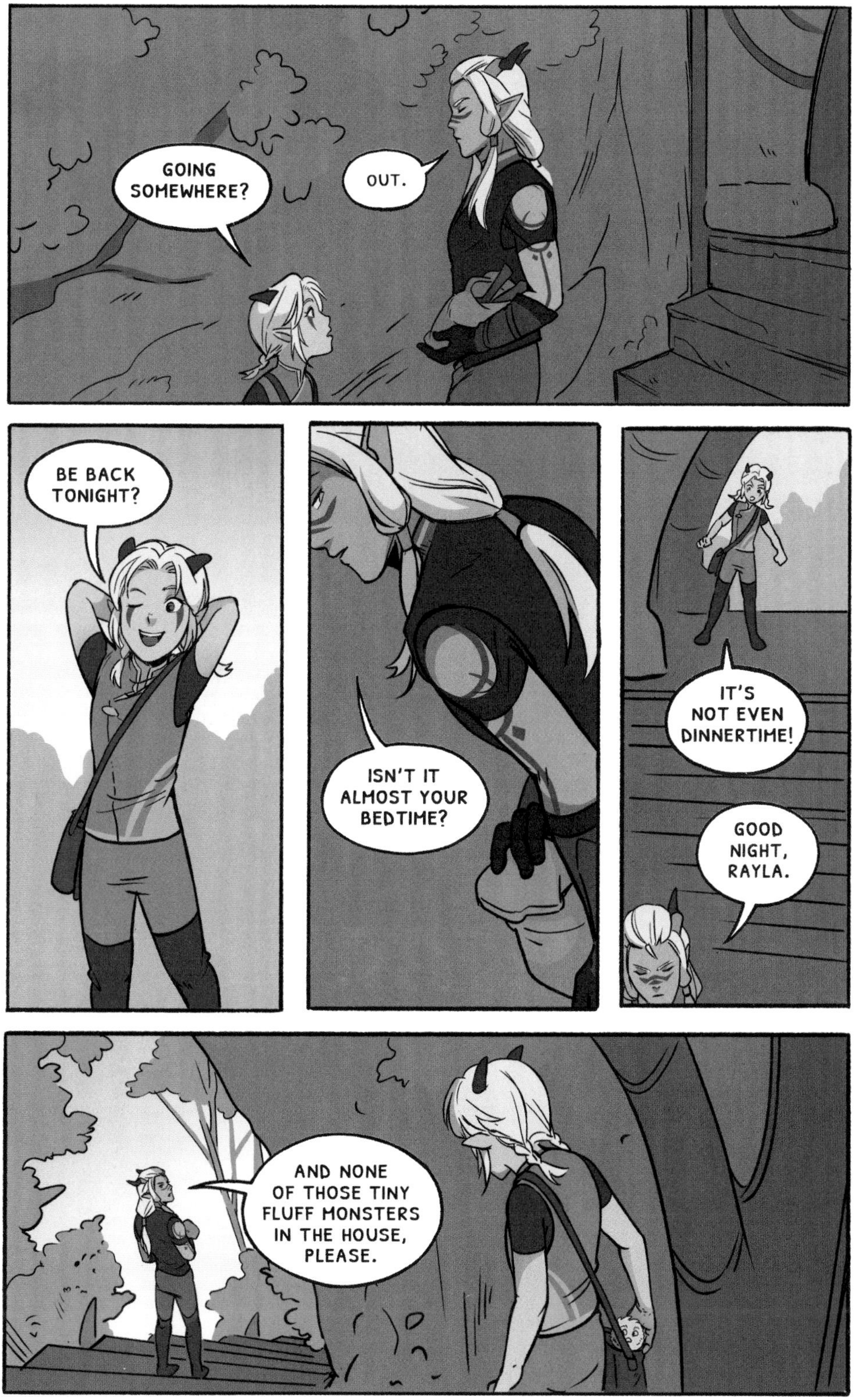
GOING SOMEWHERE?
OUT.
BE BACK TONIGHT?
ISN'T IT ALMOST YOUR BEDTIME?
IT'S NOT EVEN DINNERTIME!
GOOD NIGHT, RAYLA.
AND NONE OF THOSE TINY FLUFF MONSTERS IN THE HOUSE, PLEASE.

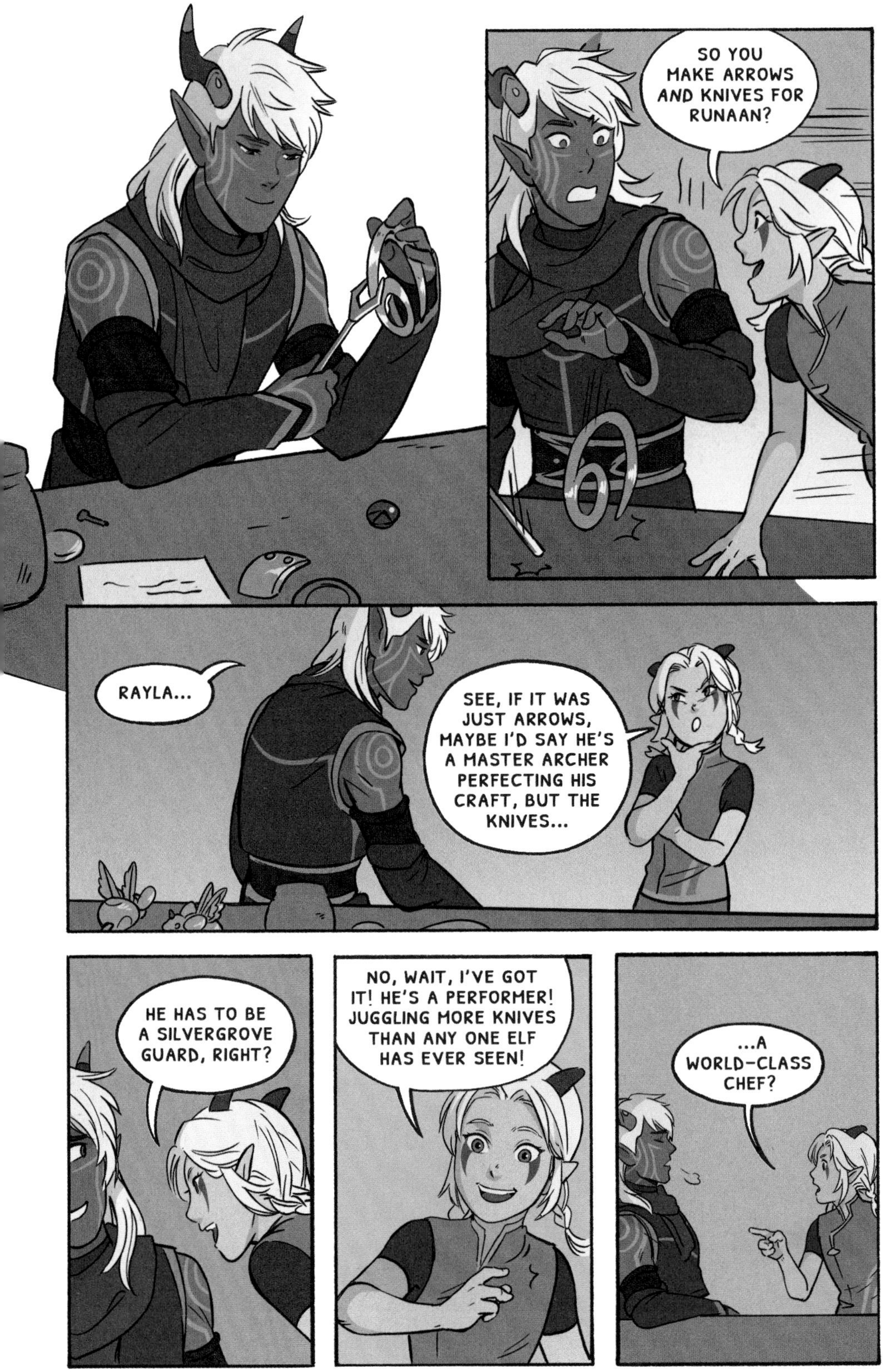
SO YOU MAKE ARROWS AND KNIVES FOR RUNAAN?
RAYLA...
SEE, IF IT WAS JUST ARROWS, MAYBE I'D SAY HE'S A MASTER ARCHER PERFECTING HIS CRAFT, BUT THE KNIVES...
HE HAS TO BE A SILVERGROVE GUARD, RIGHT?
NO, WAIT, I'VE GOT IT! HE'S A PERFORMER! JUGGLING MORE KNIVES THAN ANY ONE ELF HAS EVER SEEN!
...A WORLD-CLASS CHEF?

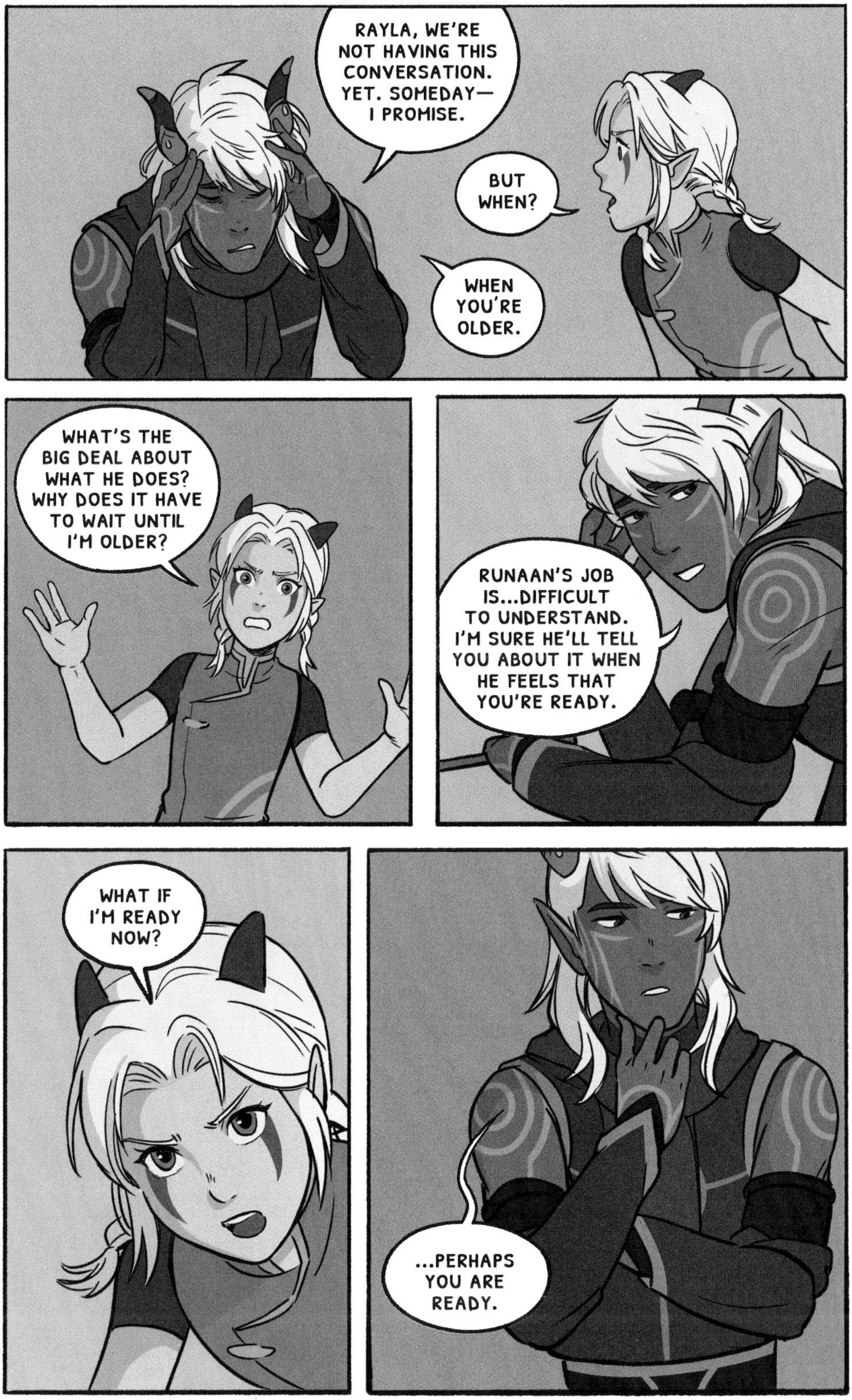
RAYLA, WE'RE NOT HAVING THIS CONVERSATION. YET. SOMEDAY— I PROMISE.
BUT WHEN?
WHEN YOU'RE OLDER.
WHAT'S THE BIG DEAL ABOUT WHAT HE DOES? WHY DOES IT HAVE TO WAIT UNTIL I'M OLDER?
RUNAAN'S JOB IS...DIFFICULT TO UNDERSTAND. I'M SURE HE'LL TELL YOU ABOUT IT WHEN HE FEELS THAT YOU'RE READY.
WHAT IF I'M READY NOW?
...PERHAPS YOU ARE READY.

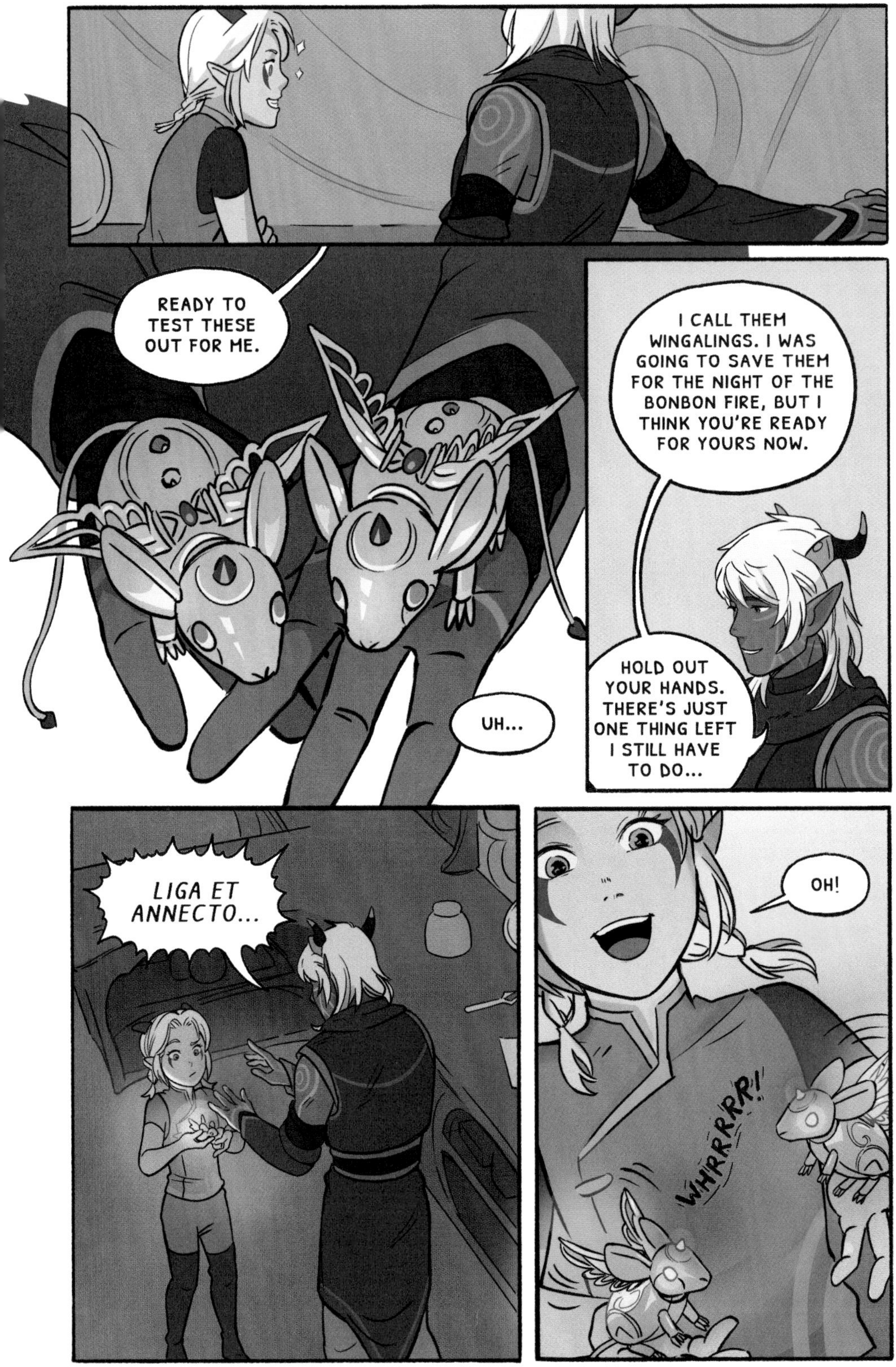
READY TO TEST THESE OUT FOR ME.
I CALL THEM WINGALINGS. I WAS GOING TO SAVE THEM FOR THE NIGHT OF THE BONBON FIRE, BUT I THINK YOU'RE READY FOR YOURS NOW.
HOLD OUT YOUR HANDS. THERE'S JUST ONE THING LEFT I STILL HAVE TO DO...
UH...
LIGA ET ANNECTO...
OH!
WHRRRR!

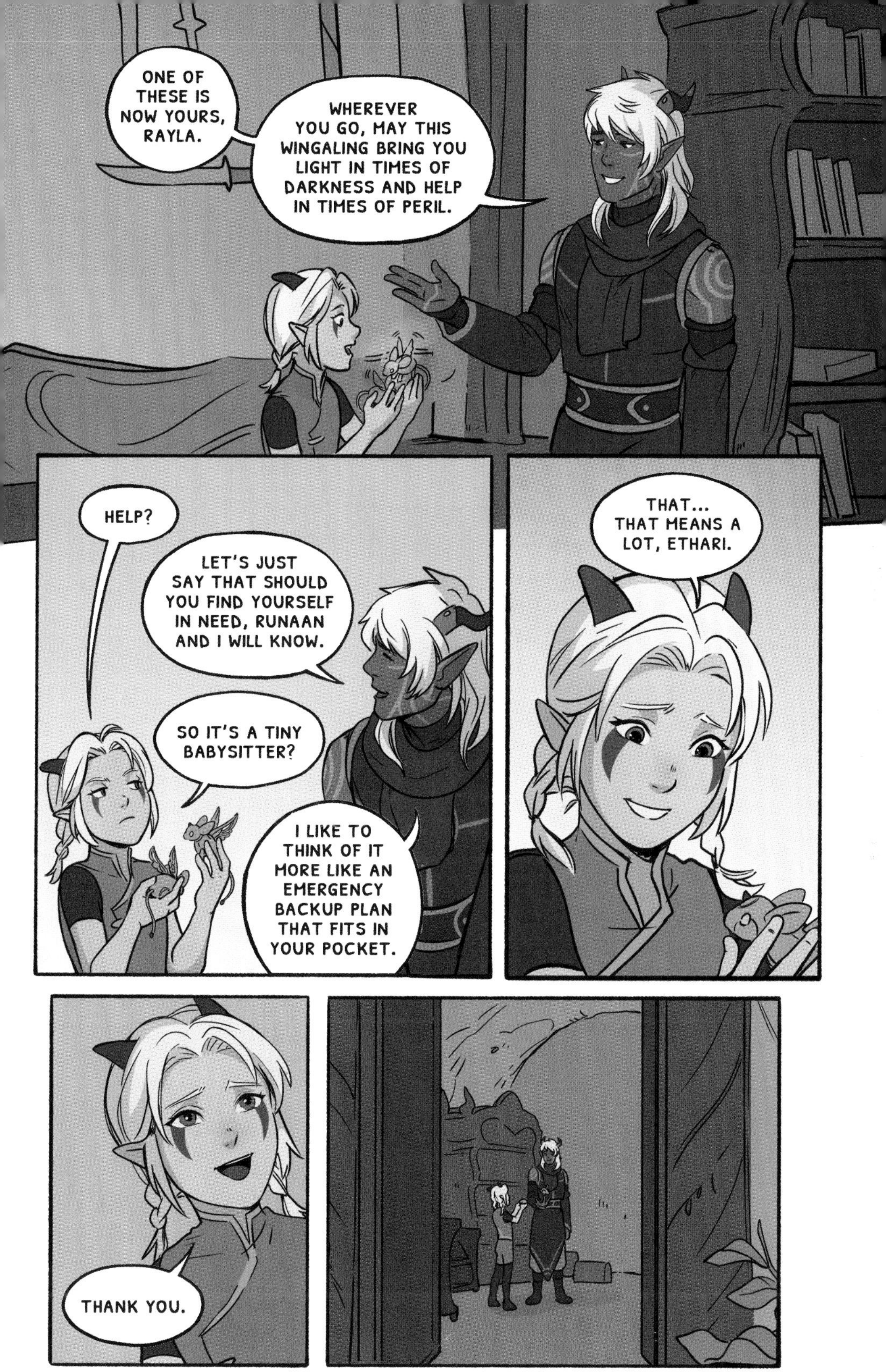
ONE OF THESE IS NOW YOURS, RAYLA.
WHEREVER YOU GO, MAY THIS WINGALING BRING YOU LIGHT IN TIMES OF DARKNESS AND HELP IN TIMES OF PERIL.
HELP?
LET'S JUST SAY THAT SHOULD YOU FIND YOURSELF IN NEED, RUNAAN AND I WILL KNOW.
SO IT'S A TINY BABYSITTER?
I LIKE TO THINK OF IT MORE LIKE AN EMERGENCY BACKUP PLAN THAT FITS IN YOUR POCKET.
THAT... THAT MEANS A LOT, ETHARI.
THANK YOU.

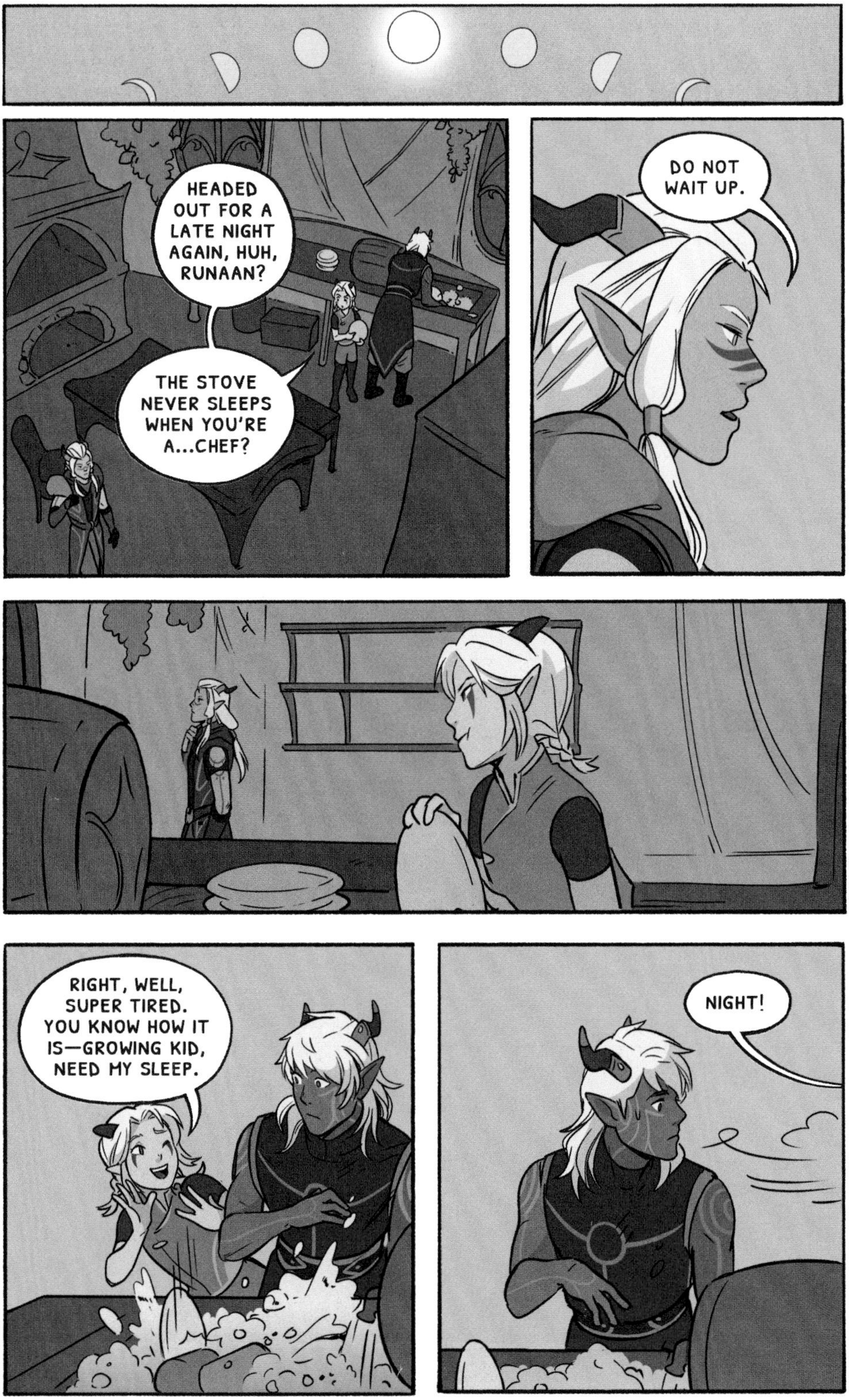
HEADED OUT FOR A LATE NIGHT AGAIN, HUH, RUNAAN?
THE STOVE NEVER SLEEPS WHEN YOU'RE A...CHEF?
DO NOT WAIT UP.
RIGHT, WELL, SUPER TIRED. YOU KNOW HOW IT IS—GROWING KID, NEED MY SLEEP.
NIGHT!

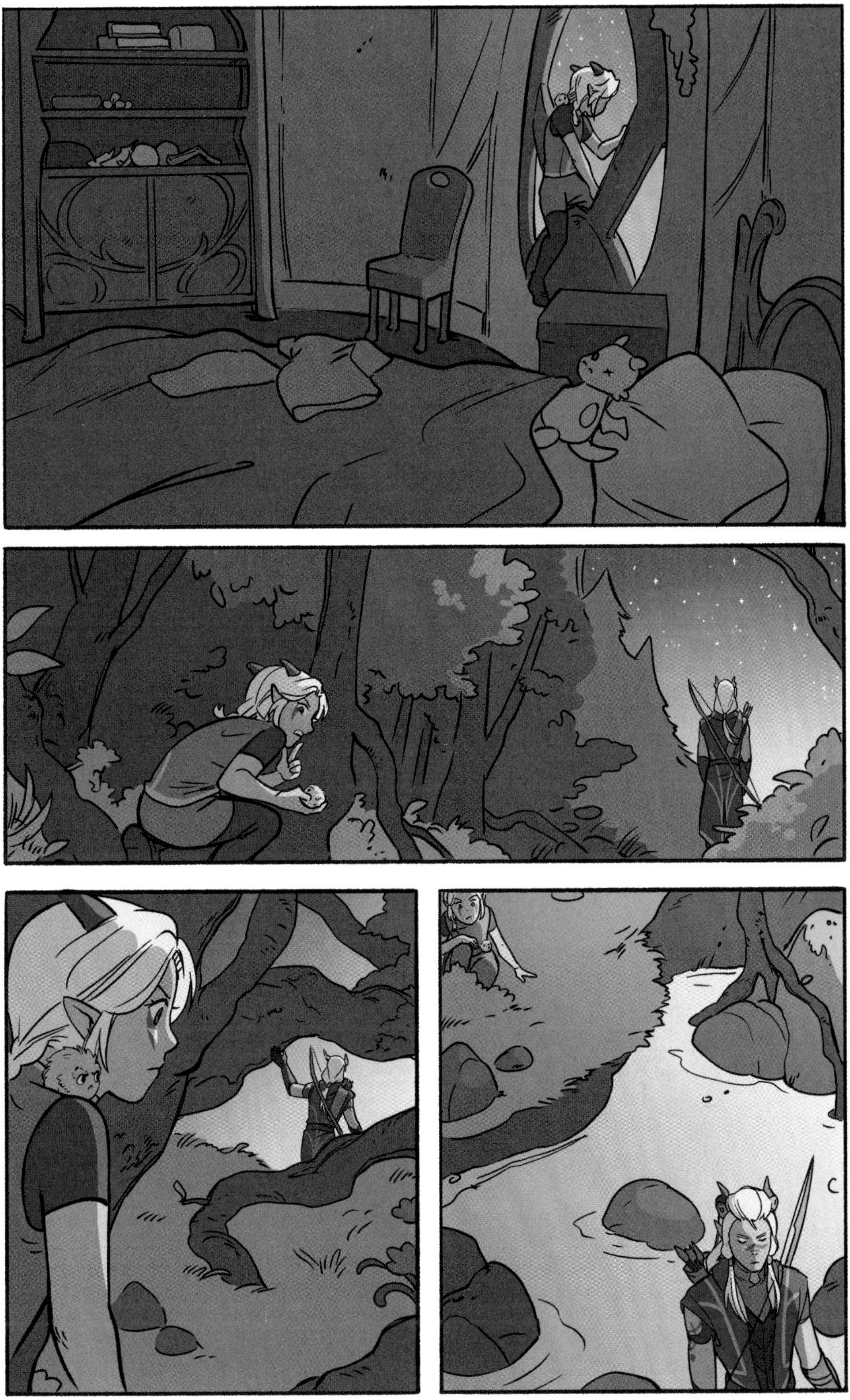

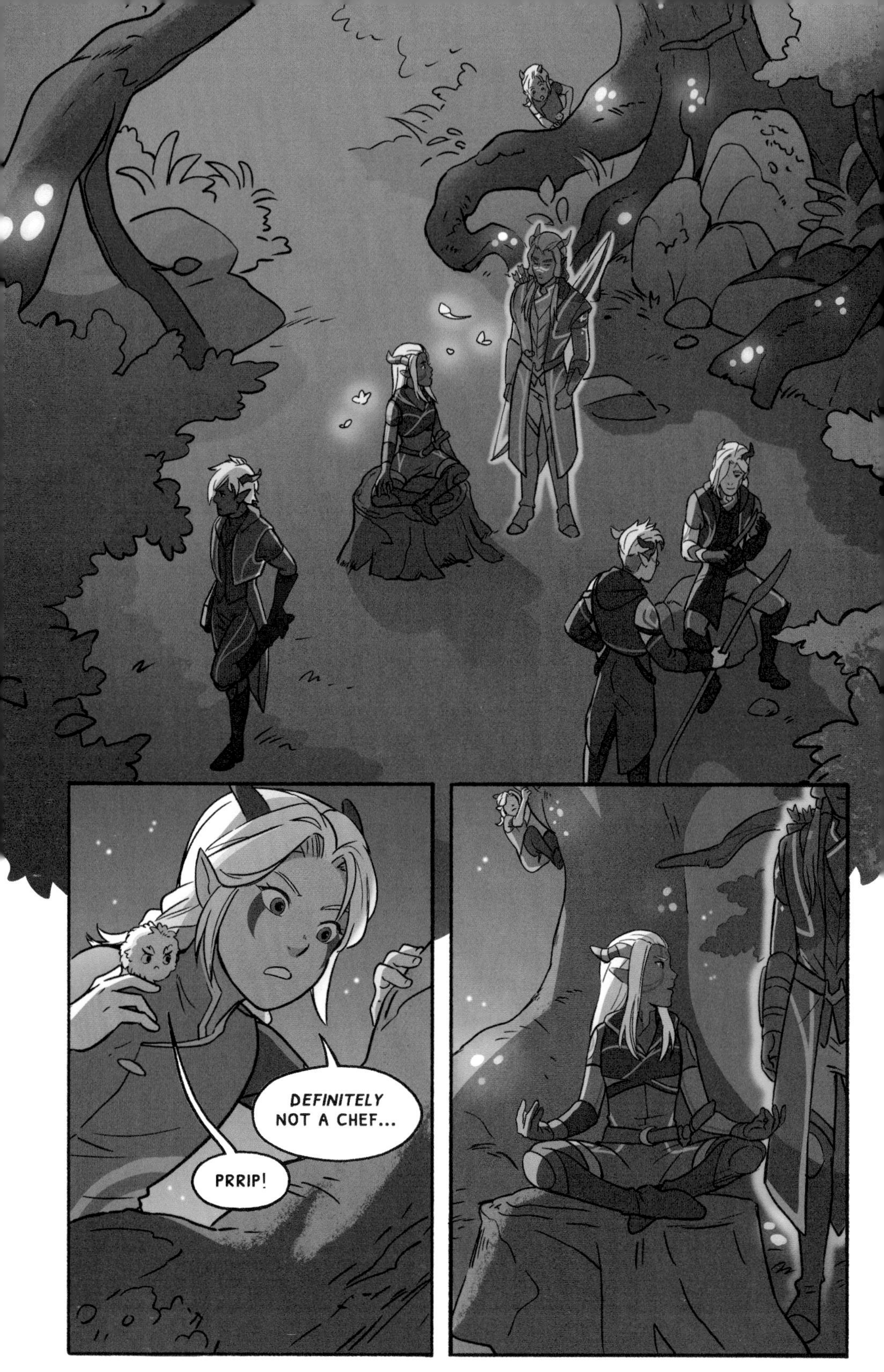
DEFINITELY NOT A CHEF...
PRRIP!

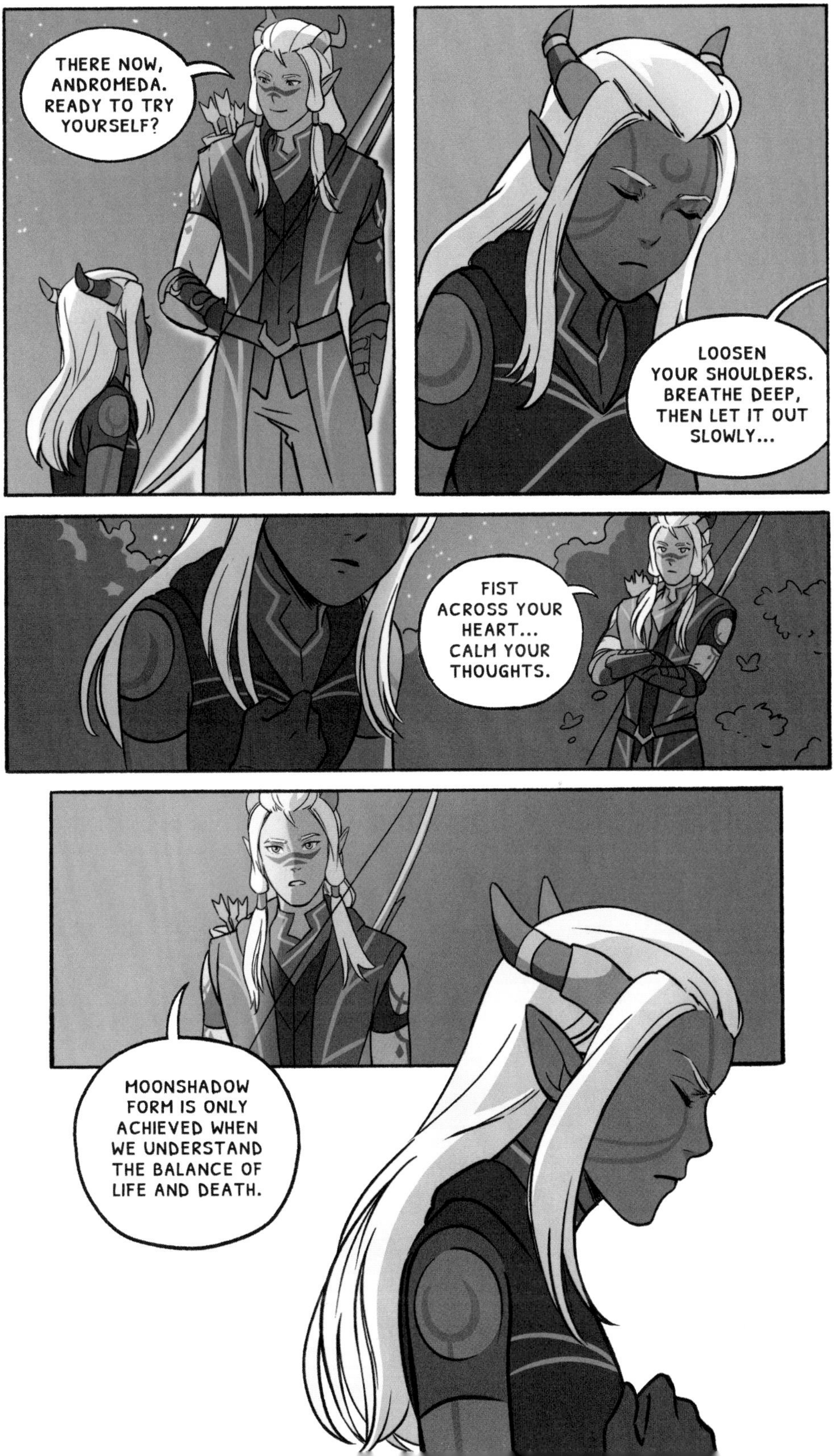
THERE NOW, ANDROMEDA. READY TO TRY YOURSELF?
LOOSEN YOUR SHOULDERS. BREATHE DEEP, THEN LET IT OUT SLOWLY...
FIST ACROSS YOUR HEART... CALM YOUR THOUGHTS.
MOONSHADOW FORM IS ONLY ACHIEVED WHEN WE UNDERSTAND THE BALANCE OF LIFE AND DEATH.

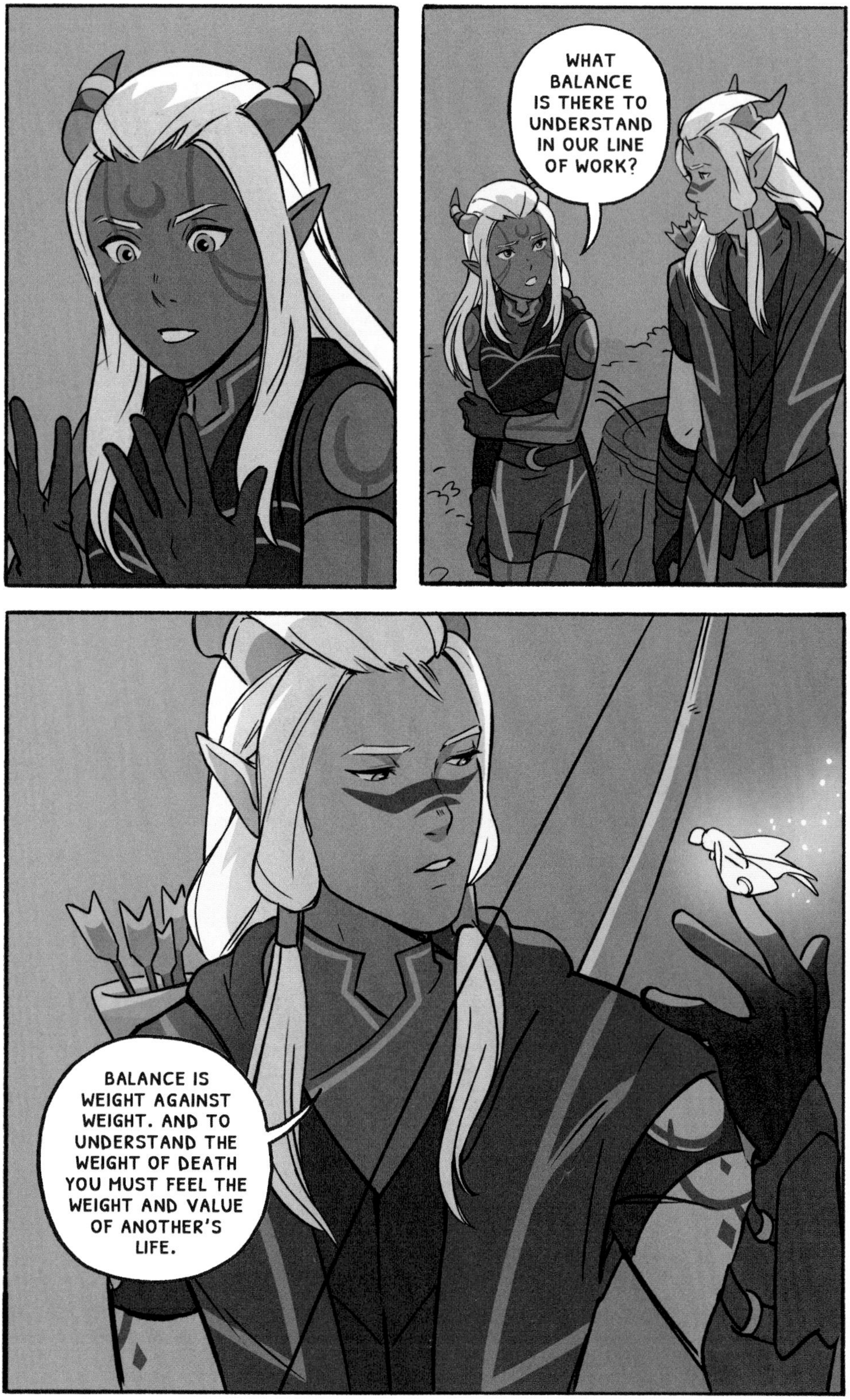
WHAT BALANCE IS THERE TO UNDERSTAND IN OUR LINE OF WORK?
BALANCE IS WEIGHT AGAINST WEIGHT. AND TO UNDERSTAND THE WEIGHT OF DEATH YOU MUST FEEL THE WEIGHT AND VALUE OF ANOTHER'S LIFE.

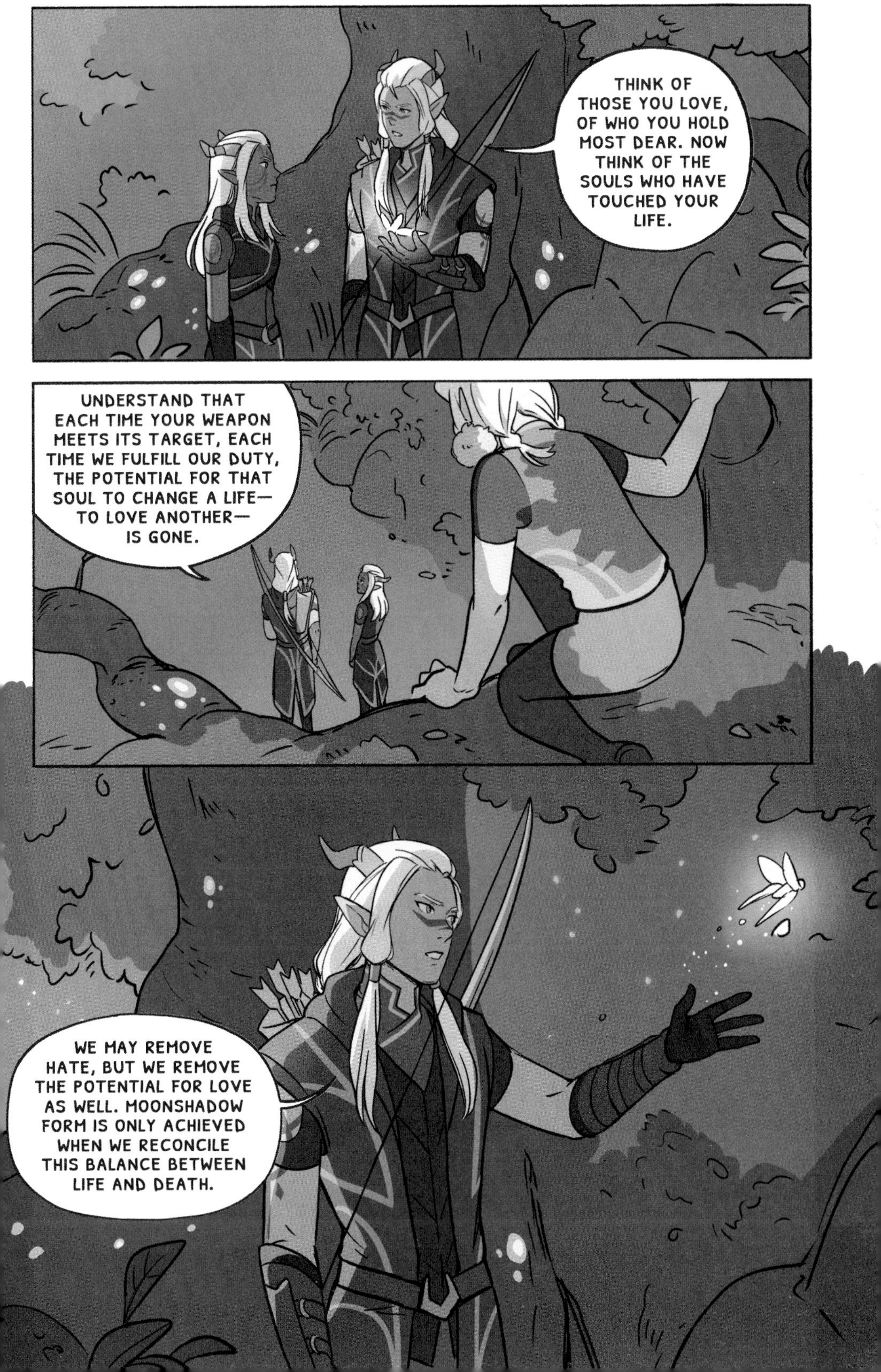
THINK OF THOSE YOU LOVE, OF WHO YOU HOLD MOST DEAR. NOW THINK OF THE SOULS WHO HAVE TOUCHED YOUR LIFE.
UNDERSTAND THAT EACH TIME YOUR WEAPON MEETS ITS TARGET, EACH TIME WE FULFILL OUR DUTY, THE POTENTIAL FOR THAT SOUL TO CHANGE A LIFE— TO LOVE ANOTHER— IS GONE.
WE MAY REMOVE HATE, BUT WE REMOVE THE POTENTIAL FOR LOVE AS WELL. MOONSHADOW FORM IS ONLY ACHIEVED WHEN WE RECONCILE THIS BALANCE BETWEEN LIFE AND DEATH.

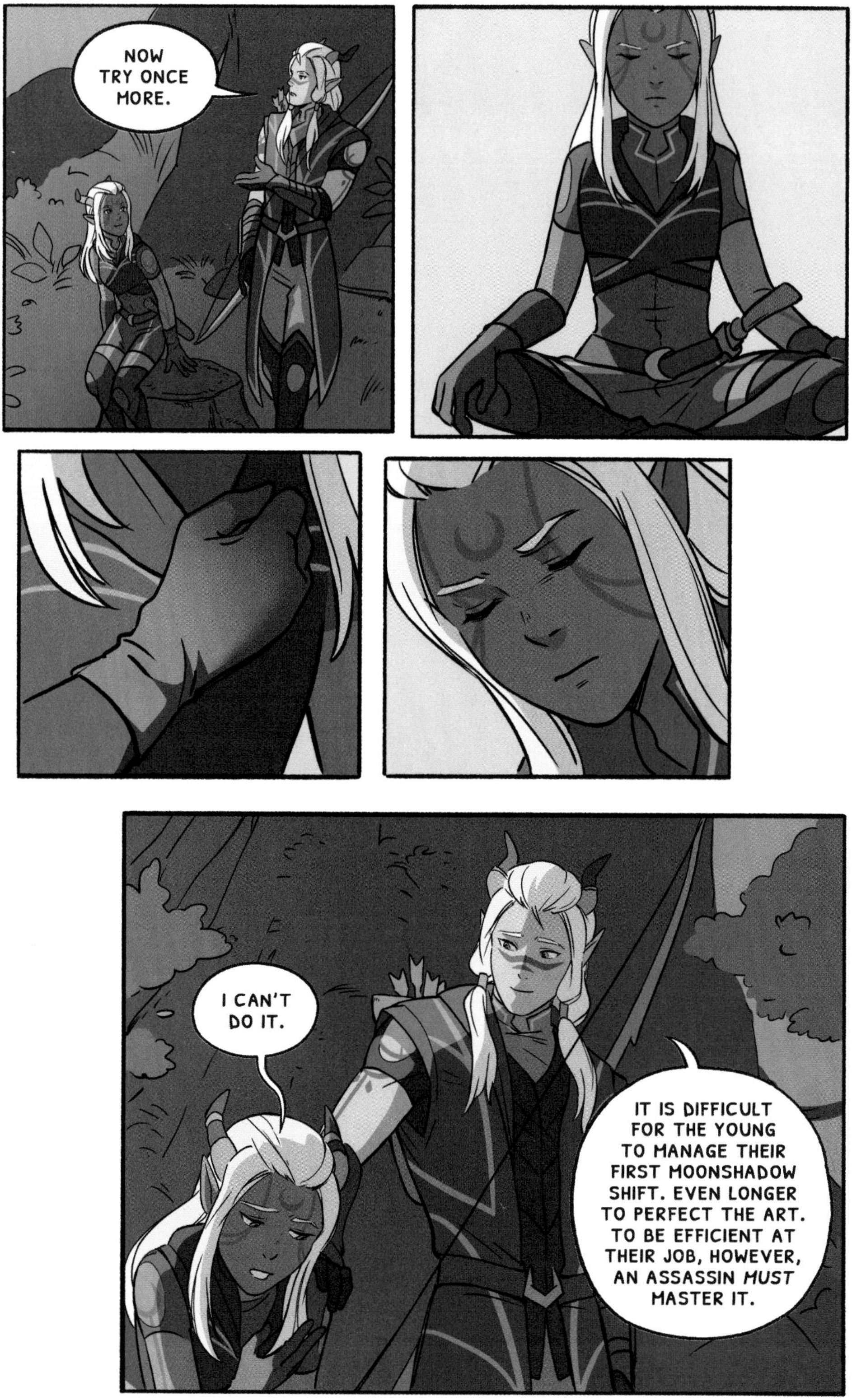
NOW TRY ONCE MORE.
I CAN'T DO IT.
IT IS DIFFICULT FOR THE YOUNG TO MANAGE THEIR FIRST MOONSHADOW SHIFT. EVEN LONGER TO PERFECT THE ART. TO BE EFFICIENT AT THEIR JOB, HOWEVER, AN ASSASSIN *MUST* MASTER IT.

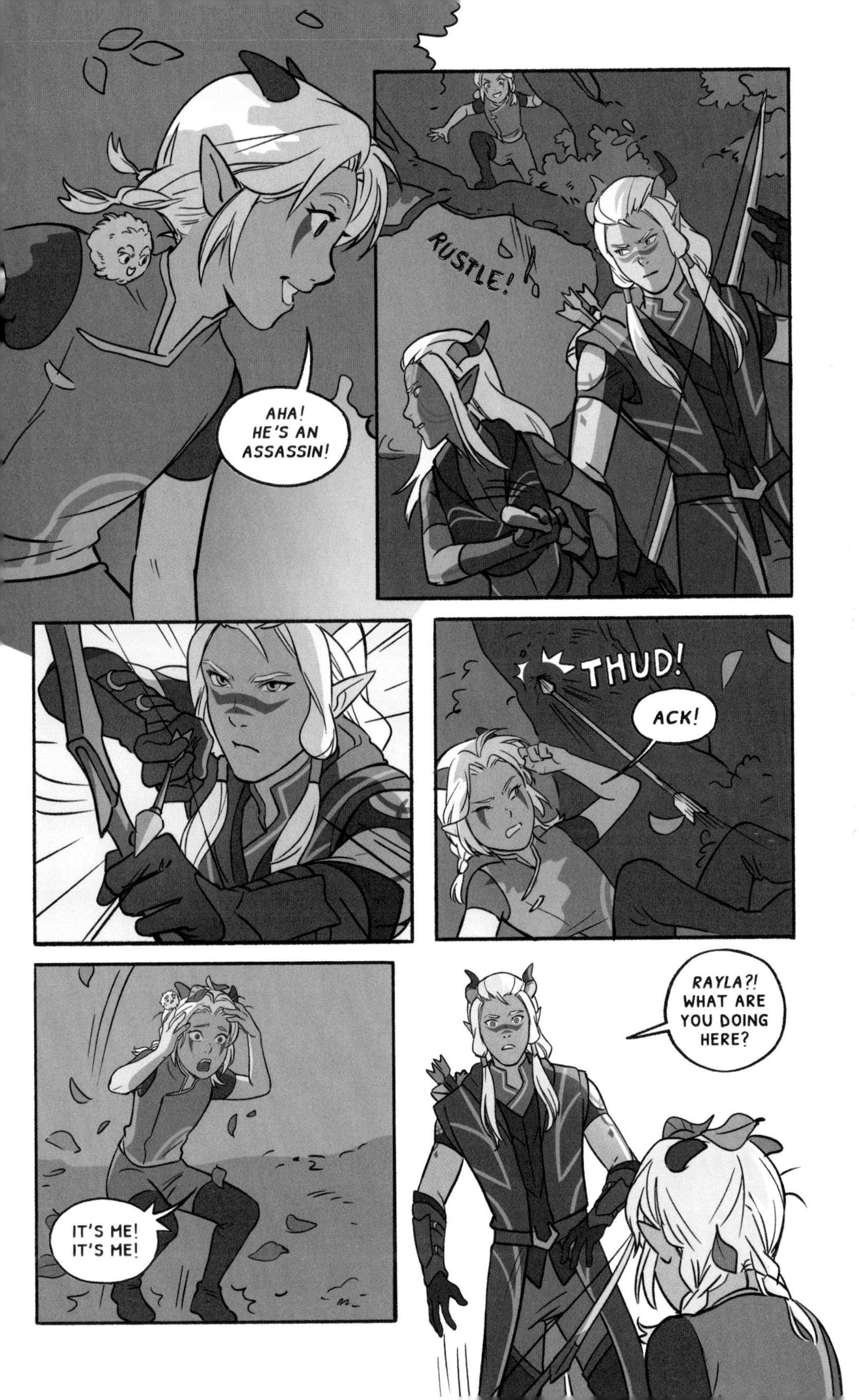
AHA! HE'S AN ASSASSIN!
RUSTLE!
THUD!
ACK!
IT'S ME! IT'S ME!
RAYLA?! WHAT ARE YOU DOING HERE?

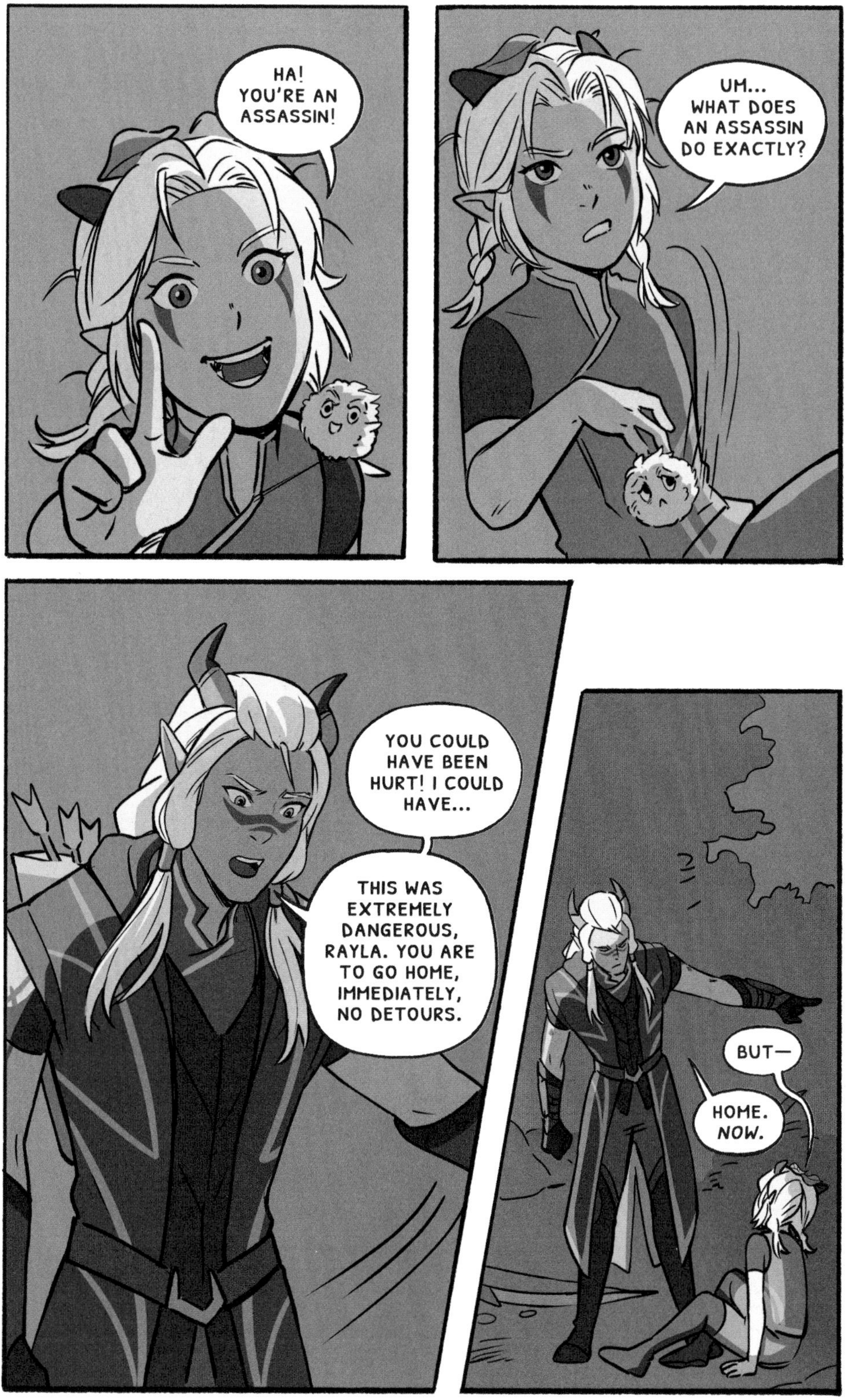
HA!
YOU'RE AN ASSASSIN!
UM... WHAT DOES AN ASSASSIN DO EXACTLY?
YOU COULD HAVE BEEN HURT! I COULD HAVE...
THIS WAS EXTREMELY DANGEROUS, RAYLA. YOU ARE TO GO HOME, IMMEDIATELY, NO DETOURS.
BUT—
HOME. *NOW.*

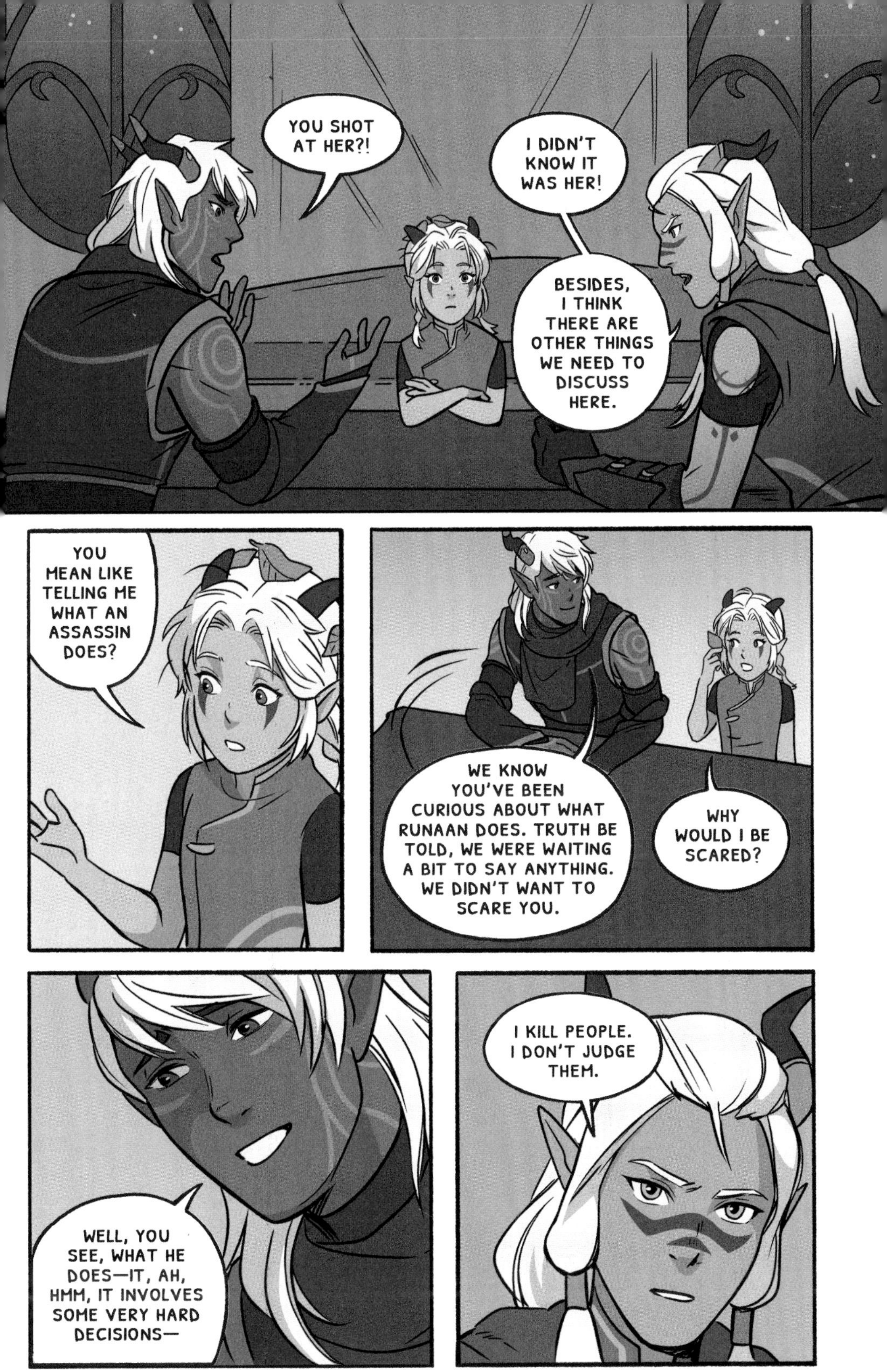

YOU SHOT AT HER?!
I DIDN'T KNOW IT WAS HER!
BESIDES, I THINK THERE ARE OTHER THINGS WE NEED TO DISCUSS HERE.
YOU MEAN LIKE TELLING ME WHAT AN ASSASSIN DOES?
WE KNOW YOU'VE BEEN CURIOUS ABOUT WHAT RUNAAN DOES. TRUTH BE TOLD, WE WERE WAITING A BIT TO SAY ANYTHING. WE DIDN'T WANT TO SCARE YOU.
WHY WOULD I BE SCARED?
WELL, YOU SEE, WHAT HE DOES—IT, AH, HMM, IT INVOLVES SOME VERY HARD DECISIONS—
I KILL PEOPLE. I DON'T JUDGE THEM.

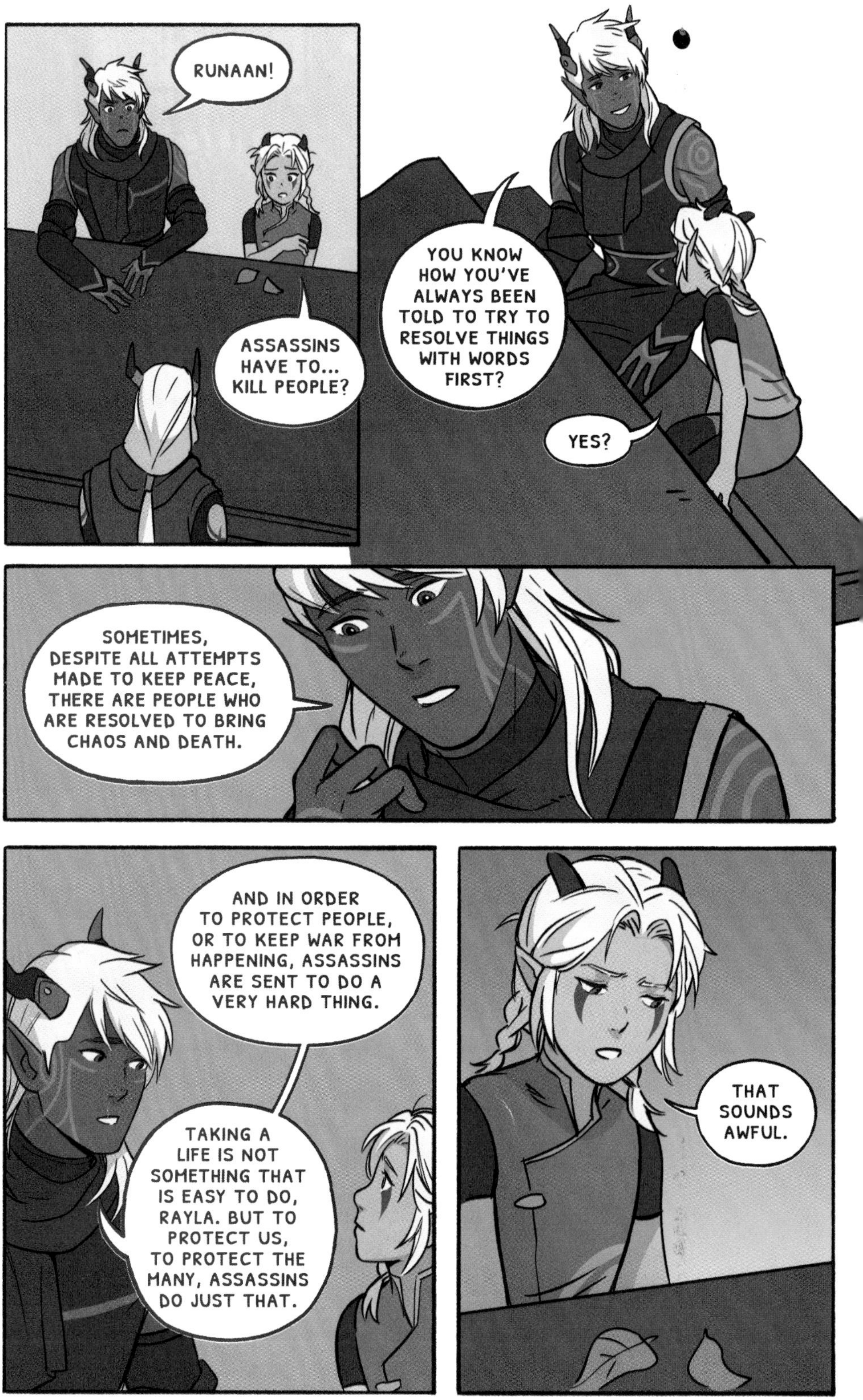
RUNAAN!
ASSASSINS HAVE TO... KILL PEOPLE?
YOU KNOW HOW YOU'VE ALWAYS BEEN TOLD TO TRY TO RESOLVE THINGS WITH WORDS FIRST?
YES?
SOMETIMES, DESPITE ALL ATTEMPTS MADE TO KEEP PEACE, THERE ARE PEOPLE WHO ARE RESOLVED TO BRING CHAOS AND DEATH.
AND IN ORDER TO PROTECT PEOPLE, OR TO KEEP WAR FROM HAPPENING, ASSASSINS ARE SENT TO DO A VERY HARD THING.
TAKING A LIFE IS NOT SOMETHING THAT IS EASY TO DO, RAYLA. BUT TO PROTECT US, TO PROTECT THE MANY, ASSASSINS DO JUST THAT.
THAT SOUNDS AWFUL.

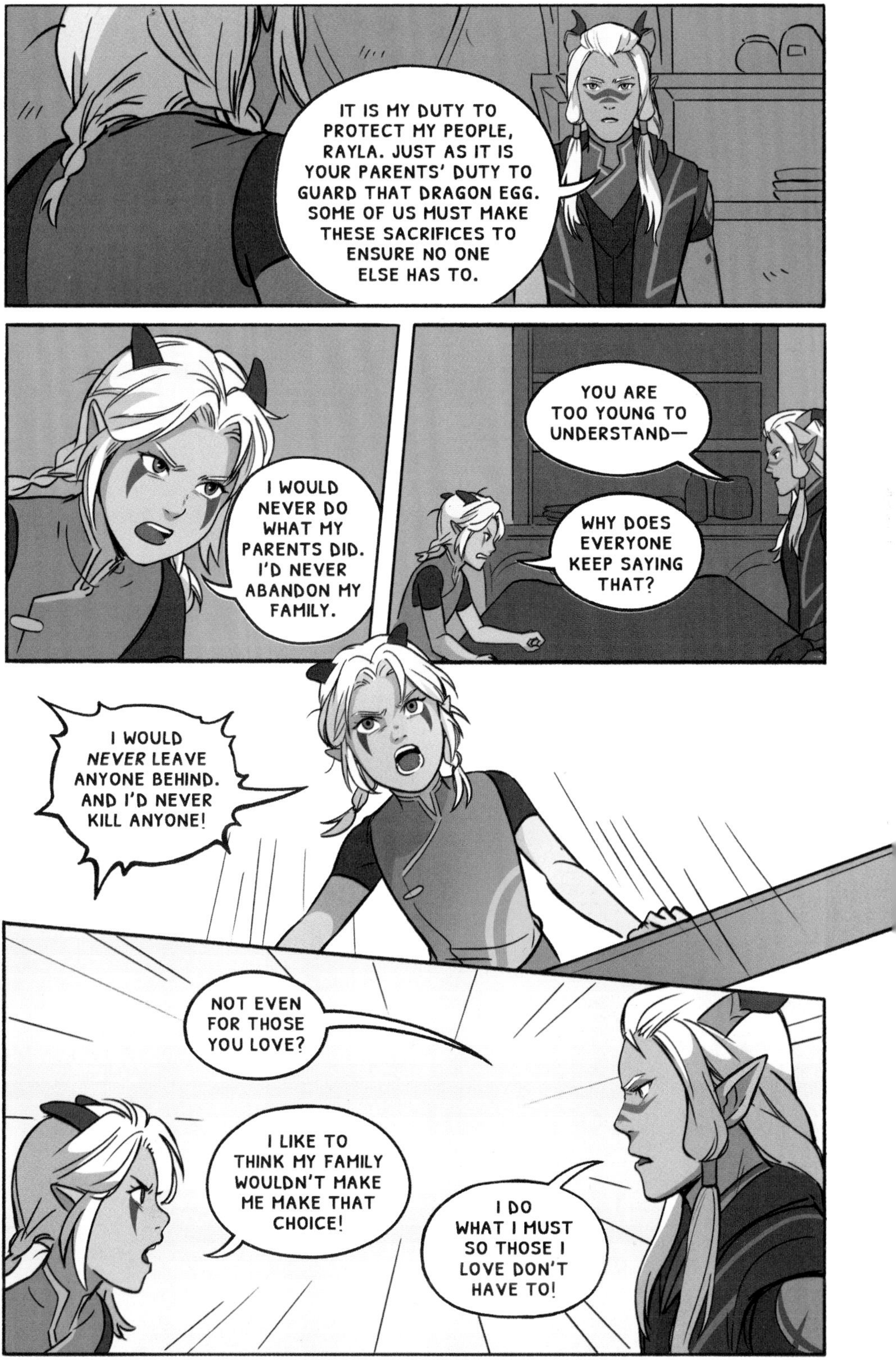
IT IS MY DUTY TO PROTECT MY PEOPLE, RAYLA. JUST AS IT IS YOUR PARENTS' DUTY TO GUARD THAT DRAGON EGG. SOME OF US MUST MAKE THESE SACRIFICES TO ENSURE NO ONE ELSE HAS TO.
I WOULD NEVER DO WHAT MY PARENTS DID. I'D NEVER ABANDON MY FAMILY.
YOU ARE TOO YOUNG TO UNDERSTAND—
WHY DOES EVERYONE KEEP SAYING THAT?
I WOULD *NEVER* LEAVE ANYONE BEHIND. AND I'D NEVER KILL ANYONE!
NOT EVEN FOR THOSE YOU LOVE?
I LIKE TO THINK MY FAMILY WOULDN'T MAKE ME MAKE THAT CHOICE!
I DO WHAT I MUST SO THOSE I LOVE DON'T HAVE TO!

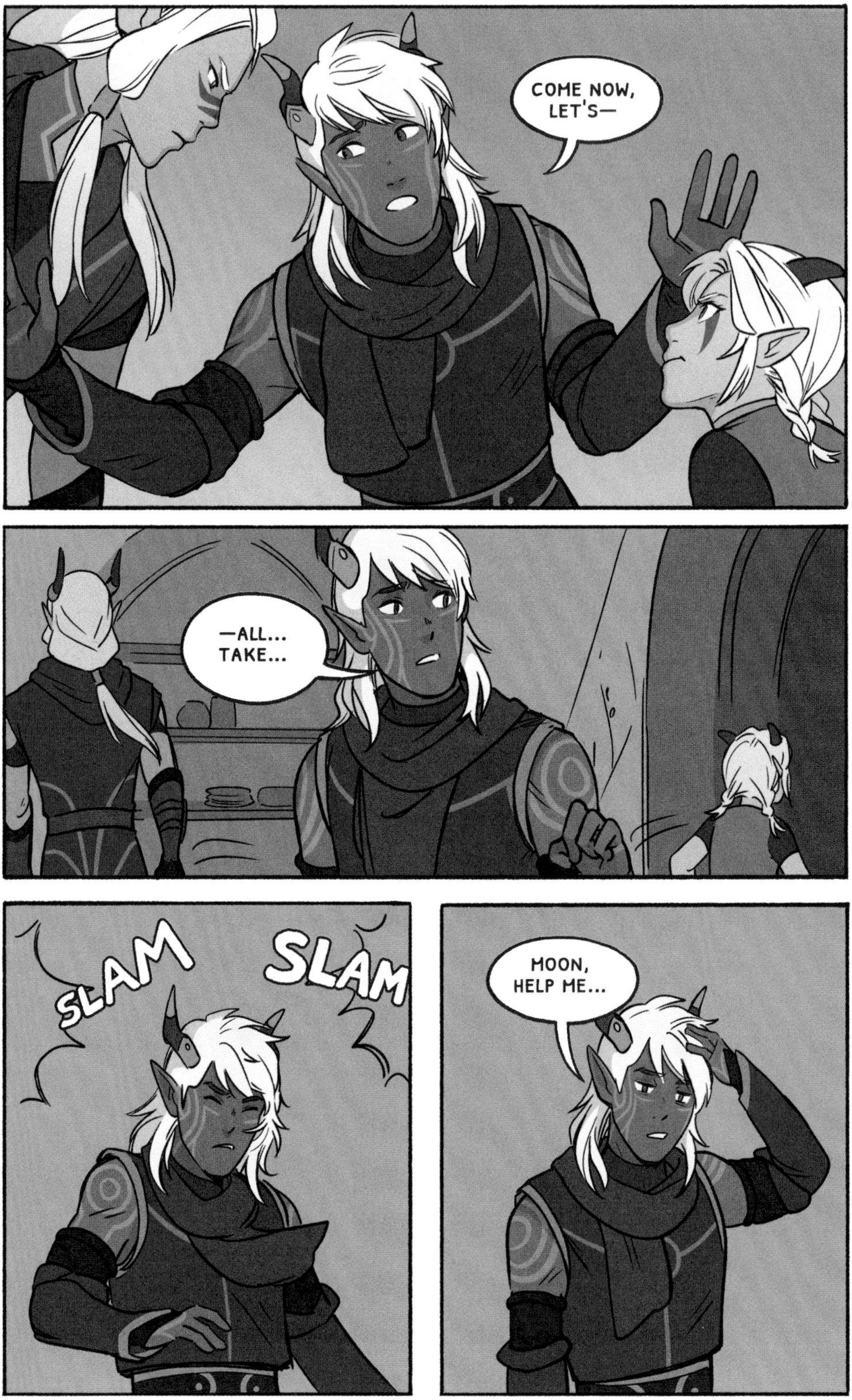
COME NOW, LET'S—
—ALL... TAKE...
SLAM
SLAM
MOON, HELP ME...

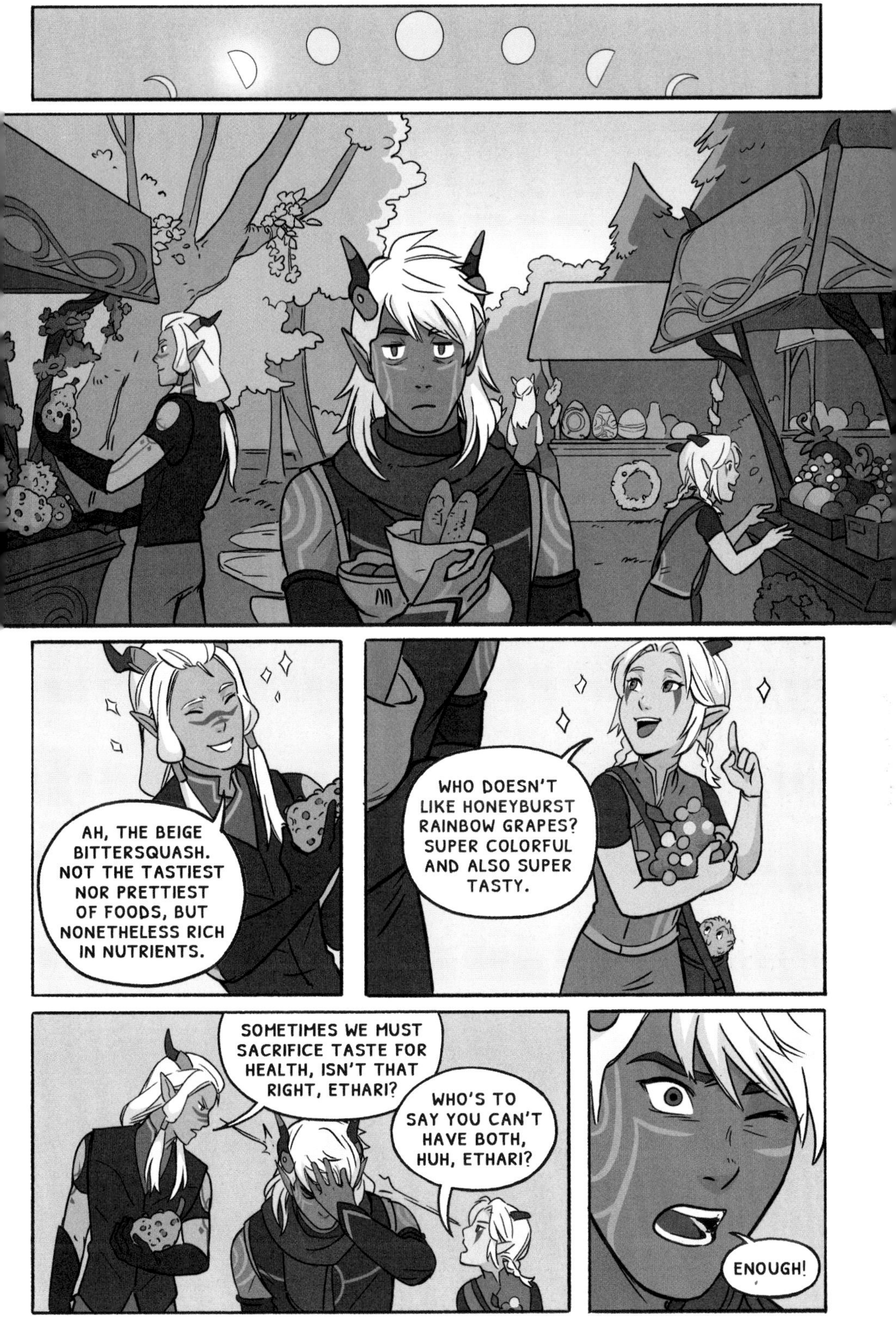
AH, THE BEIGE BITTERSQUASH. NOT THE TASTIEST NOR PRETTIEST OF FOODS, BUT NONETHELESS RICH IN NUTRIENTS.
WHO DOESN'T LIKE HONEYBURST RAINBOW GRAPES? SUPER COLORFUL AND ALSO SUPER TASTY.
SOMETIMES WE MUST SACRIFICE TASTE FOR HEALTH, ISN'T THAT RIGHT, ETHARI?
WHO'S TO SAY YOU CAN'T HAVE BOTH, HUH, ETHARI?
ENOUGH!

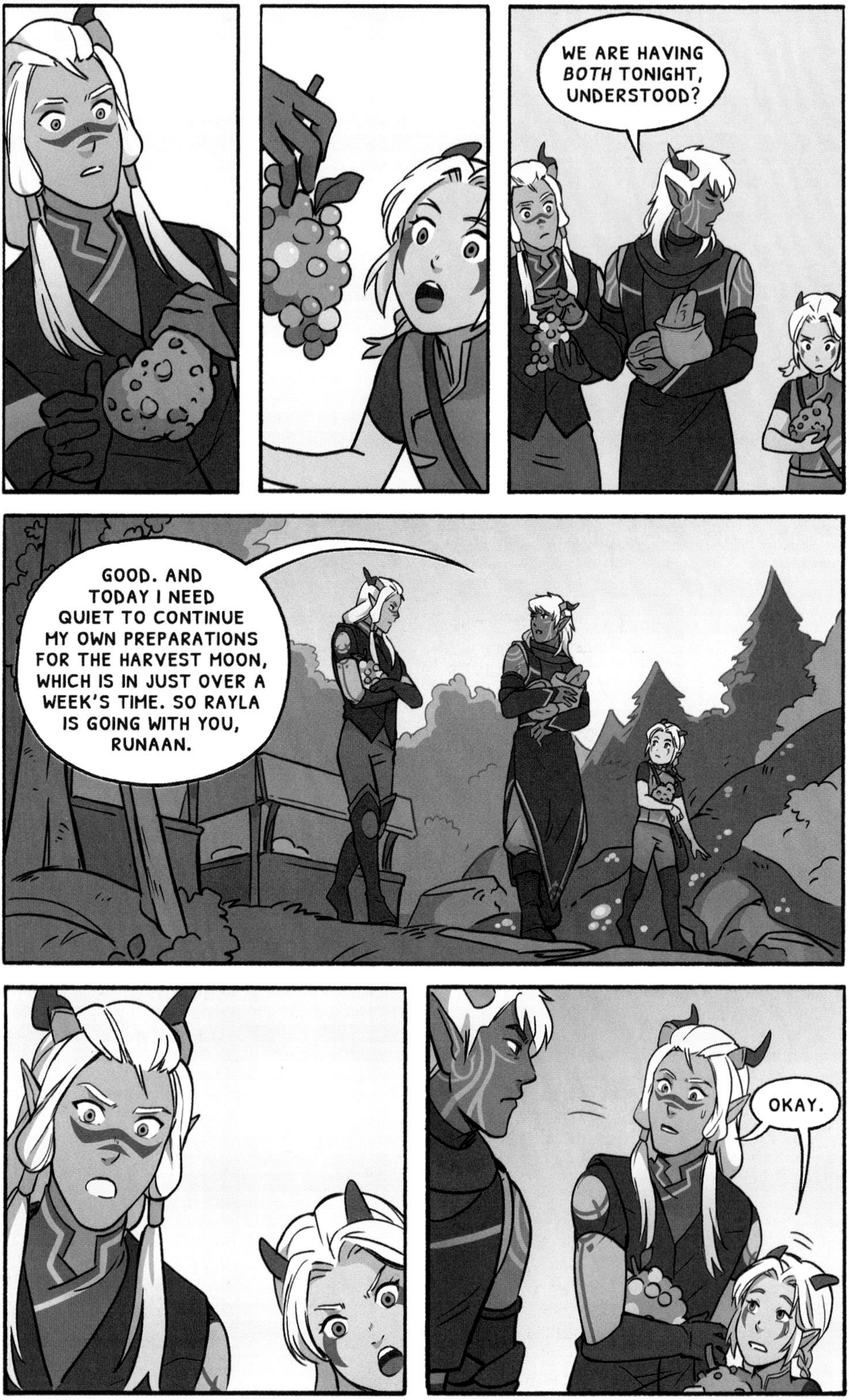
WE ARE HAVING *BOTH* TONIGHT, UNDERSTOOD?
GOOD. AND TODAY I NEED QUIET TO CONTINUE MY OWN PREPARATIONS FOR THE HARVEST MOON, WHICH IS IN JUST OVER A WEEK'S TIME. SO RAYLA IS GOING WITH YOU, RUNAAN.
OKAY.

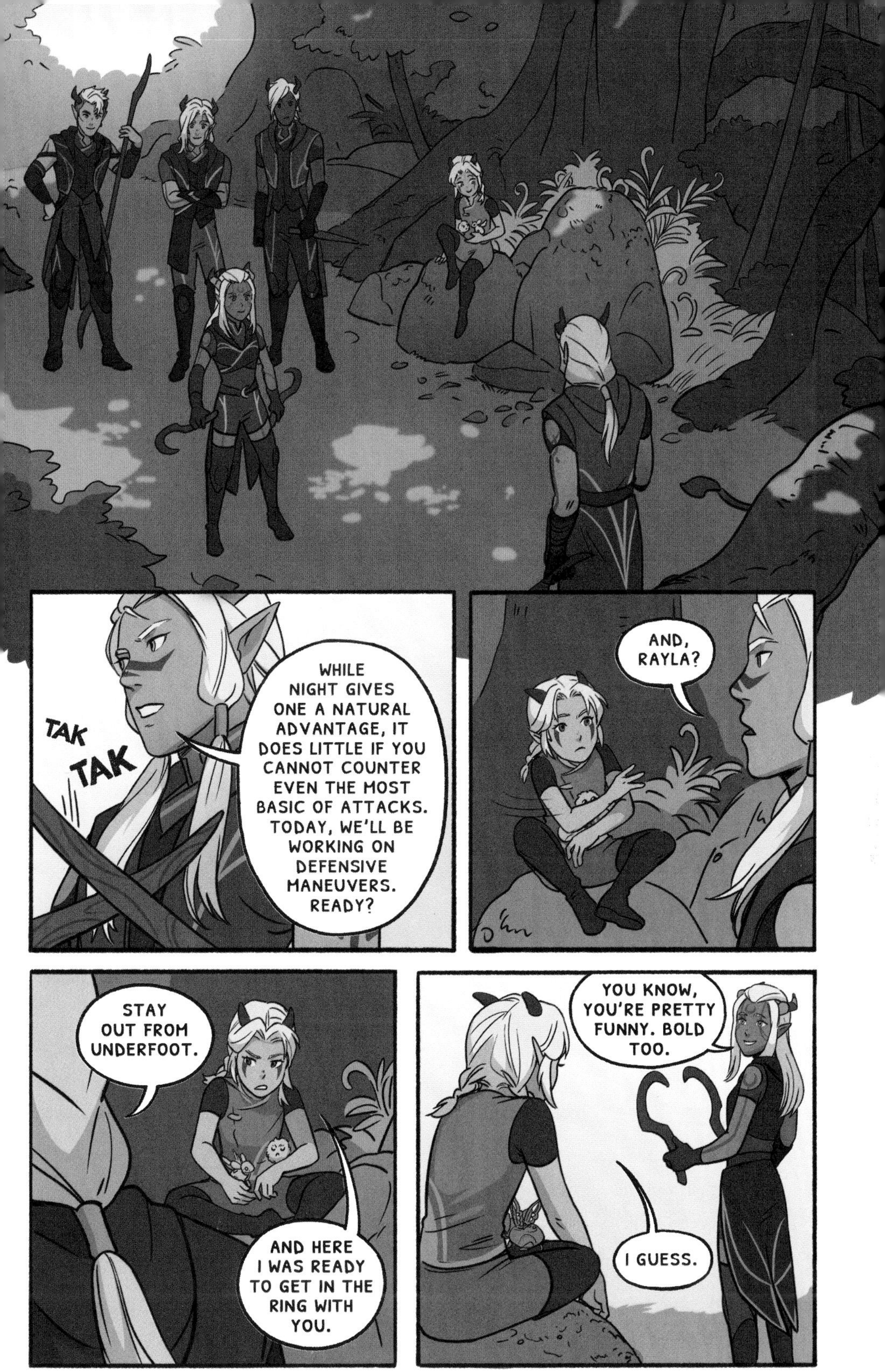
TAK
TAK
WHILE NIGHT GIVES ONE A NATURAL ADVANTAGE, IT DOES LITTLE IF YOU CANNOT COUNTER EVEN THE MOST BASIC OF ATTACKS. TODAY, WE'LL BE WORKING ON DEFENSIVE MANEUVERS. READY?
AND, RAYLA?
STAY OUT FROM UNDERFOOT.
AND HERE I WAS READY TO GET IN THE RING WITH YOU.
YOU KNOW, YOU'RE PRETTY FUNNY. BOLD TOO.
I GUESS.

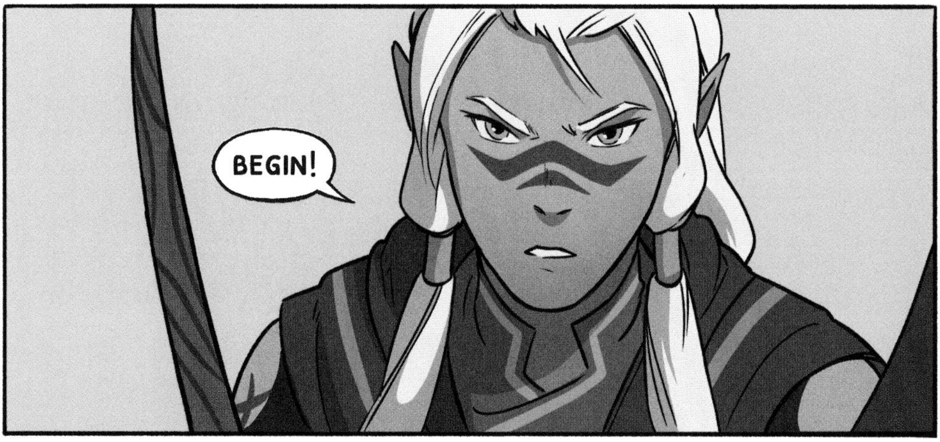
BEGIN!

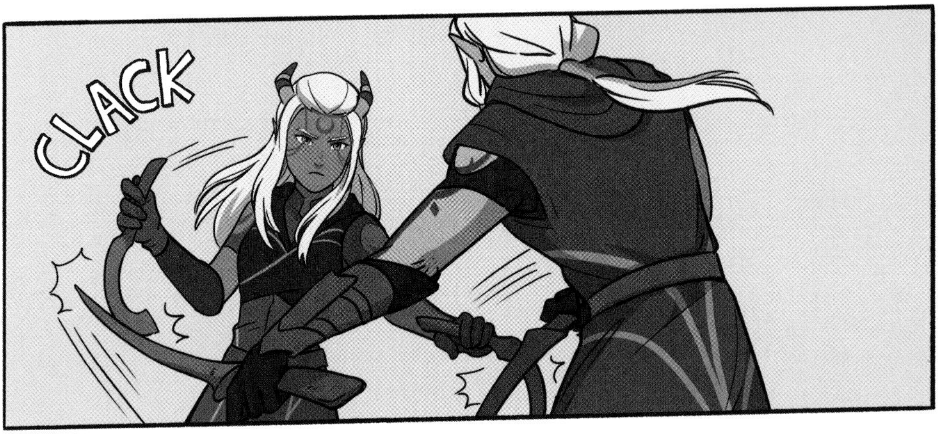
CLACK

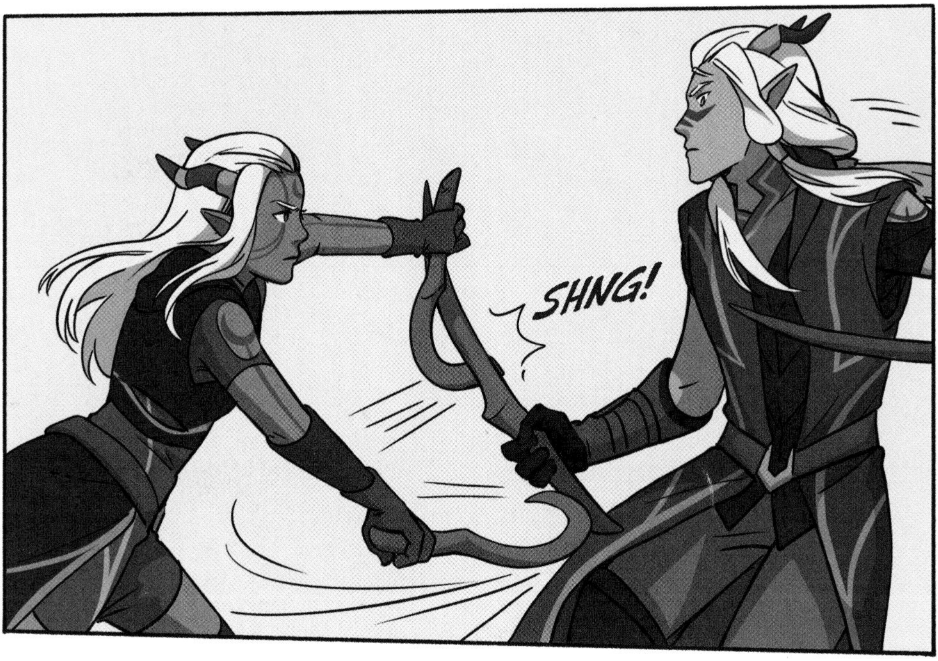
SHNG!

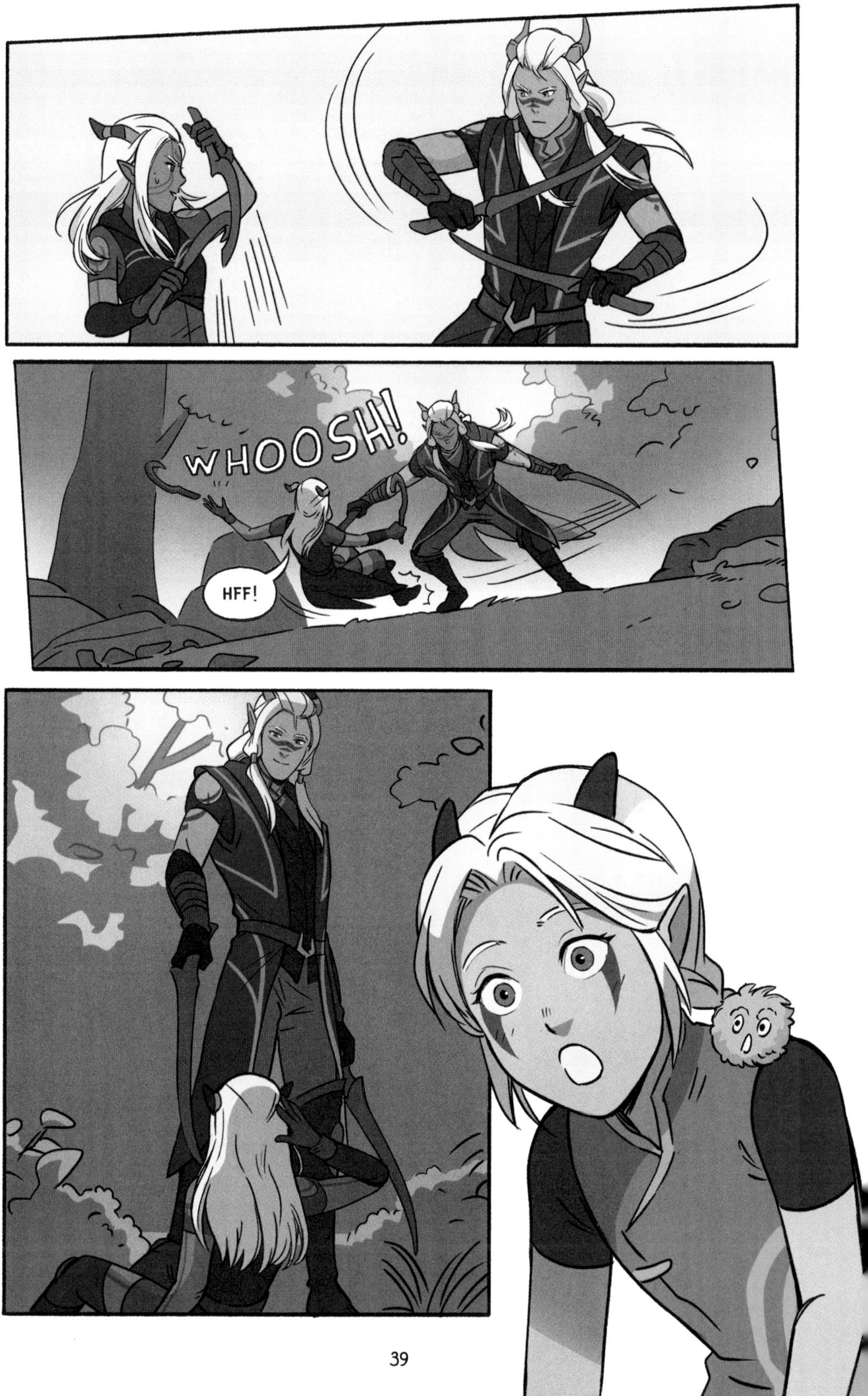
WHOOSH!
HFF!

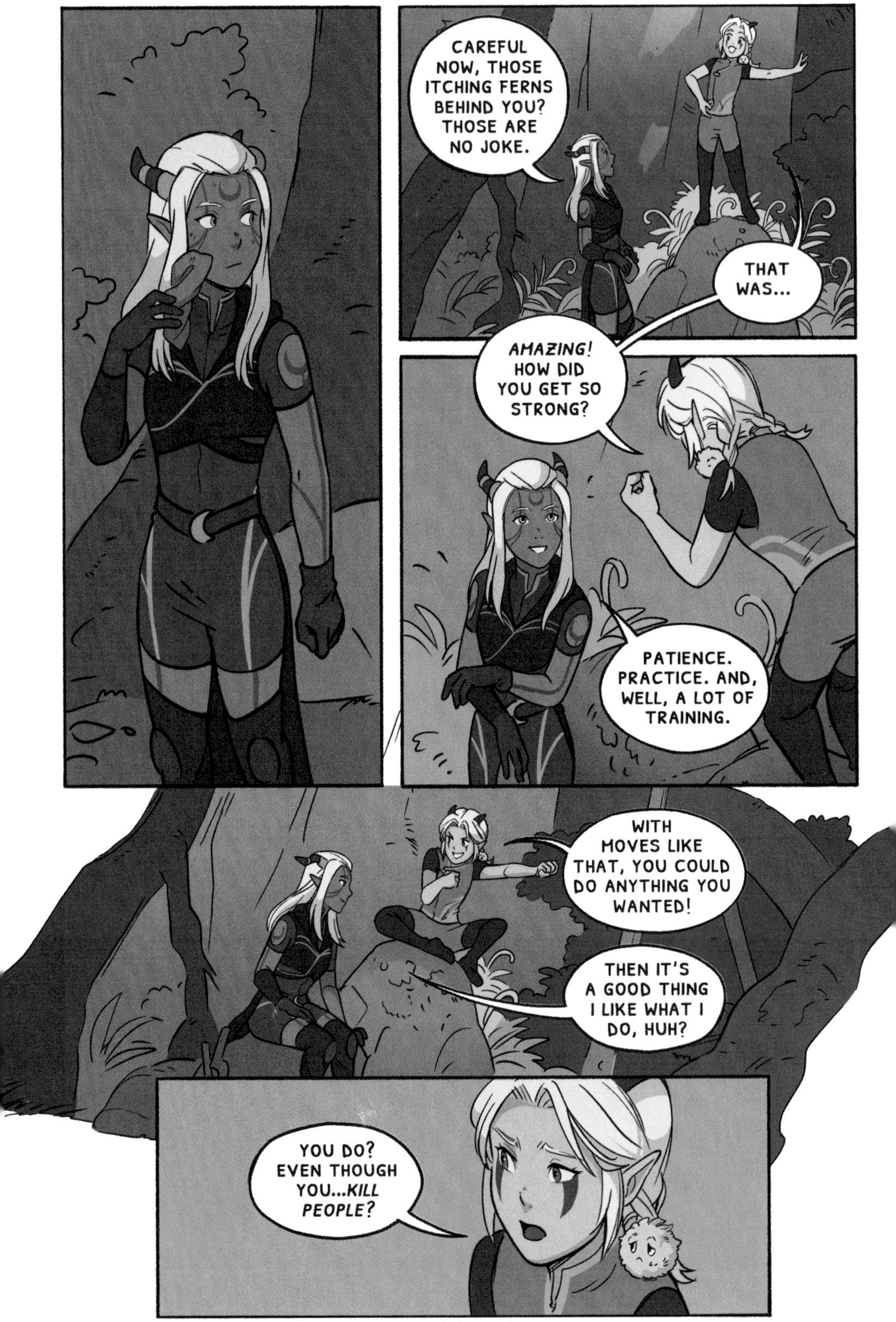
CAREFUL NOW, THOSE ITCHING FERNS BEHIND YOU? THOSE ARE NO JOKE.
THAT WAS...
AMAZING! HOW DID YOU GET SO STRONG?
PATIENCE. PRACTICE. AND, WELL, A LOT OF TRAINING.
WITH MOVES LIKE THAT, YOU COULD DO ANYTHING YOU WANTED!
THEN IT'S A GOOD THING I LIKE WHAT I DO, HUH?
YOU DO? EVEN THOUGH YOU...*KILL PEOPLE*?

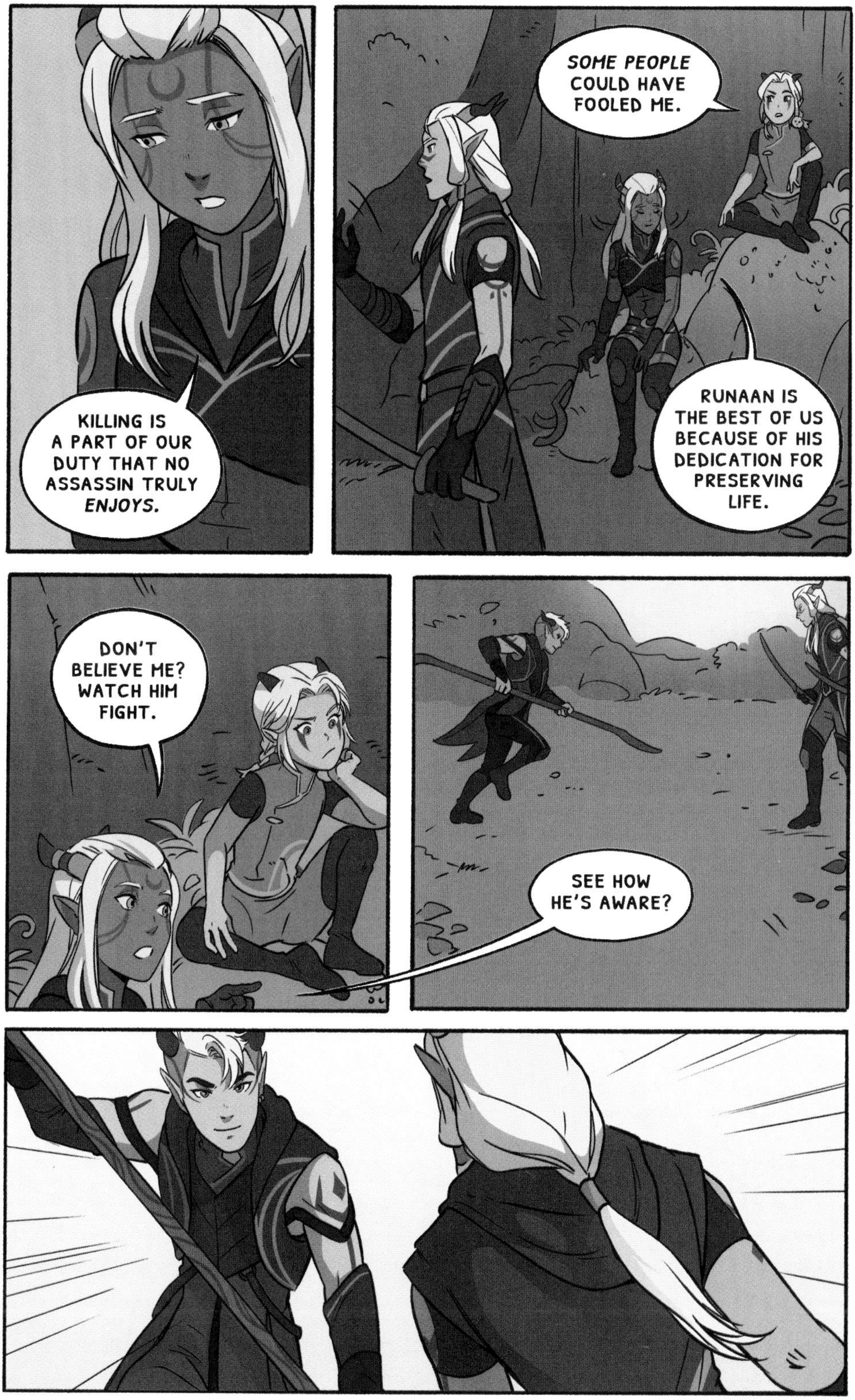
KILLING IS A PART OF OUR DUTY THAT NO ASSASSIN TRULY *ENJOYS.*
SOME PEOPLE COULD HAVE FOOLED ME.
RUNAAN IS THE BEST OF US BECAUSE OF HIS DEDICATION FOR PRESERVING LIFE.
DON'T BELIEVE ME? WATCH HIM FIGHT.
SEE HOW HE'S AWARE?

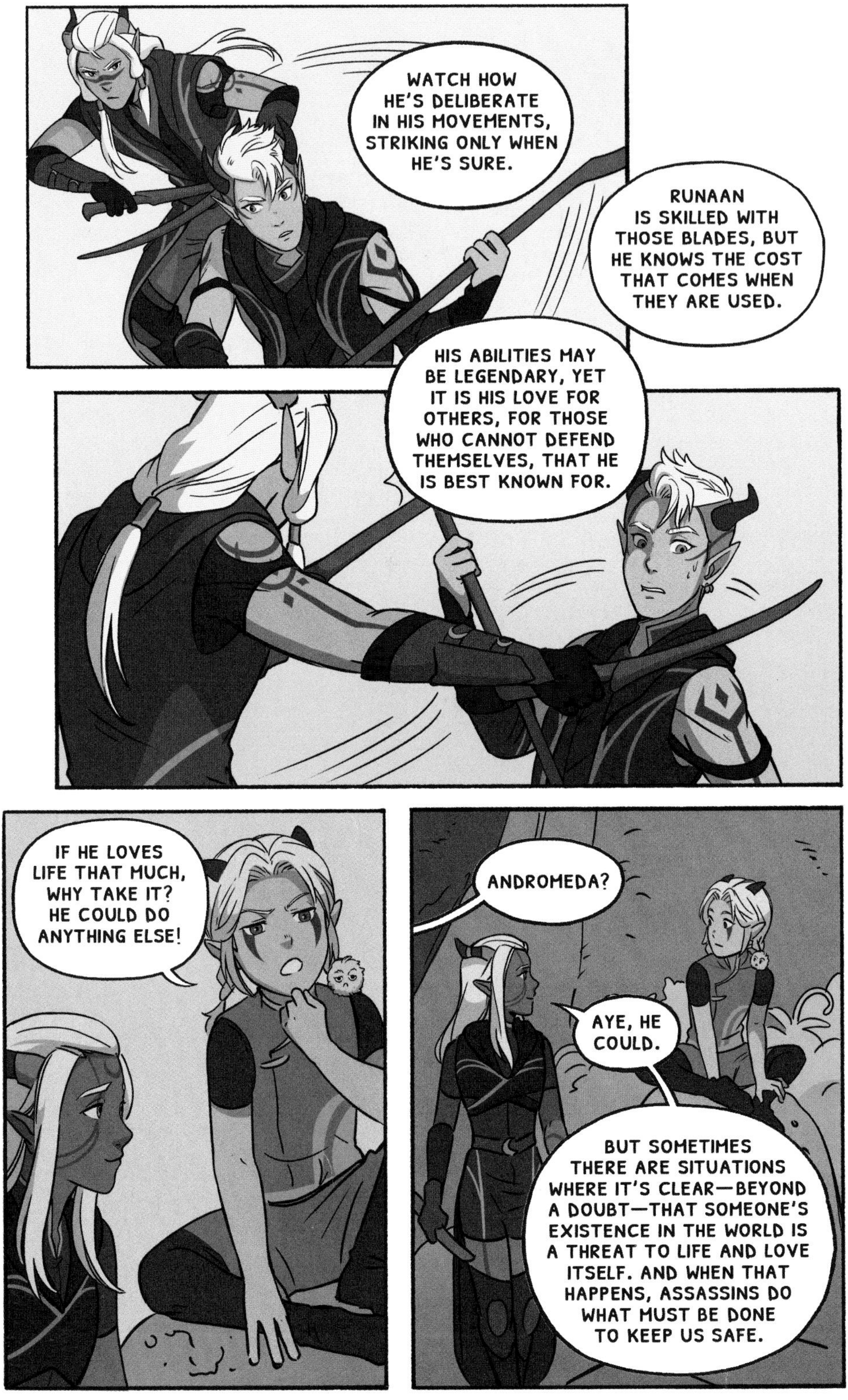
WATCH HOW HE'S DELIBERATE IN HIS MOVEMENTS, STRIKING ONLY WHEN HE'S SURE.
RUNAAN IS SKILLED WITH THOSE BLADES, BUT HE KNOWS THE COST THAT COMES WHEN THEY ARE USED.
HIS ABILITIES MAY BE LEGENDARY, YET IT IS HIS LOVE FOR OTHERS, FOR THOSE WHO CANNOT DEFEND THEMSELVES, THAT HE IS BEST KNOWN FOR.
IF HE LOVES LIFE THAT MUCH, WHY TAKE IT? HE COULD DO ANYTHING ELSE!
ANDROMEDA?
AYE, HE COULD.
BUT SOMETIMES THERE ARE SITUATIONS WHERE IT'S CLEAR—BEYOND A DOUBT—THAT SOMEONE'S EXISTENCE IN THE WORLD IS A THREAT TO LIFE AND LOVE ITSELF. AND WHEN THAT HAPPENS, ASSASSINS DO WHAT MUST BE DONE TO KEEP US SAFE.

CHIIIIRP?

HYAH!

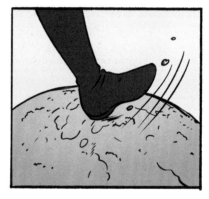

AAAAAARGH!

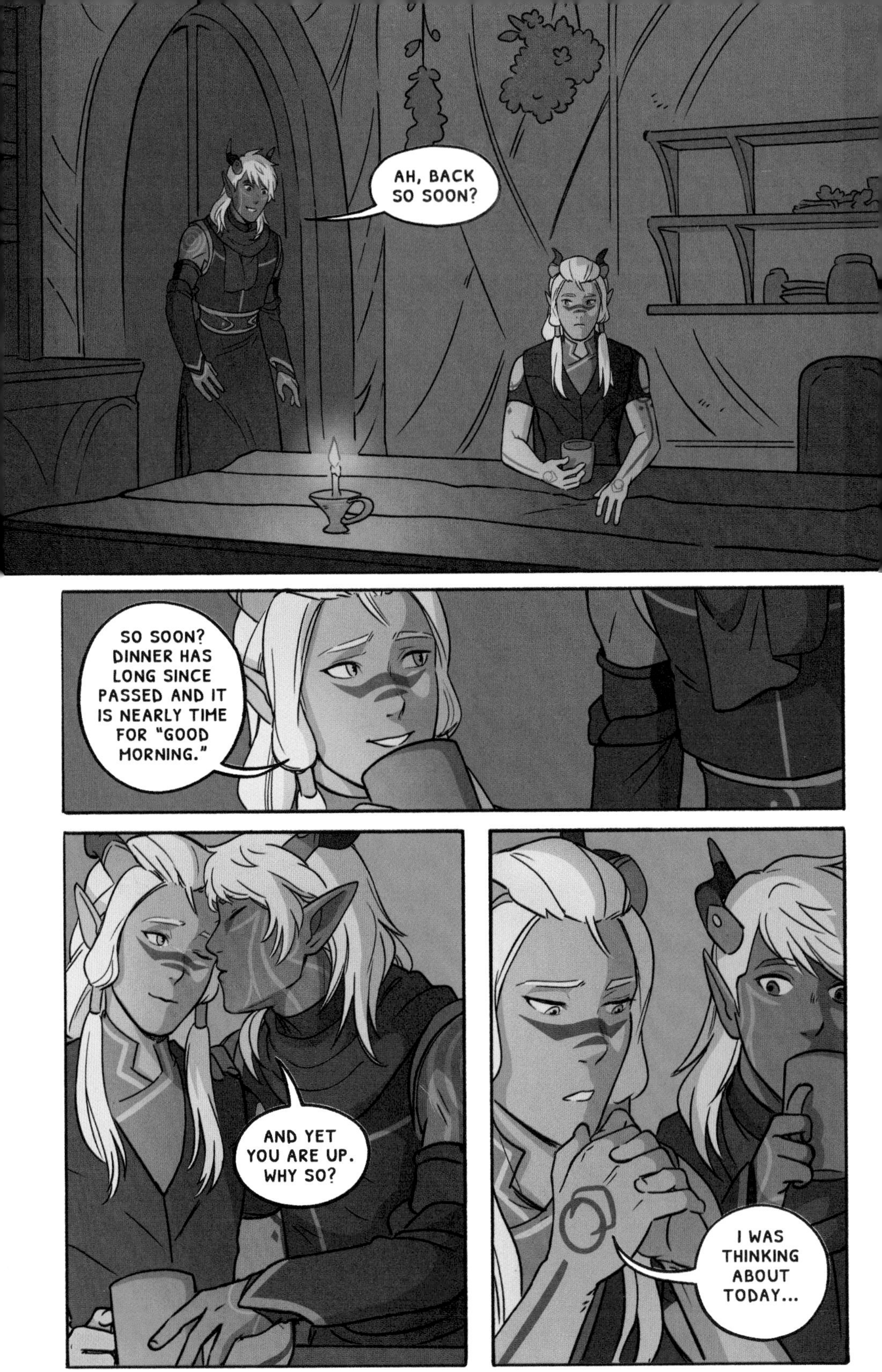
AH, BACK SO SOON?
SO SOON? DINNER HAS LONG SINCE PASSED AND IT IS NEARLY TIME FOR "GOOD MORNING."
AND YET YOU ARE UP. WHY SO?
I WAS THINKING ABOUT TODAY...

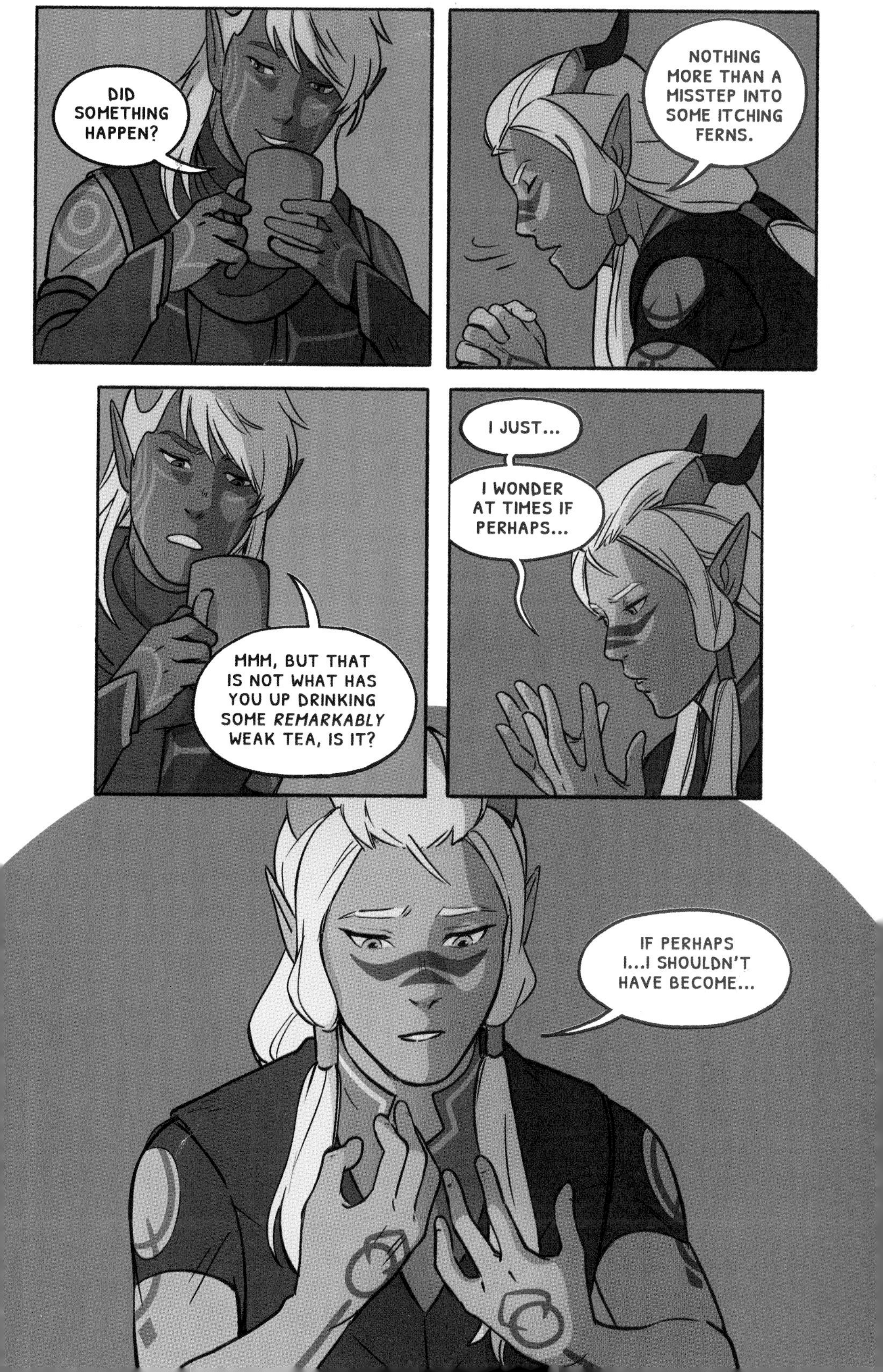
DID SOMETHING HAPPEN?
NOTHING MORE THAN A MISSTEP INTO SOME ITCHING FERNS.
MMM, BUT THAT IS NOT WHAT HAS YOU UP DRINKING SOME *REMARKABLY* WEAK TEA, IS IT?
I JUST...
I WONDER AT TIMES IF PERHAPS...
IF PERHAPS I...I SHOULDN'T HAVE BECOME...

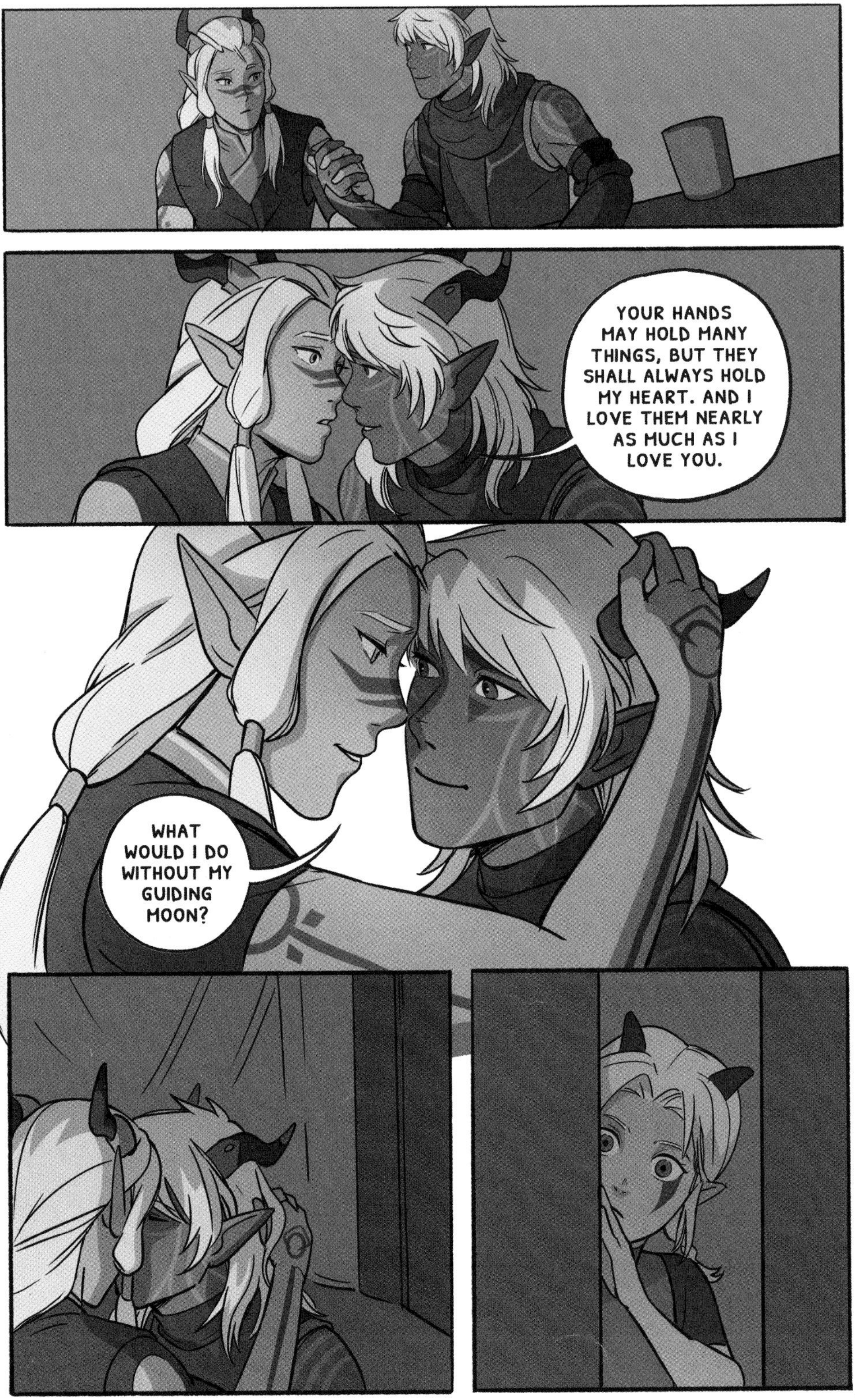
YOUR HANDS MAY HOLD MANY THINGS, BUT THEY SHALL ALWAYS HOLD MY HEART. AND I LOVE THEM NEARLY AS MUCH AS I LOVE YOU.
WHAT WOULD I DO WITHOUT MY GUIDING MOON?

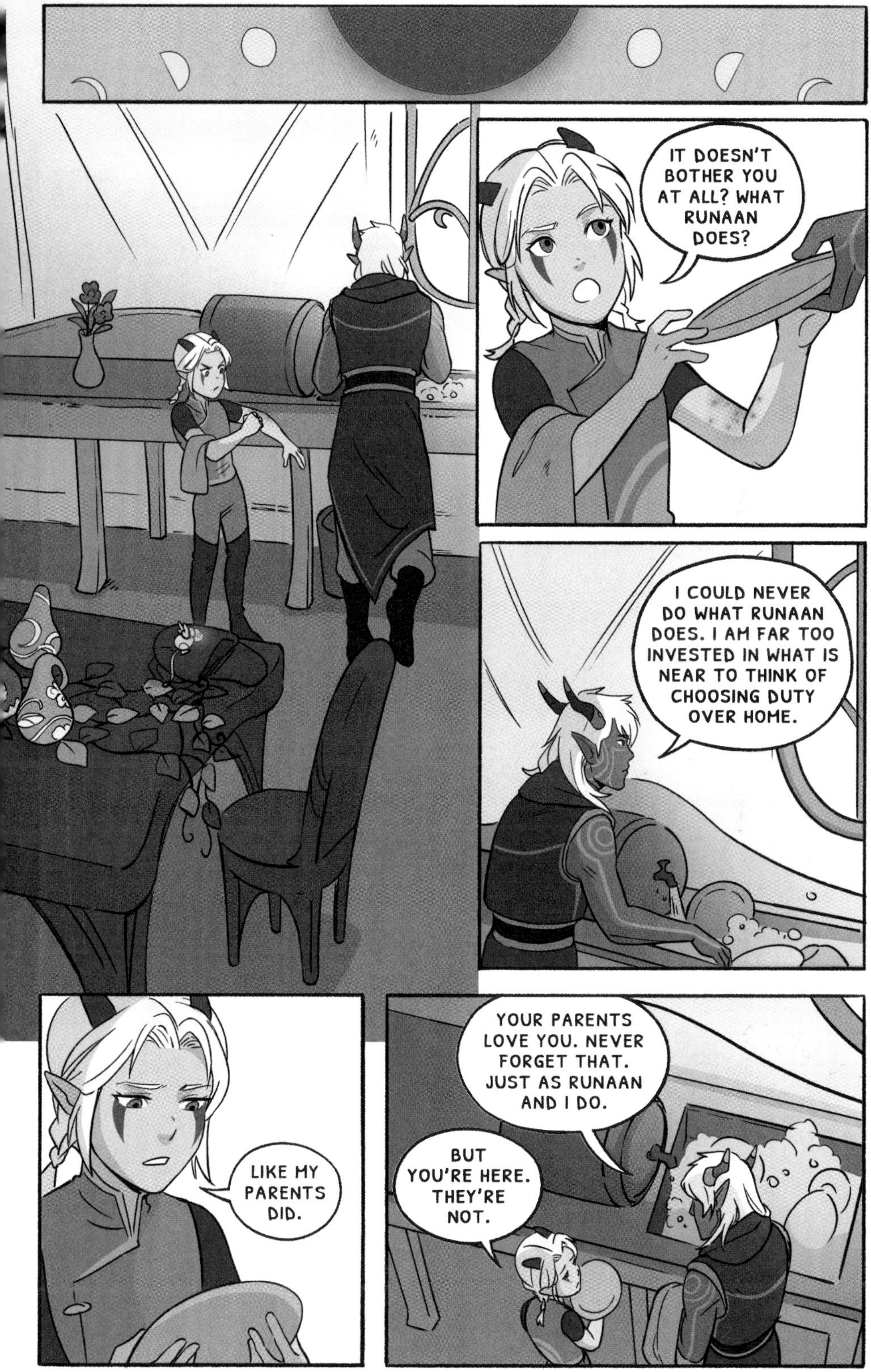
IT DOESN'T BOTHER YOU AT ALL? WHAT RUNAAN DOES?
I COULD NEVER DO WHAT RUNAAN DOES. I AM FAR TOO INVESTED IN WHAT IS NEAR TO THINK OF CHOOSING DUTY OVER HOME.
LIKE MY PARENTS DID.
YOUR PARENTS LOVE YOU. NEVER FORGET THAT. JUST AS RUNAAN AND I DO.
BUT YOU'RE HERE. THEY'RE NOT.

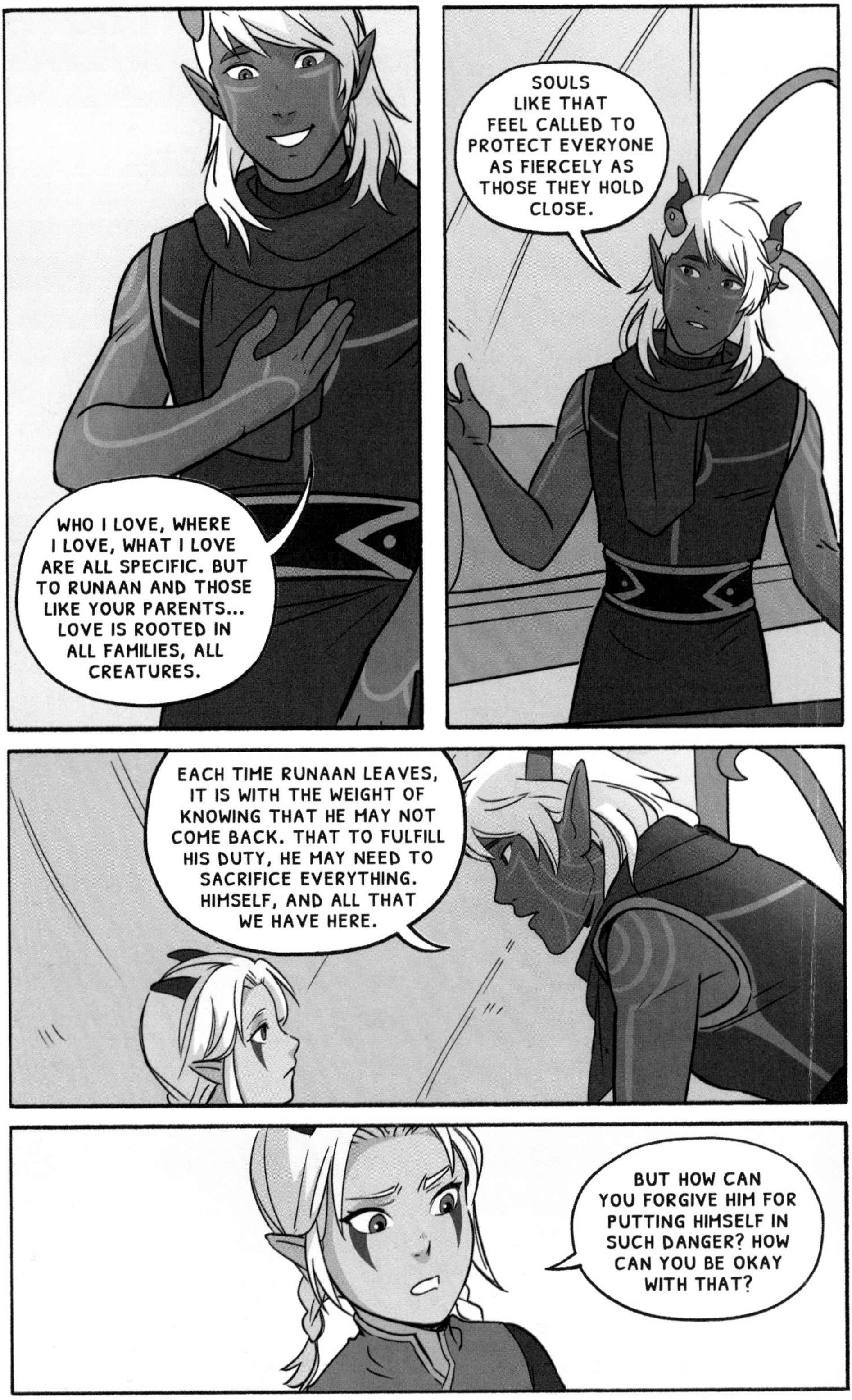
WHO I LOVE, WHERE I LOVE, WHAT I LOVE ARE ALL SPECIFIC. BUT TO RUNAAN AND THOSE LIKE YOUR PARENTS... LOVE IS ROOTED IN ALL FAMILIES, ALL CREATURES.
SOULS LIKE THAT FEEL CALLED TO PROTECT EVERYONE AS FIERCELY AS THOSE THEY HOLD CLOSE.
EACH TIME RUNAAN LEAVES, IT IS WITH THE WEIGHT OF KNOWING THAT HE MAY NOT COME BACK. THAT TO FULFILL HIS DUTY, HE MAY NEED TO SACRIFICE EVERYTHING. HIMSELF, AND ALL THAT WE HAVE HERE.
BUT HOW CAN YOU FORGIVE HIM FOR PUTTING HIMSELF IN SUCH DANGER? HOW CAN YOU BE OKAY WITH THAT?

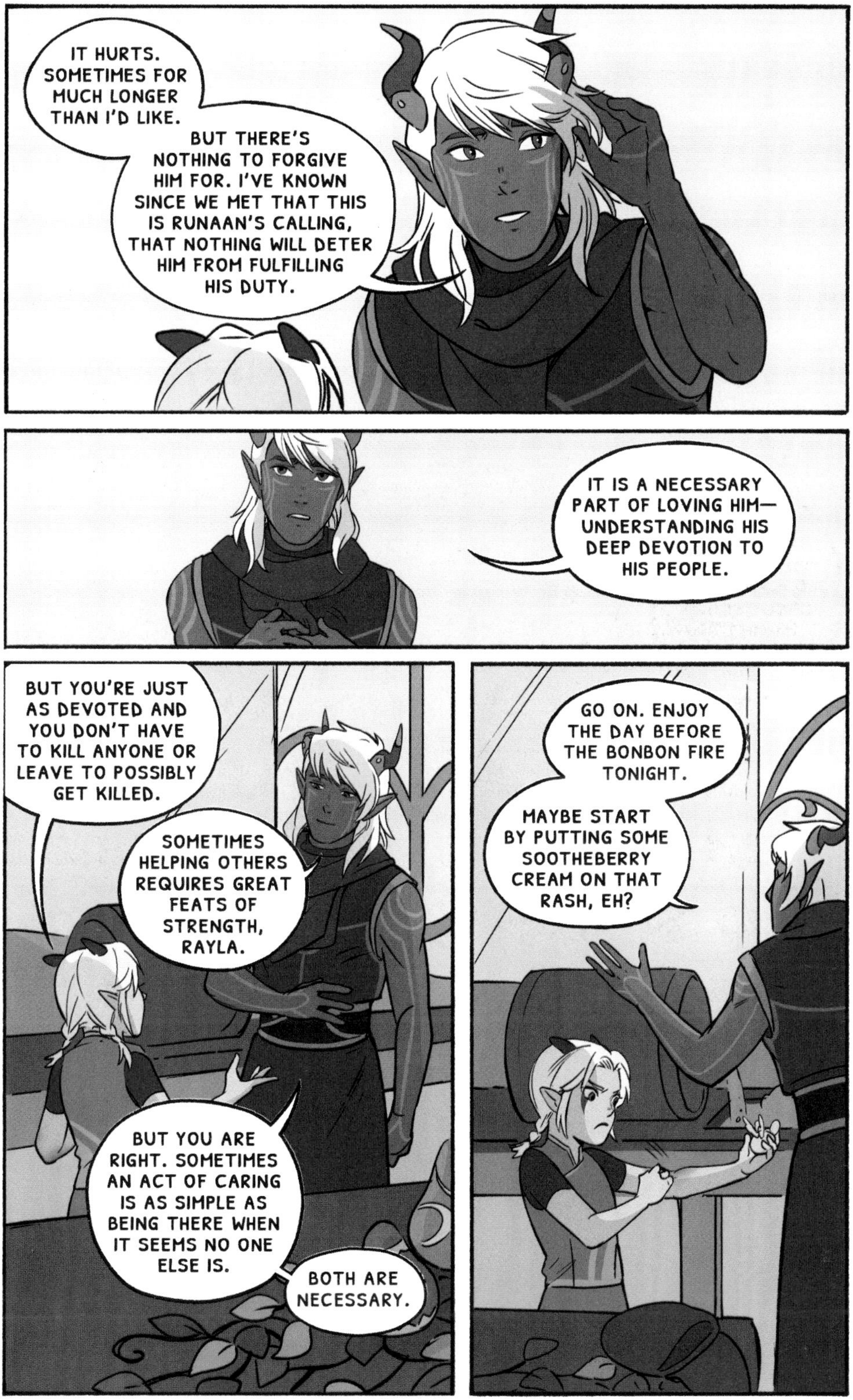
IT HURTS. SOMETIMES FOR MUCH LONGER THAN I'D LIKE.
BUT THERE'S NOTHING TO FORGIVE HIM FOR. I'VE KNOWN SINCE WE MET THAT THIS IS RUNAAN'S CALLING, THAT NOTHING WILL DETER HIM FROM FULFILLING HIS DUTY.
IT IS A NECESSARY PART OF LOVING HIM— UNDERSTANDING HIS DEEP DEVOTION TO HIS PEOPLE.
BUT YOU'RE JUST AS DEVOTED AND YOU DON'T HAVE TO KILL ANYONE OR LEAVE TO POSSIBLY GET KILLED.
SOMETIMES HELPING OTHERS REQUIRES GREAT FEATS OF STRENGTH, RAYLA.
BUT YOU ARE RIGHT. SOMETIMES AN ACT OF CARING IS AS SIMPLE AS BEING THERE WHEN IT SEEMS NO ONE ELSE IS.
BOTH ARE NECESSARY.
GO ON. ENJOY THE DAY BEFORE THE BONBON FIRE TONIGHT.
MAYBE START BY PUTTING SOME SOOTHEBERRY CREAM ON THAT RASH, EH?

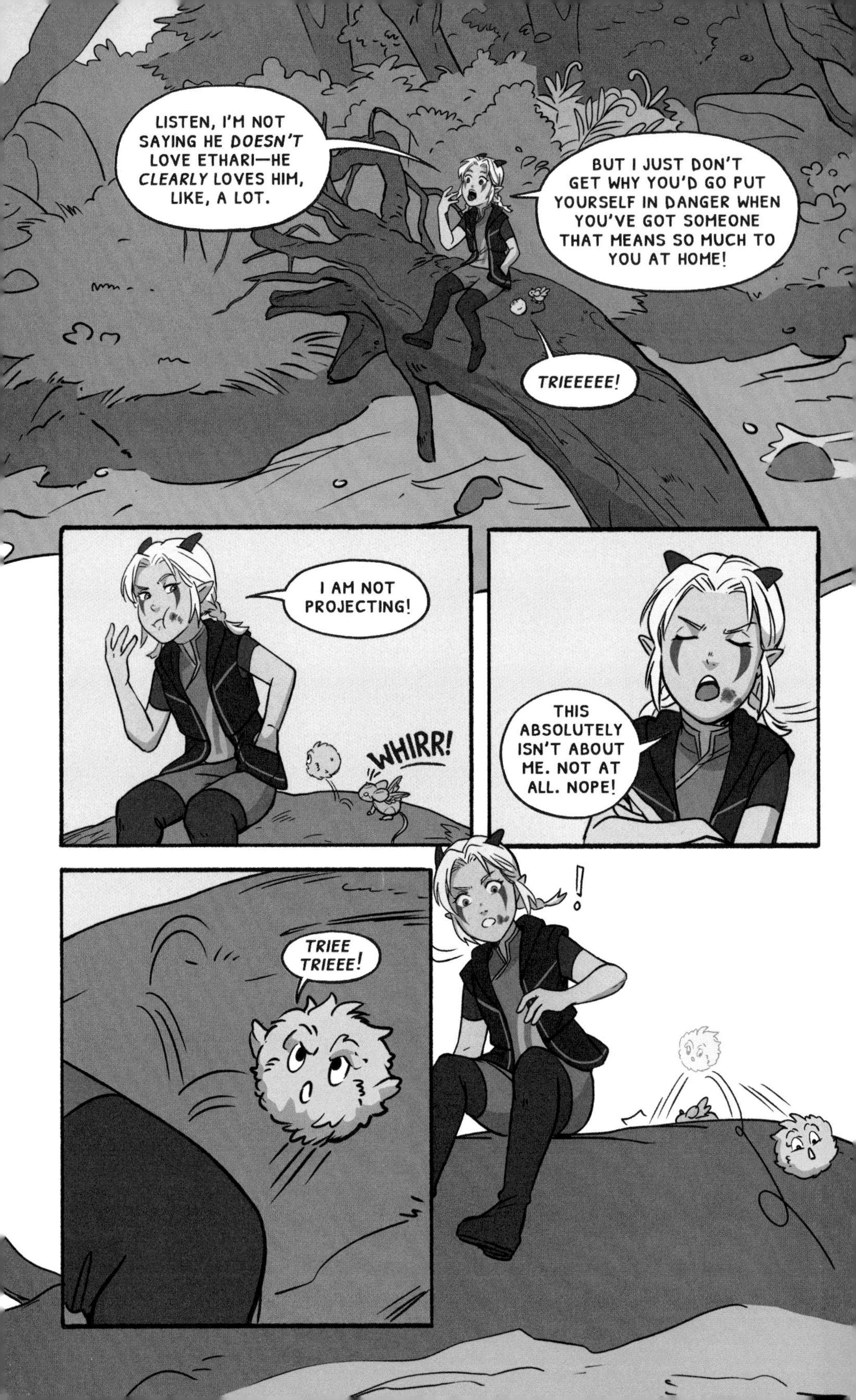
LISTEN, I'M NOT SAYING HE *DOESN'T* LOVE ETHARI—HE *CLEARLY* LOVES HIM, LIKE, A LOT.
BUT I JUST DON'T GET WHY YOU'D GO PUT YOURSELF IN DANGER WHEN YOU'VE GOT SOMEONE THAT MEANS SO MUCH TO YOU AT HOME!
TRIEEEEE!
I AM NOT PROJECTING!
WHIRR!
THIS ABSOLUTELY ISN'T ABOUT ME. NOT AT ALL. NOPE!
!
TRIEE TRIEEE!

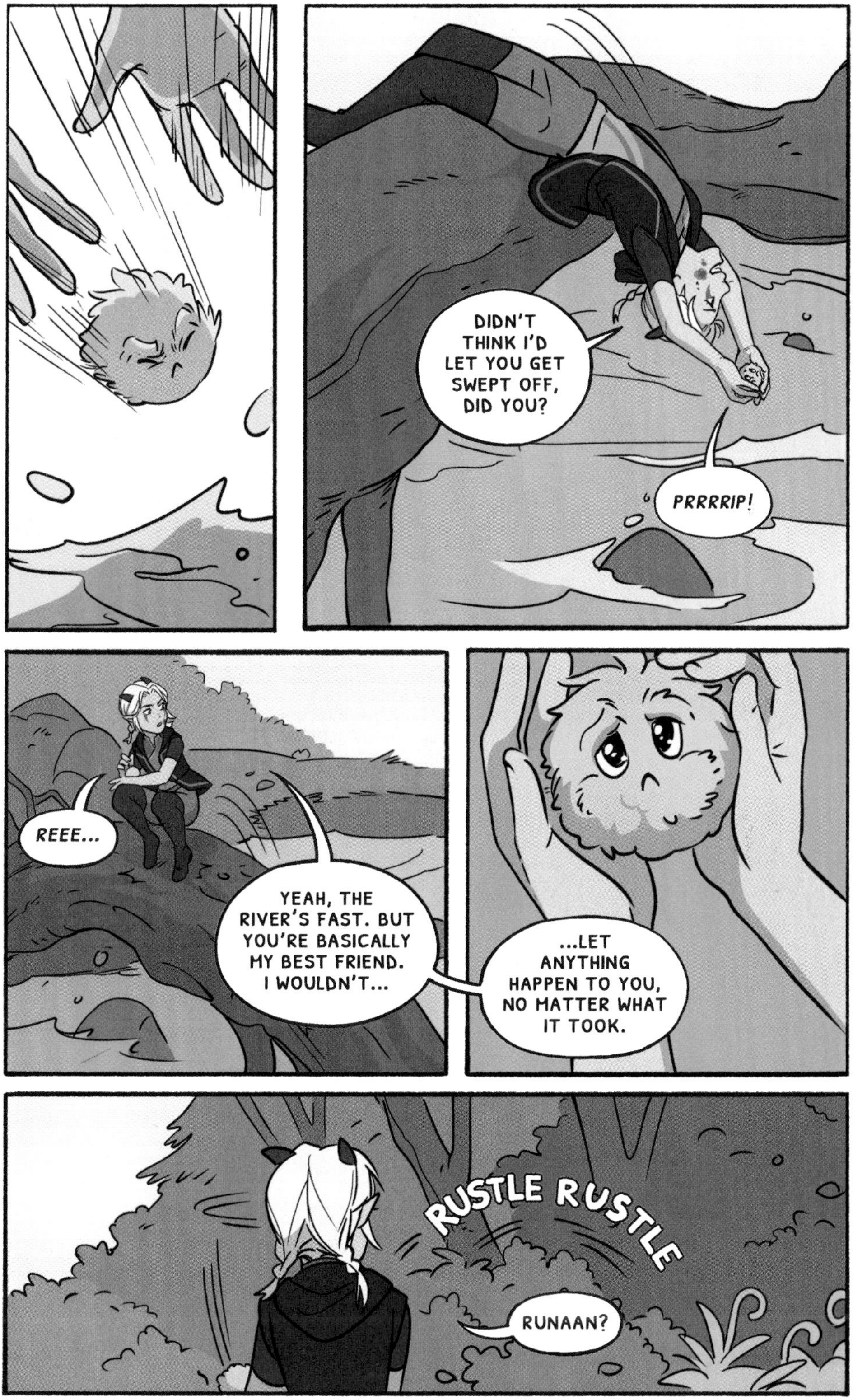
DIDN'T THINK I'D LET YOU GET SWEPT OFF, DID YOU?
PRRRRIP!
REEE...
YEAH, THE RIVER'S FAST. BUT YOU'RE BASICALLY MY BEST FRIEND. I WOULDN'T...
...LET ANYTHING HAPPEN TO YOU, NO MATTER WHAT IT TOOK.
RUSTLE RUSTLE
RUNAAN?

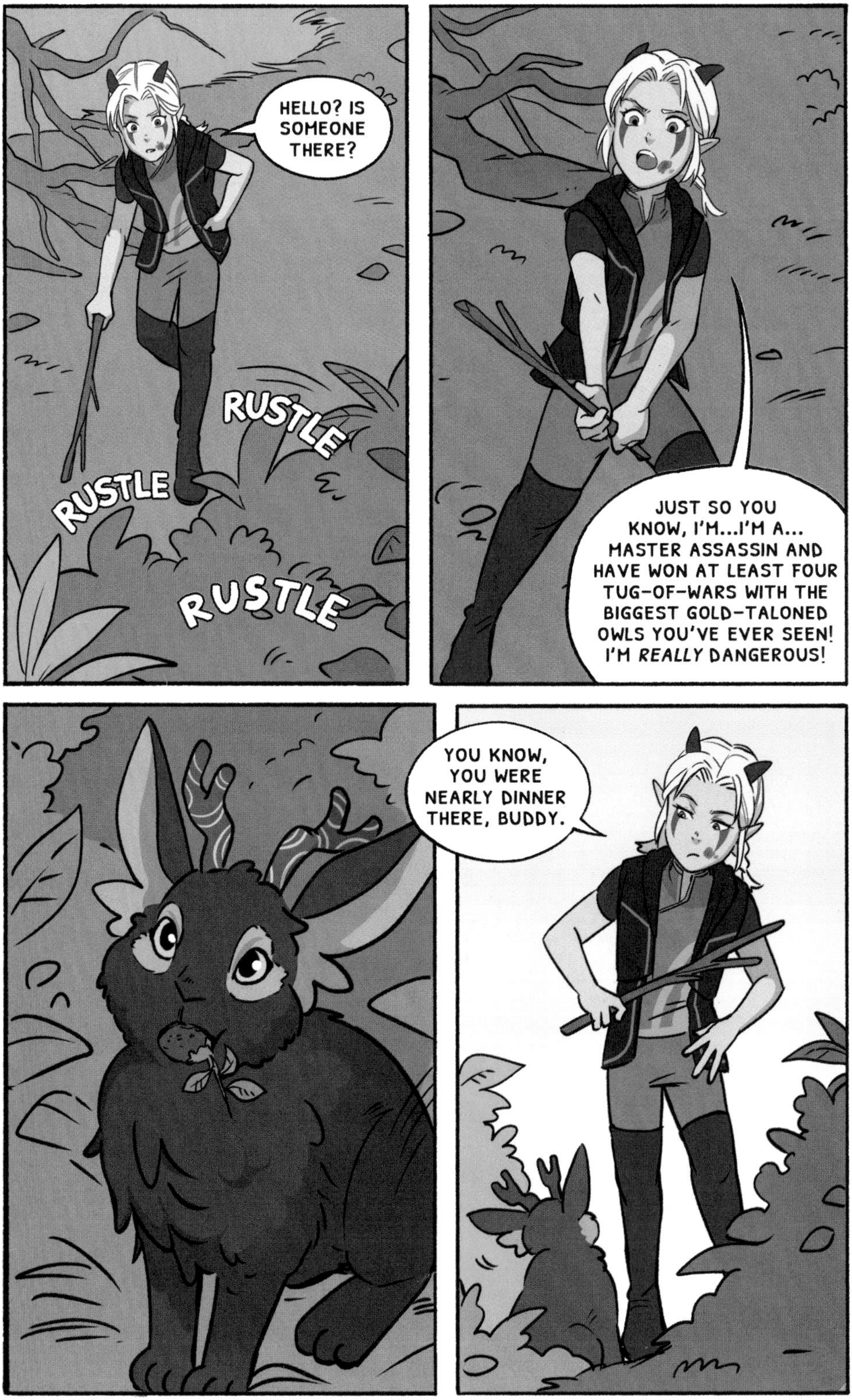
HELLO? IS SOMEONE THERE?
RUSTLE
RUSTLE
RUSTLE
JUST SO YOU KNOW, I'M...I'M A... MASTER ASSASSIN AND HAVE WON AT LEAST FOUR TUG-OF-WARS WITH THE BIGGEST GOLD-TALONED OWLS YOU'VE EVER SEEN! I'M *REALLY* DANGEROUS!
YOU KNOW, YOU WERE NEARLY DINNER THERE, BUDDY.

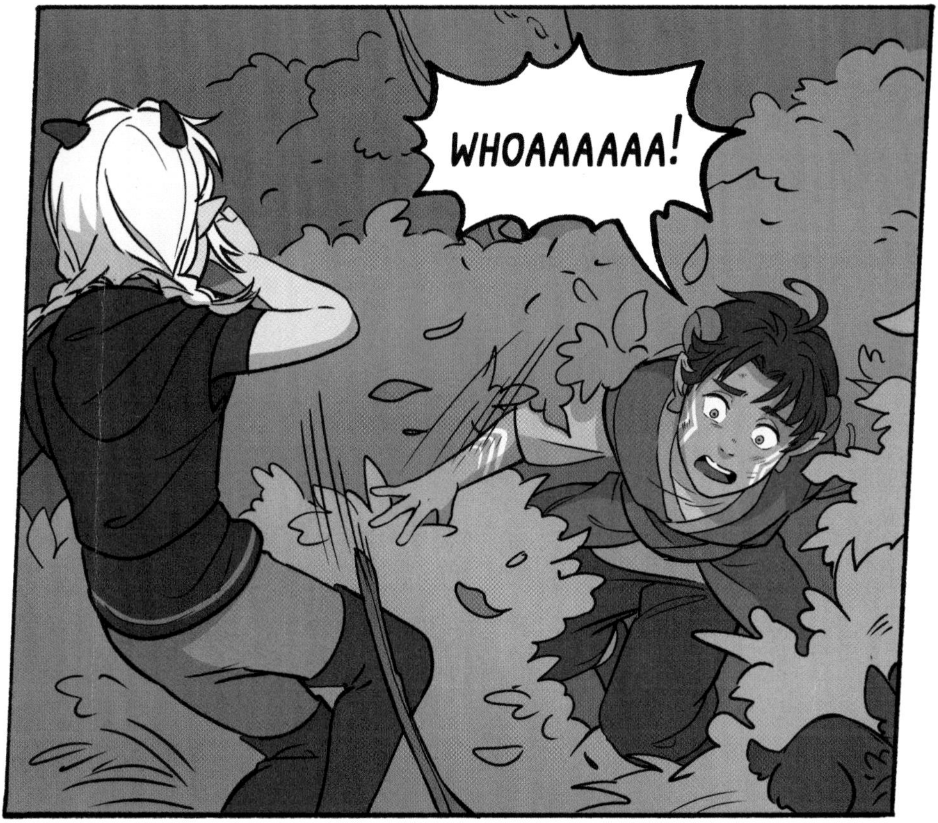
WHOAAAAAA!

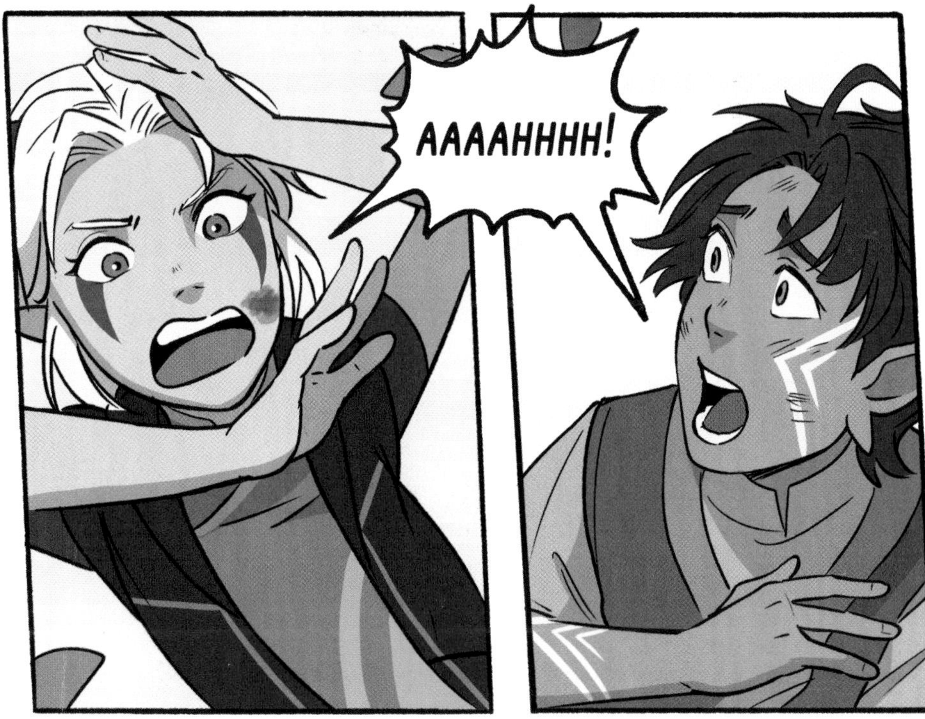
AAAAHHHH!

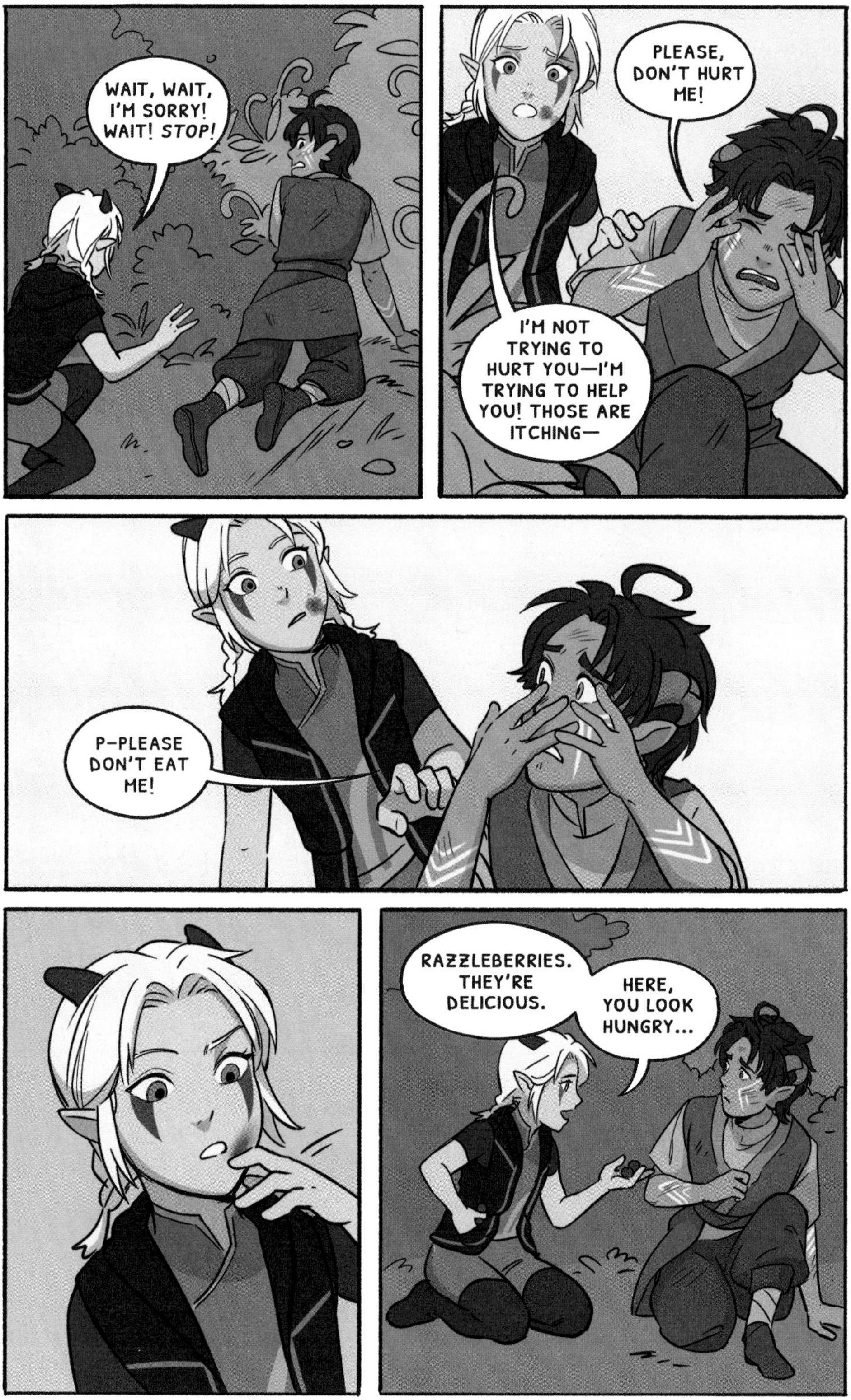
WAIT, WAIT, I'M SORRY! WAIT! *STOP!*
PLEASE, DON'T HURT ME!
I'M NOT TRYING TO HURT YOU—I'M TRYING TO HELP YOU! THOSE ARE ITCHING—
P-PLEASE DON'T EAT ME!
RAZZLEBERRIES. THEY'RE DELICIOUS.
HERE, YOU LOOK HUNGRY...

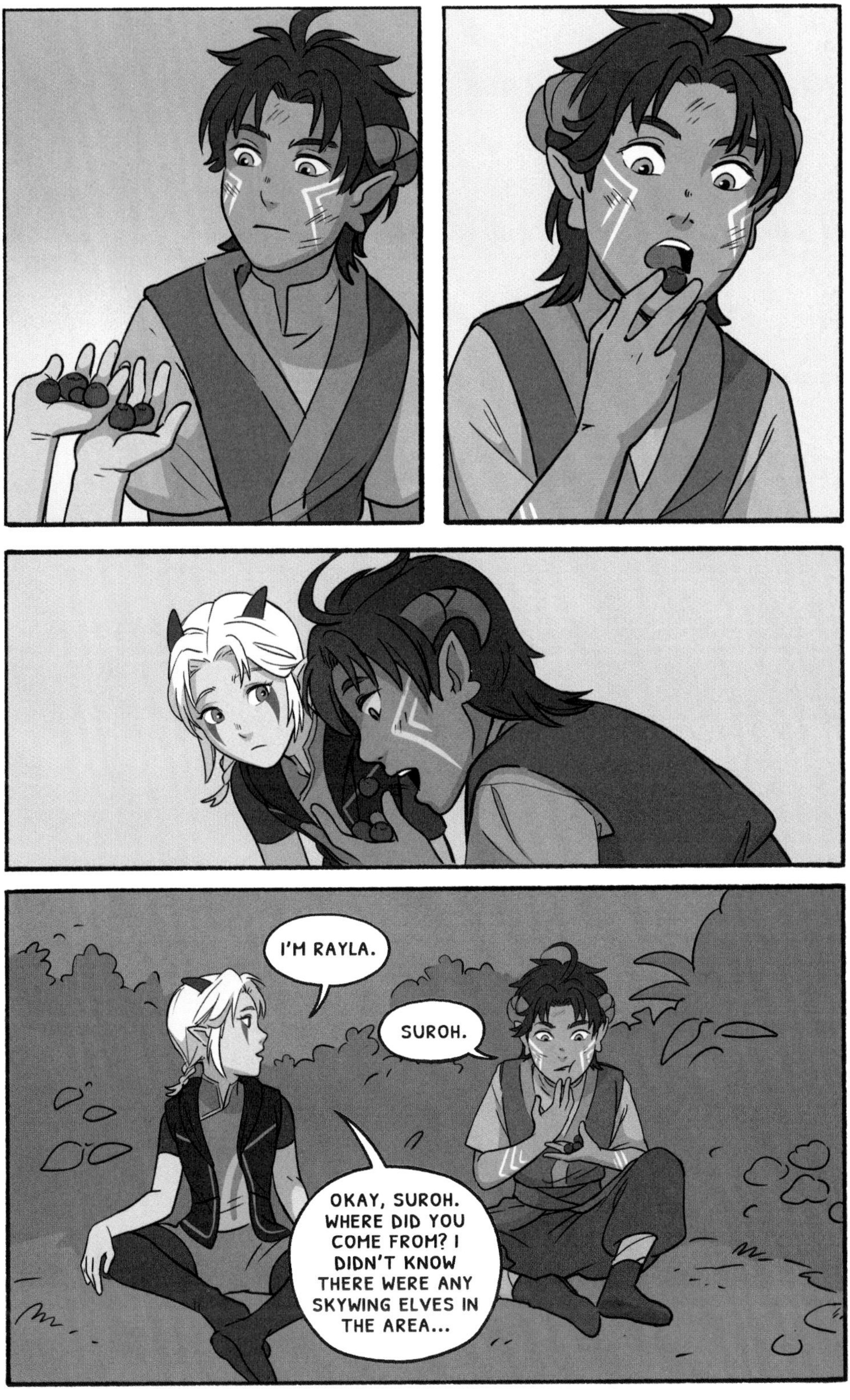
I'M RAYLA.
SUROH.
OKAY, SUROH. WHERE DID YOU COME FROM? I DIDN'T KNOW THERE WERE ANY SKYWING ELVES IN THE AREA...

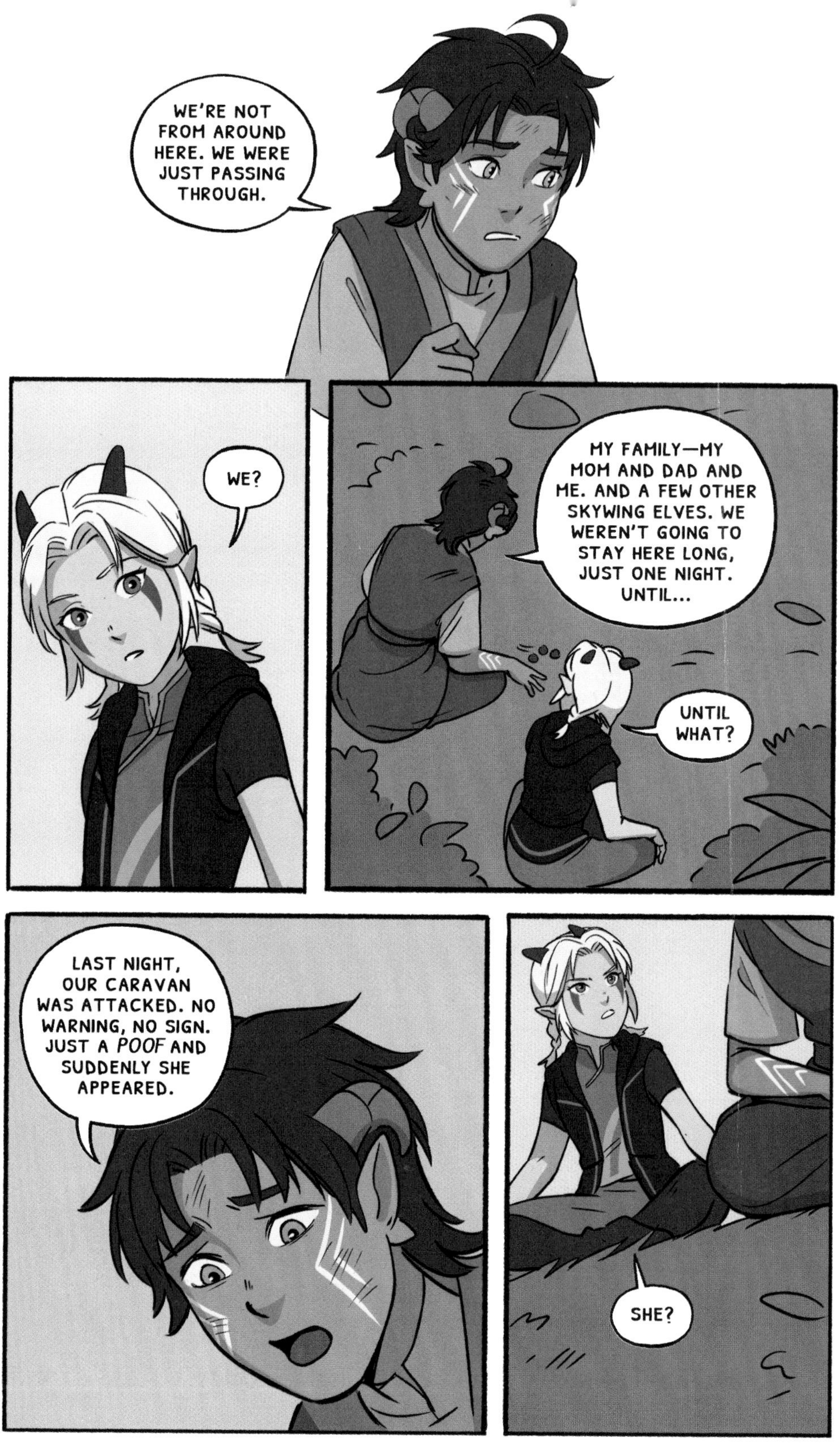
WE'RE NOT FROM AROUND HERE. WE WERE JUST PASSING THROUGH.
WE?
MY FAMILY—MY MOM AND DAD AND ME. AND A FEW OTHER SKYWING ELVES. WE WEREN'T GOING TO STAY HERE LONG, JUST ONE NIGHT. UNTIL...
UNTIL WHAT?
LAST NIGHT, OUR CARAVAN WAS ATTACKED. NO WARNING, NO SIGN. JUST A *POOF* AND SUDDENLY SHE APPEARED.
SHE?

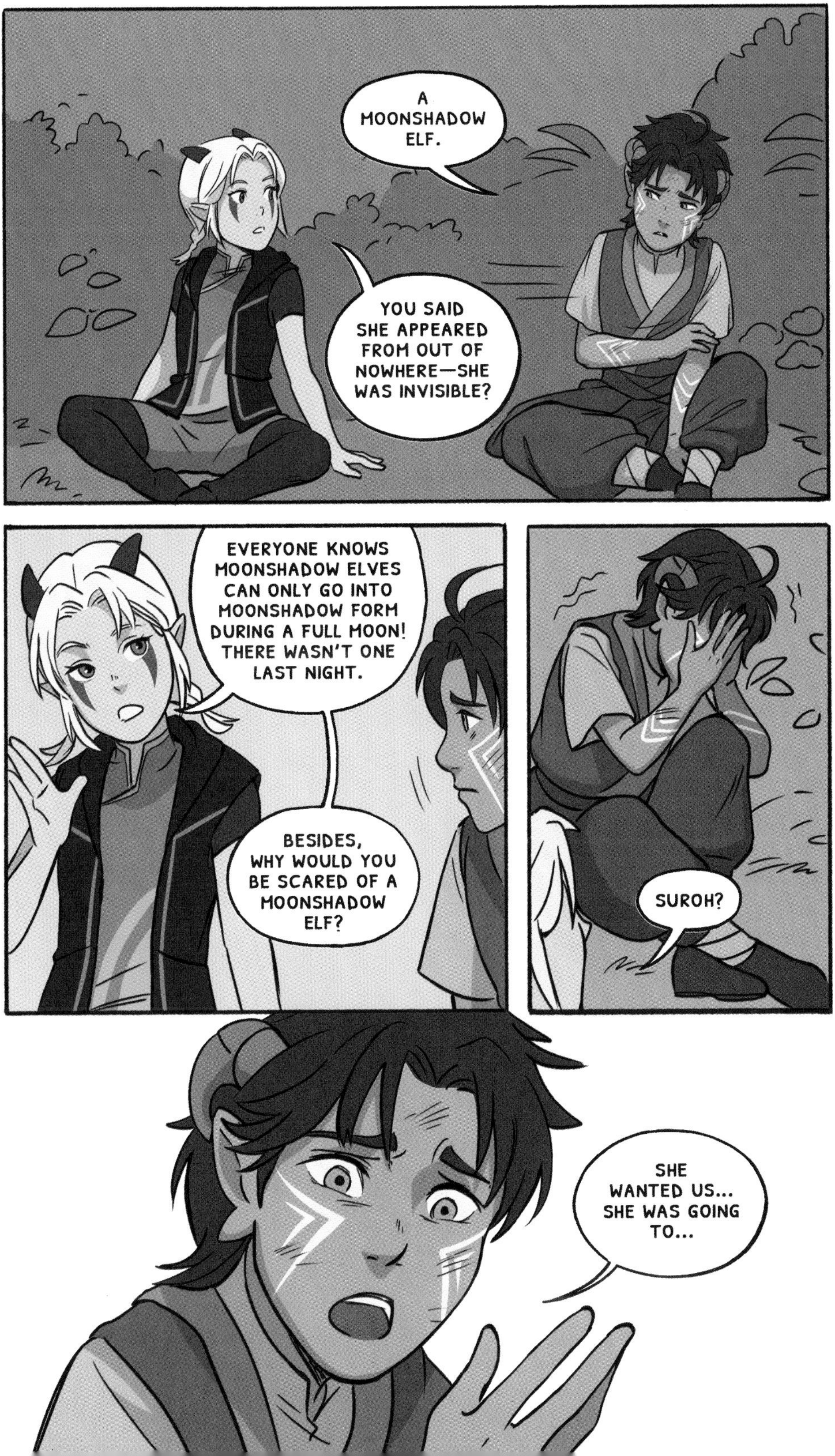
A MOONSHADOW ELF.
YOU SAID SHE APPEARED FROM OUT OF NOWHERE—SHE WAS INVISIBLE?
EVERYONE KNOWS MOONSHADOW ELVES CAN ONLY GO INTO MOONSHADOW FORM DURING A FULL MOON! THERE WASN'T ONE LAST NIGHT.
BESIDES, WHY WOULD YOU BE SCARED OF A MOONSHADOW ELF?
SUROH?
SHE WANTED US... SHE WAS GOING TO...

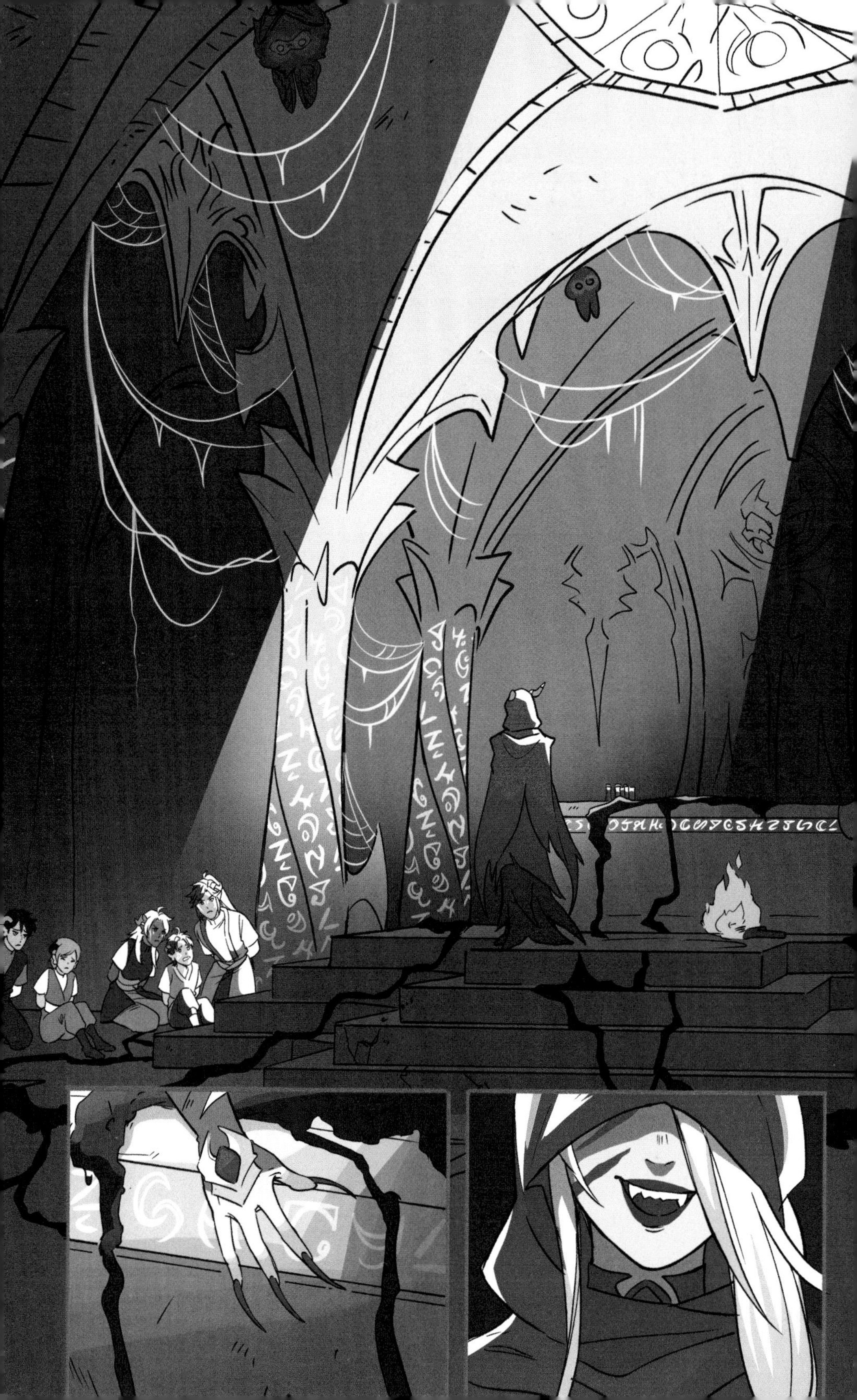

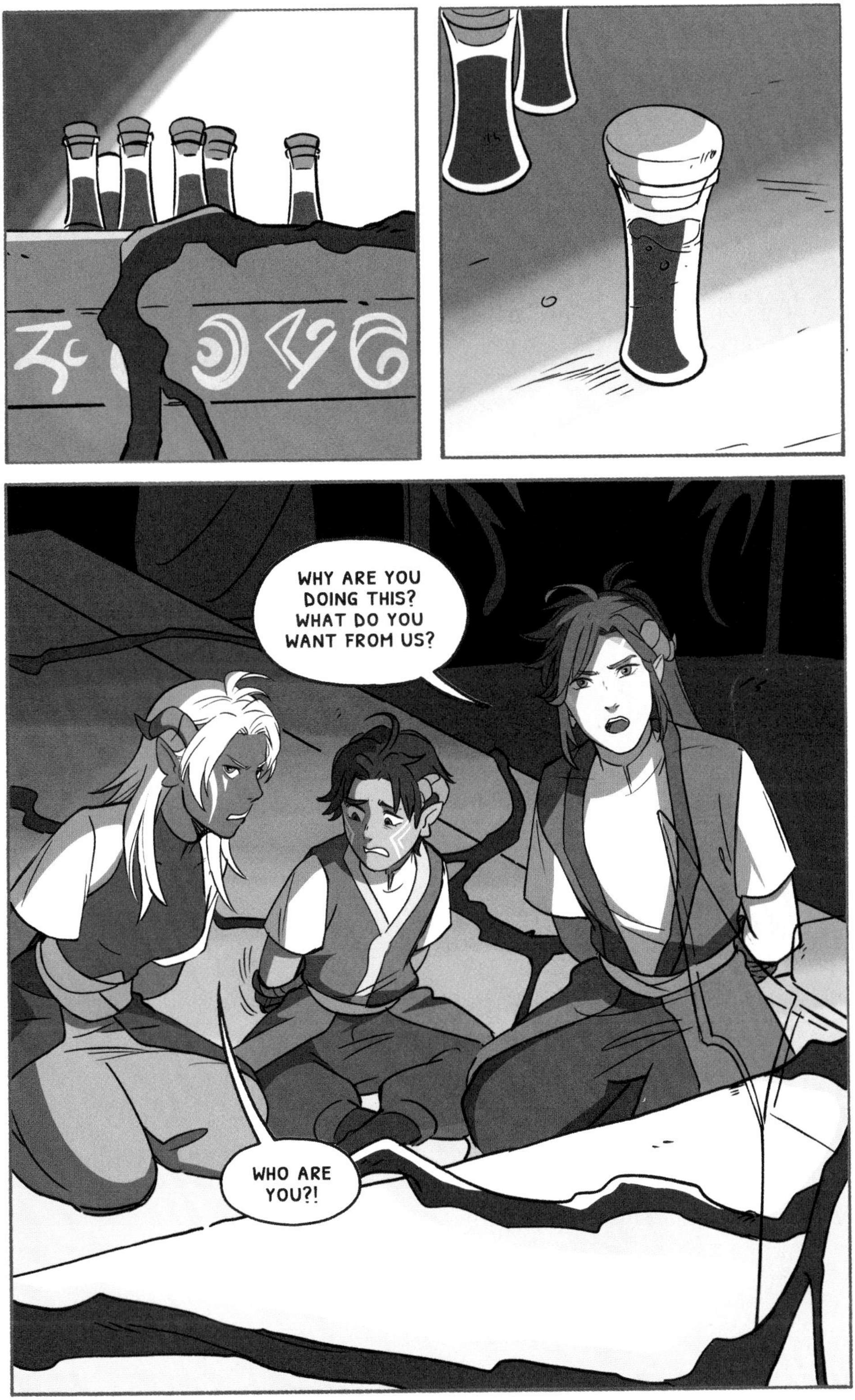
WHY ARE YOU DOING THIS? WHAT DO YOU WANT FROM US?
WHO ARE YOU?!

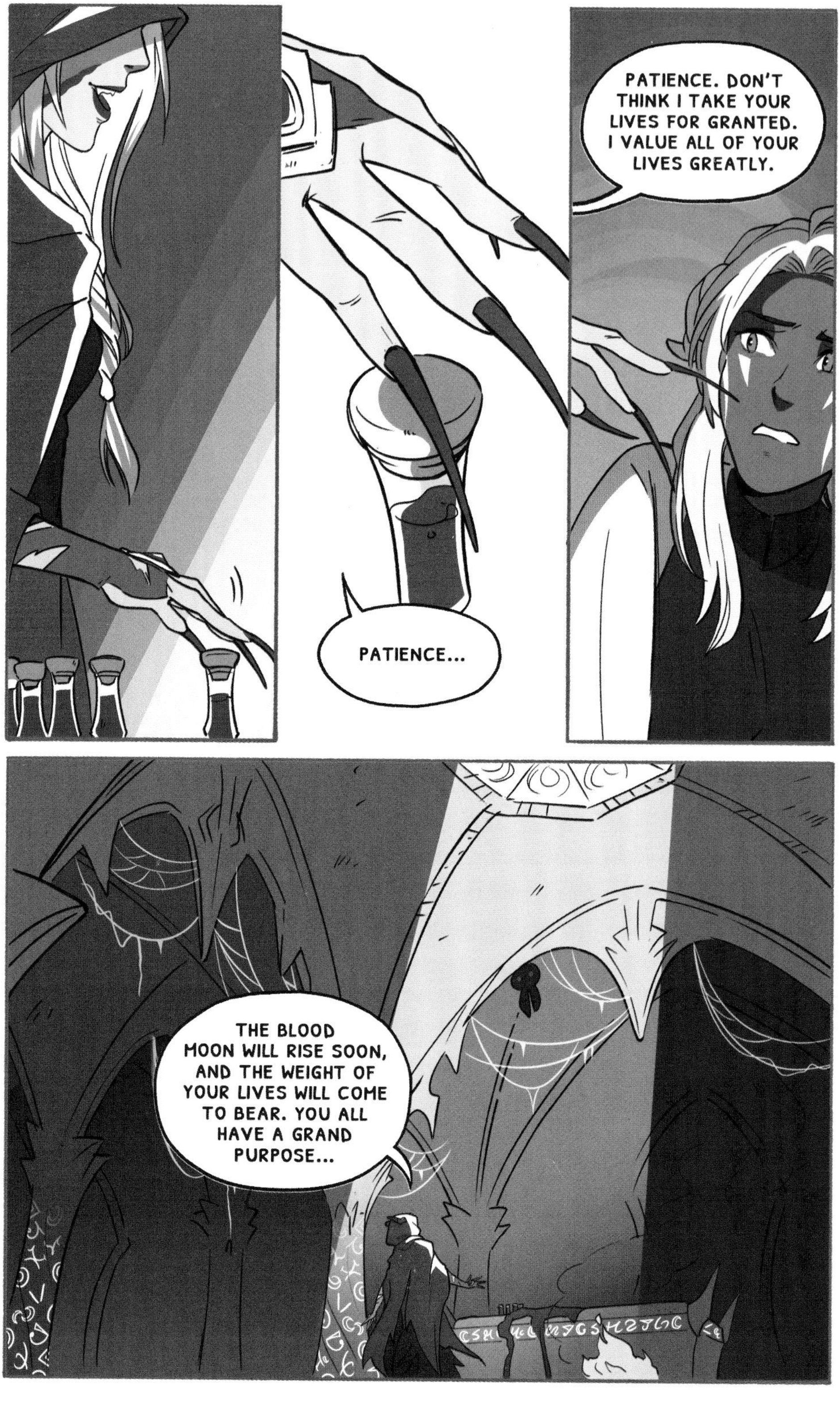
PATIENCE...
PATIENCE. DON'T THINK I TAKE YOUR LIVES FOR GRANTED. I VALUE ALL OF YOUR LIVES GREATLY.
THE BLOOD MOON WILL RISE SOON, AND THE WEIGHT OF YOUR LIVES WILL COME TO BEAR. YOU ALL HAVE A GRAND PURPOSE...

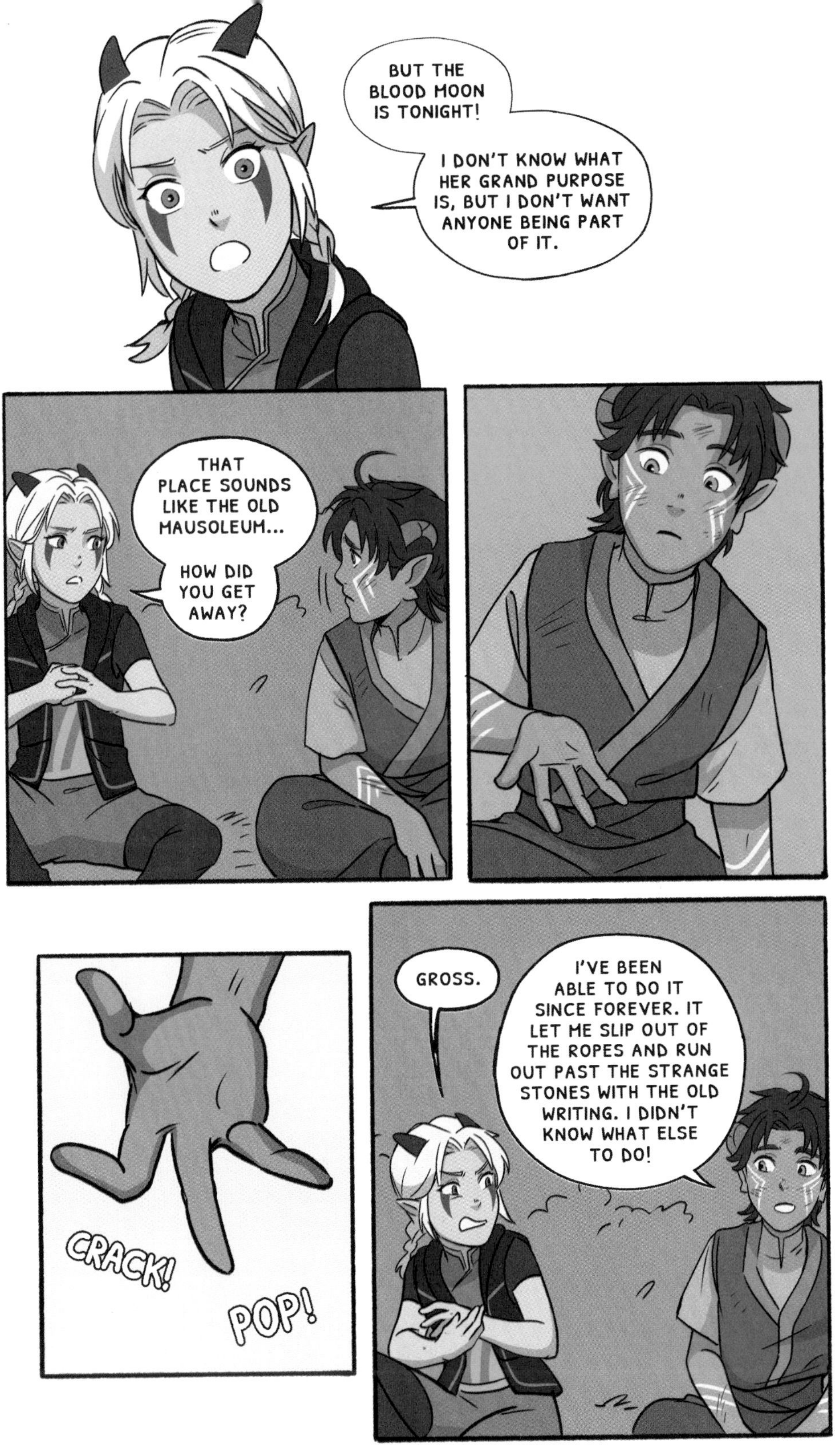
BUT THE BLOOD MOON IS TONIGHT!
I DON'T KNOW WHAT HER GRAND PURPOSE IS, BUT I DON'T WANT ANYONE BEING PART OF IT.
THAT PLACE SOUNDS LIKE THE OLD MAUSOLEUM...
HOW DID YOU GET AWAY?
CRACK!
POP!
GROSS.
I'VE BEEN ABLE TO DO IT SINCE FOREVER. IT LET ME SLIP OUT OF THE ROPES AND RUN OUT PAST THE STRANGE STONES WITH THE OLD WRITING. I DIDN'T KNOW WHAT ELSE TO DO!

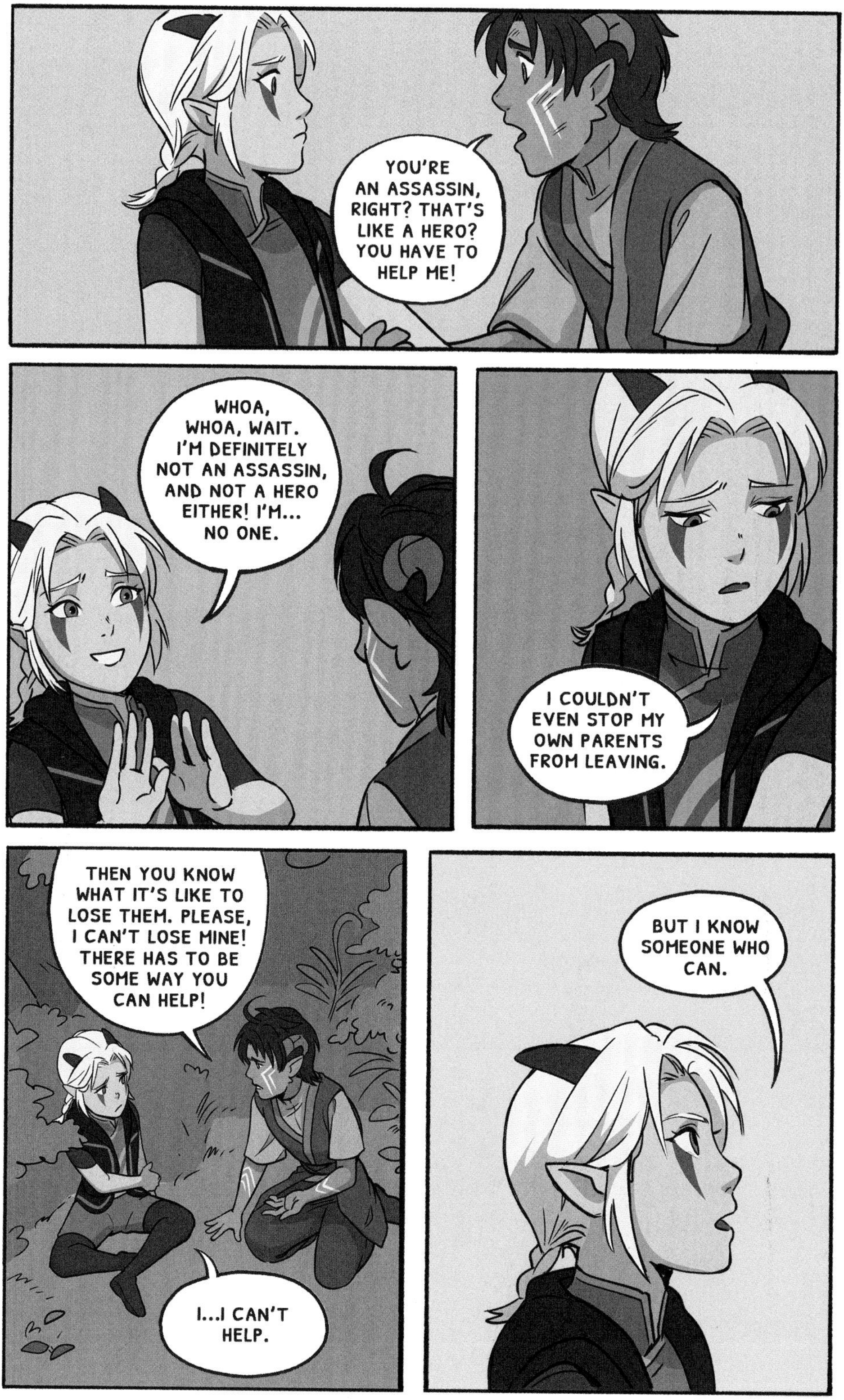
YOU'RE AN ASSASSIN, RIGHT? THAT'S LIKE A HERO? YOU HAVE TO HELP ME!
WHOA, WHOA, WAIT. I'M DEFINITELY NOT AN ASSASSIN, AND NOT A HERO EITHER! I'M... NO ONE.
I COULDN'T EVEN STOP MY OWN PARENTS FROM LEAVING.
THEN YOU KNOW WHAT IT'S LIKE TO LOSE THEM. PLEASE, I CAN'T LOSE MINE! THERE HAS TO BE SOME WAY YOU CAN HELP!
I...I CAN'T HELP.
BUT I KNOW SOMEONE WHO CAN.

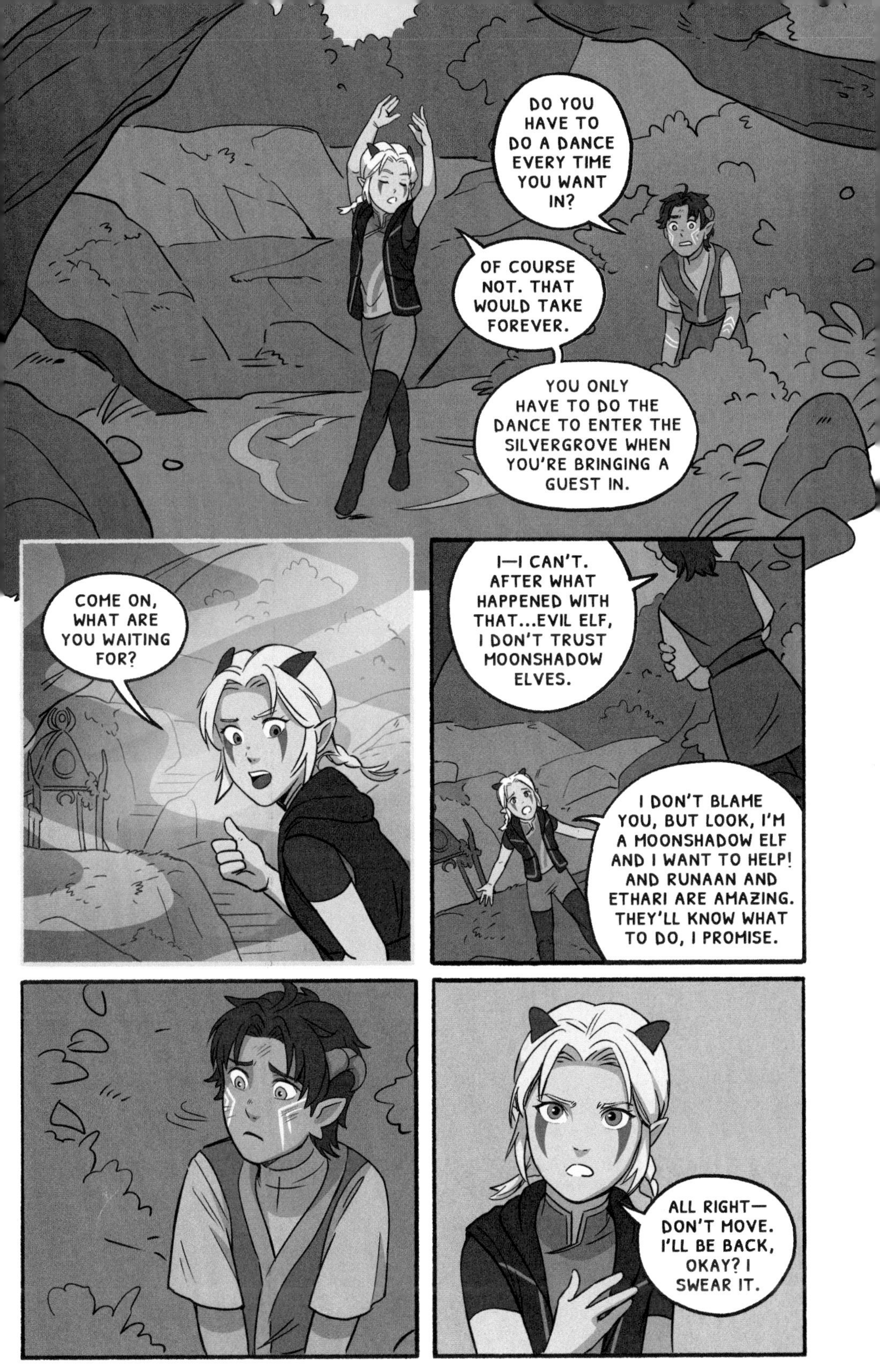
DO YOU HAVE TO DO A DANCE EVERY TIME YOU WANT IN?
OF COURSE NOT. THAT WOULD TAKE FOREVER.
YOU ONLY HAVE TO DO THE DANCE TO ENTER THE SILVERGROVE WHEN YOU'RE BRINGING A GUEST IN.
COME ON, WHAT ARE YOU WAITING FOR?
I—I CAN'T. AFTER WHAT HAPPENED WITH THAT...EVIL ELF, I DON'T TRUST MOONSHADOW ELVES.
I DON'T BLAME YOU, BUT LOOK, I'M A MOONSHADOW ELF AND I WANT TO HELP! AND RUNAAN AND ETHARI ARE AMAZING. THEY'LL KNOW WHAT TO DO, I PROMISE.
ALL RIGHT—DON'T MOVE. I'LL BE BACK, OKAY? I SWEAR IT.

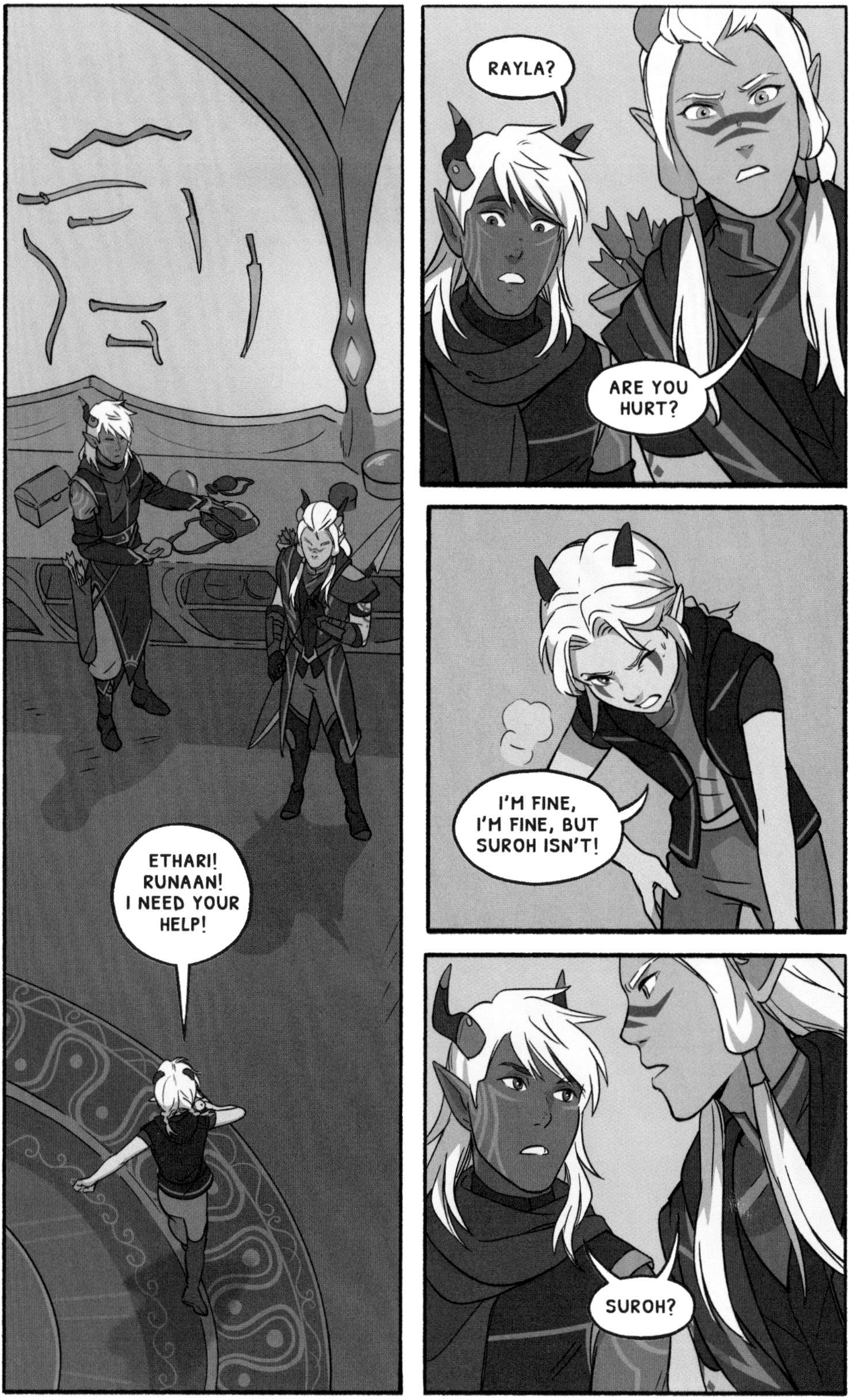
ETHARI! RUNAAN! I NEED YOUR HELP!
RAYLA?
ARE YOU HURT?
I'M FINE, I'M FINE, BUT SUROH ISN'T!
SUROH?

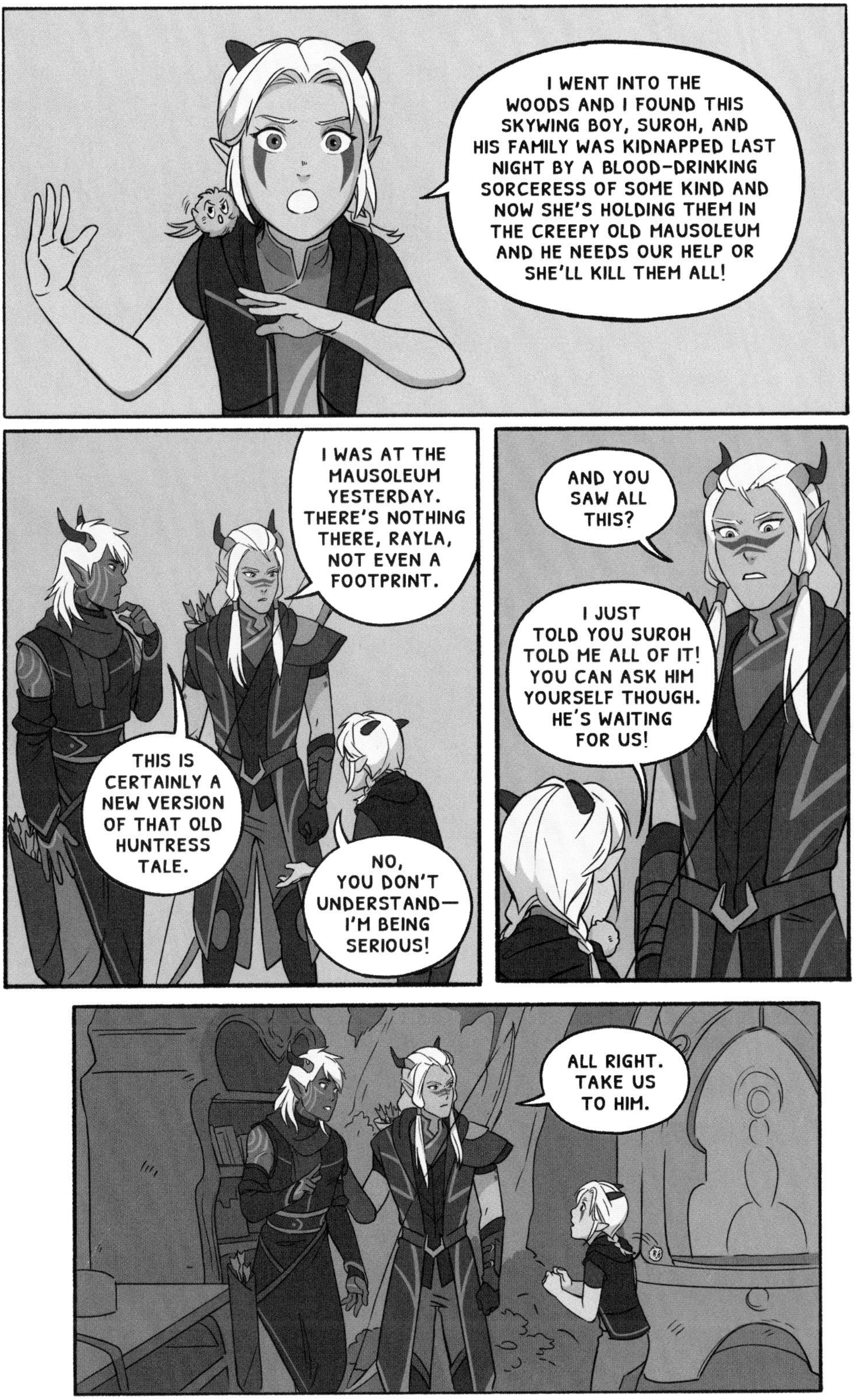
I WENT INTO THE WOODS AND I FOUND THIS SKYWING BOY, SUROH, AND HIS FAMILY WAS KIDNAPPED LAST NIGHT BY A BLOOD-DRINKING SORCERESS OF SOME KIND AND NOW SHE'S HOLDING THEM IN THE CREEPY OLD MAUSOLEUM AND HE NEEDS OUR HELP OR SHE'LL KILL THEM ALL!
I WAS AT THE MAUSOLEUM YESTERDAY. THERE'S NOTHING THERE, RAYLA, NOT EVEN A FOOTPRINT.
THIS IS CERTAINLY A NEW VERSION OF THAT OLD HUNTRESS TALE.
NO, YOU DON'T UNDERSTAND— I'M BEING SERIOUS!
AND YOU SAW ALL THIS?
I JUST TOLD YOU SUROH TOLD ME ALL OF IT! YOU CAN ASK HIM YOURSELF THOUGH. HE'S WAITING FOR US!
ALL RIGHT. TAKE US TO HIM.

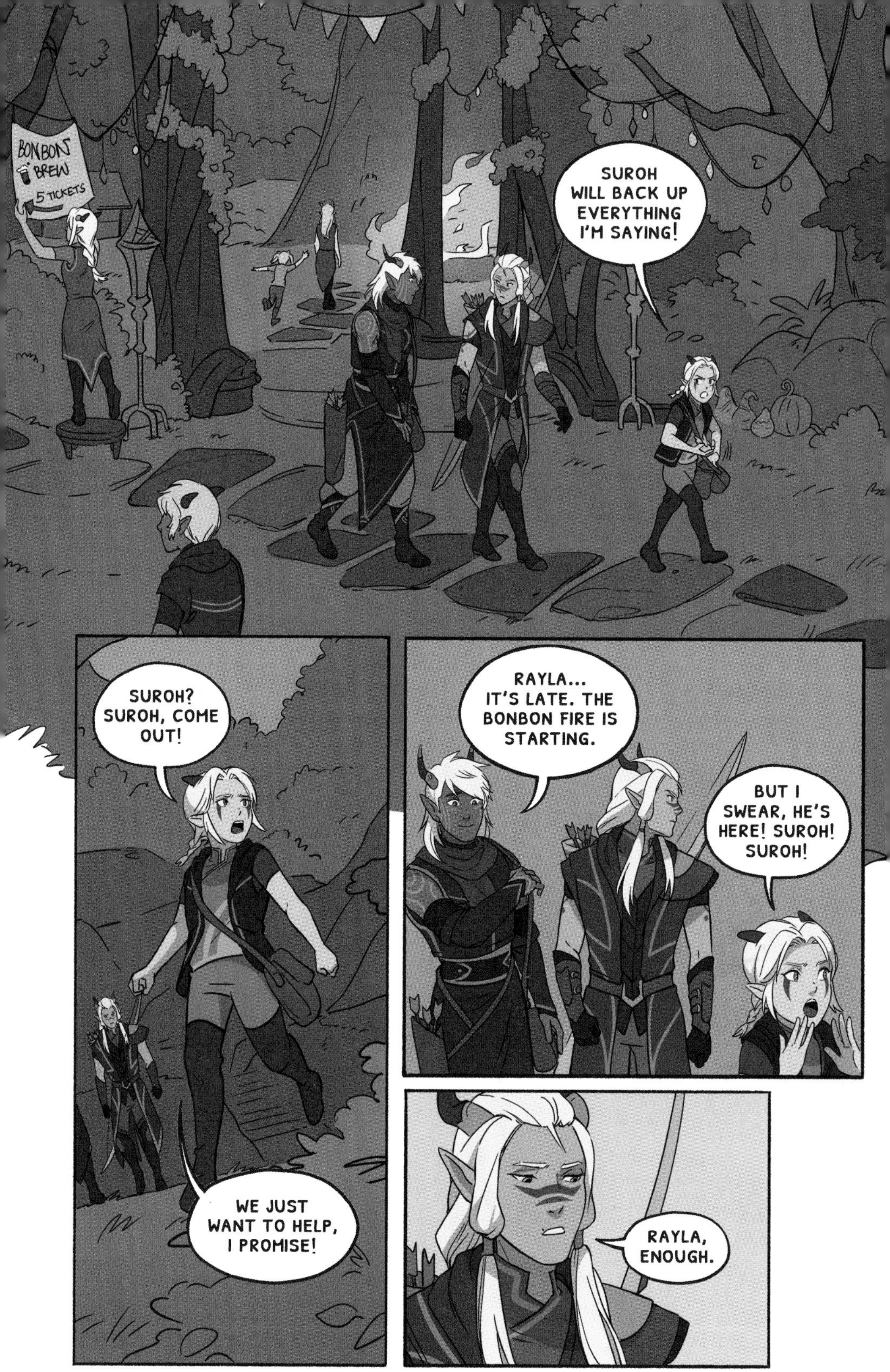
BONBON BREW
5 TICKETS
SUROH WILL BACK UP EVERYTHING I'M SAYING!
SUROH? SUROH, COME OUT!
WE JUST WANT TO HELP, I PROMISE!
RAYLA... IT'S LATE. THE BONBON FIRE IS STARTING.
BUT I SWEAR, HE'S HERE! SUROH! SUROH!
RAYLA, ENOUGH.

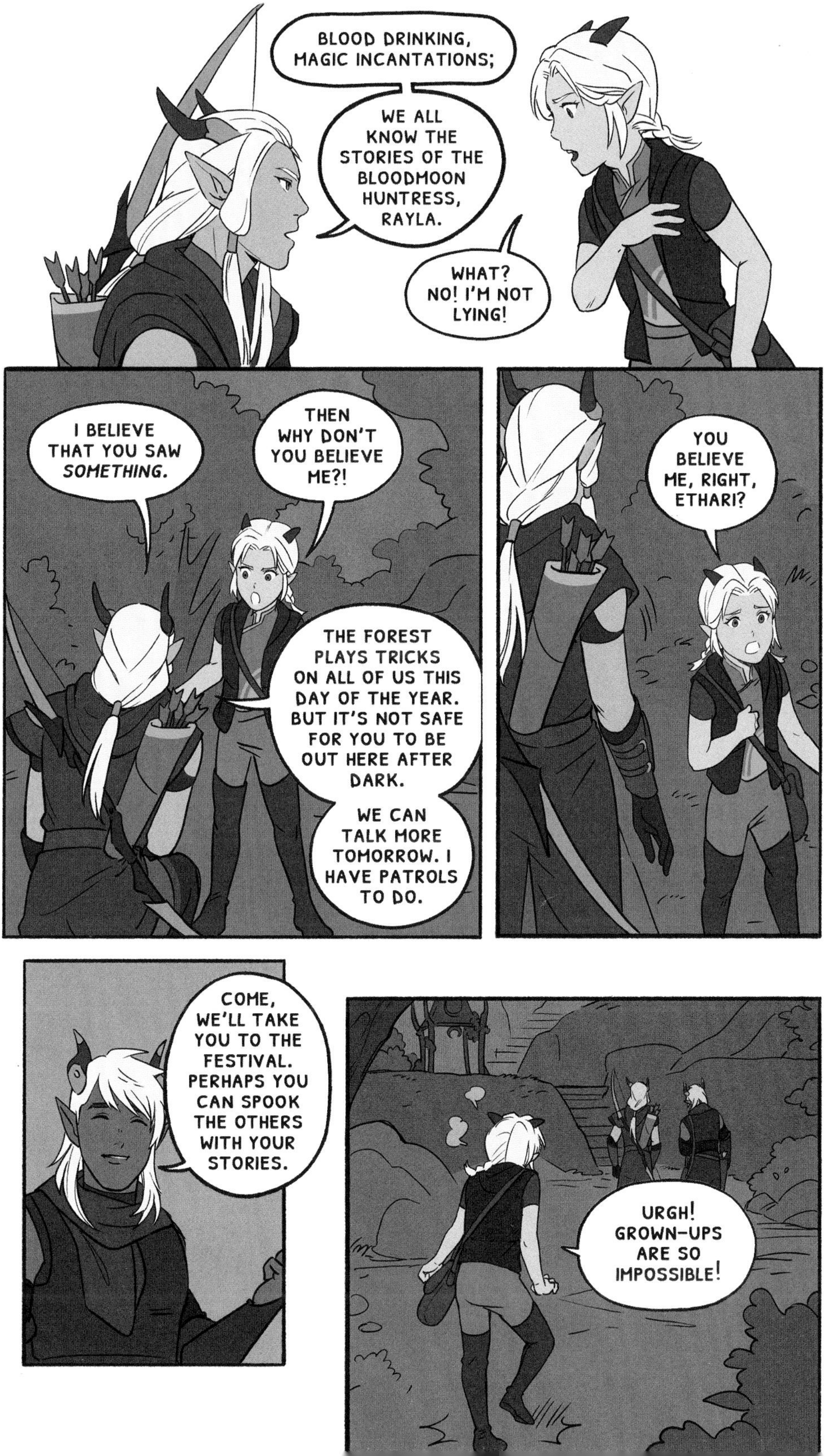
BLOOD DRINKING, MAGIC INCANTATIONS;
WE ALL KNOW THE STORIES OF THE BLOODMOON HUNTRESS, RAYLA.
WHAT? NO! I'M NOT LYING!
I BELIEVE THAT YOU SAW *SOMETHING.*
THEN WHY DON'T YOU BELIEVE ME?!
THE FOREST PLAYS TRICKS ON ALL OF US THIS DAY OF THE YEAR. BUT IT'S NOT SAFE FOR YOU TO BE OUT HERE AFTER DARK.
WE CAN TALK MORE TOMORROW. I HAVE PATROLS TO DO.
YOU BELIEVE ME, RIGHT, ETHARI?
COME, WE'LL TAKE YOU TO THE FESTIVAL. PERHAPS YOU CAN SPOOK THE OTHERS WITH YOUR STORIES.
URGH! GROWN-UPS ARE SO IMPOSSIBLE!

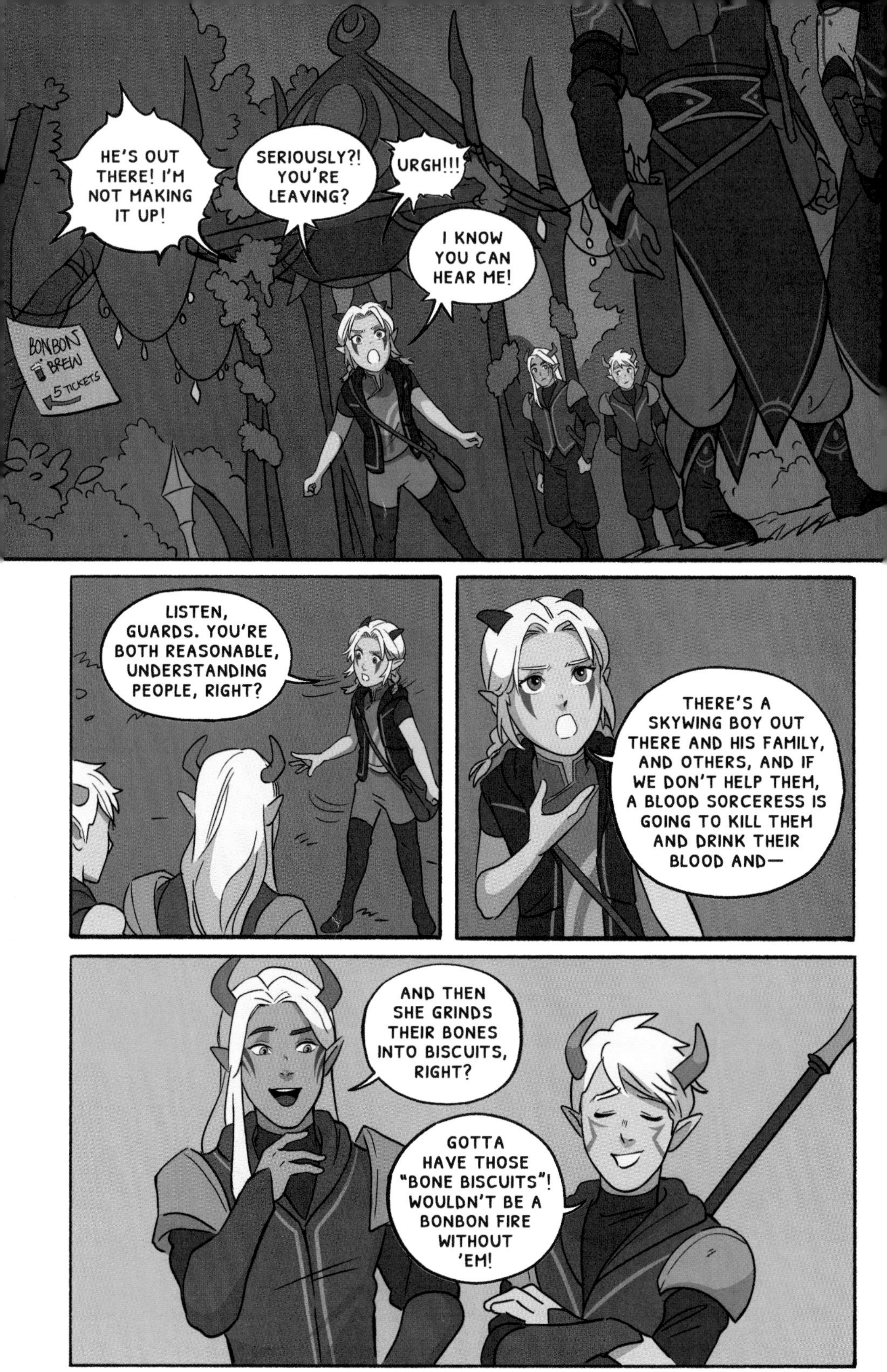
HE'S OUT THERE! I'M NOT MAKING IT UP!
SERIOUSLY?! YOU'RE LEAVING?
URGH!!!
I KNOW YOU CAN HEAR ME!
BONBONS BREW 5 TICKETS
LISTEN, GUARDS. YOU'RE BOTH REASONABLE, UNDERSTANDING PEOPLE, RIGHT?
THERE'S A SKYWING BOY OUT THERE AND HIS FAMILY, AND OTHERS, AND IF WE DON'T HELP THEM, A BLOOD SORCERESS IS GOING TO KILL THEM AND DRINK THEIR BLOOD AND—
AND THEN SHE GRINDS THEIR BONES INTO BISCUITS, RIGHT?
GOTTA HAVE THOSE "BONE BISCUITS"! WOULDN'T BE A BONBON FIRE WITHOUT 'EM!

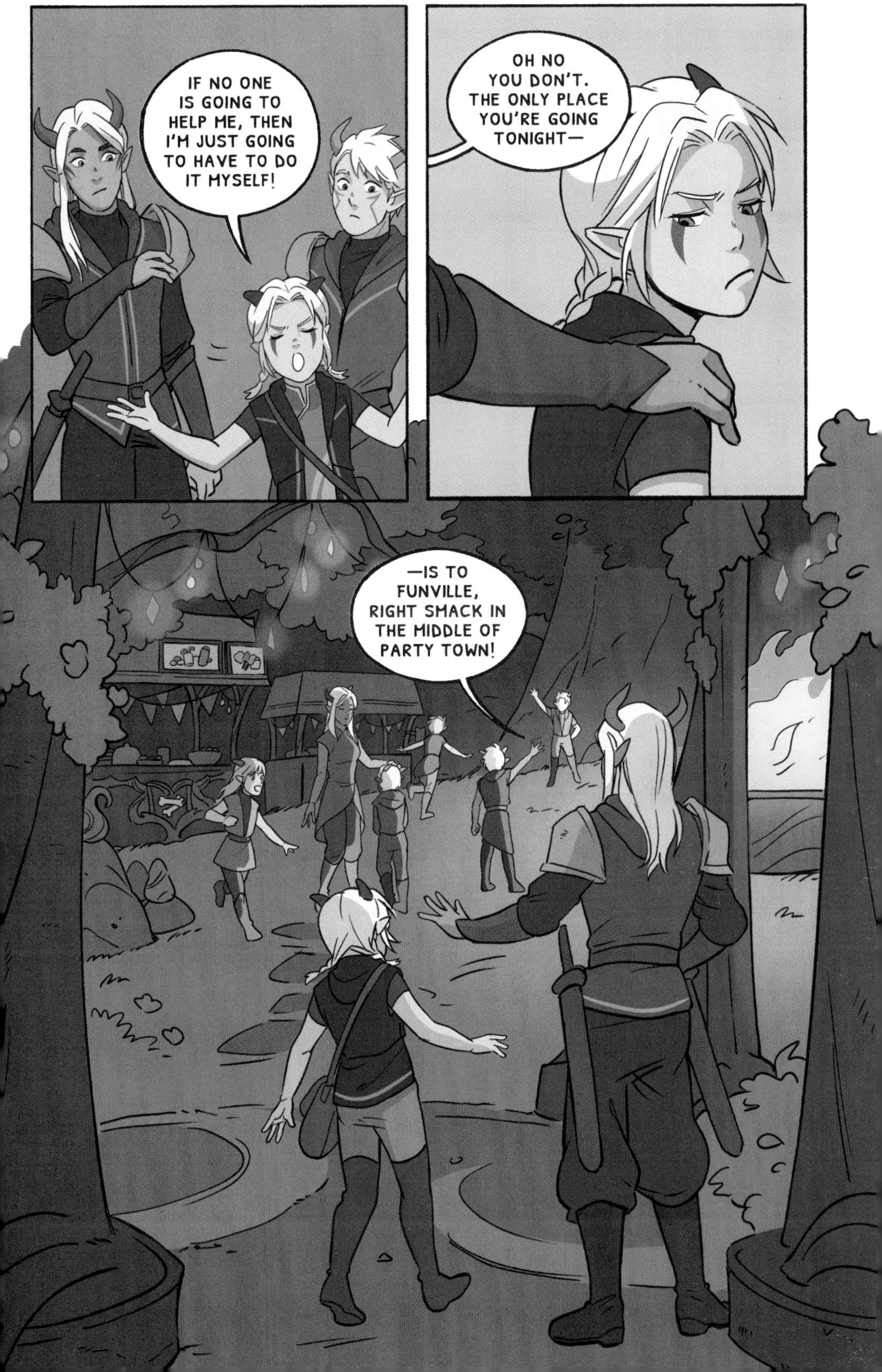
IF NO ONE IS GOING TO HELP ME, THEN I'M JUST GOING TO HAVE TO DO IT MYSELF!
OH NO YOU DON'T. THE ONLY PLACE YOU'RE GOING TONIGHT—
—IS TO FUNVILLE, RIGHT SMACK IN THE MIDDLE OF PARTY TOWN!

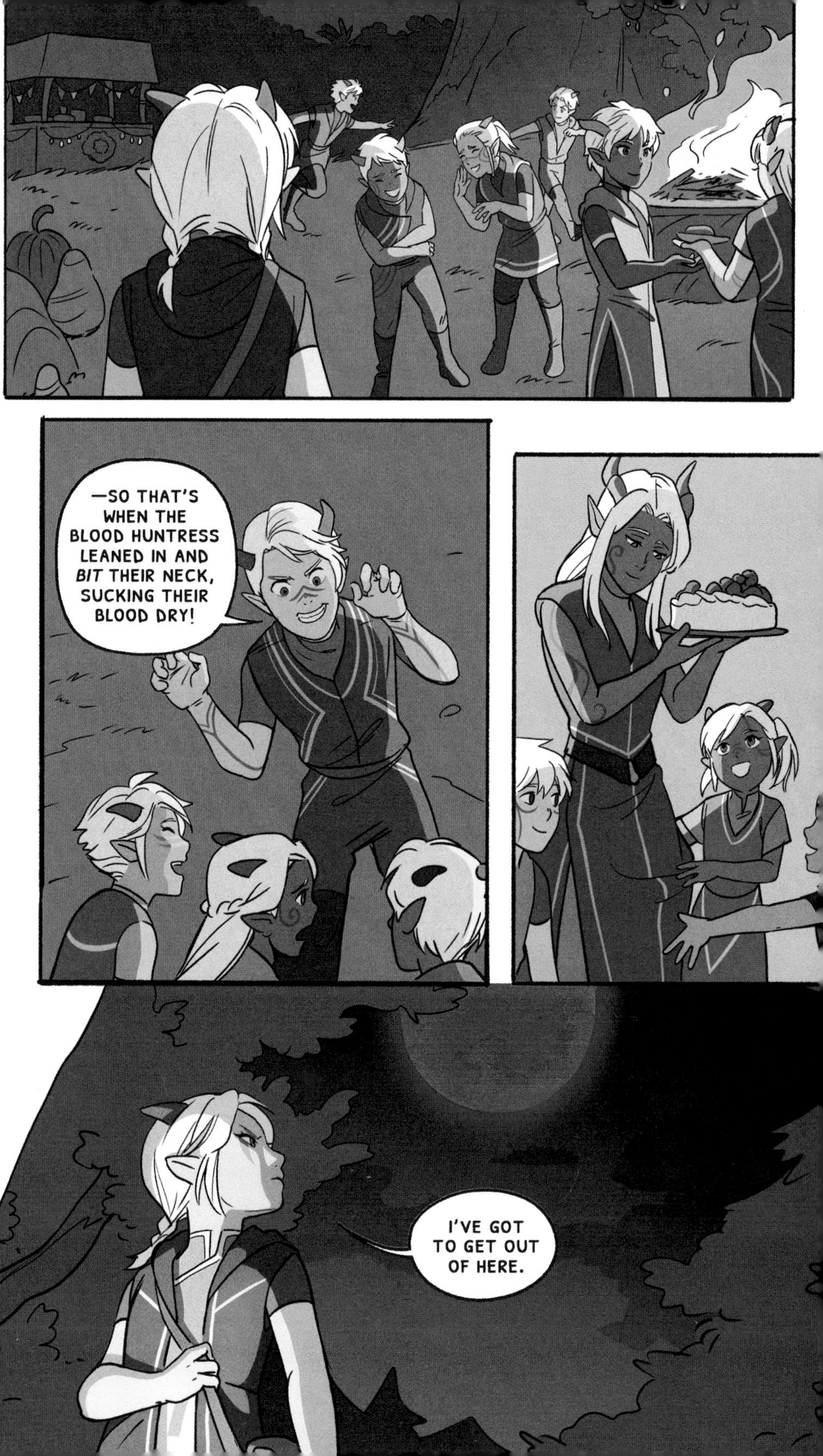
—SO THAT'S WHEN THE BLOOD HUNTRESS LEANED IN AND *BIT* THEIR NECK, SUCKING THEIR BLOOD DRY!
I'VE GOT TO GET OUT OF HERE.

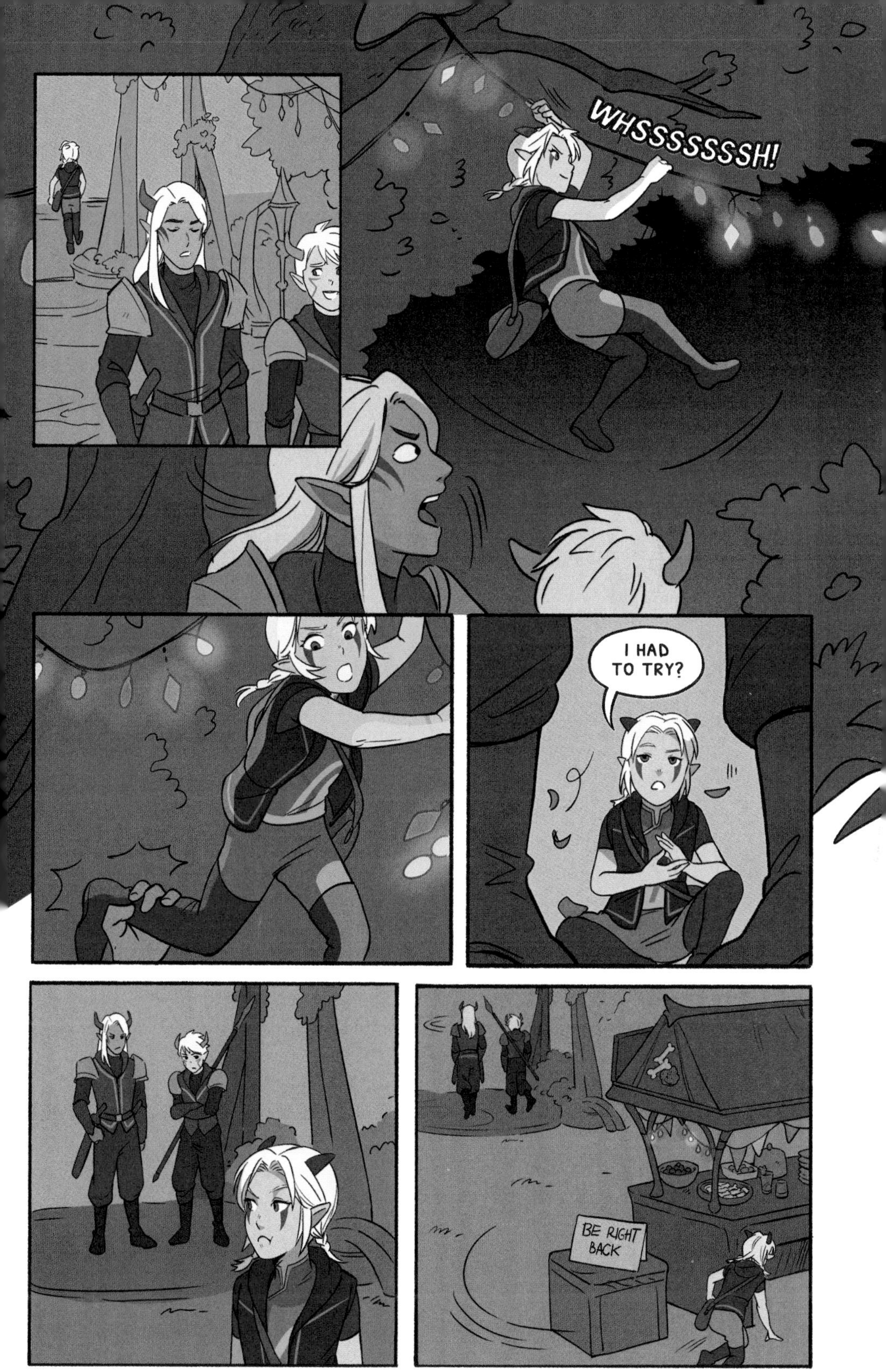
WHSSSSSSSH!
I HAD TO TRY?
BE RIGHT BACK

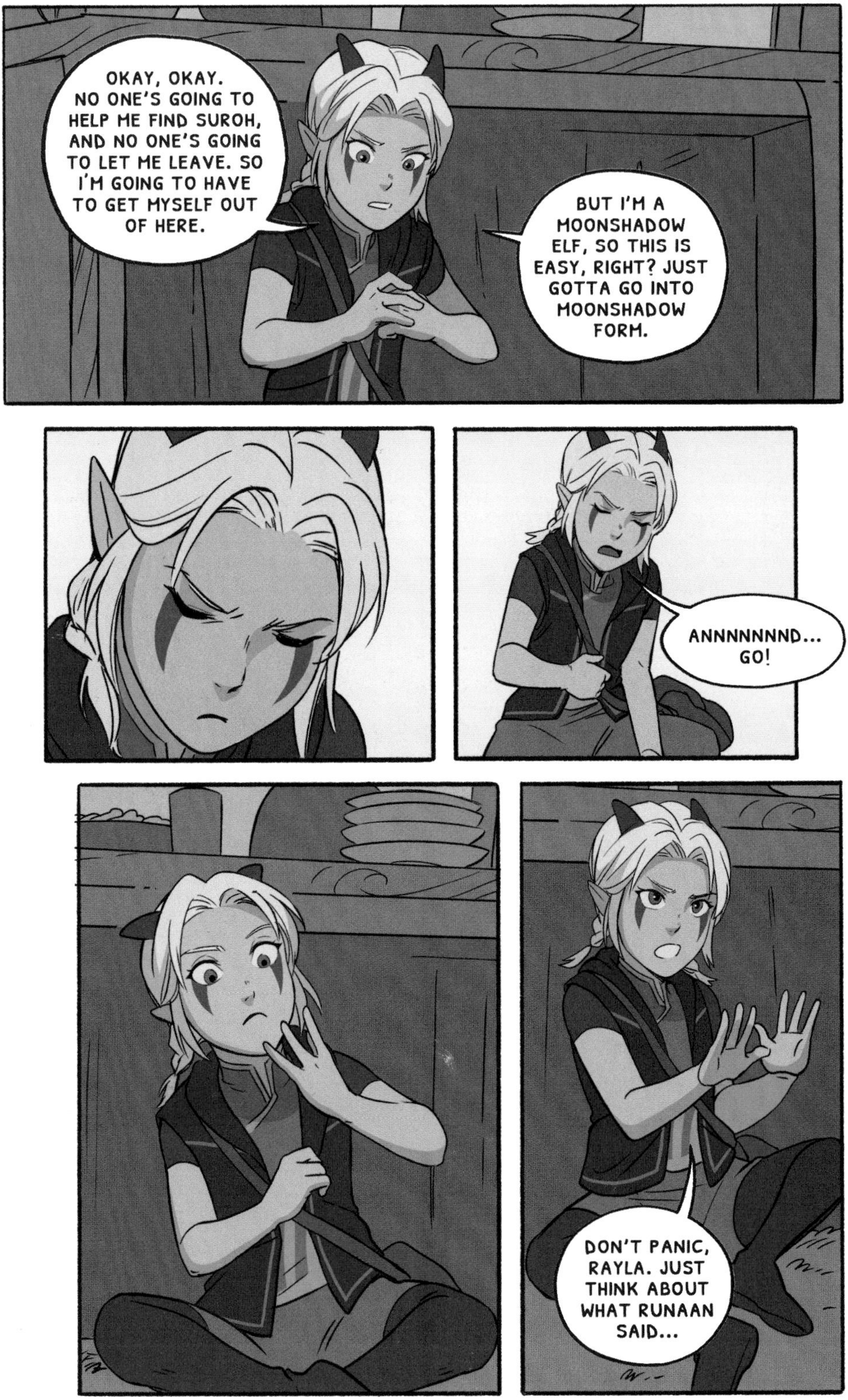
OKAY, OKAY. NO ONE'S GOING TO HELP ME FIND SUROH, AND NO ONE'S GOING TO LET ME LEAVE. SO I'M GOING TO HAVE TO GET MYSELF OUT OF HERE.
BUT I'M A MOONSHADOW ELF, SO THIS IS EASY, RIGHT? JUST GOTTA GO INTO MOONSHADOW FORM.
ANNNNNNND... GO!
DON'T PANIC, RAYLA. JUST THINK ABOUT WHAT RUNAAN SAID...

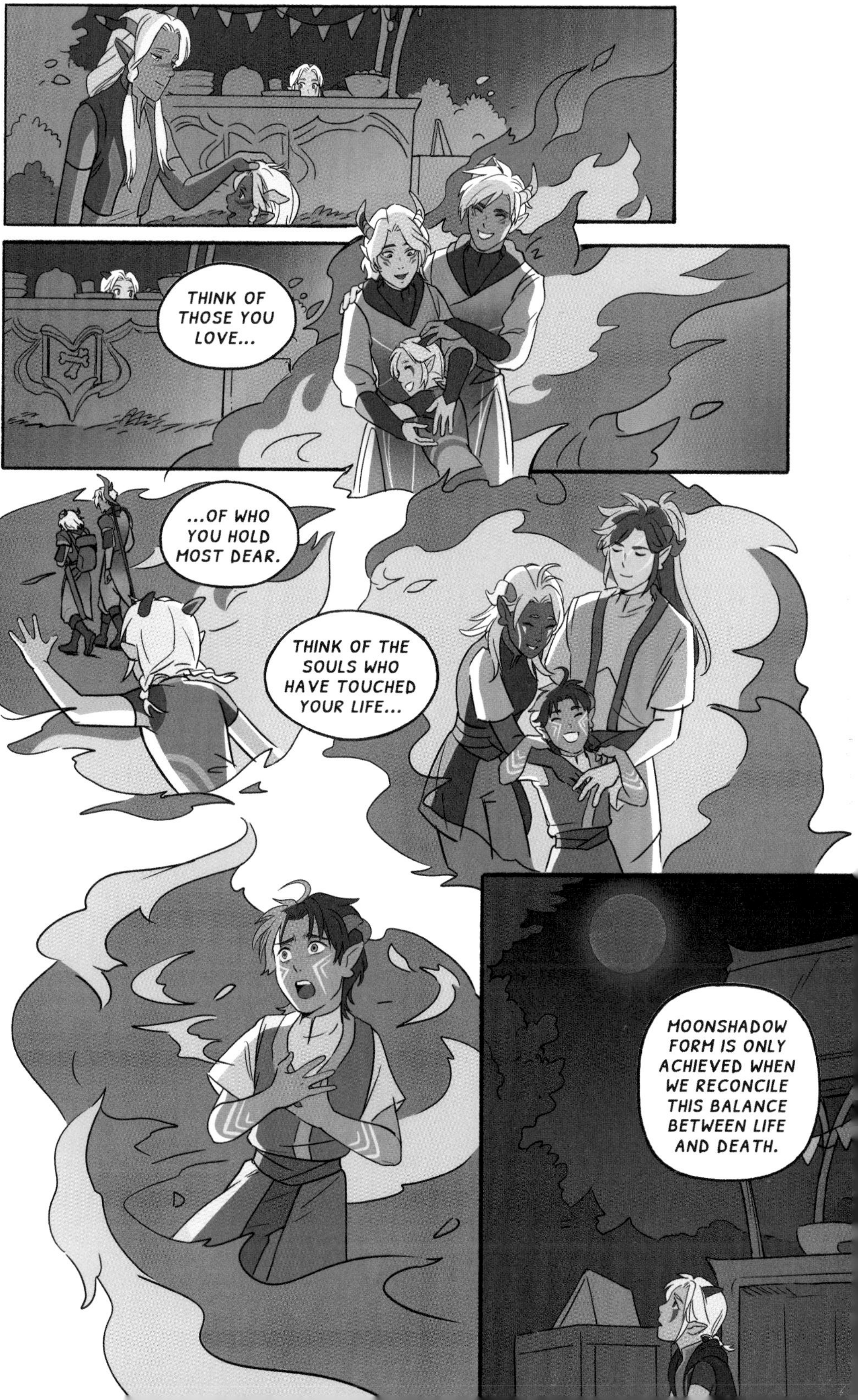
THINK OF THOSE YOU LOVE...
...OF WHO YOU HOLD MOST DEAR.
THINK OF THE SOULS WHO HAVE TOUCHED YOUR LIFE...
MOONSHADOW FORM IS ONLY ACHIEVED WHEN WE RECONCILE THIS BALANCE BETWEEN LIFE AND DEATH.

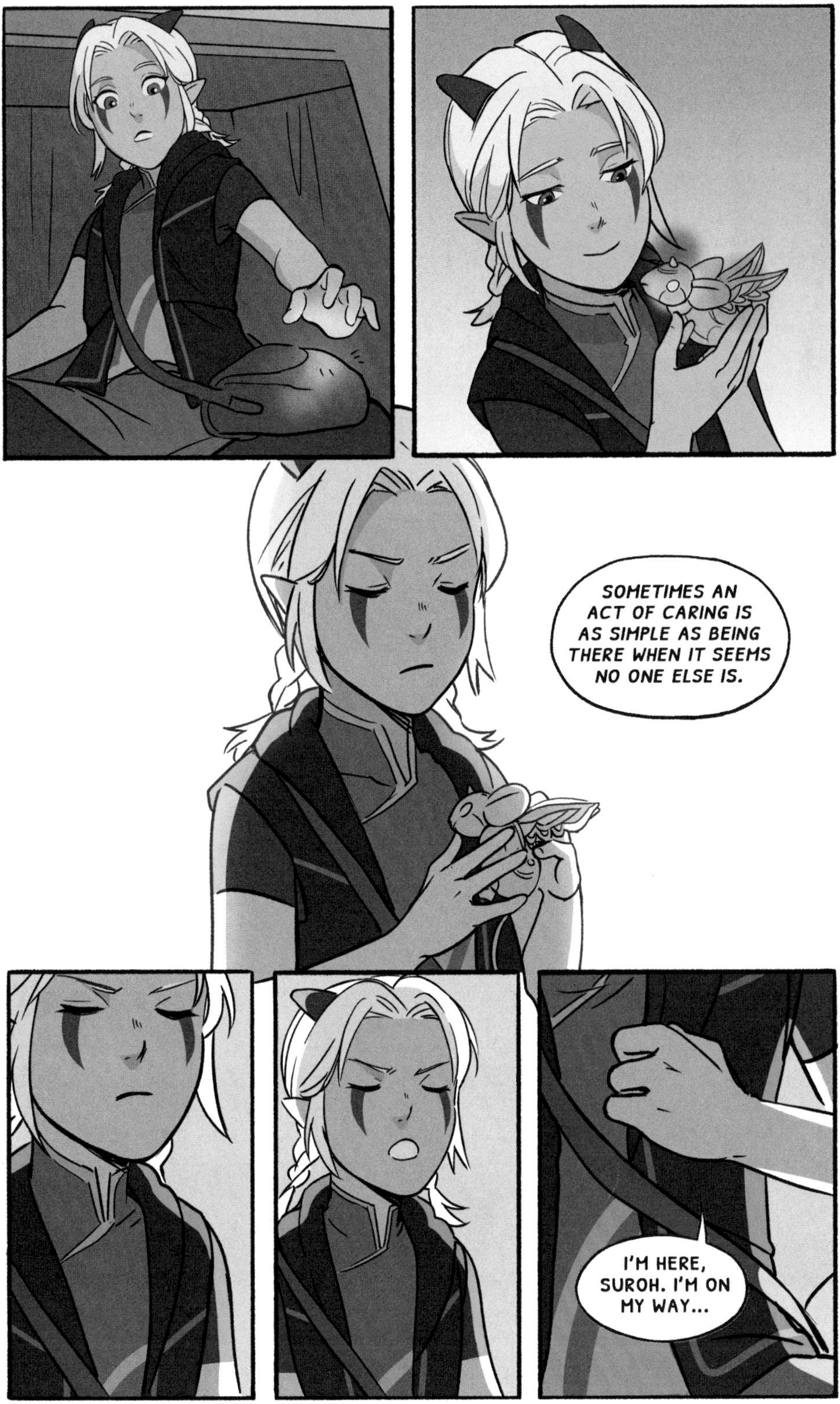
SOMETIMES AN ACT OF CARING IS AS SIMPLE AS BEING THERE WHEN IT SEEMS NO ONE ELSE IS.
I'M HERE, SUROH. I'M ON MY WAY...

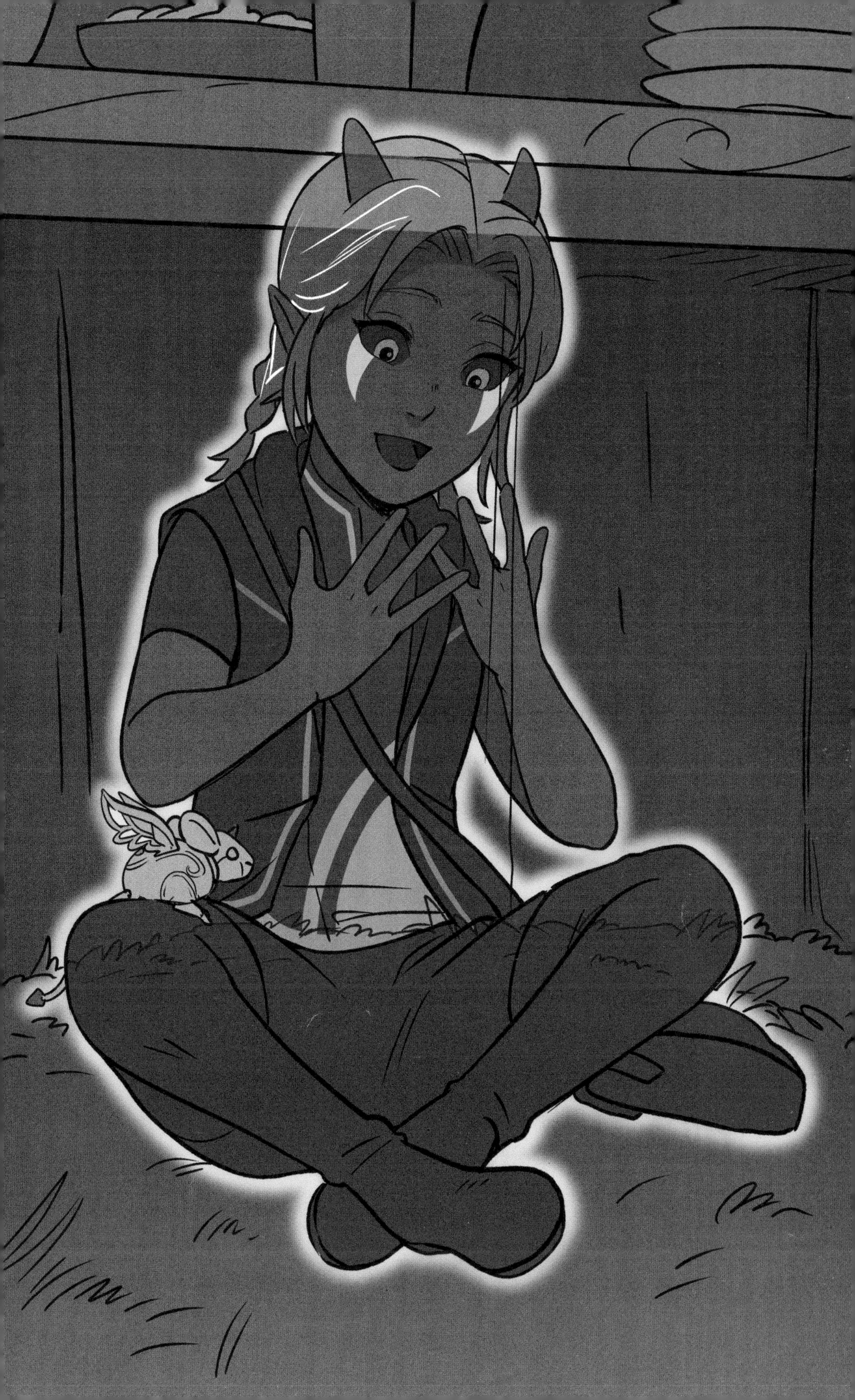

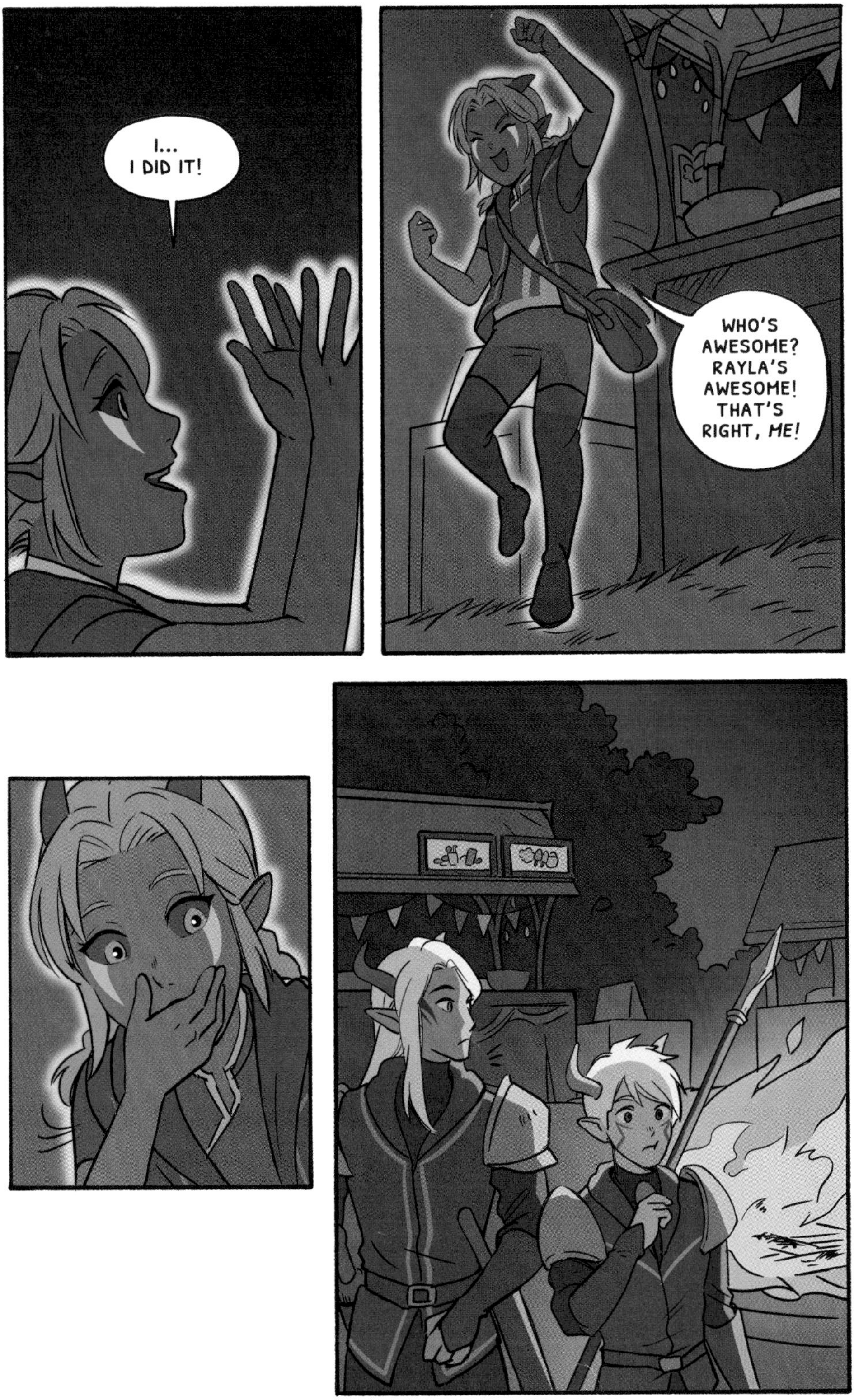
I...
I DID IT!
WHO'S AWESOME? RAYLA'S AWESOME! THAT'S RIGHT, *ME*!

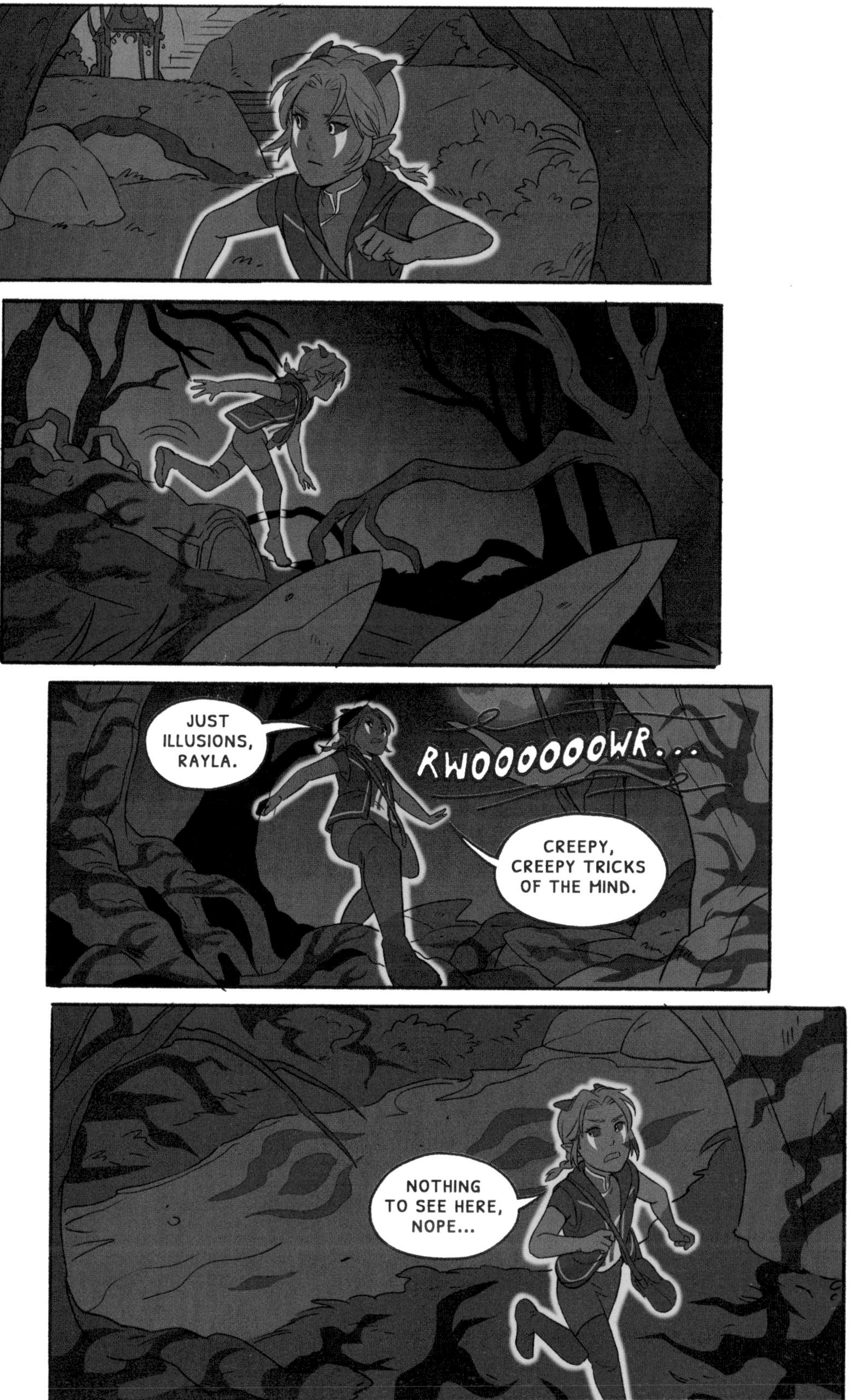
JUST ILLUSIONS, RAYLA.
RWOOOOOOWR...
CREEPY, CREEPY TRICKS OF THE MIND.
NOTHING TO SEE HERE, NOPE...

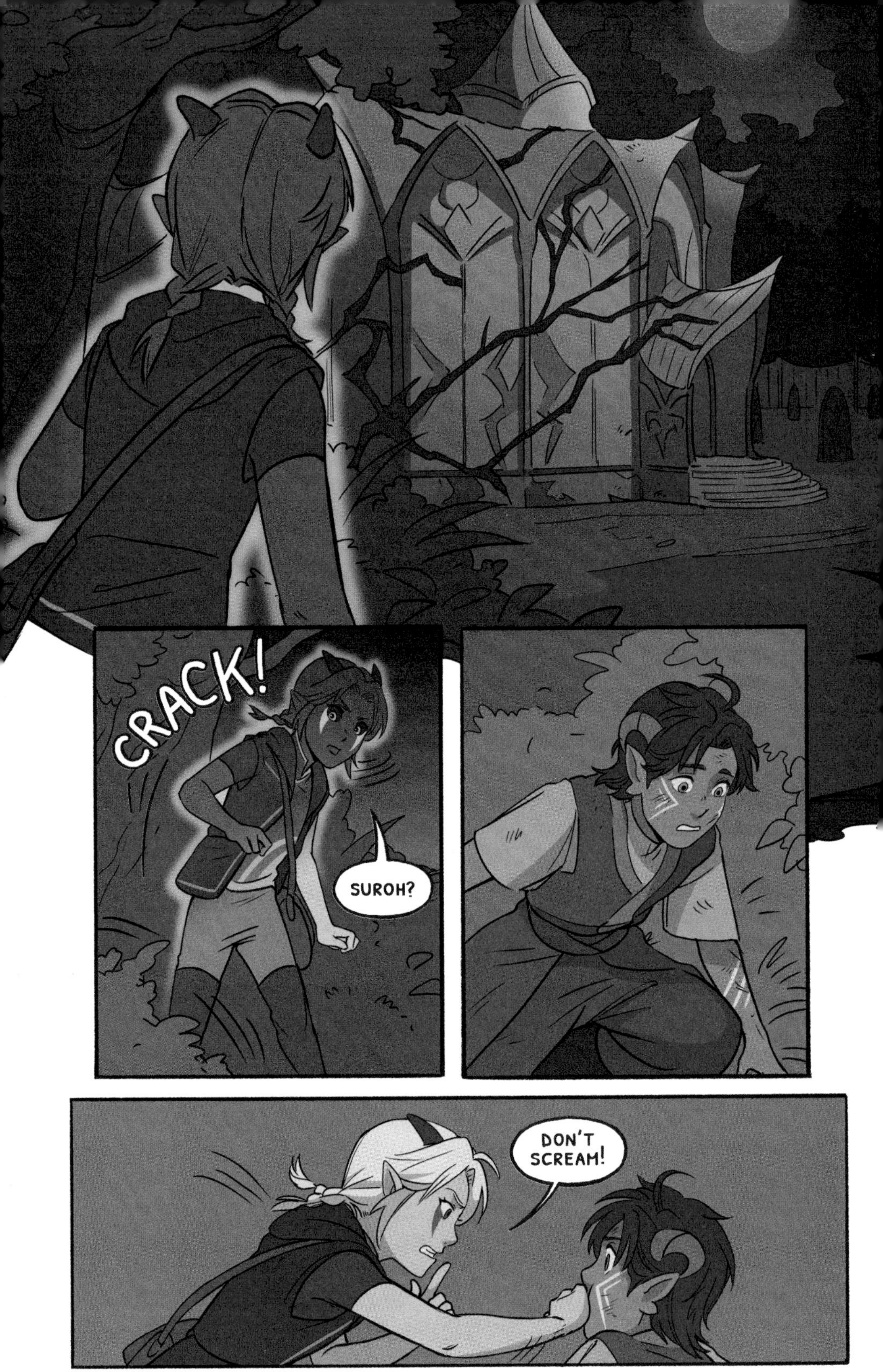
CRACK!
SUROH?
DON'T SCREAM!

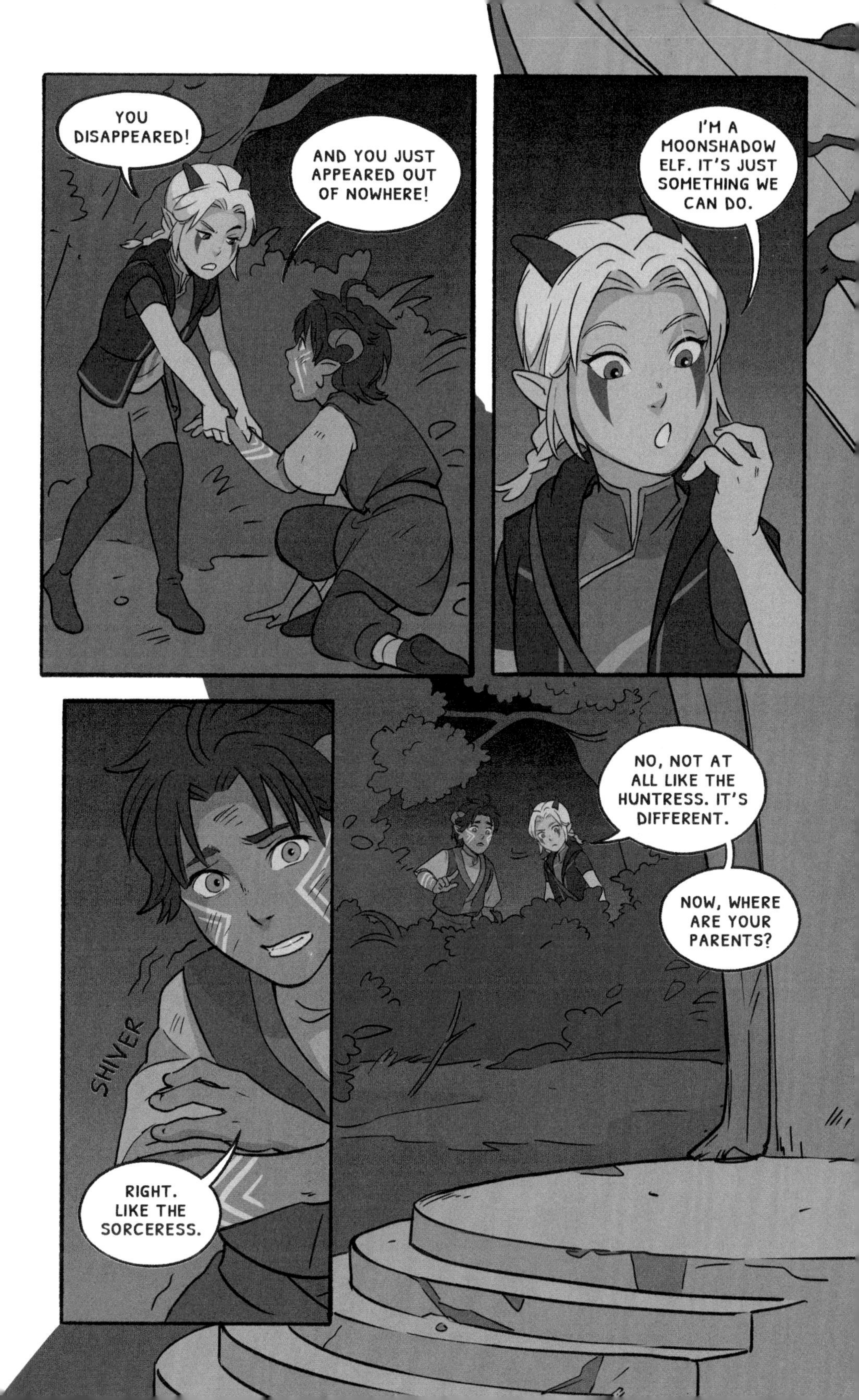
YOU DISAPPEARED!
AND YOU JUST APPEARED OUT OF NOWHERE!
I'M A MOONSHADOW ELF. IT'S JUST SOMETHING WE CAN DO.
SHIVER
RIGHT. LIKE THE SORCERESS.
NO, NOT AT ALL LIKE THE HUNTRESS. IT'S DIFFERENT.
NOW, WHERE ARE YOUR PARENTS?

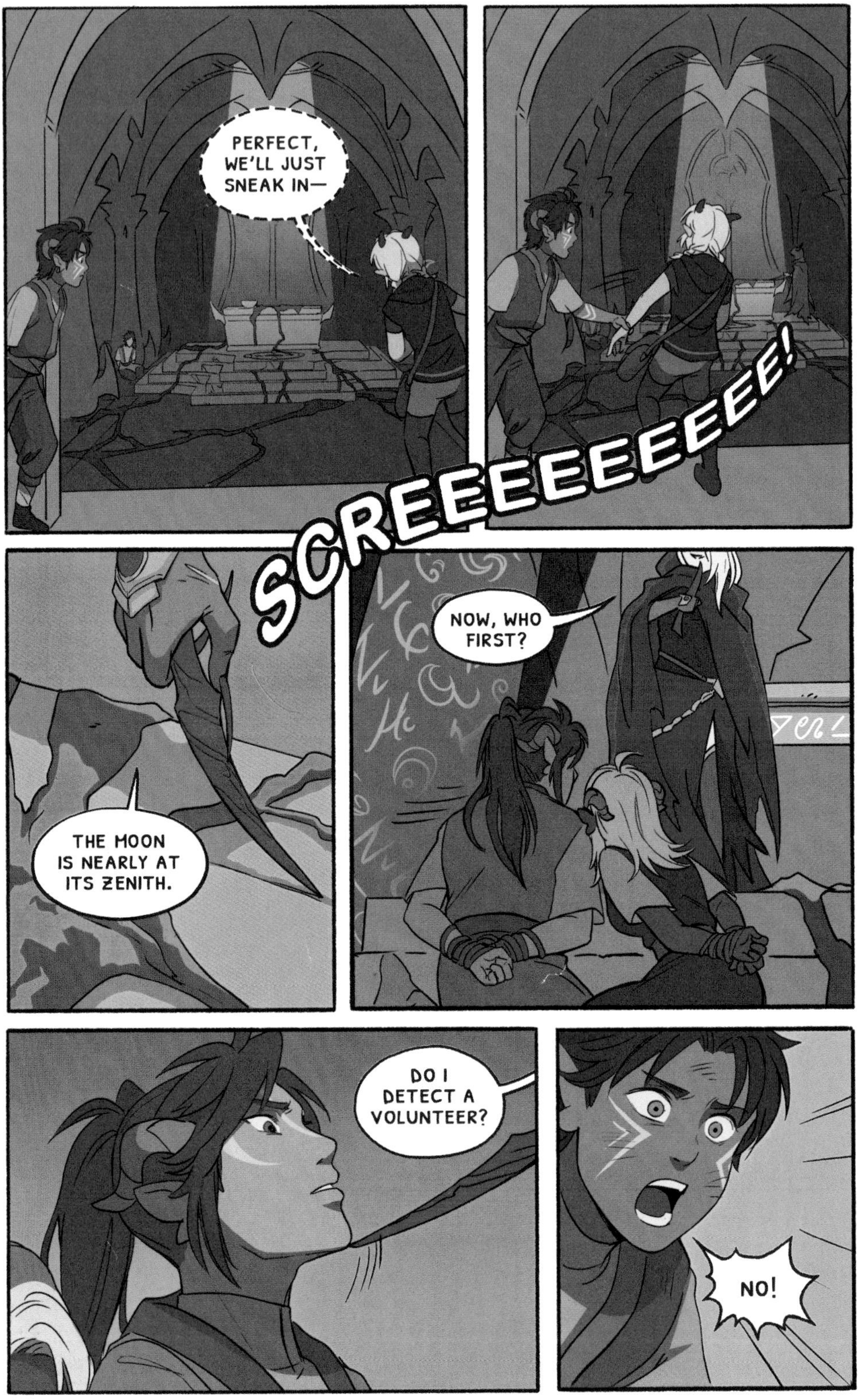
PERFECT, WE'LL JUST SNEAK IN—
SCREEEEEEEEEEEE!
THE MOON IS NEARLY AT ITS ZENITH.
NOW, WHO FIRST?
DO I DETECT A VOLUNTEER?
NO!

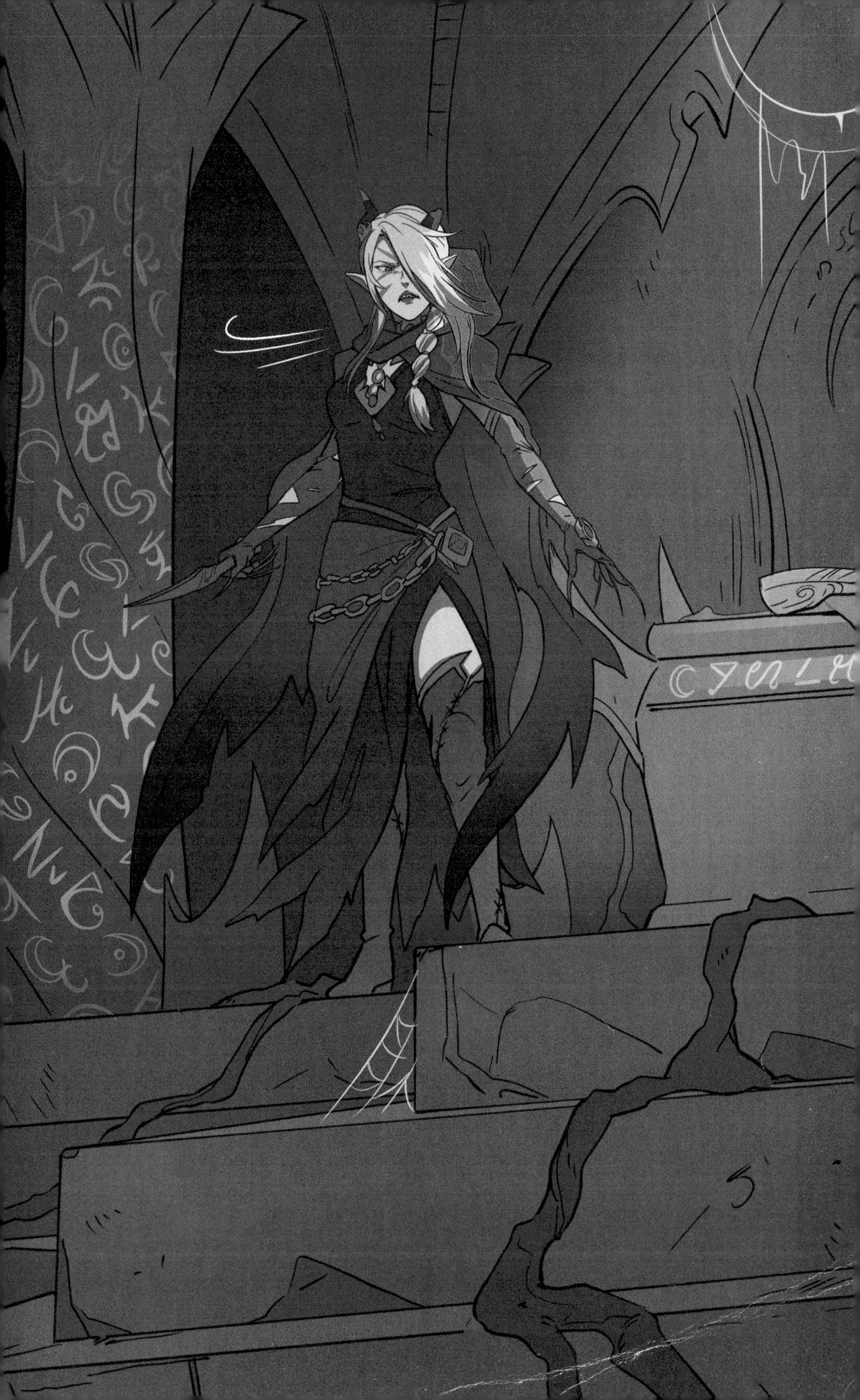

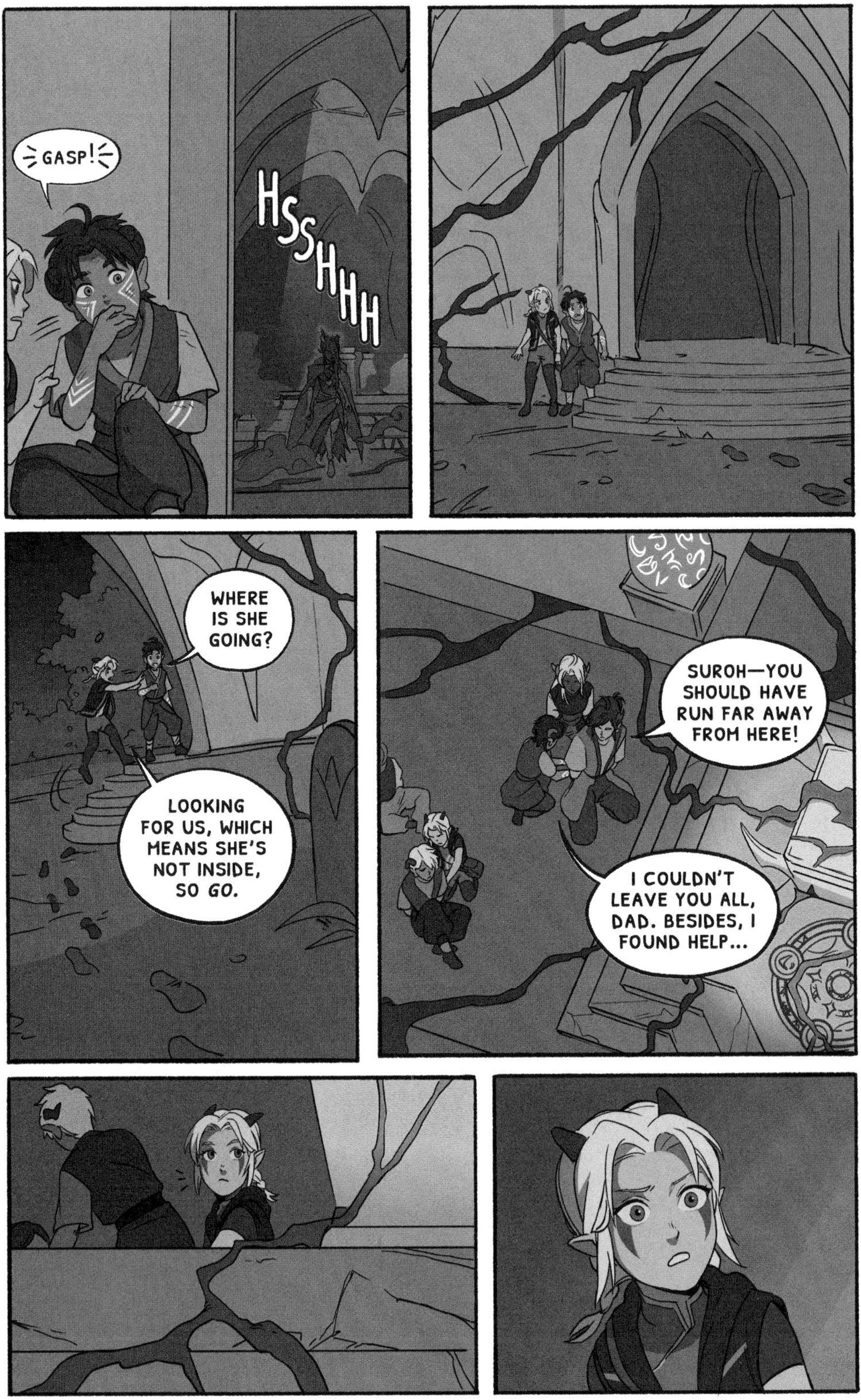
GASP!
HSSHHHH
WHERE IS SHE GOING?
LOOKING FOR US, WHICH MEANS SHE'S NOT INSIDE, SO GO.
SUROH—YOU SHOULD HAVE RUN FAR AWAY FROM HERE!
I COULDN'T LEAVE YOU ALL, DAD. BESIDES, I FOUND HELP...

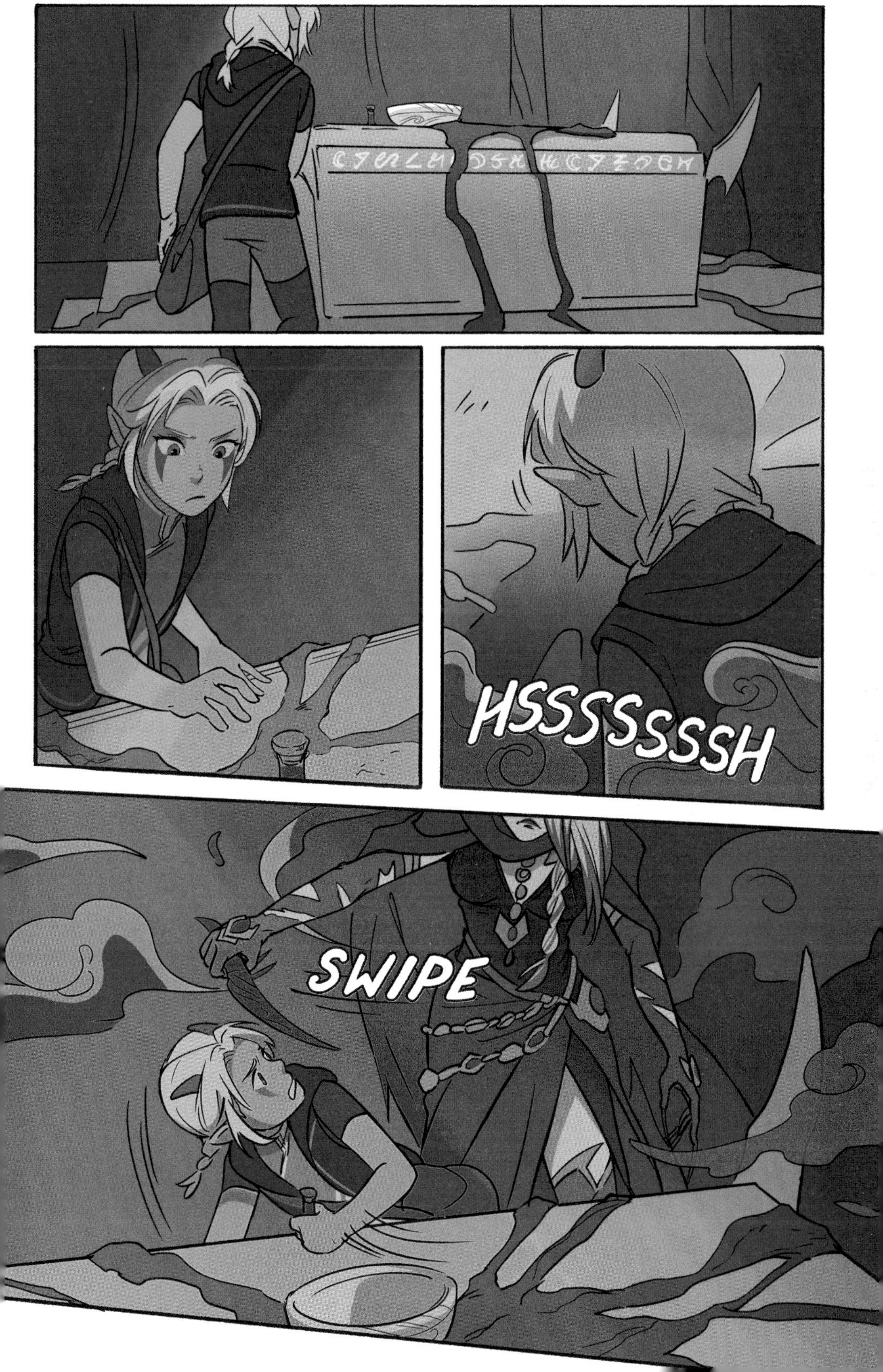
HSSSSSSSH
SWIPE

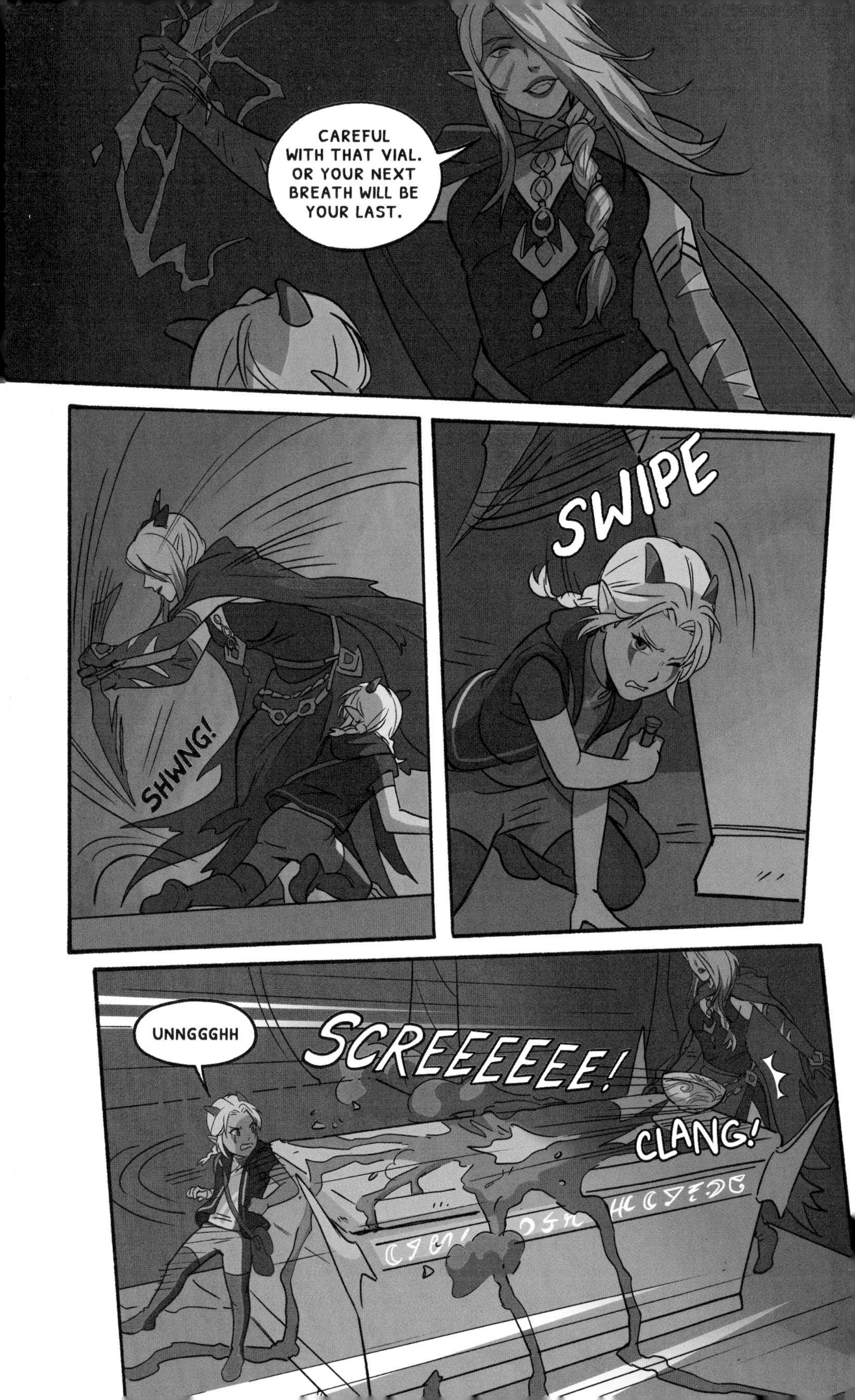
CAREFUL WITH THAT VIAL. OR YOUR NEXT BREATH WILL BE YOUR LAST.
SHWNG!
SWIPE
UNNGGGHH
SCREEEEEEE!
CLANG!

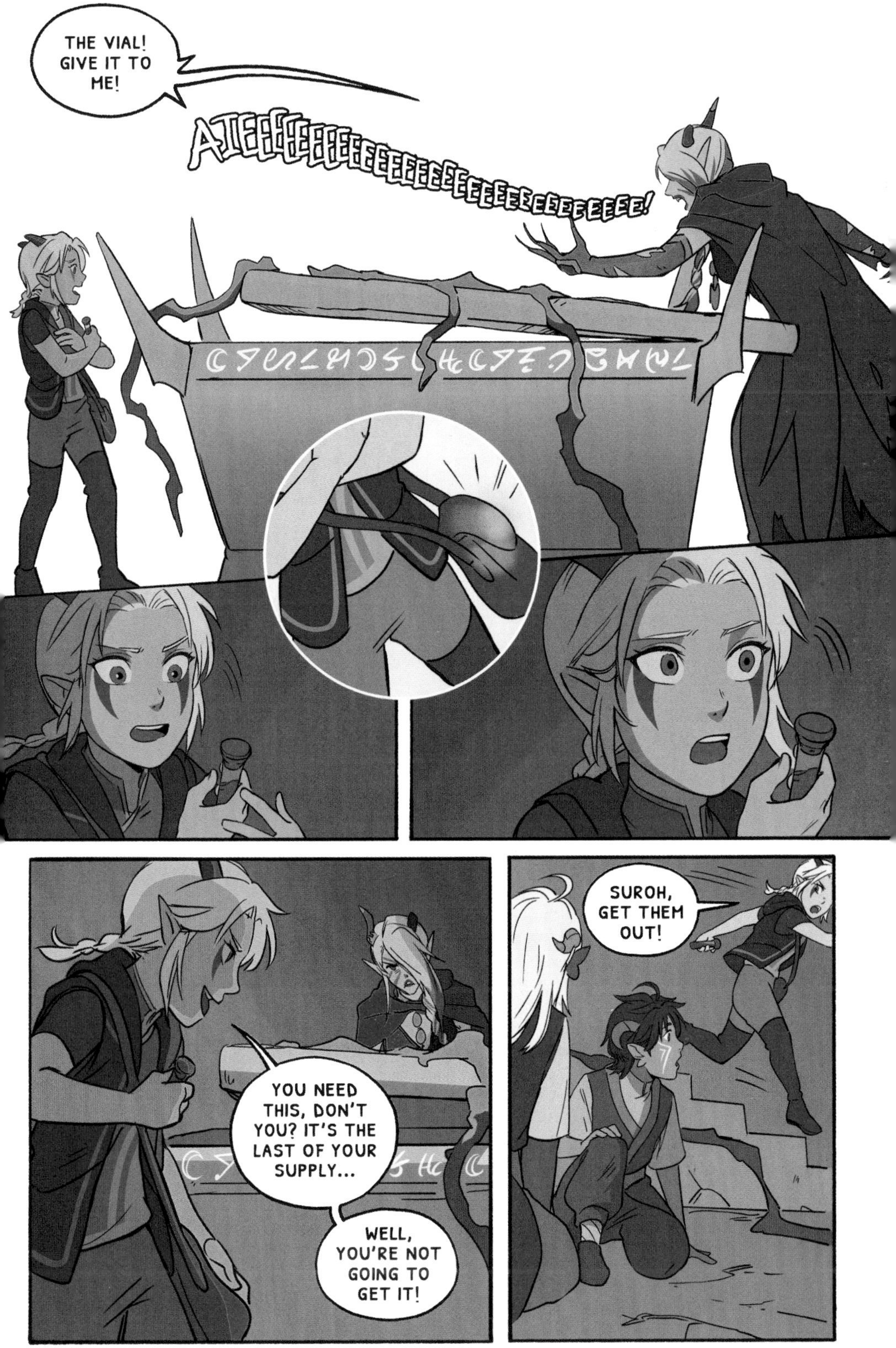
THE VIAL! GIVE IT TO ME!
AIEEEEEEEEEEEEEEEEEEEEEEEEEEEEEEEE!
YOU NEED THIS, DON'T YOU? IT'S THE LAST OF YOUR SUPPLY...
WELL, YOU'RE NOT GOING TO GET IT!
SUROH, GET THEM OUT!

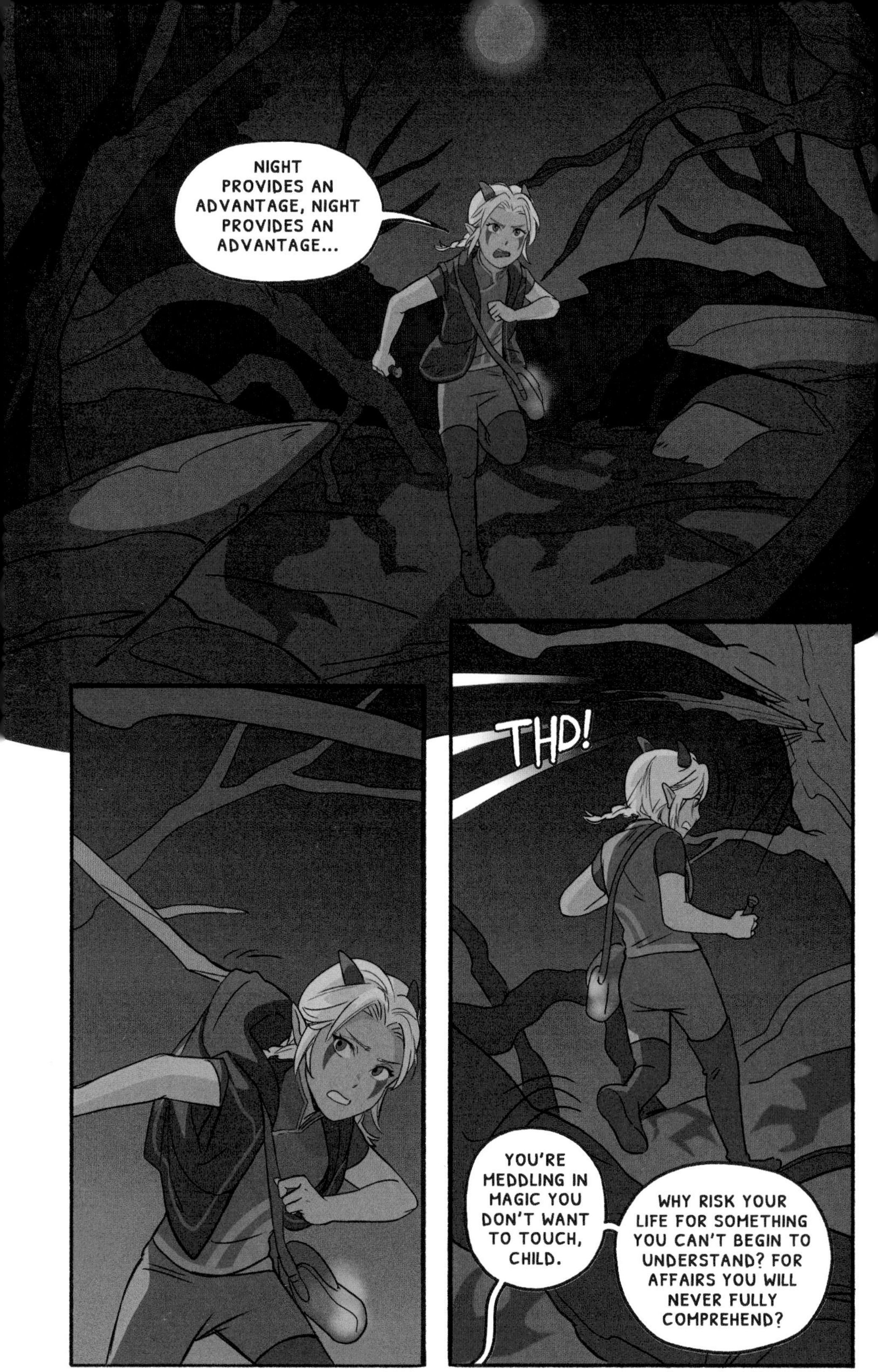
NIGHT PROVIDES AN ADVANTAGE, NIGHT PROVIDES AN ADVANTAGE...
THD!
YOU'RE MEDDLING IN MAGIC YOU DON'T WANT TO TOUCH, CHILD.
WHY RISK YOUR LIFE FOR SOMETHING YOU CAN'T BEGIN TO UNDERSTAND? FOR AFFAIRS YOU WILL NEVER FULLY COMPREHEND?

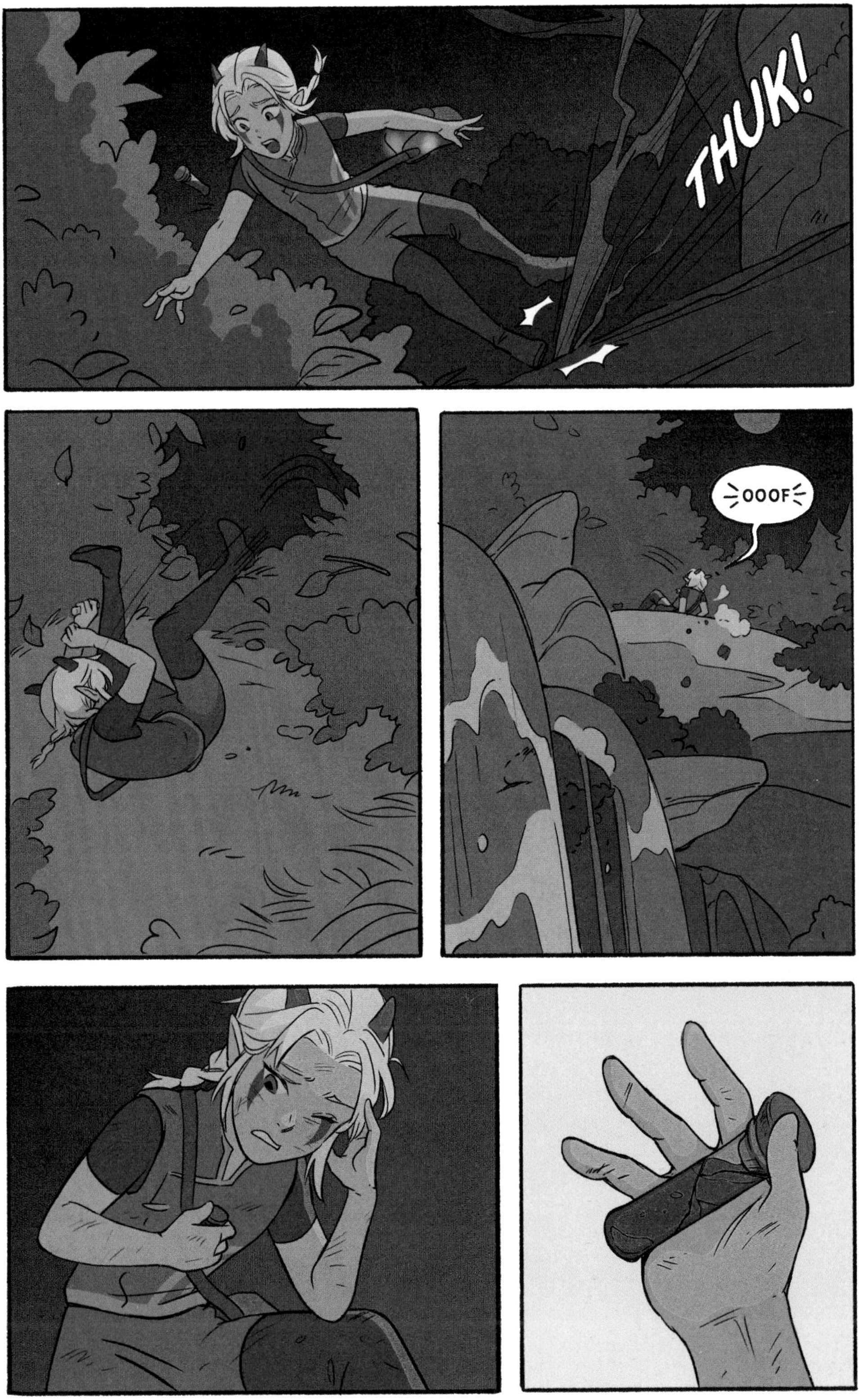
THUK!
OOOF

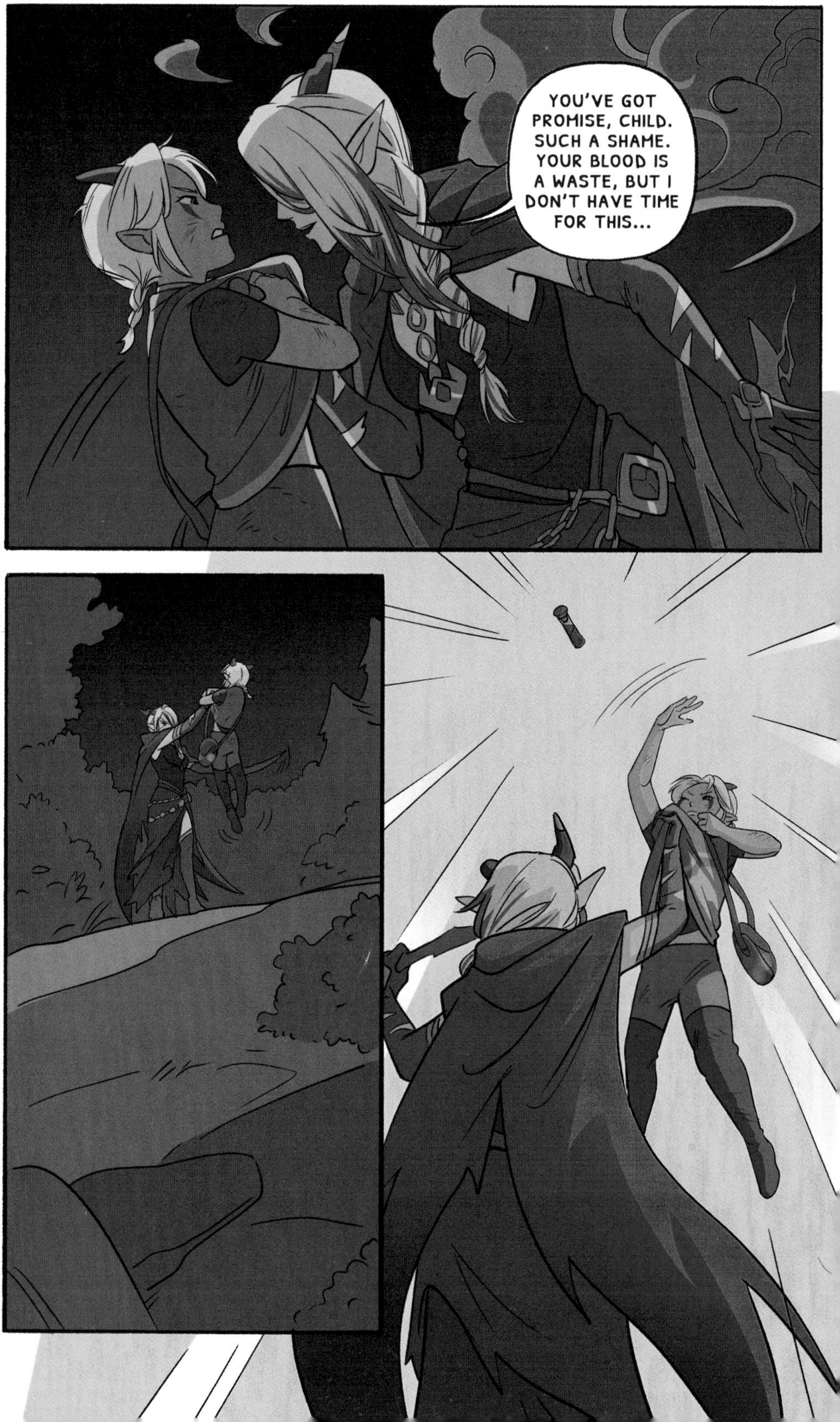
YOU'VE GOT PROMISE, CHILD. SUCH A SHAME. YOUR BLOOD IS A WASTE, BUT I DON'T HAVE TIME FOR THIS...

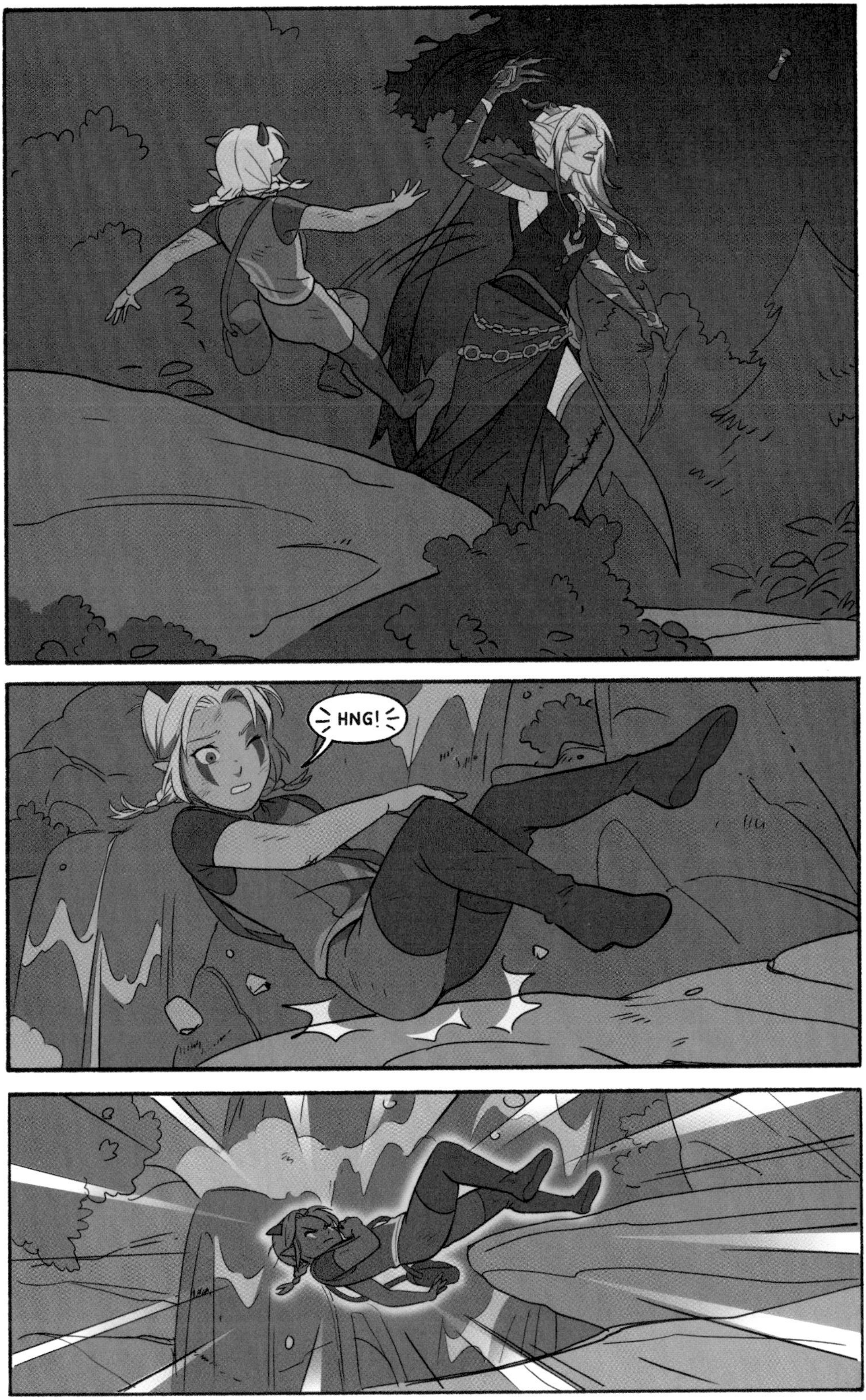
HNG!

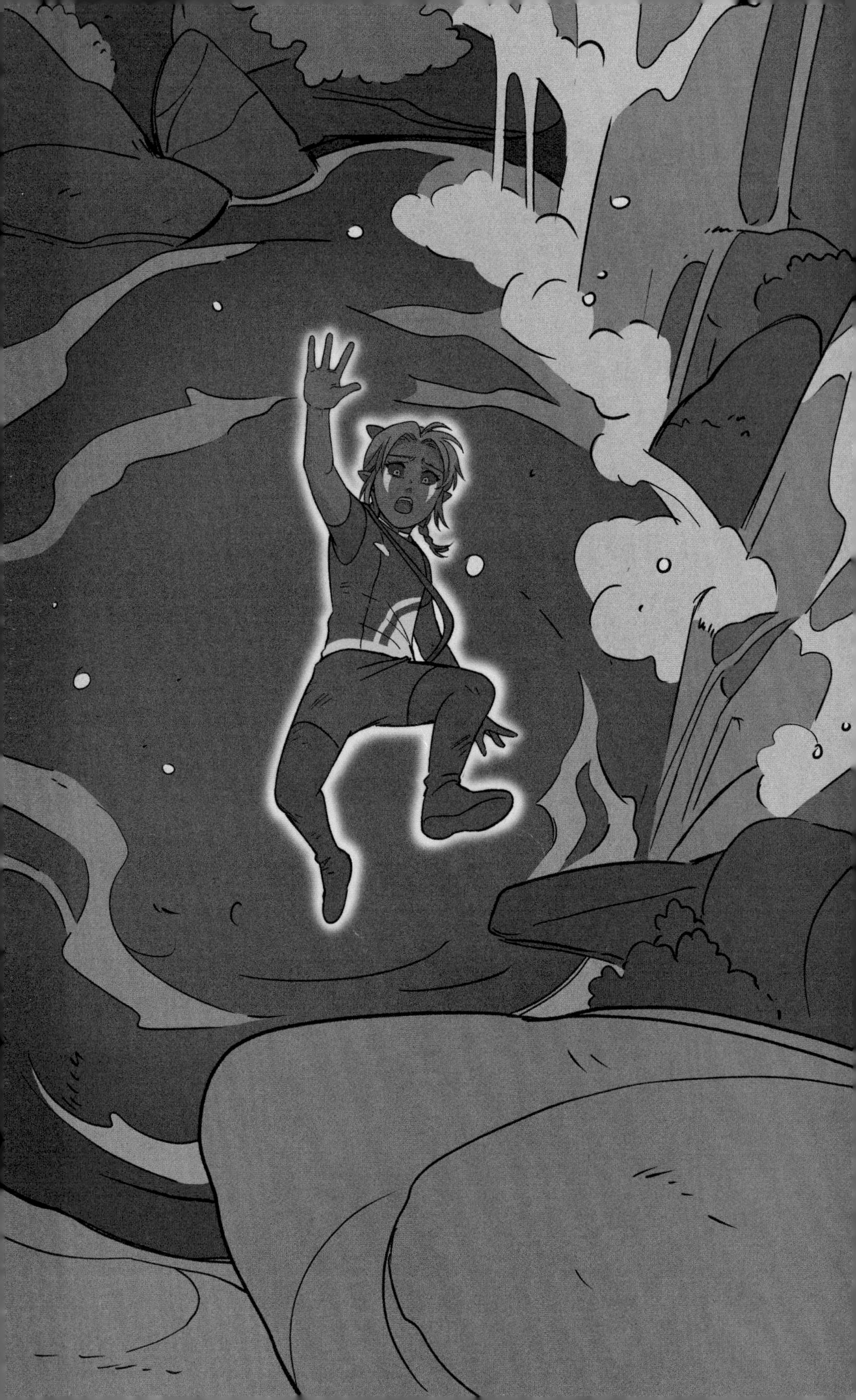

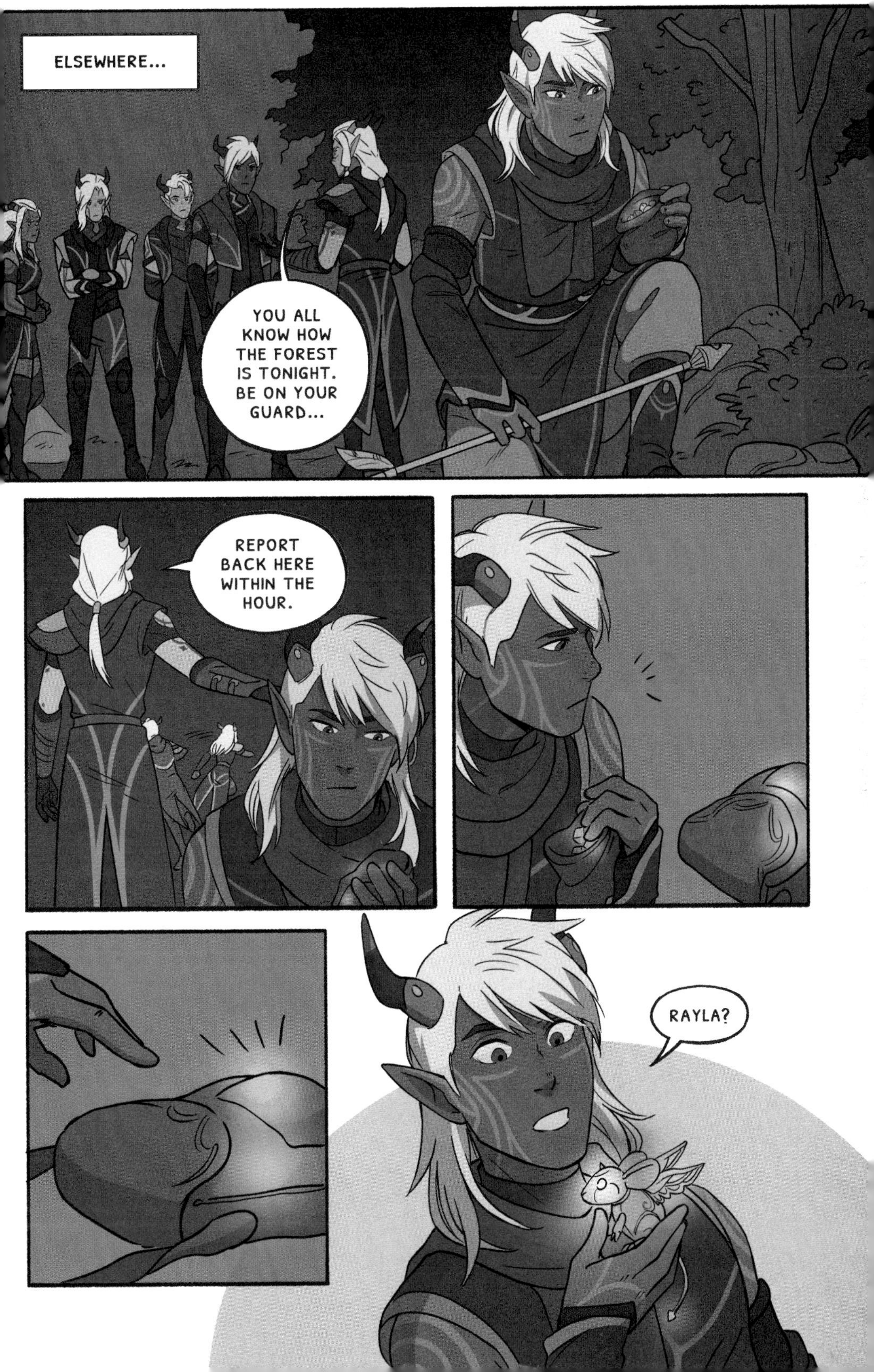
ELSEWHERE...
YOU ALL KNOW HOW THE FOREST IS TONIGHT. BE ON YOUR GUARD...
REPORT BACK HERE WITHIN THE HOUR.
RAYLA?

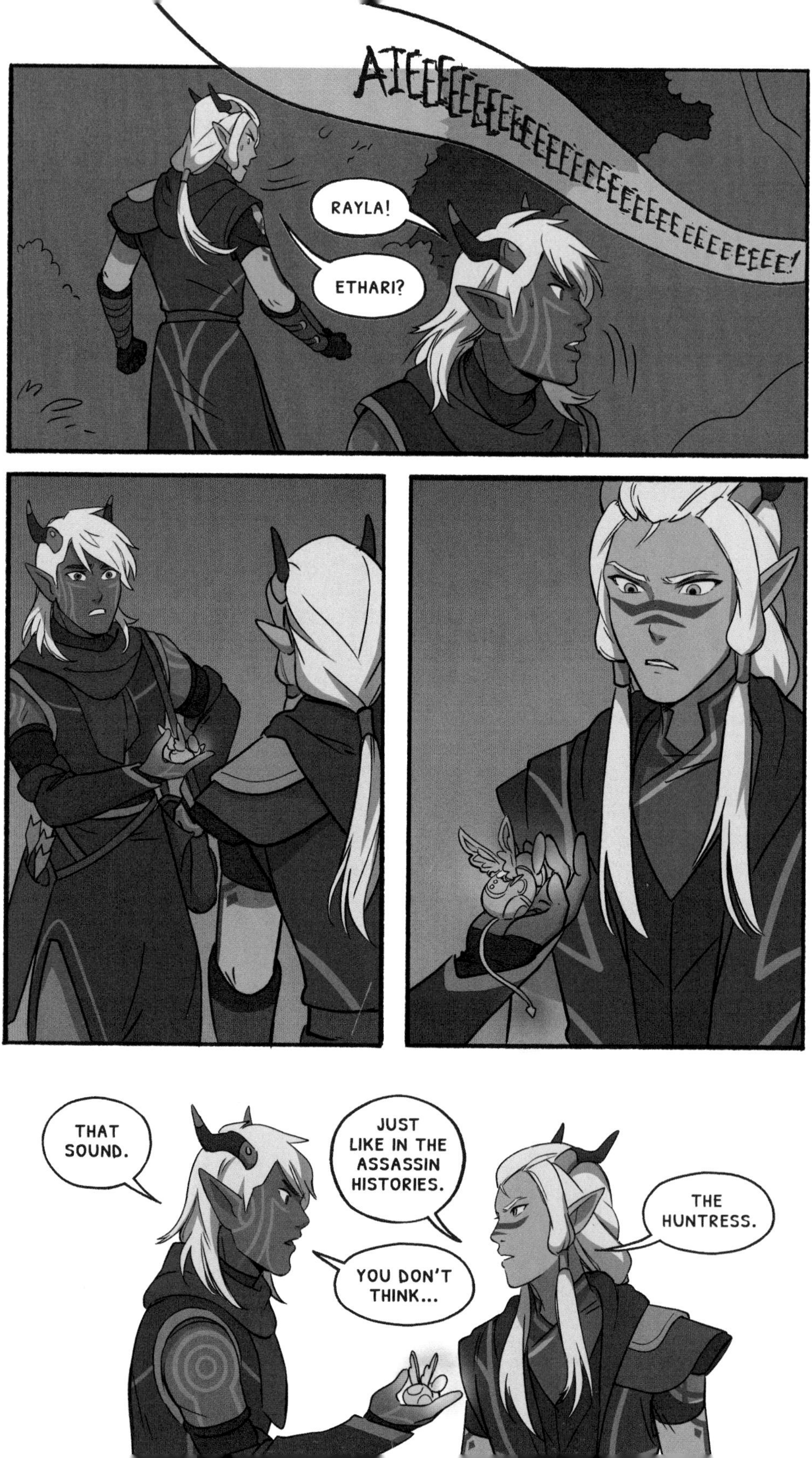
AIEEEEEEEEEEEEEEEEEEEEEEEEEEEEEEEEE!
RAYLA!
ETHARI?
THAT SOUND.
JUST LIKE IN THE ASSASSIN HISTORIES.
YOU DON'T THINK...
THE HUNTRESS.

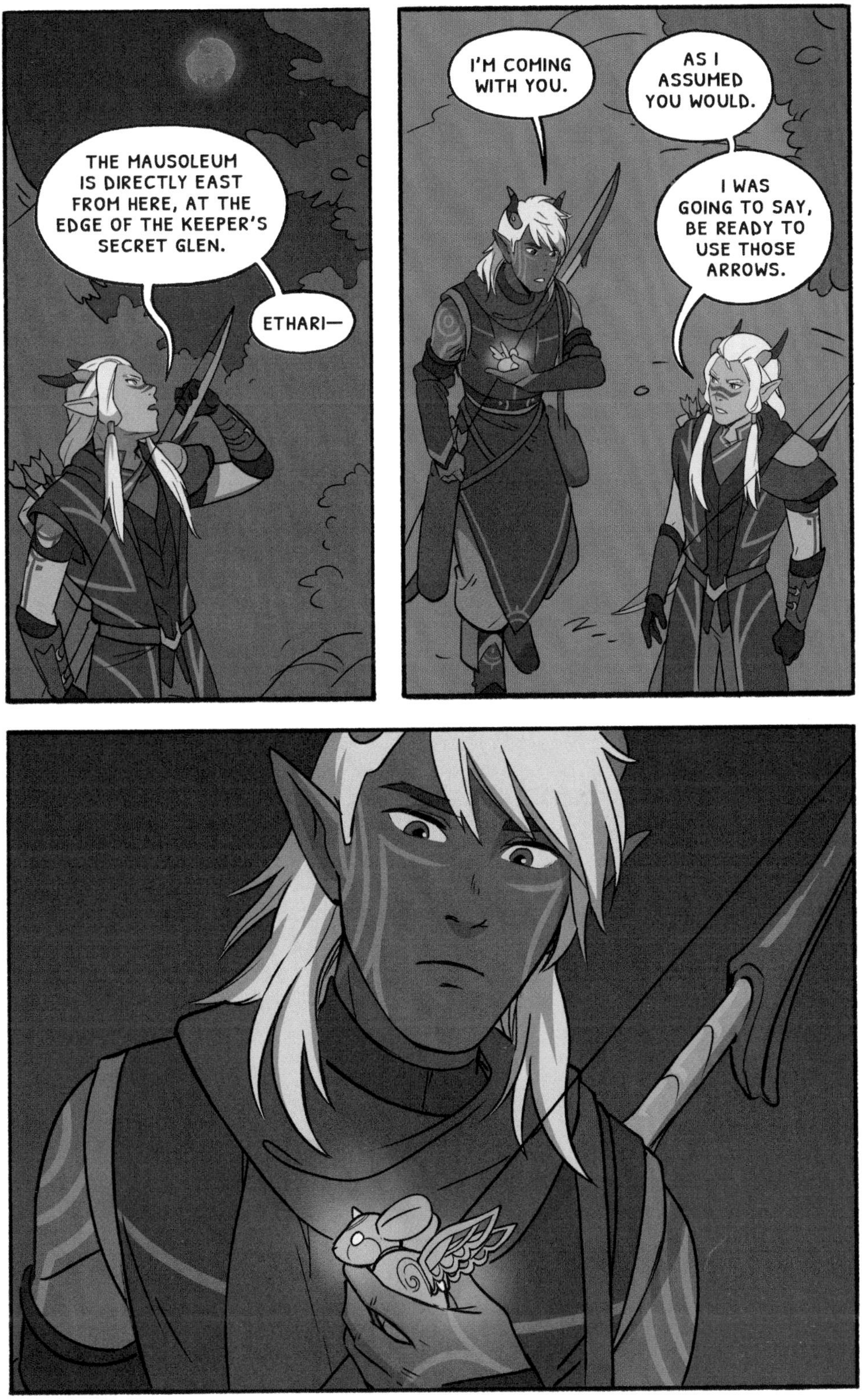
THE MAUSOLEUM IS DIRECTLY EAST FROM HERE, AT THE EDGE OF THE KEEPER'S SECRET GLEN.
ETHARI—
I'M COMING WITH YOU.
AS I ASSUMED YOU WOULD.
I WAS GOING TO SAY, BE READY TO USE THOSE ARROWS.

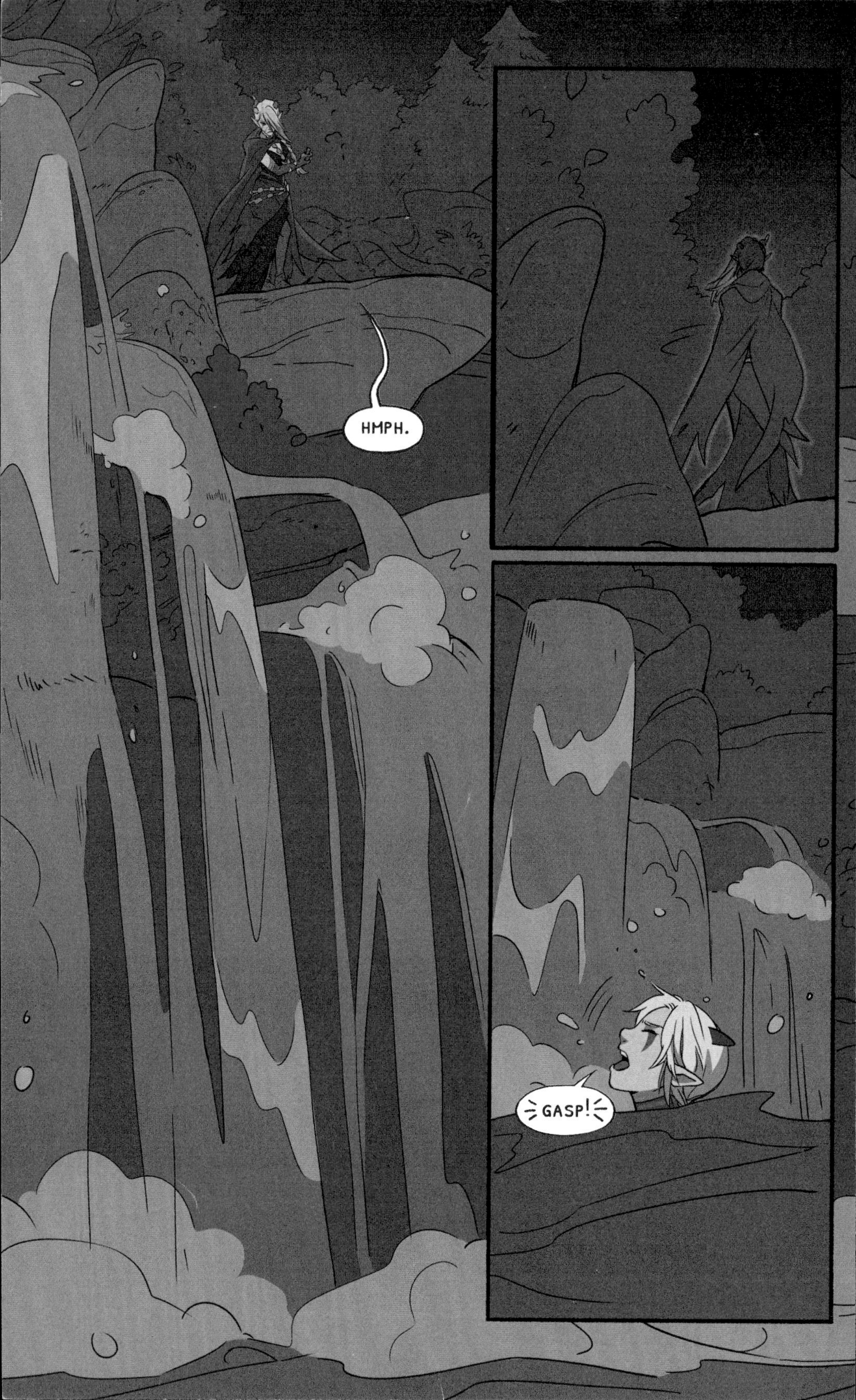
HMPH.
GASP!

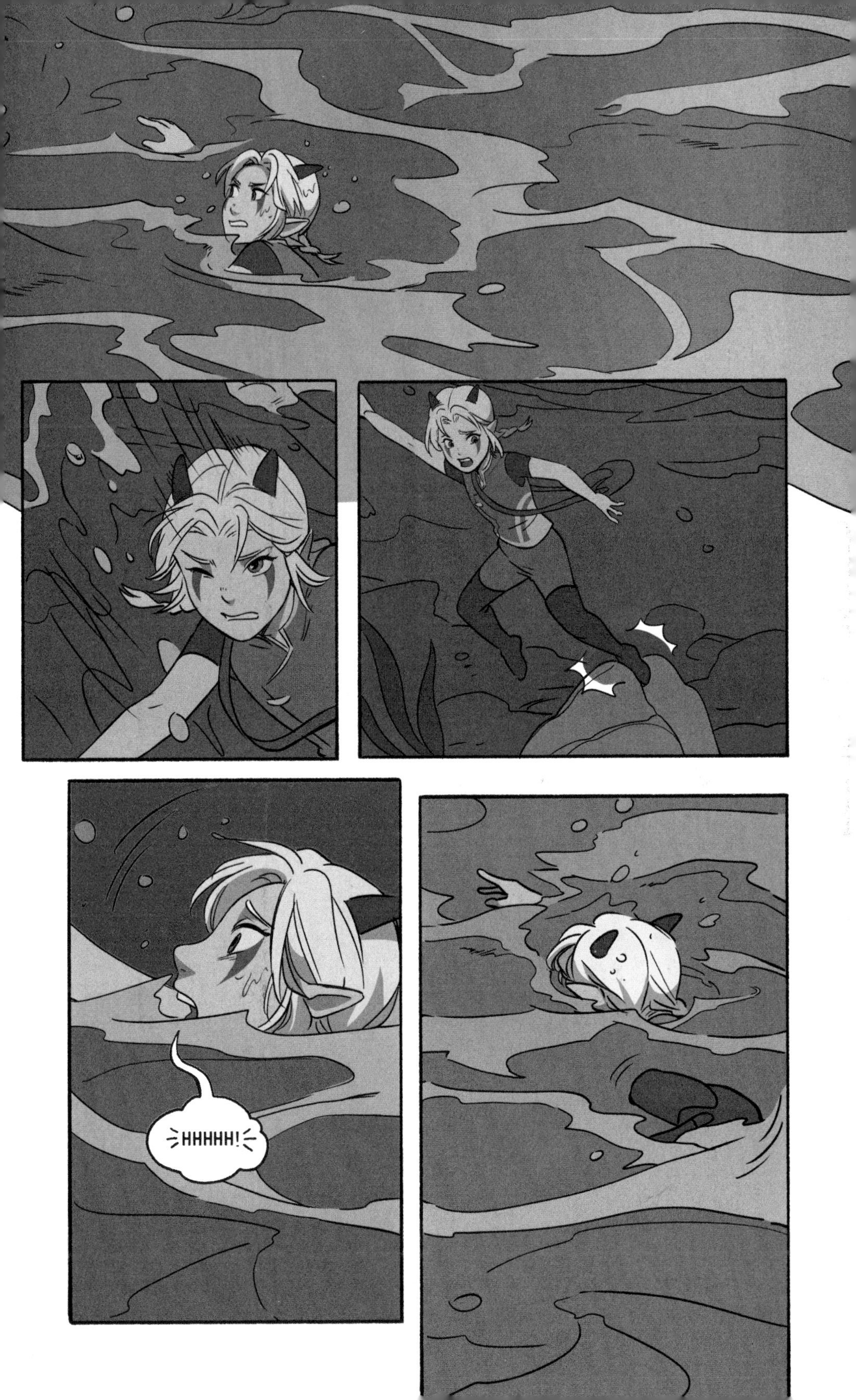
HHHHH!

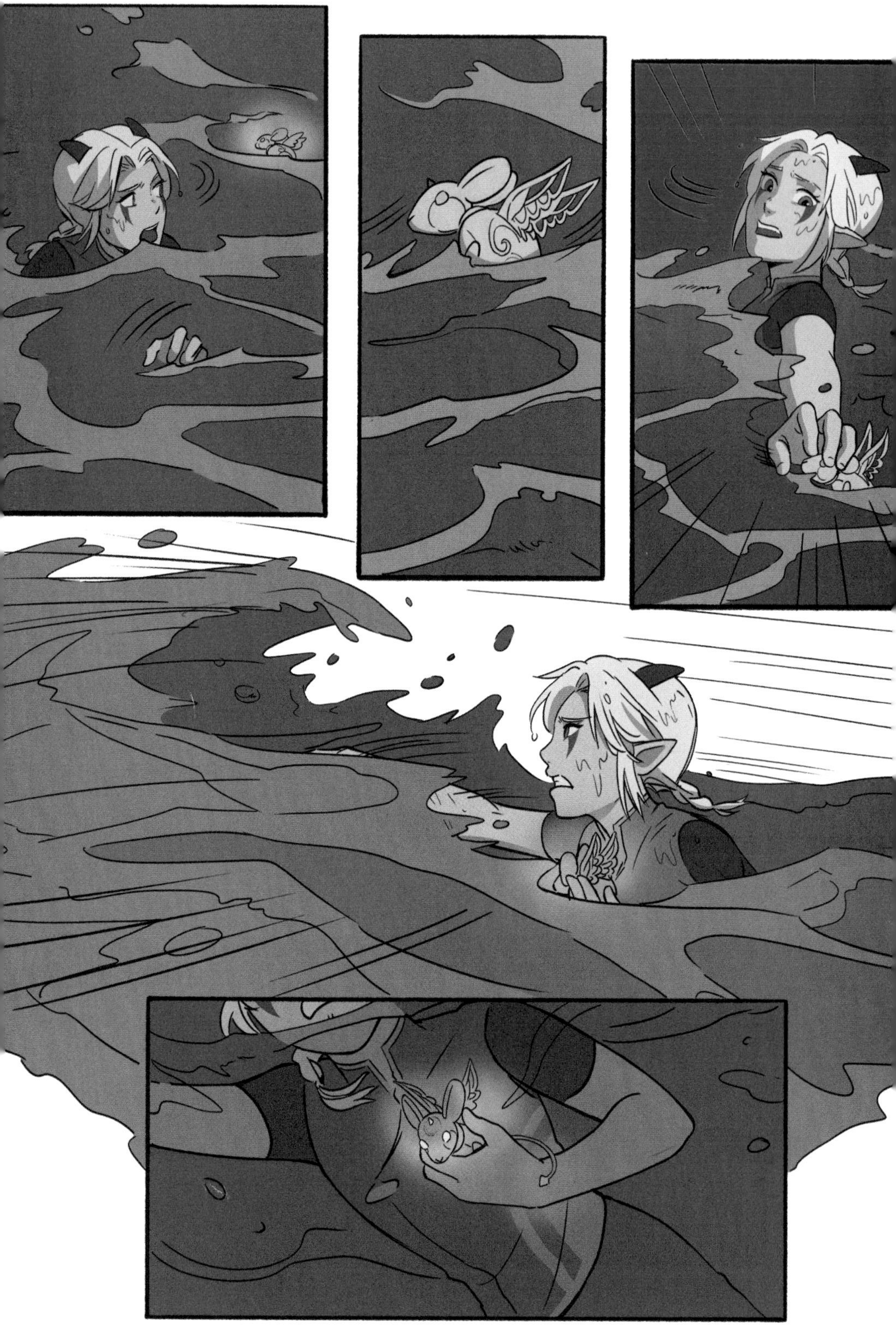

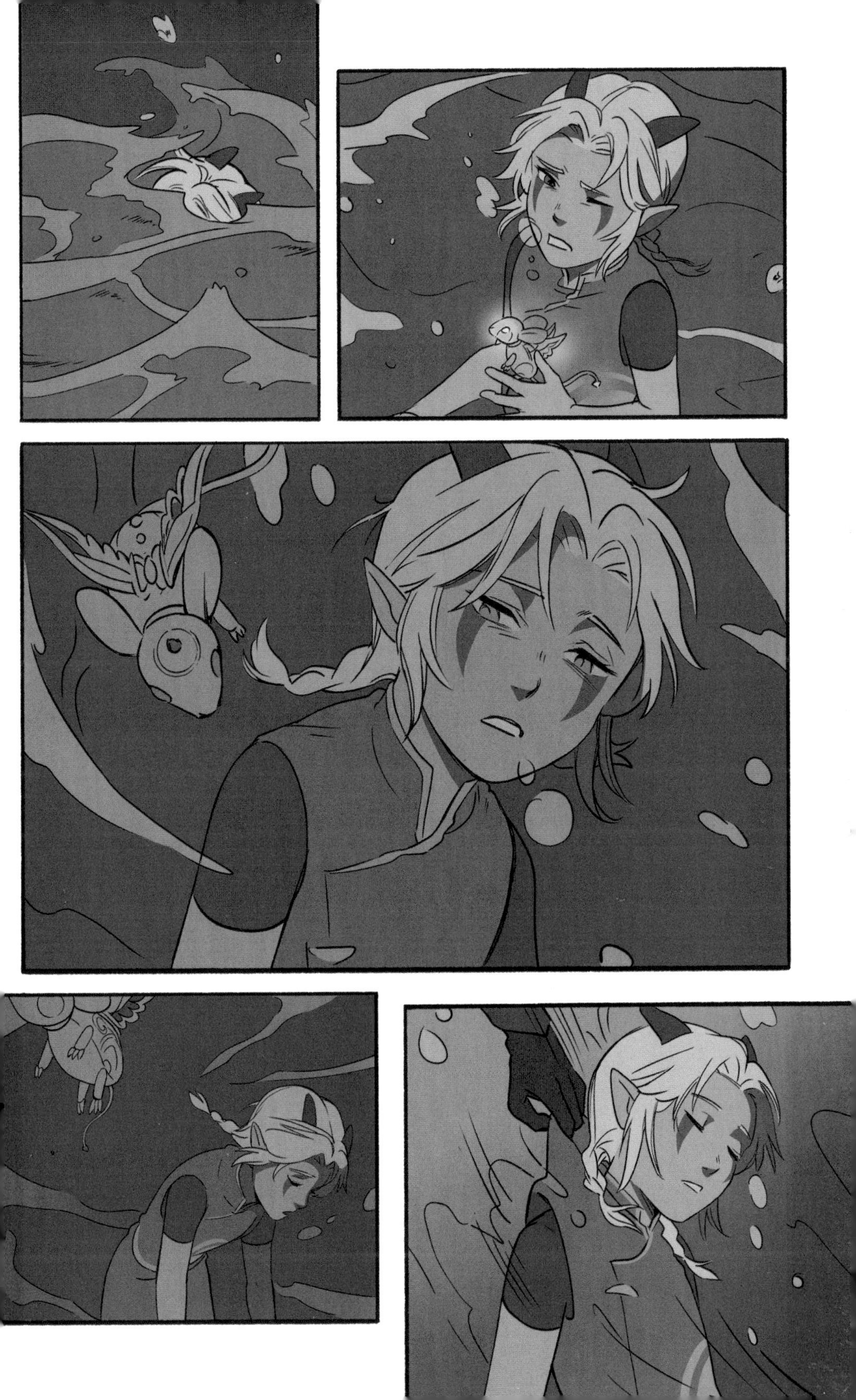

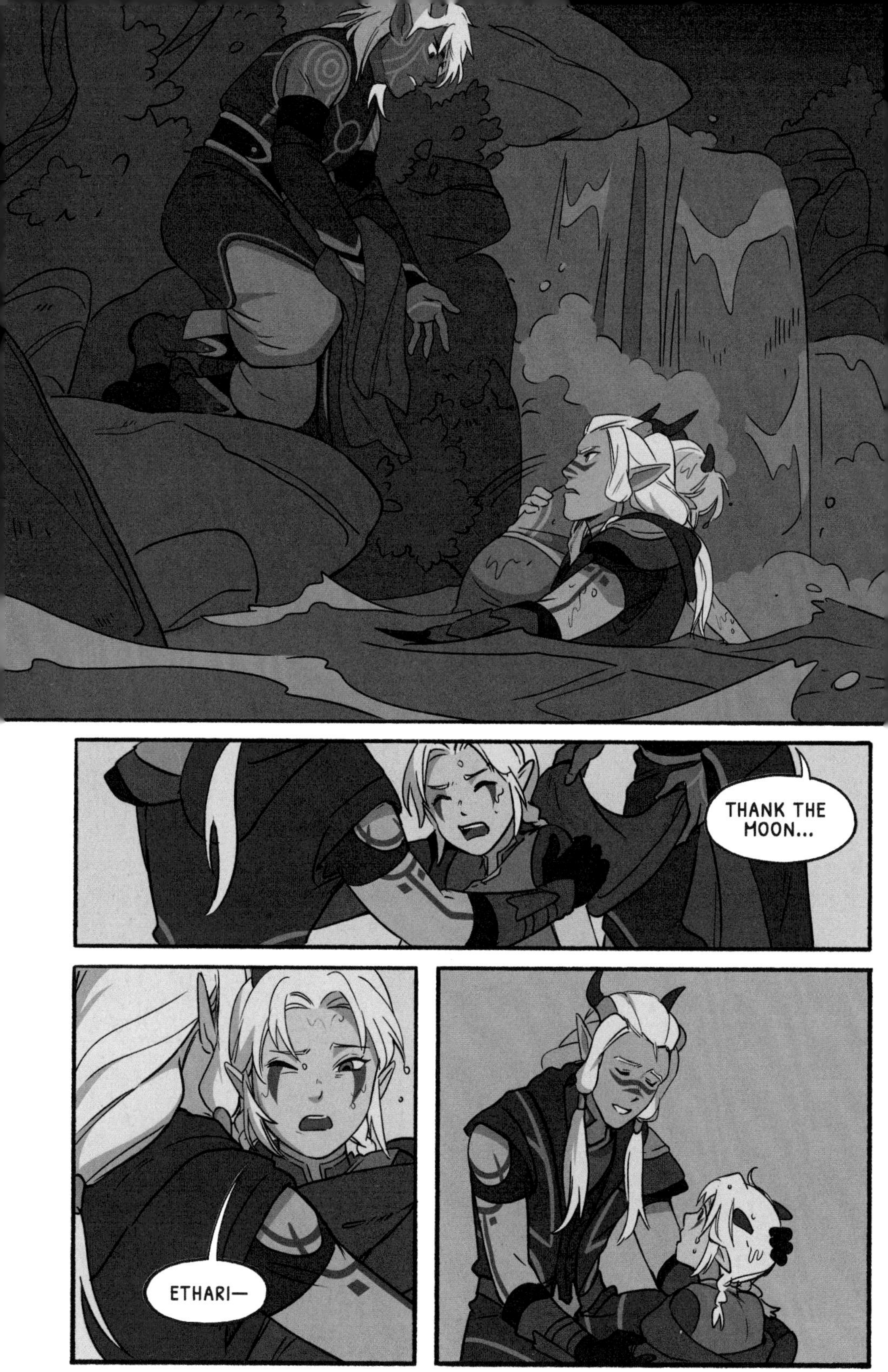
THANK THE MOON...
ETHARI—

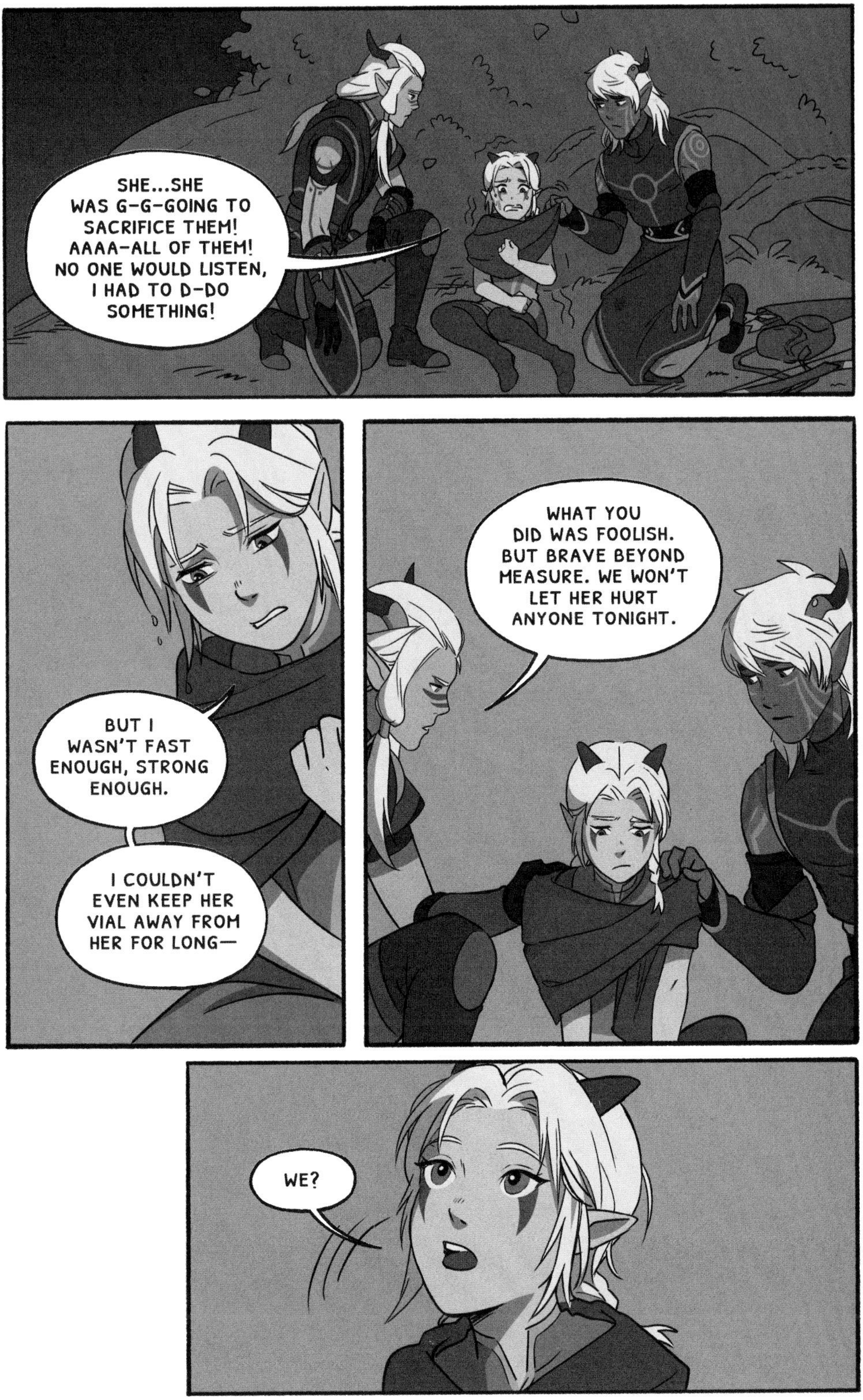
SHE...SHE WAS G-G-GOING TO SACRIFICE THEM! AAAA-ALL OF THEM! NO ONE WOULD LISTEN, I HAD TO D-DO SOMETHING!
BUT I WASN'T FAST ENOUGH, STRONG ENOUGH.
I COULDN'T EVEN KEEP HER VIAL AWAY FROM HER FOR LONG—
WHAT YOU DID WAS FOOLISH. BUT BRAVE BEYOND MEASURE. WE WON'T LET HER HURT ANYONE TONIGHT.
WE?

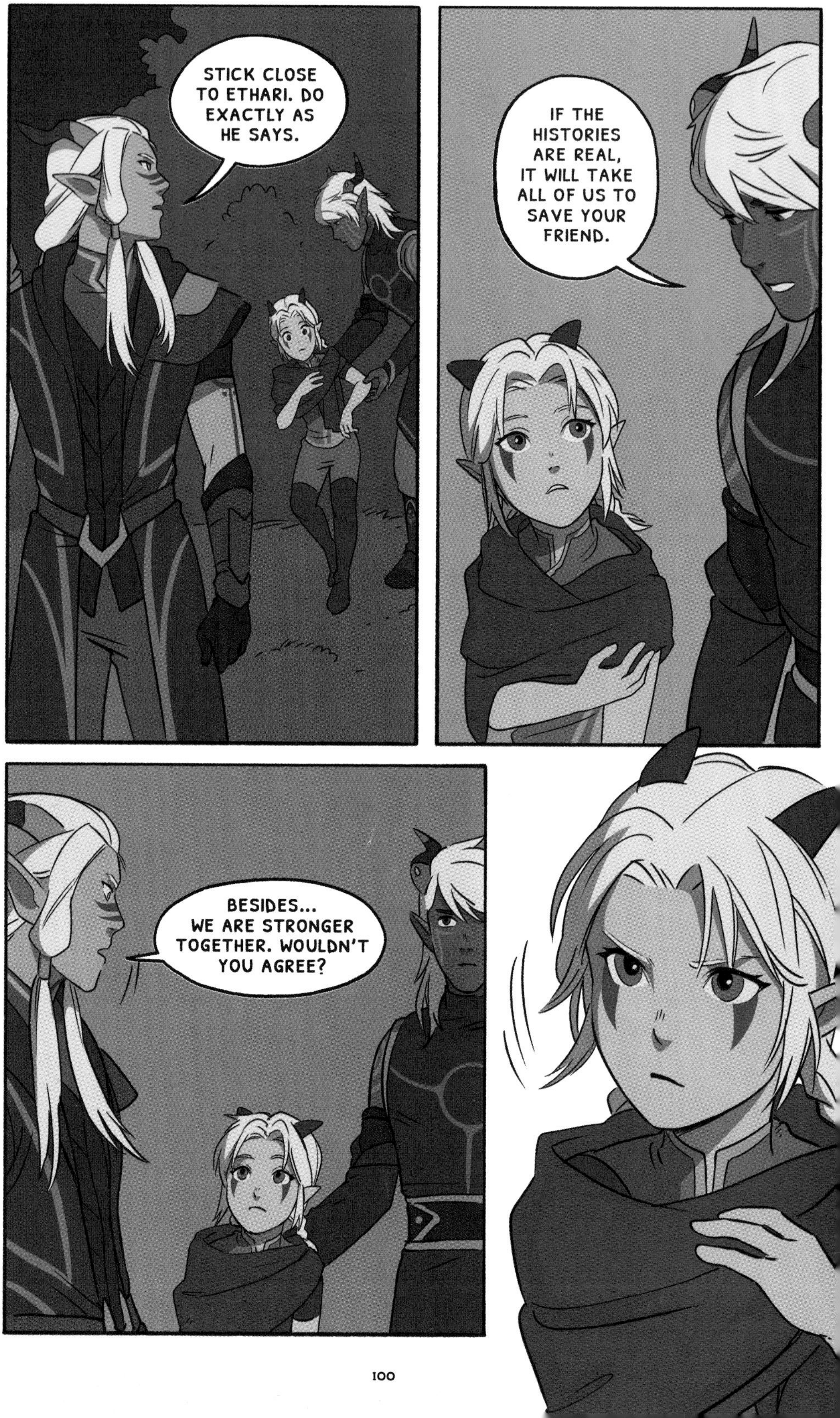
STICK CLOSE TO ETHARI. DO EXACTLY AS HE SAYS.
IF THE HISTORIES ARE REAL, IT WILL TAKE ALL OF US TO SAVE YOUR FRIEND.
BESIDES... WE ARE STRONGER TOGETHER. WOULDN'T YOU AGREE?

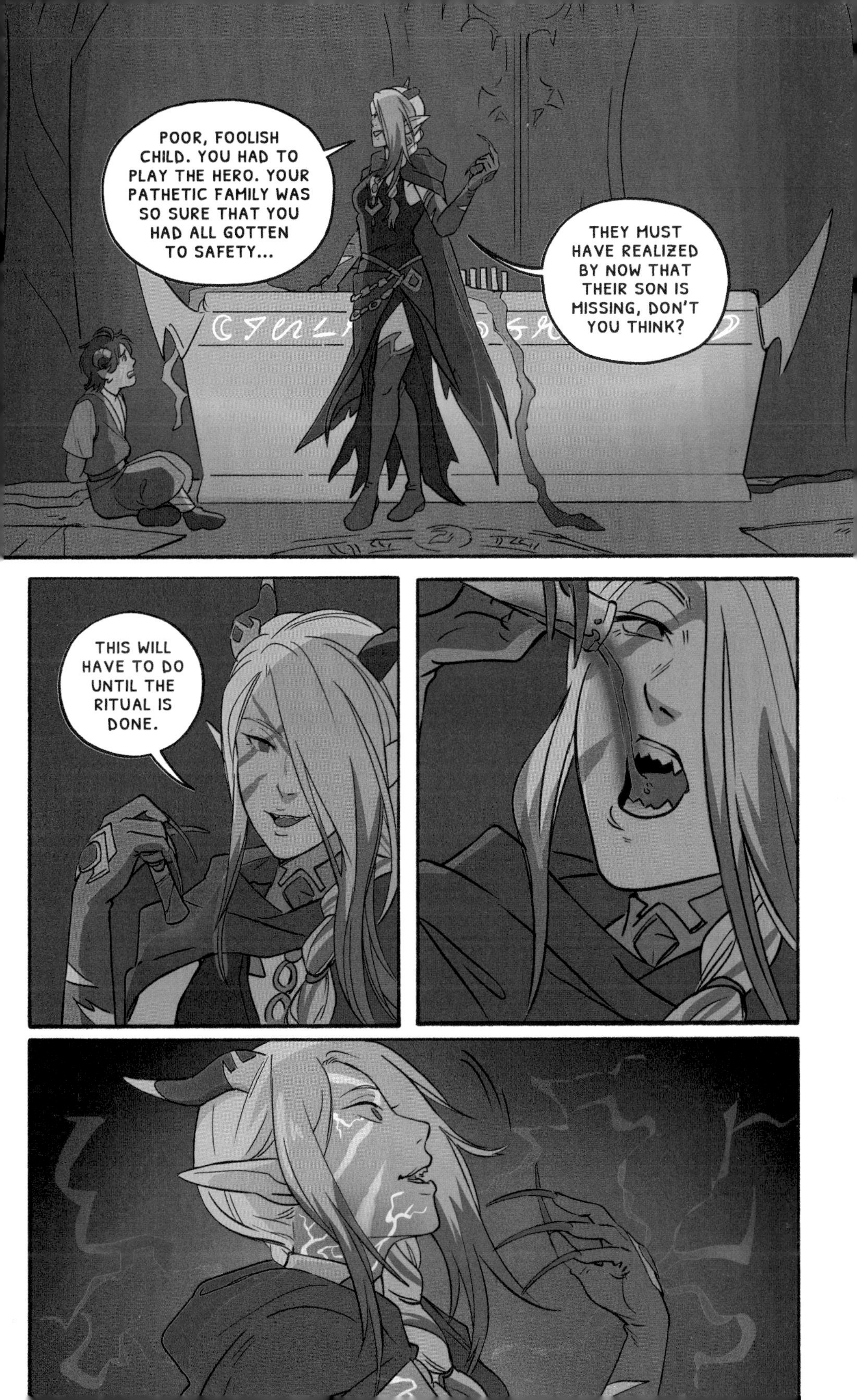
POOR, FOOLISH CHILD. YOU HAD TO PLAY THE HERO. YOUR PATHETIC FAMILY WAS SO SURE THAT YOU HAD ALL GOTTEN TO SAFETY...
THEY MUST HAVE REALIZED BY NOW THAT THEIR SON IS MISSING, DON'T YOU THINK?
THIS WILL HAVE TO DO UNTIL THE RITUAL IS DONE.

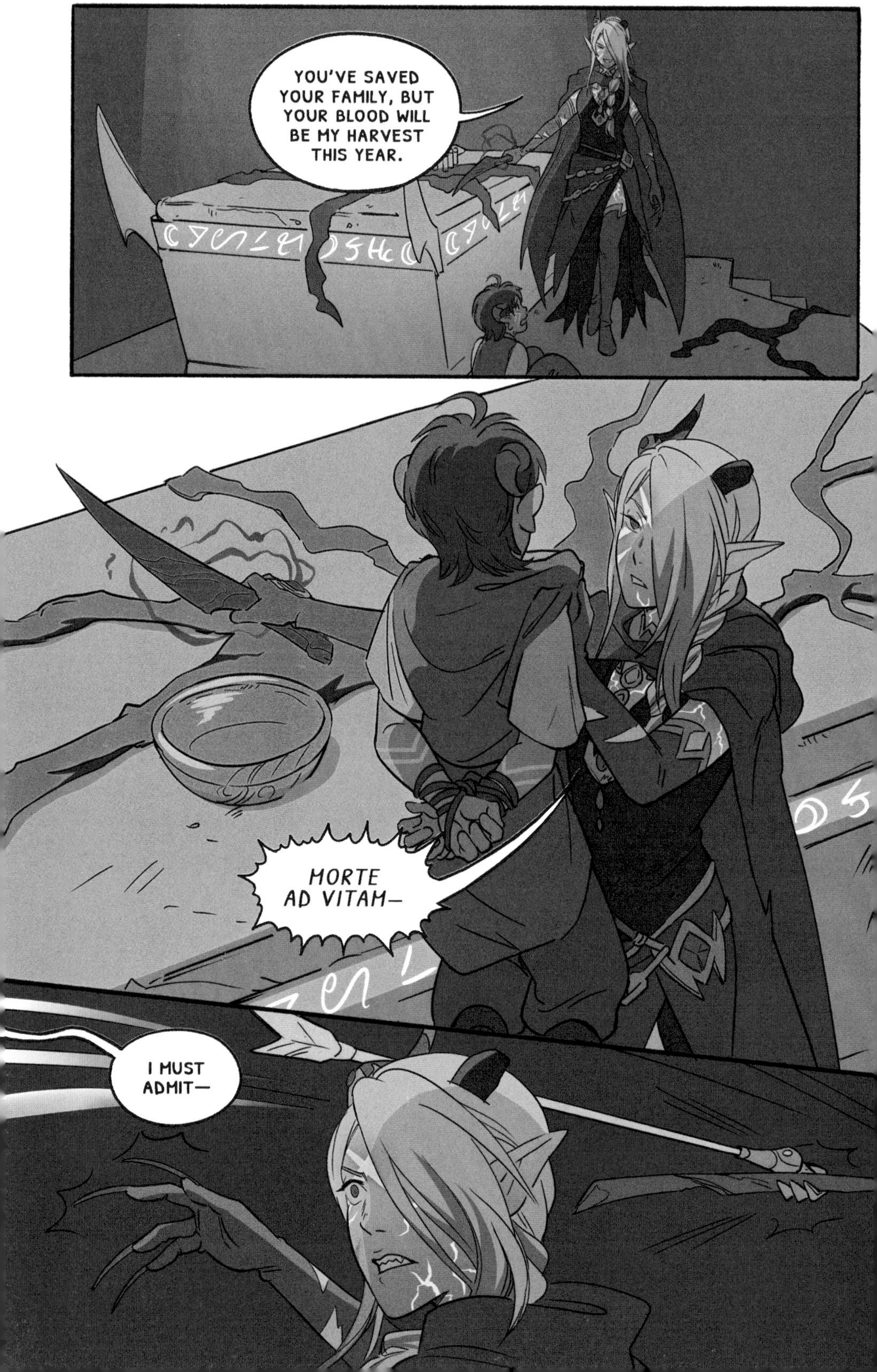
YOU'VE SAVED YOUR FAMILY, BUT YOUR BLOOD WILL BE MY HARVEST THIS YEAR.
MORTE AD VITAM—
I MUST ADMIT—

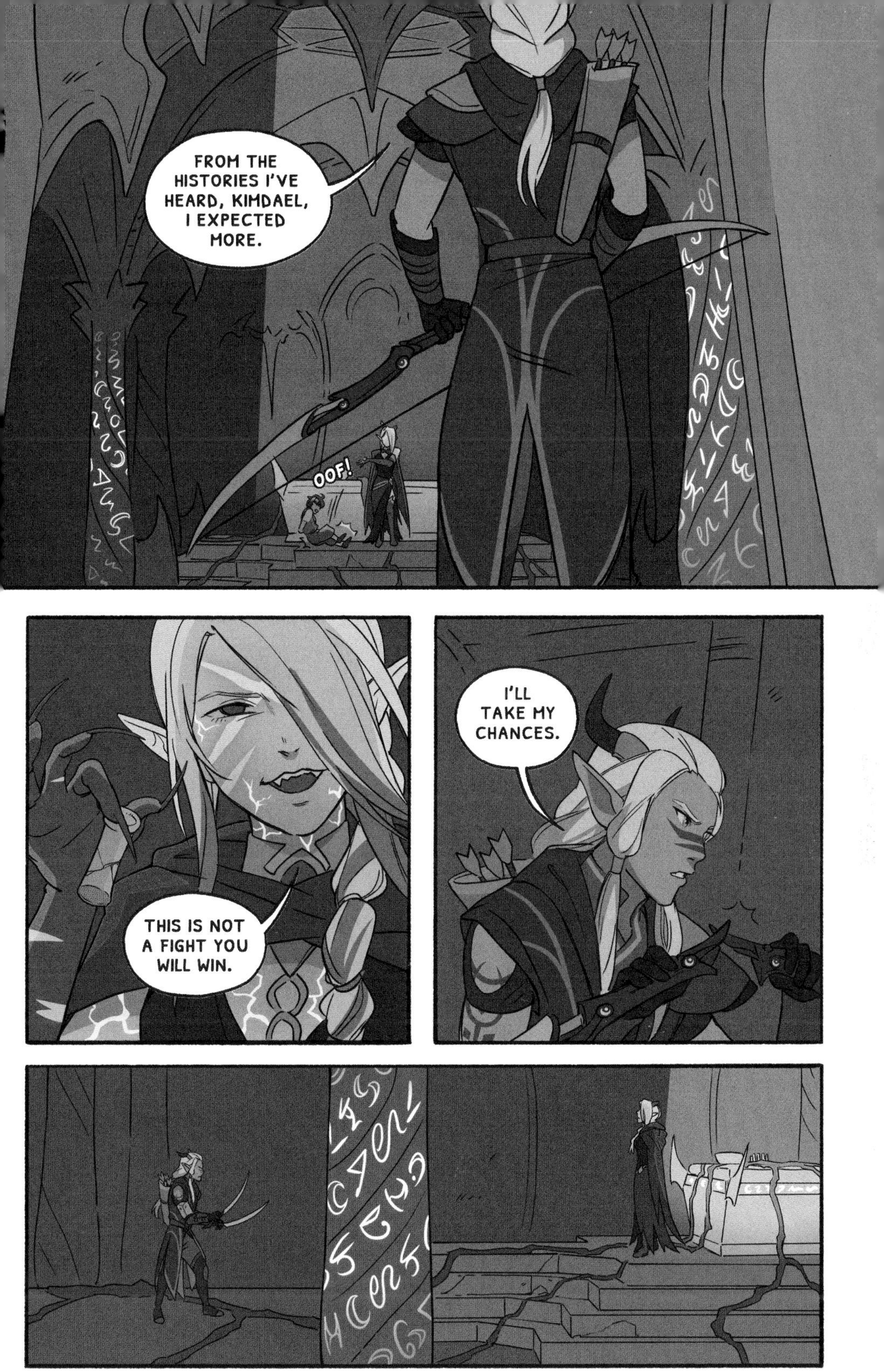
FROM THE HISTORIES I'VE HEARD, KIMDAEL, I EXPECTED MORE.
OOF!
THIS IS NOT A FIGHT YOU WILL WIN.
I'LL TAKE MY CHANCES.

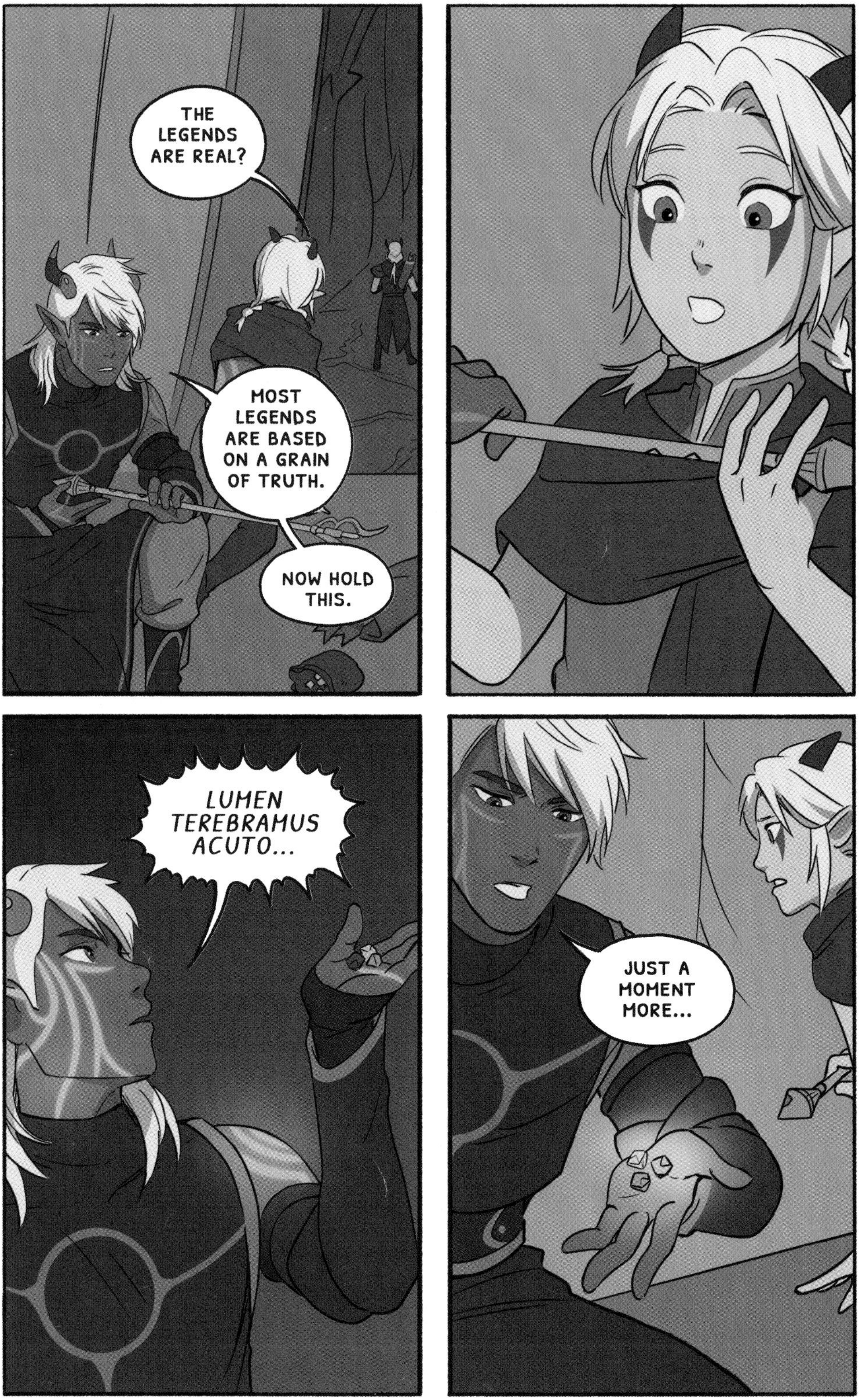
THE LEGENDS ARE REAL?
MOST LEGENDS ARE BASED ON A GRAIN OF TRUTH.
NOW HOLD THIS.
LUMEN TEREBRAMUS ACUTO...
JUST A MOMENT MORE...

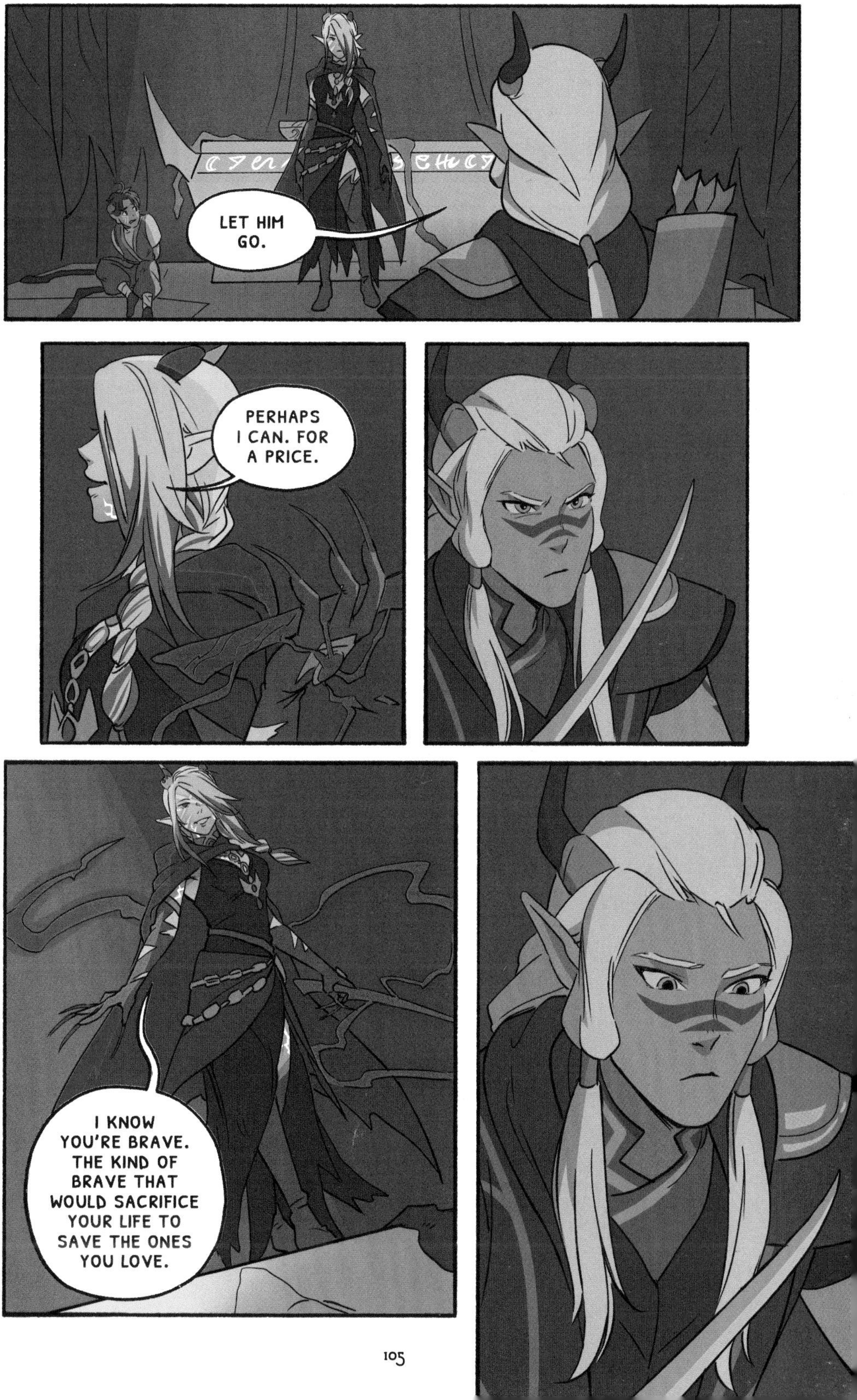
LET HIM GO.
PERHAPS I CAN. FOR A PRICE.
I KNOW YOU'RE BRAVE. THE KIND OF BRAVE THAT WOULD SACRIFICE YOUR LIFE TO SAVE THE ONES YOU LOVE.

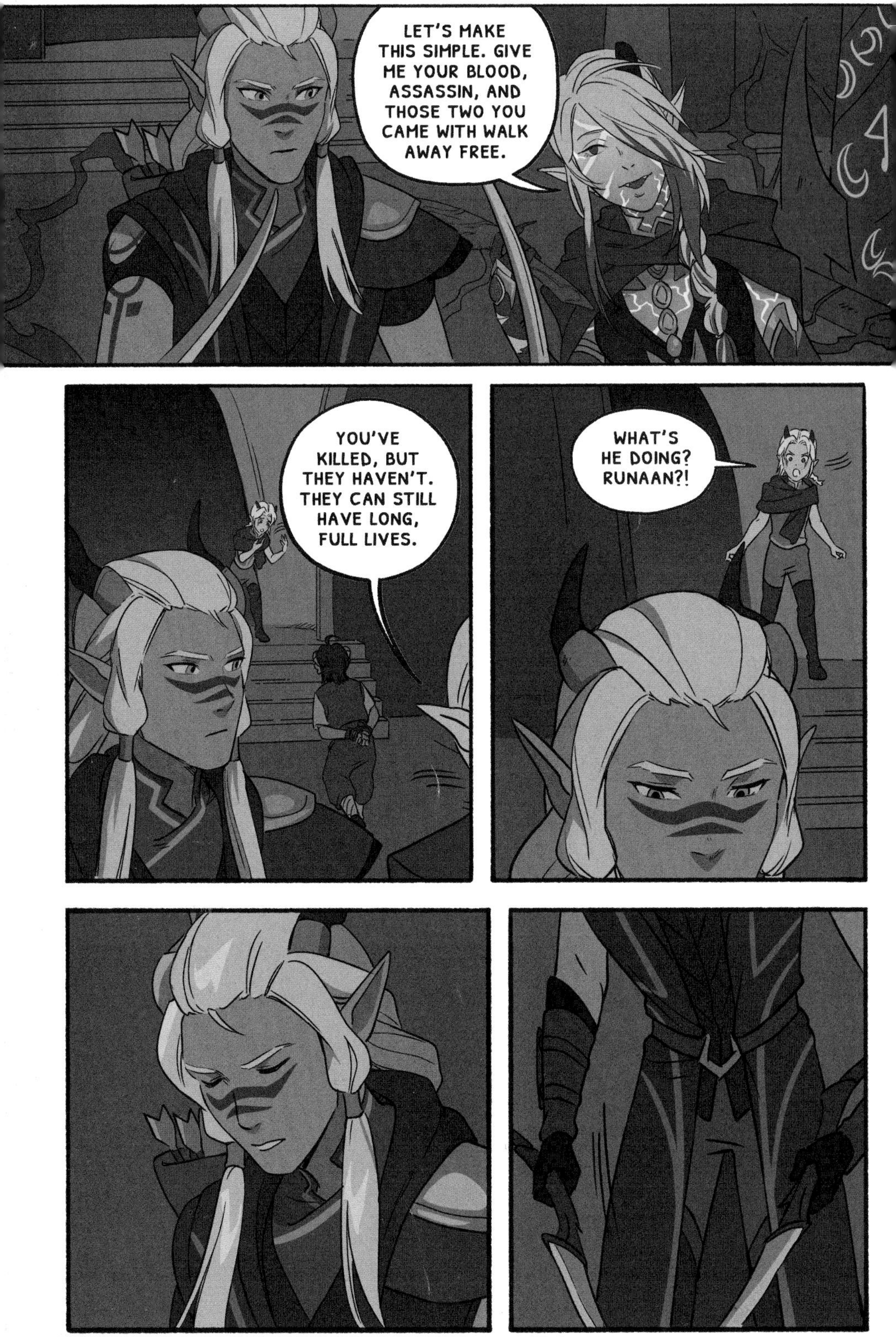
LET'S MAKE THIS SIMPLE. GIVE ME YOUR BLOOD, ASSASSIN, AND THOSE TWO YOU CAME WITH WALK AWAY FREE.
YOU'VE KILLED, BUT THEY HAVEN'T. THEY CAN STILL HAVE LONG, FULL LIVES.
WHAT'S HE DOING? RUNAAN?!

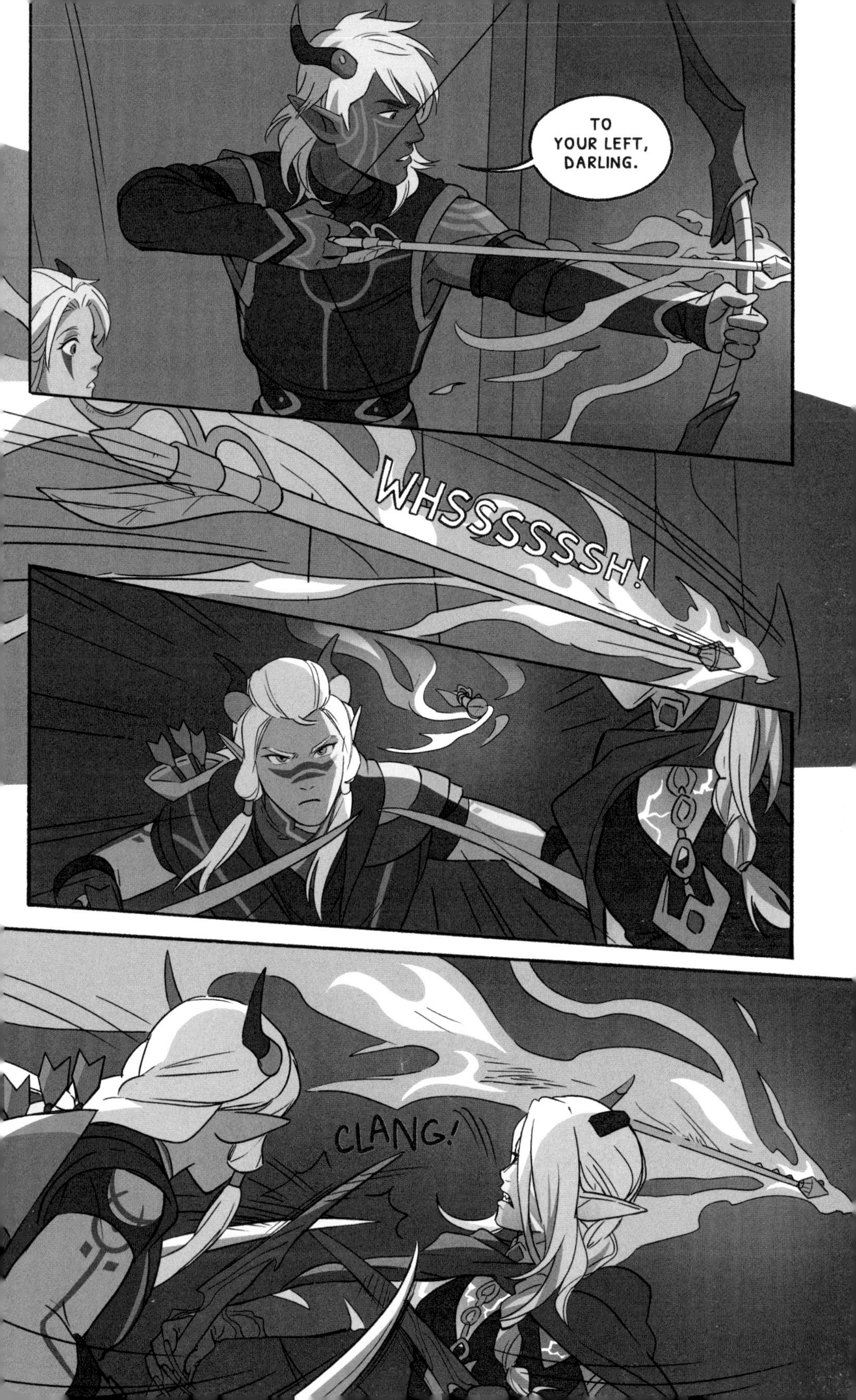
TO YOUR LEFT, DARLING.
WHSSSSSSH!
CLANG!

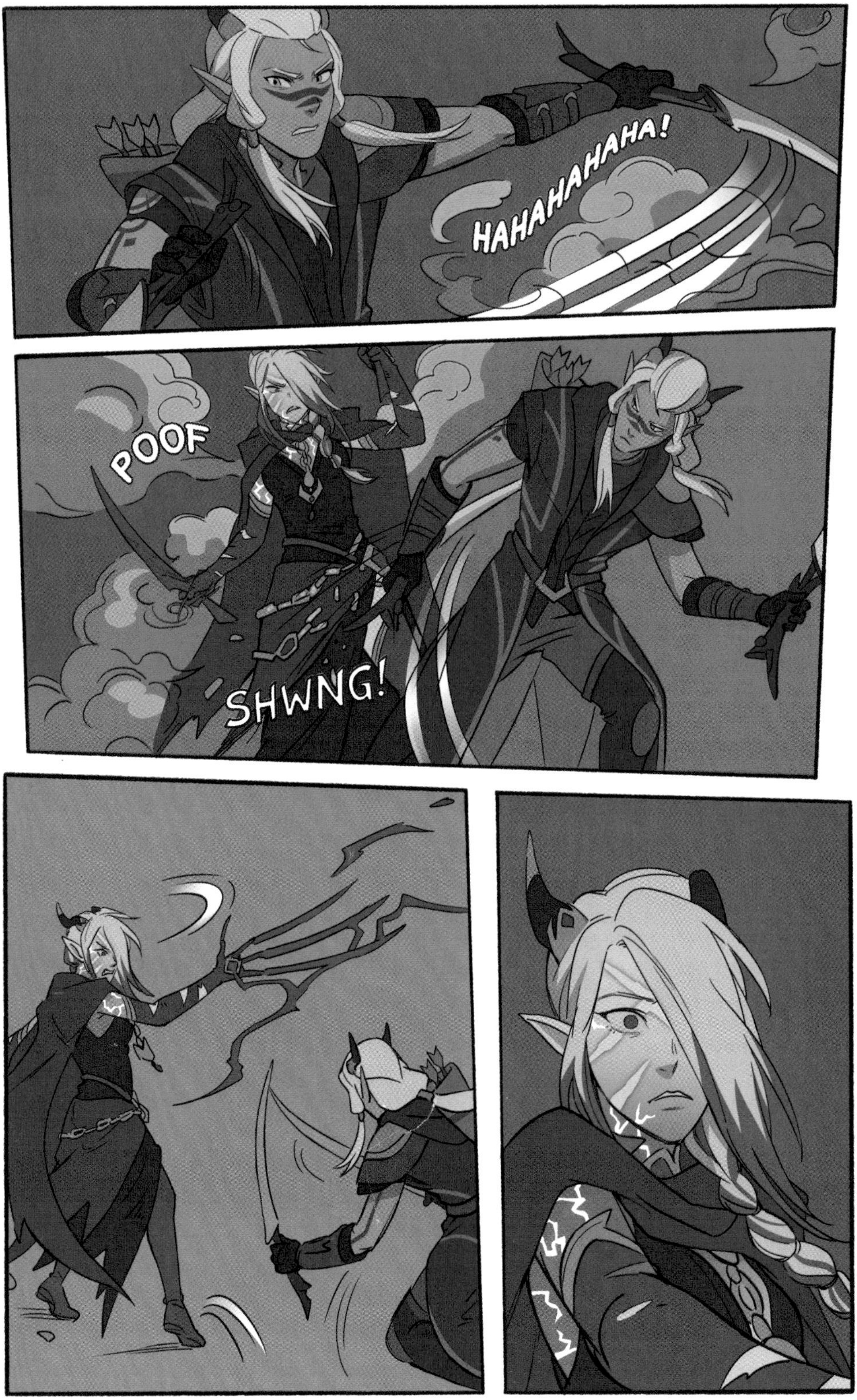
HAHAHAHAHA!
POOF
SHWNG!

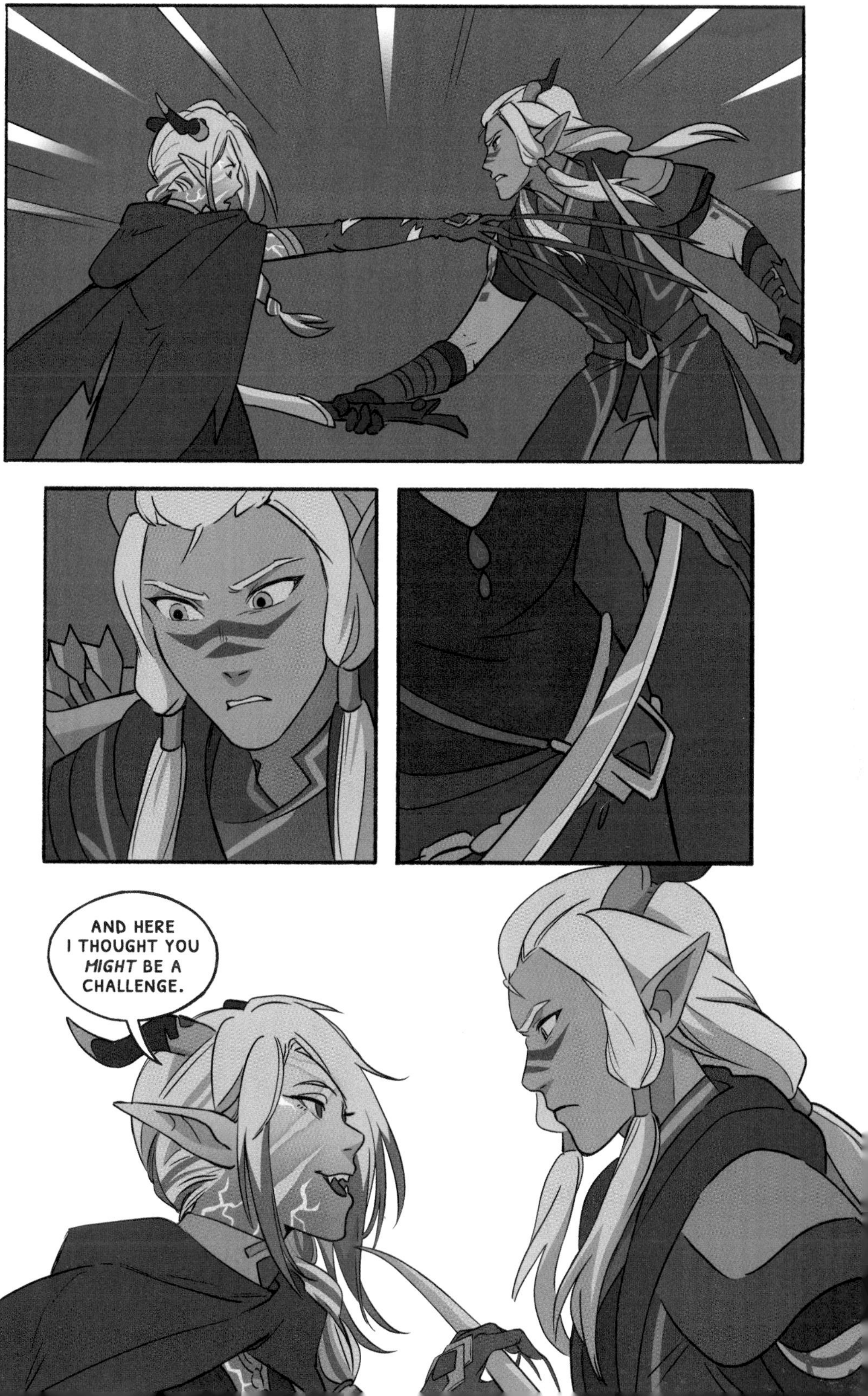
AND HERE I THOUGHT YOU *MIGHT* BE A CHALLENGE.

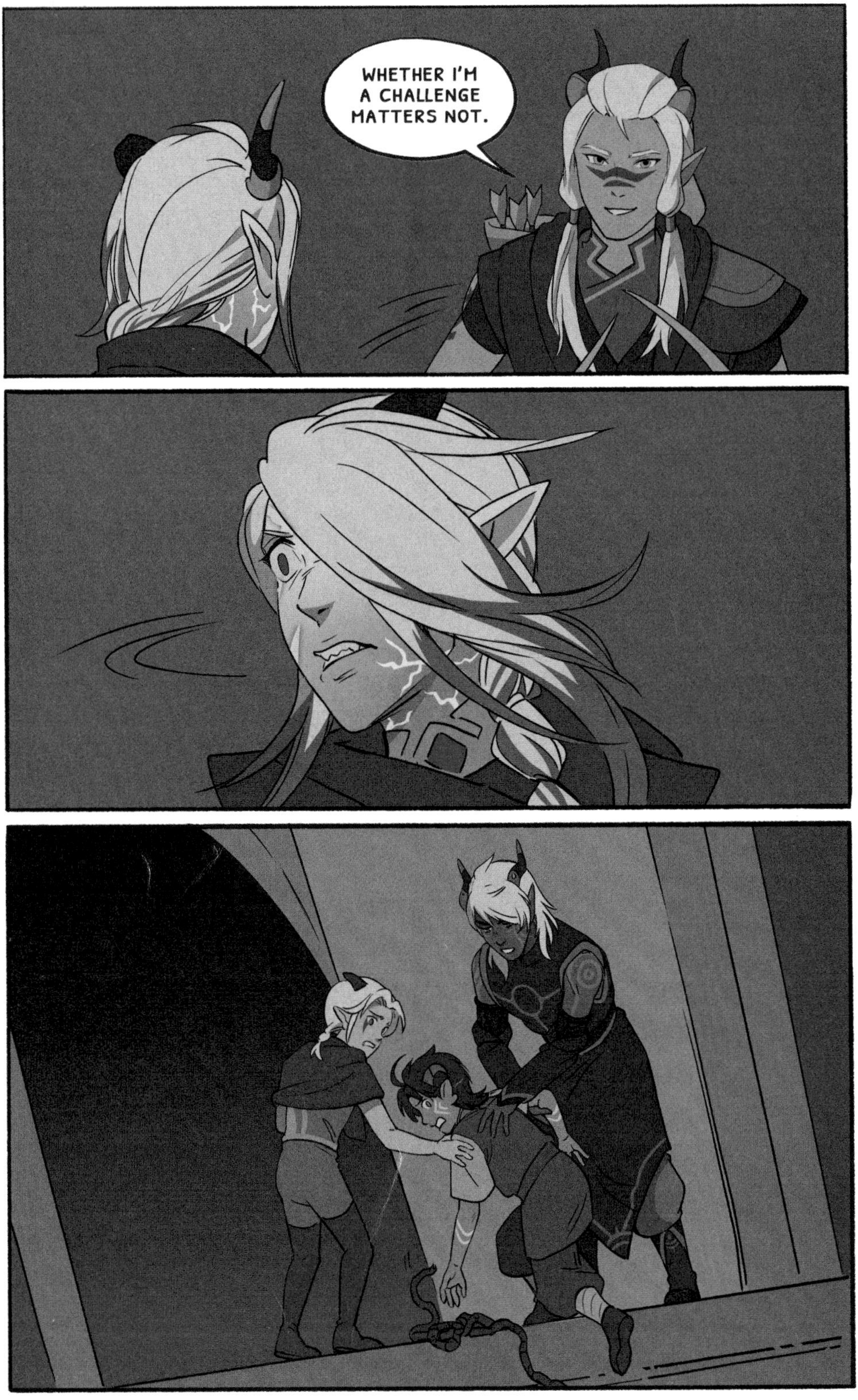
WHETHER I'M A CHALLENGE MATTERS NOT.

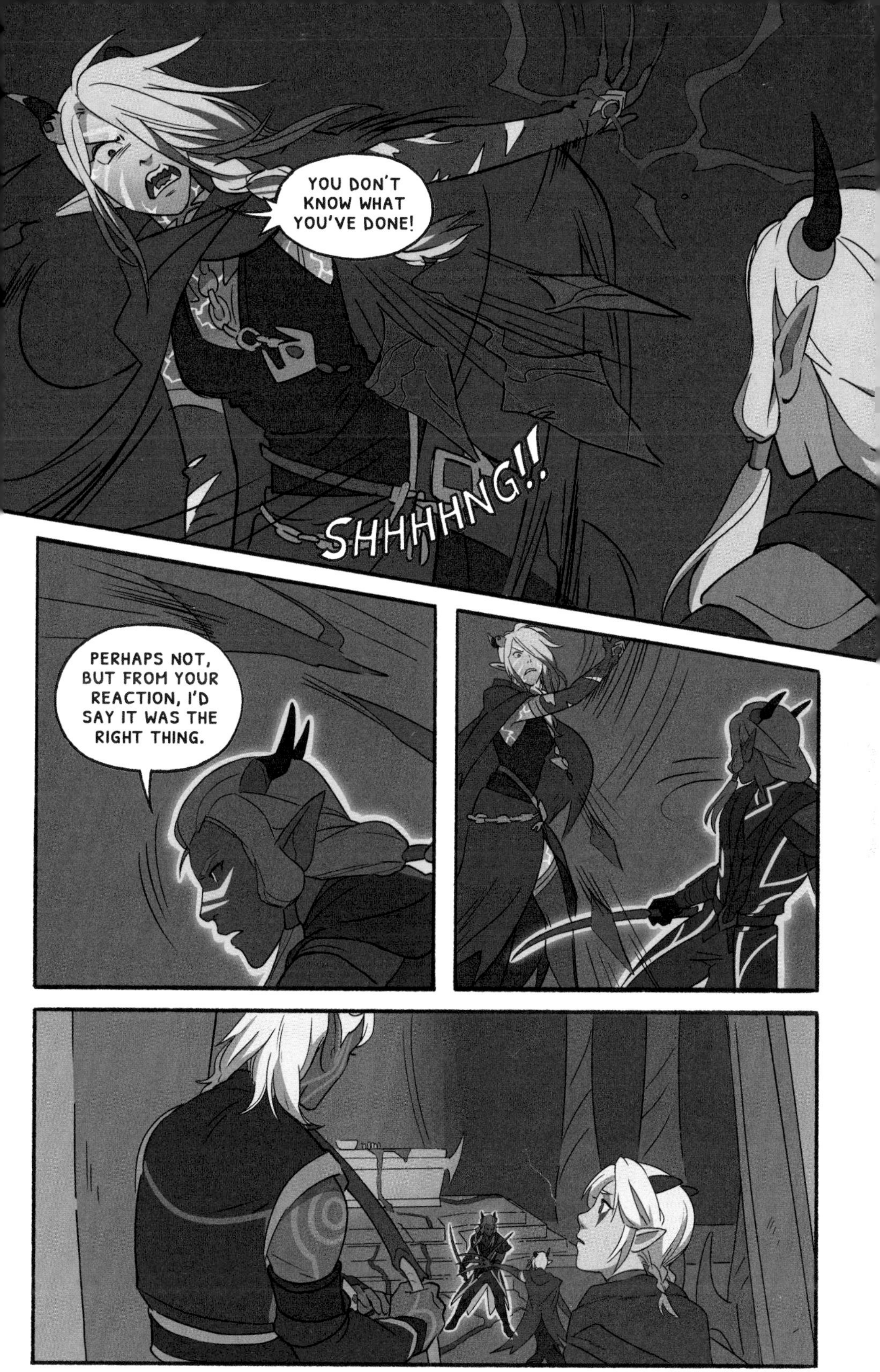
YOU DON'T KNOW WHAT YOU'VE DONE!
SHHHHNG!!
PERHAPS NOT, BUT FROM YOUR REACTION, I'D SAY IT WAS THE RIGHT THING.

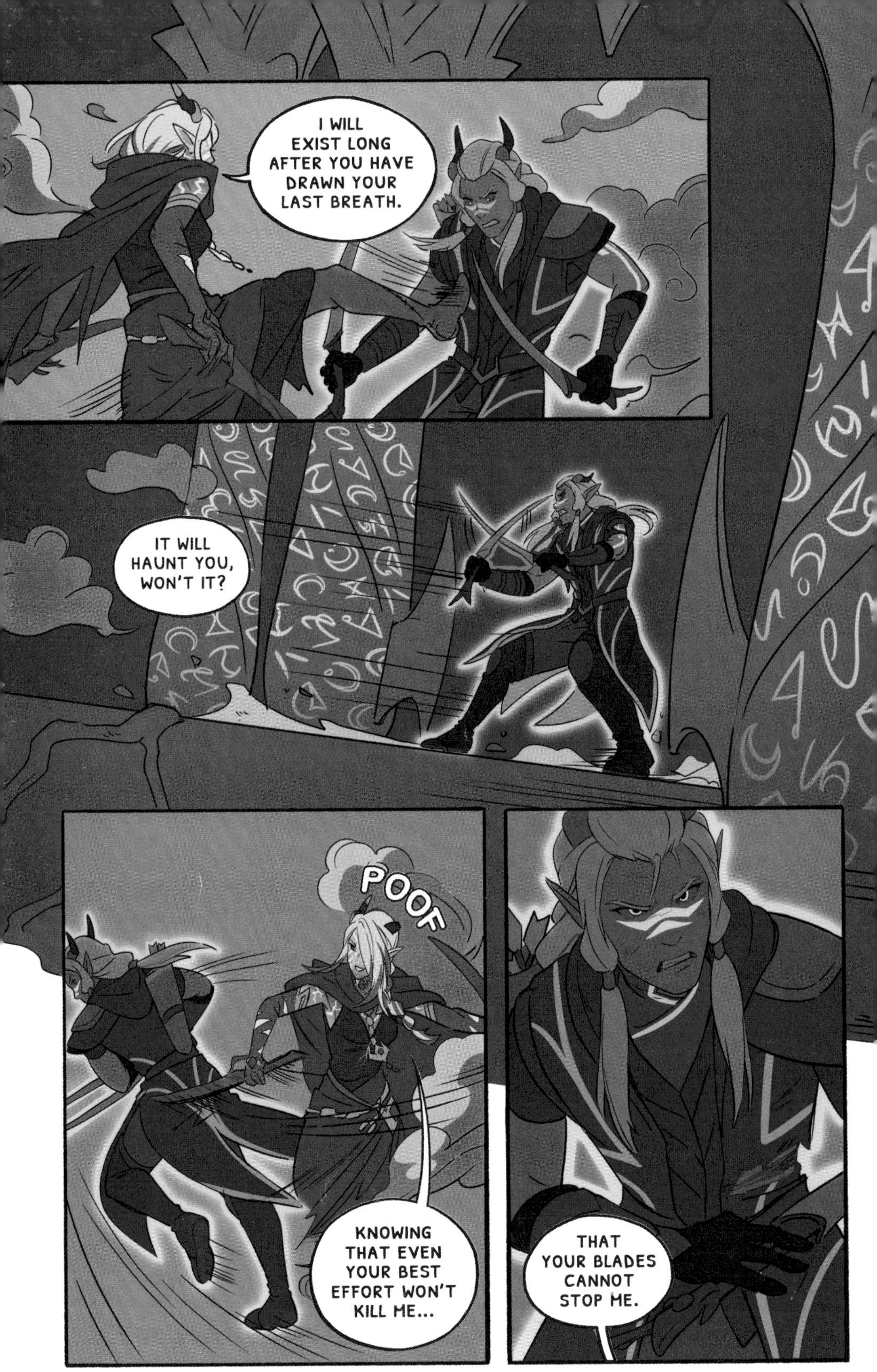
I WILL EXIST LONG AFTER YOU HAVE DRAWN YOUR LAST BREATH.
IT WILL HAUNT YOU, WON'T IT?
POOF
KNOWING THAT EVEN YOUR BEST EFFORT WON'T KILL ME...
THAT YOUR BLADES CANNOT STOP ME.

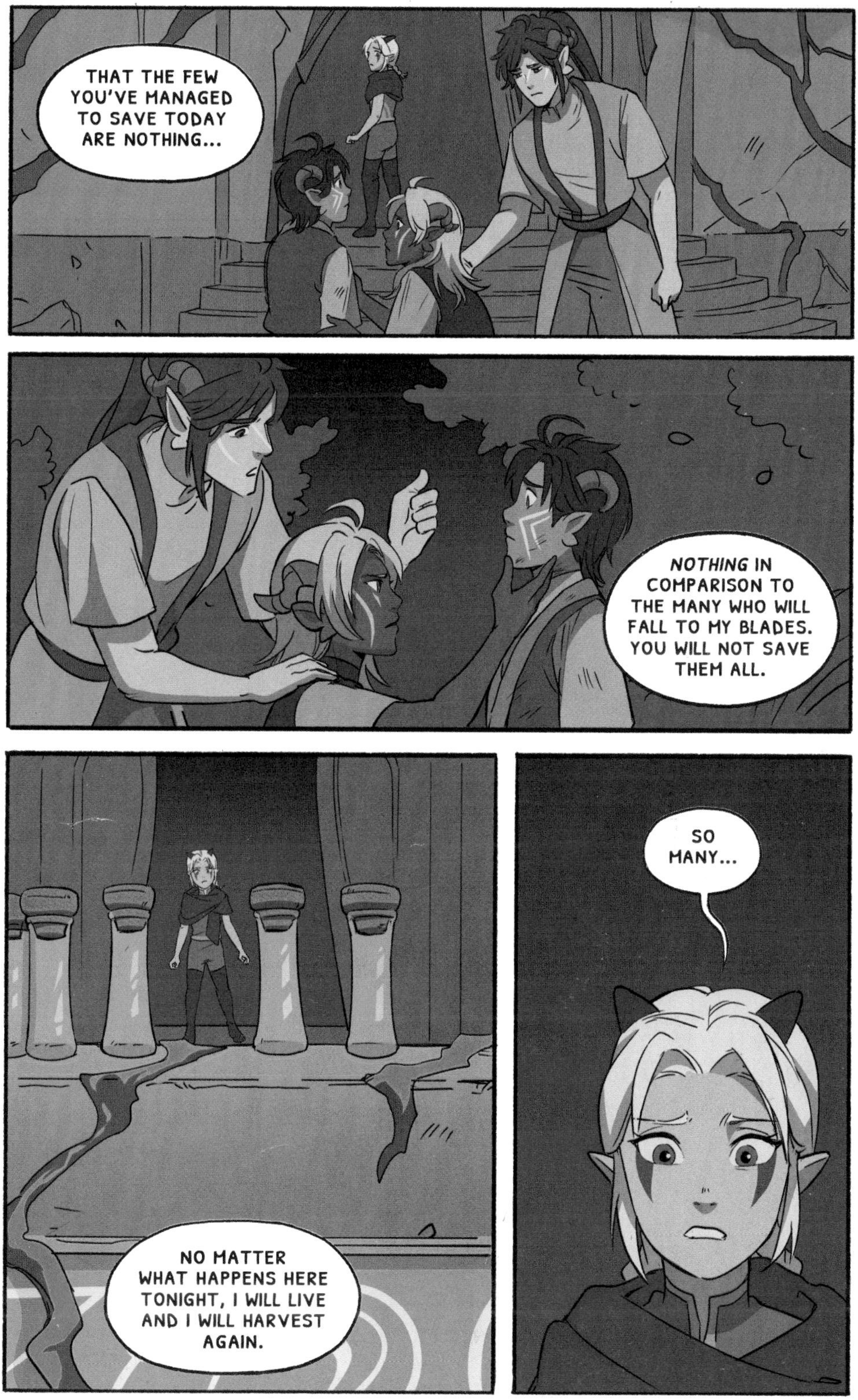
THAT THE FEW YOU'VE MANAGED TO SAVE TODAY ARE NOTHING...
NOTHING IN COMPARISON TO THE MANY WHO WILL FALL TO MY BLADES. YOU WILL NOT SAVE THEM ALL.
NO MATTER WHAT HAPPENS HERE TONIGHT, I WILL LIVE AND I WILL HARVEST AGAIN.
SO MANY...

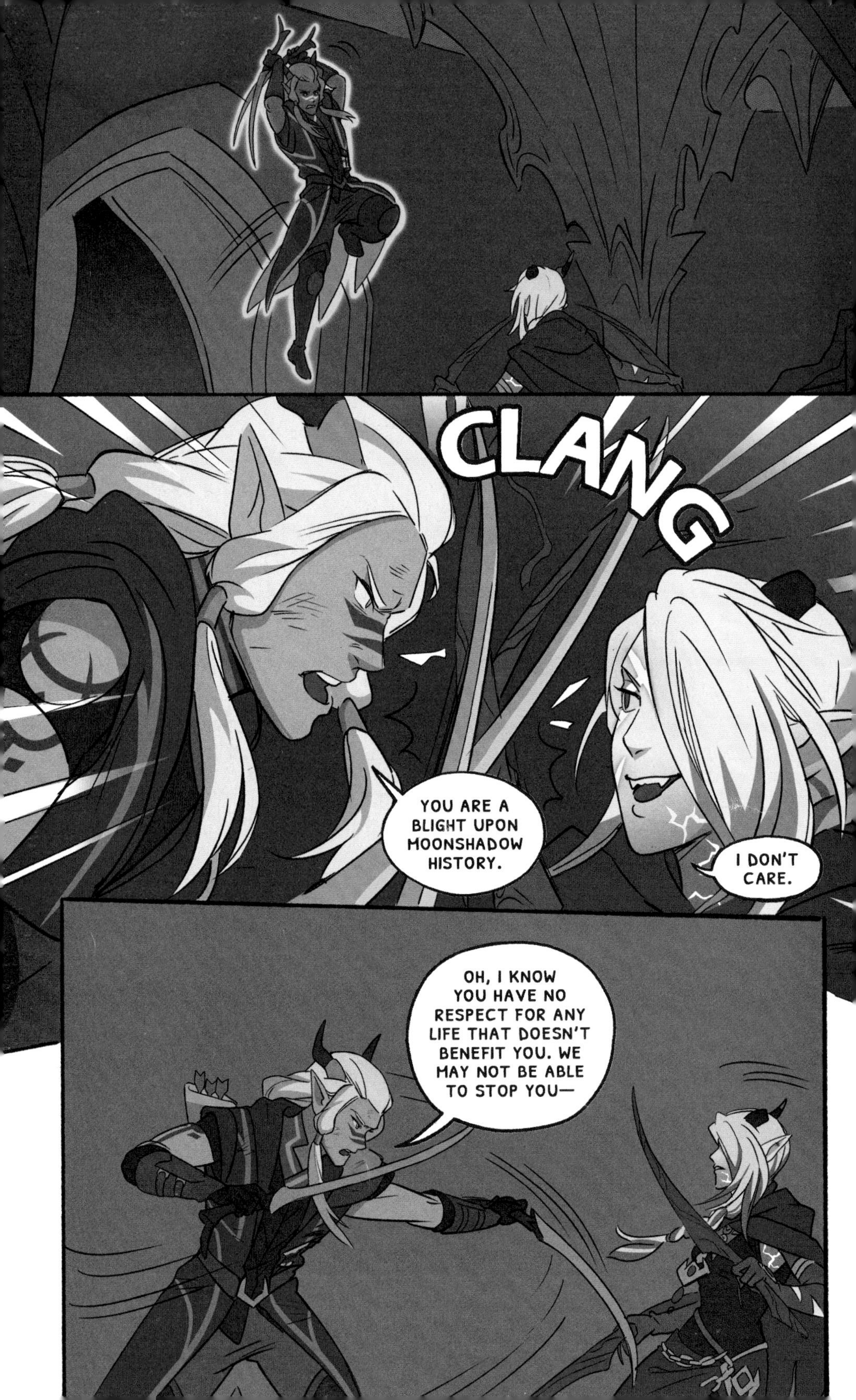
CLANG
YOU ARE A BLIGHT UPON MOONSHADOW HISTORY.
I DON'T CARE.
OH, I KNOW YOU HAVE NO RESPECT FOR ANY LIFE THAT DOESN'T BENEFIT YOU. WE MAY NOT BE ABLE TO STOP YOU—

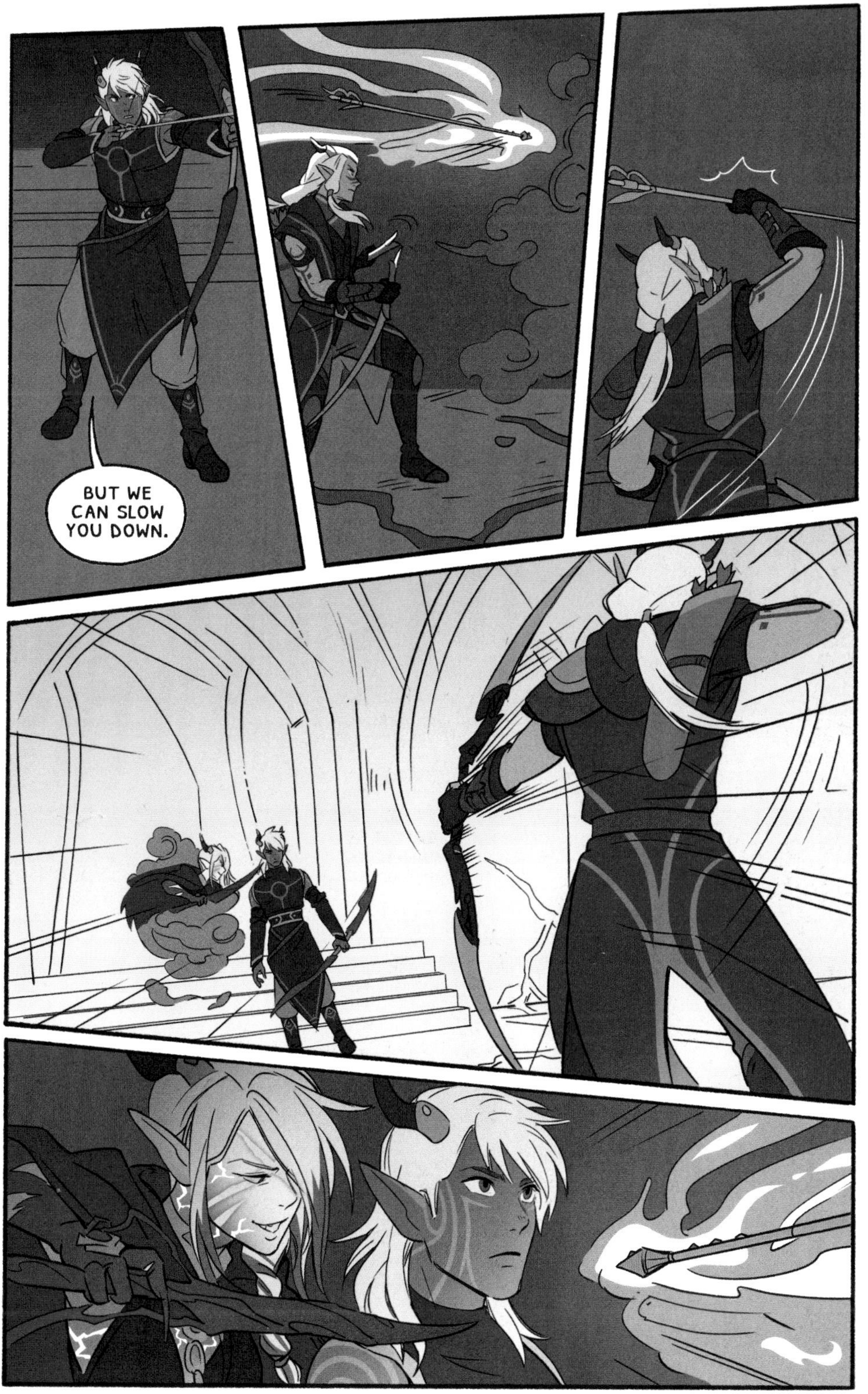
BUT WE CAN SLOW YOU DOWN.

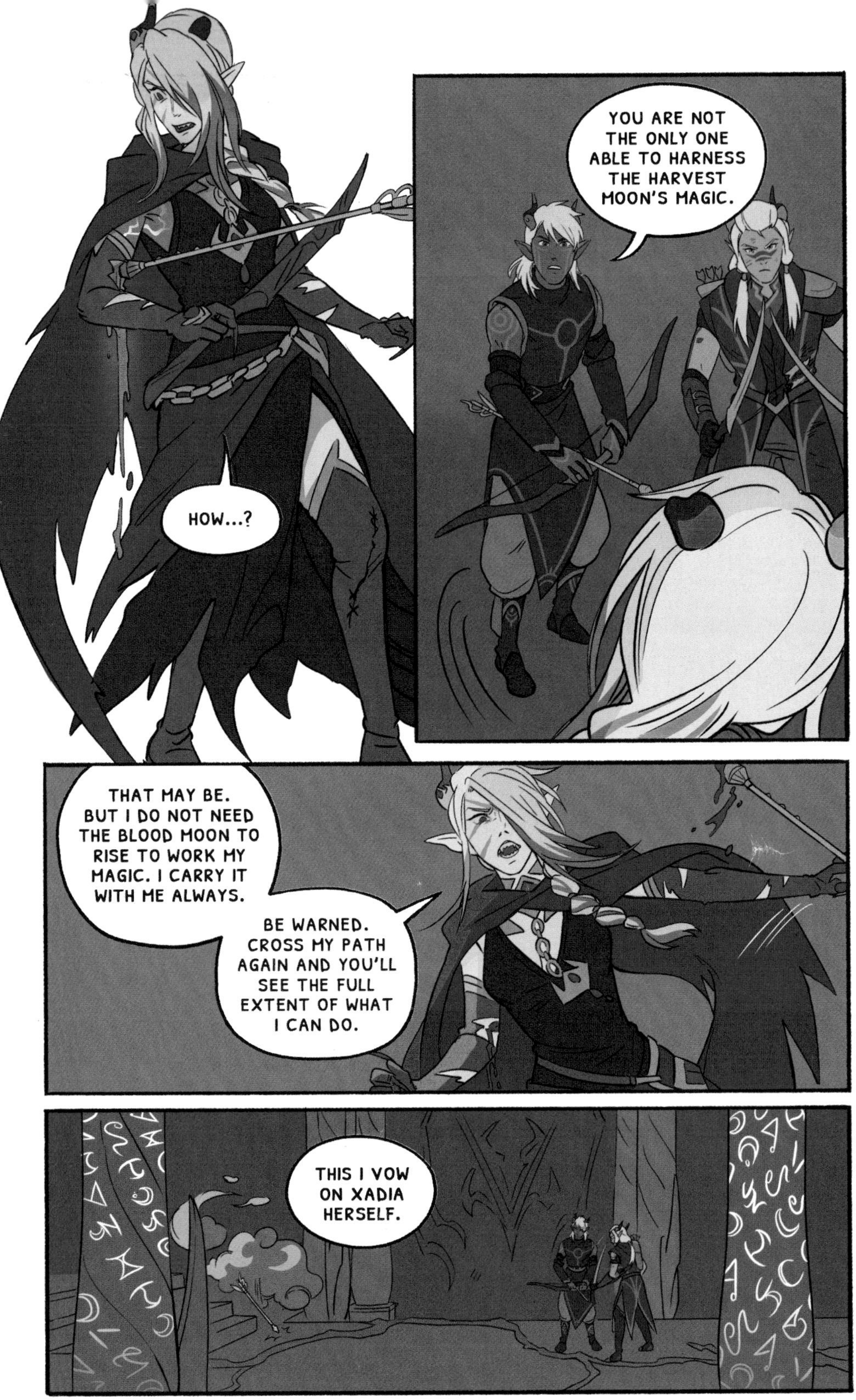
YOU ARE NOT THE ONLY ONE ABLE TO HARNESS THE HARVEST MOON'S MAGIC.
HOW...?
THAT MAY BE. BUT I DO NOT NEED THE BLOOD MOON TO RISE TO WORK MY MAGIC. I CARRY IT WITH ME ALWAYS.
BE WARNED. CROSS MY PATH AGAIN AND YOU'LL SEE THE FULL EXTENT OF WHAT I CAN DO.
THIS I VOW ON XADIA HERSELF.

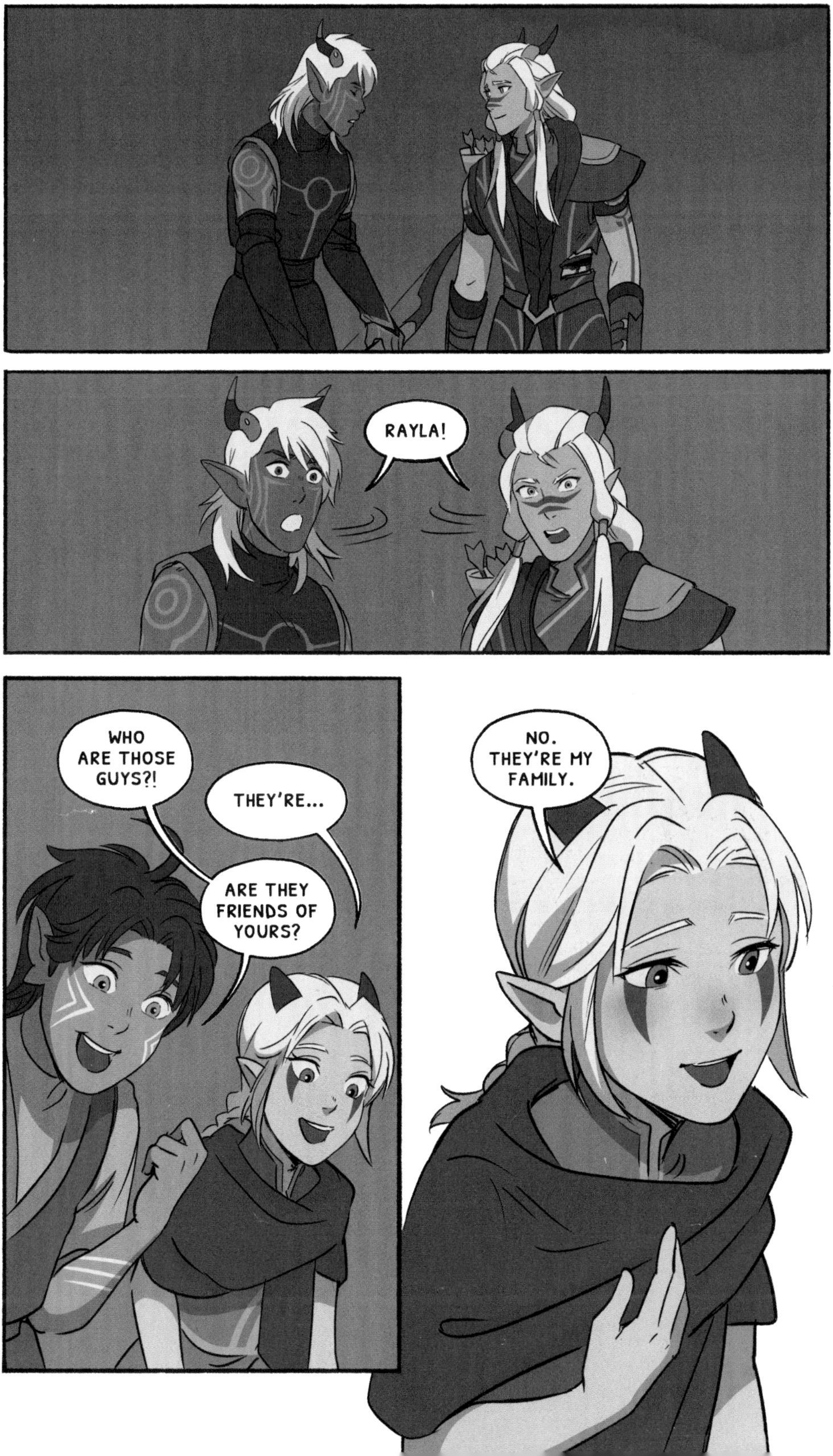
RAYLA!
WHO ARE THOSE GUYS?!
THEY'RE...
ARE THEY FRIENDS OF YOURS?
NO. THEY'RE MY FAMILY.

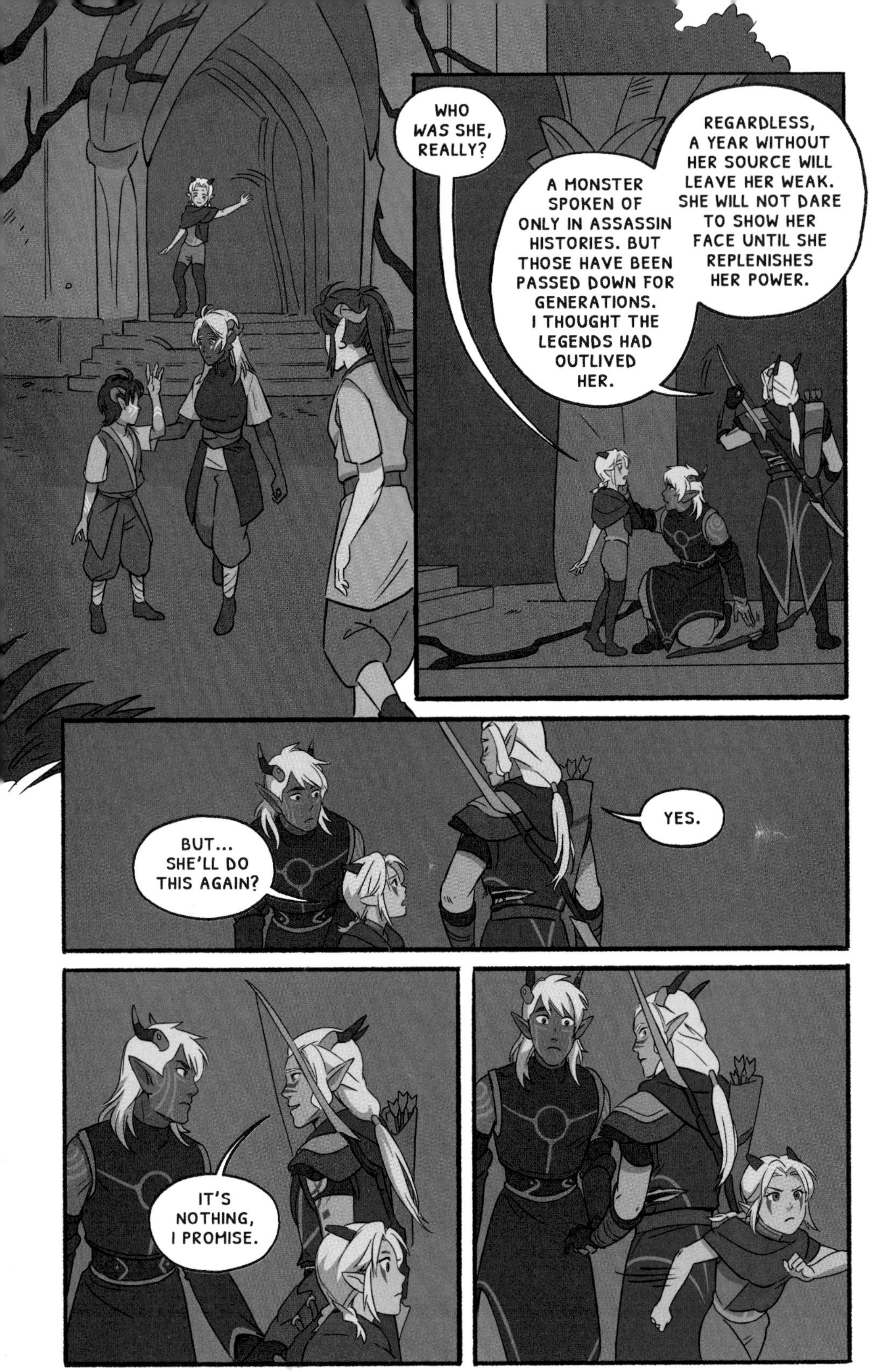
WHO WAS SHE, REALLY?
A MONSTER SPOKEN OF ONLY IN ASSASSIN HISTORIES. BUT THOSE HAVE BEEN PASSED DOWN FOR GENERATIONS. I THOUGHT THE LEGENDS HAD OUTLIVED HER.
REGARDLESS, A YEAR WITHOUT HER SOURCE WILL LEAVE HER WEAK. SHE WILL NOT DARE TO SHOW HER FACE UNTIL SHE REPLENISHES HER POWER.
BUT... SHE'LL DO THIS AGAIN?
YES.
IT'S NOTHING, I PROMISE.

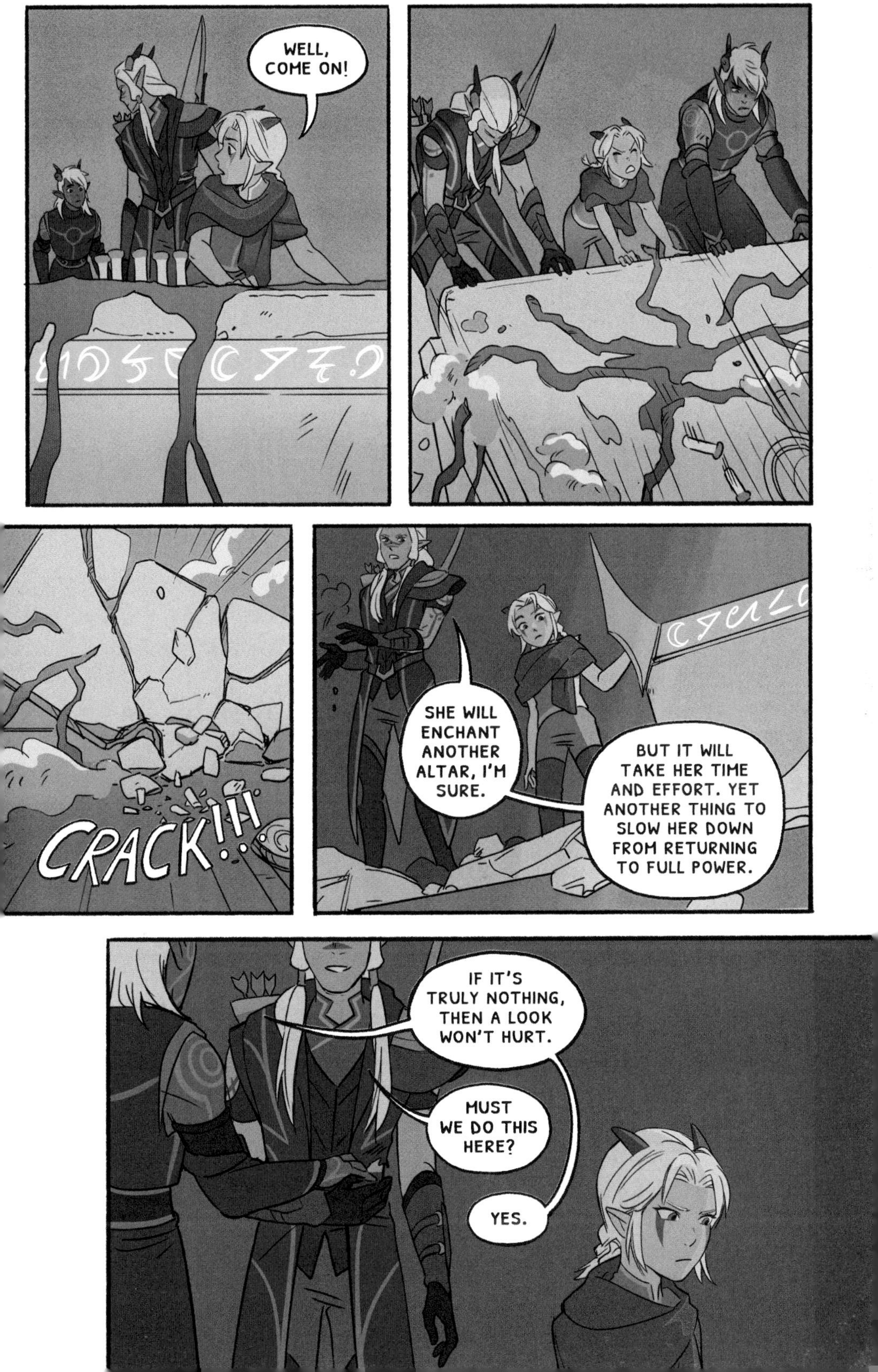
WELL, COME ON!
CRACK!!!
SHE WILL ENCHANT ANOTHER ALTAR, I'M SURE.
BUT IT WILL TAKE HER TIME AND EFFORT. YET ANOTHER THING TO SLOW HER DOWN FROM RETURNING TO FULL POWER.
IF IT'S TRULY NOTHING, THEN A LOOK WON'T HURT.
MUST WE DO THIS HERE?
YES.

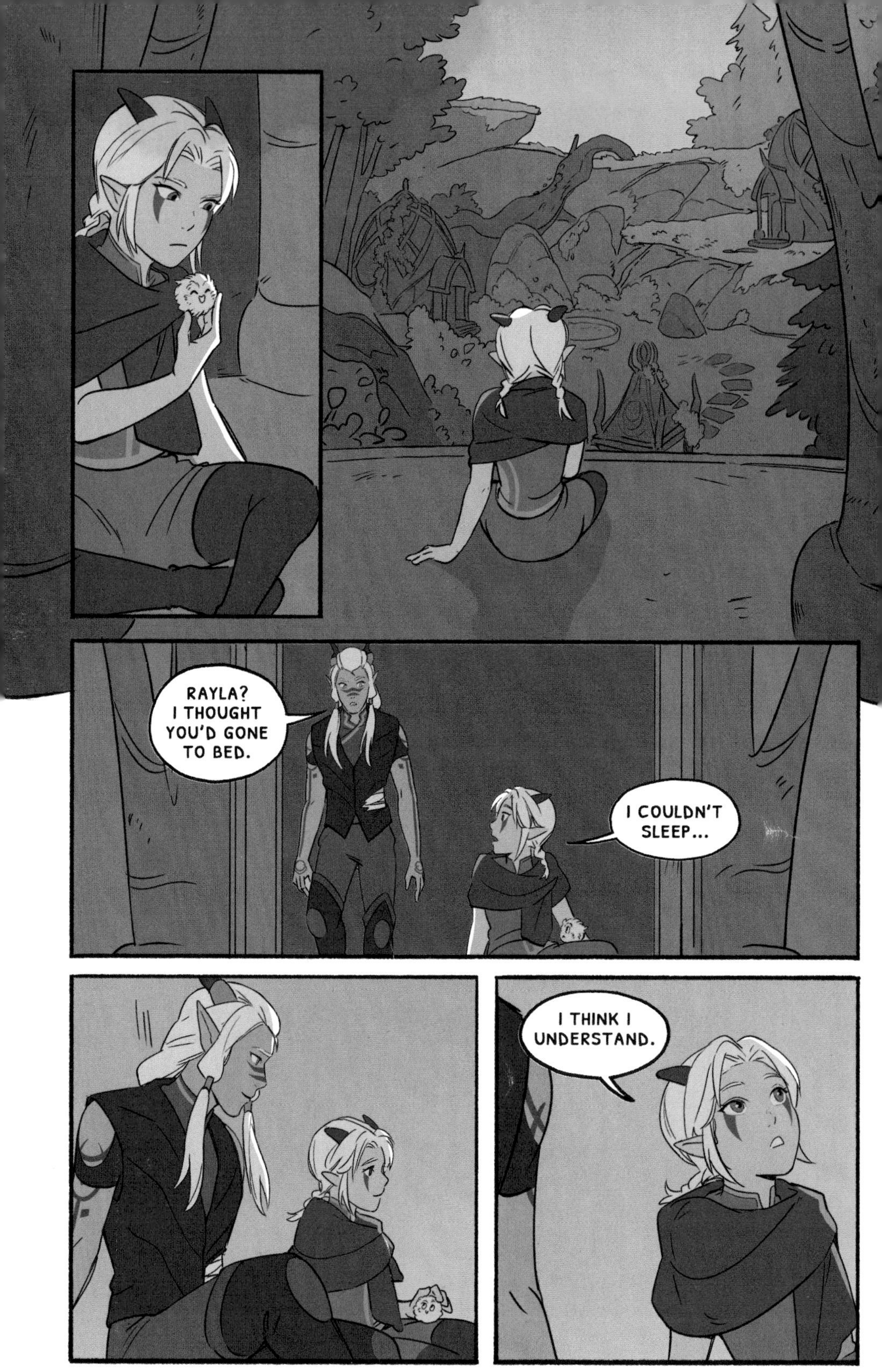
RAYLA? I THOUGHT YOU'D GONE TO BED.
I COULDN'T SLEEP...
I THINK I UNDERSTAND.

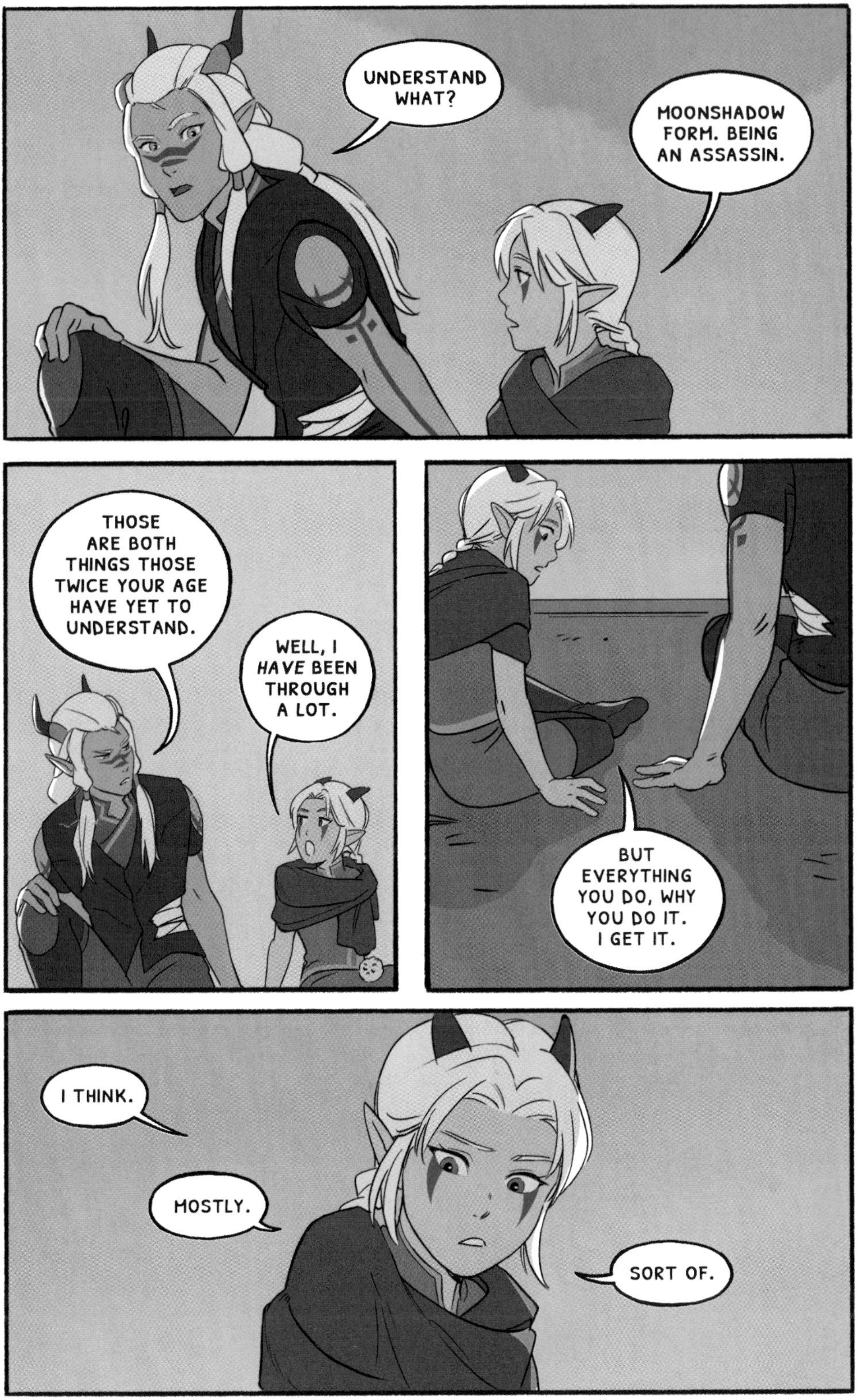
UNDERSTAND WHAT?
MOONSHADOW FORM. BEING AN ASSASSIN.
THOSE ARE BOTH THINGS THOSE TWICE YOUR AGE HAVE YET TO UNDERSTAND.
WELL, I *HAVE* BEEN THROUGH A LOT.
BUT EVERYTHING YOU DO, WHY YOU DO IT. I GET IT.
I THINK.
MOSTLY.
SORT OF.

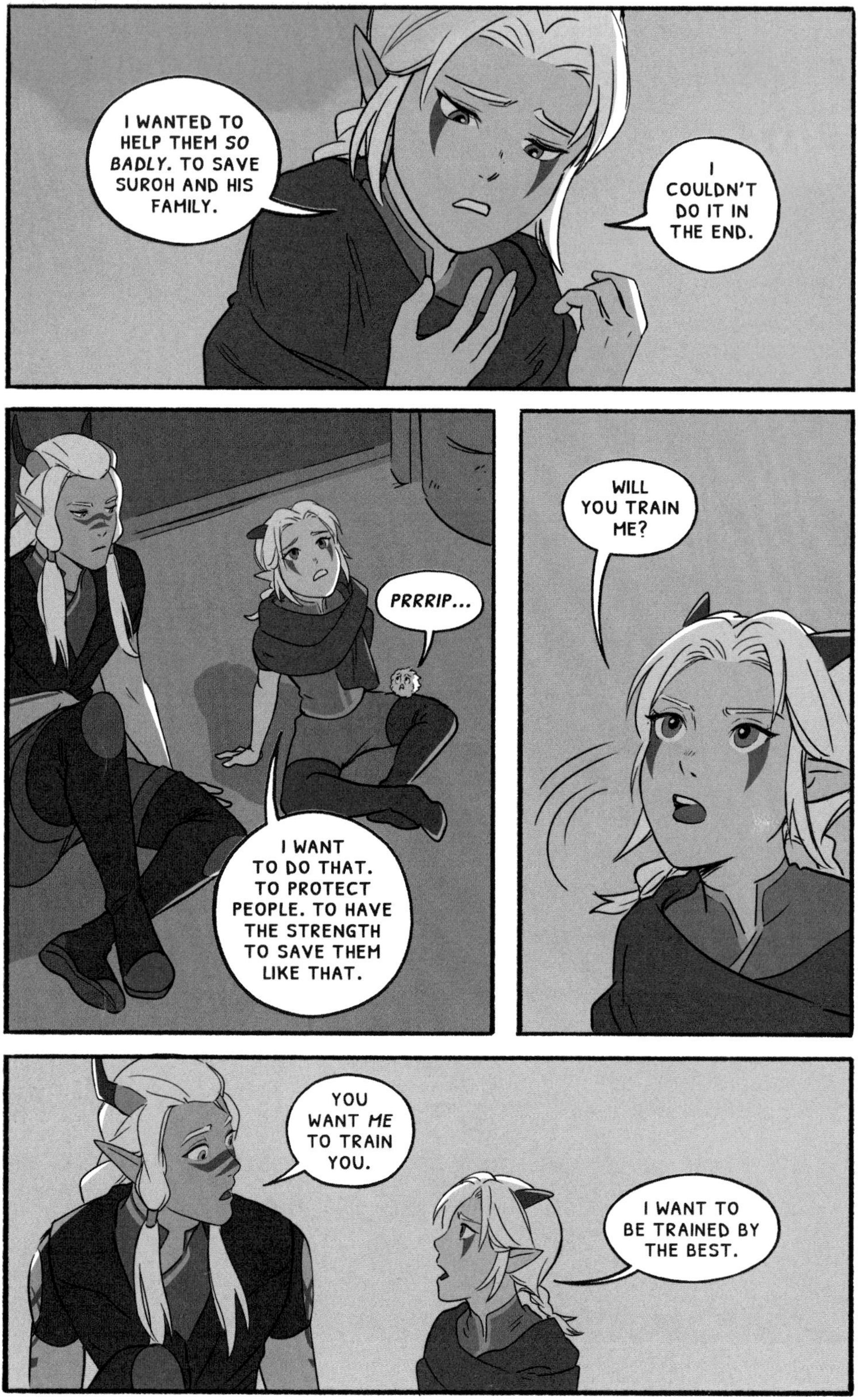
I WANTED TO HELP THEM *SO BADLY*. TO SAVE SUROH AND HIS FAMILY.
I COULDN'T DO IT IN THE END.
PRRRIP...
I WANT TO DO THAT. TO PROTECT PEOPLE. TO HAVE THE STRENGTH TO SAVE THEM LIKE THAT.
WILL YOU TRAIN ME?
YOU WANT *ME* TO TRAIN YOU.
I WANT TO BE TRAINED BY THE BEST.

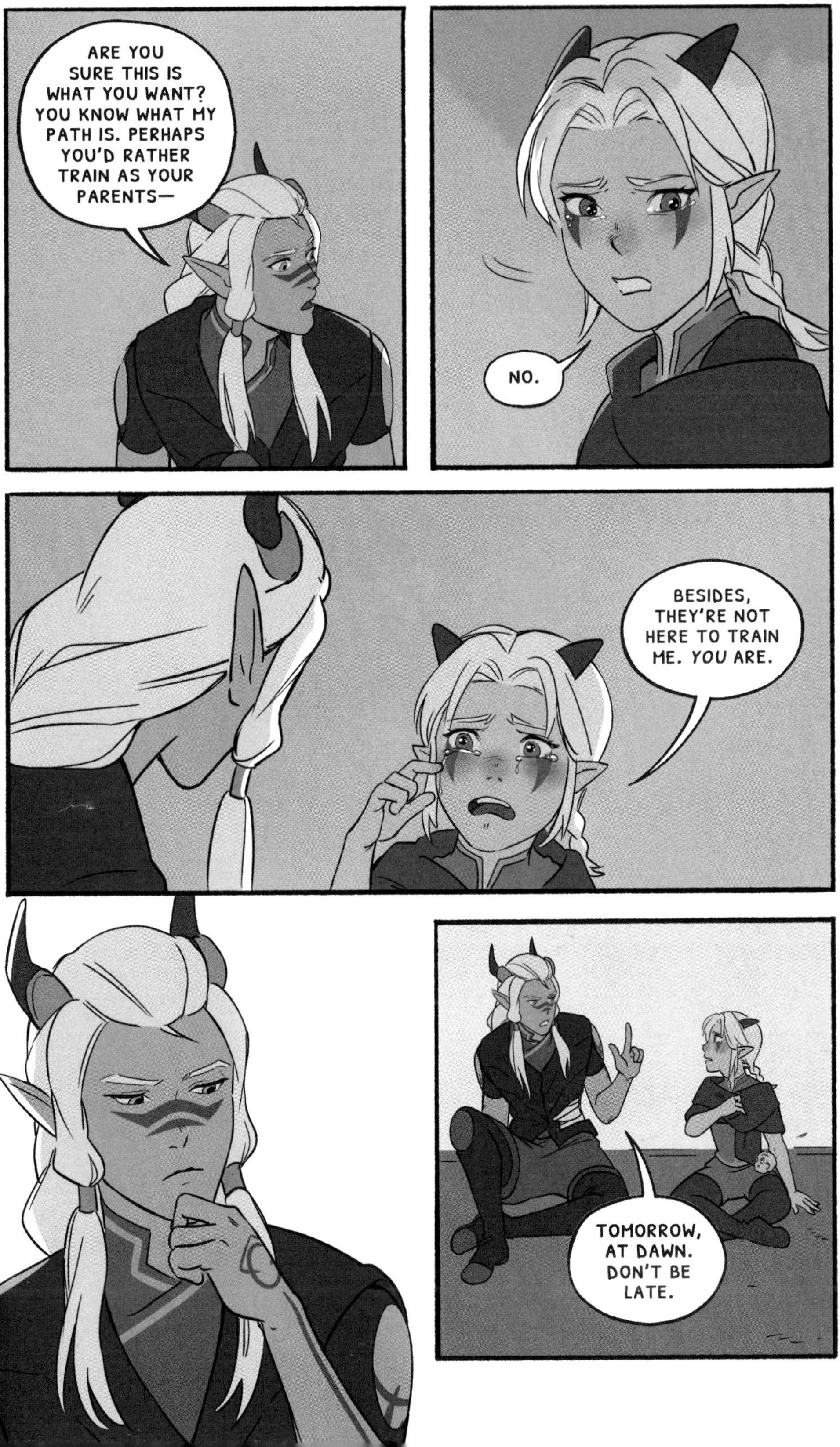
ARE YOU SURE THIS IS WHAT YOU WANT? YOU KNOW WHAT MY PATH IS. PERHAPS YOU'D RATHER TRAIN AS YOUR PARENTS—
NO.
BESIDES, THEY'RE NOT HERE TO TRAIN ME. *YOU* ARE.
TOMORROW, AT DAWN. DON'T BE LATE.

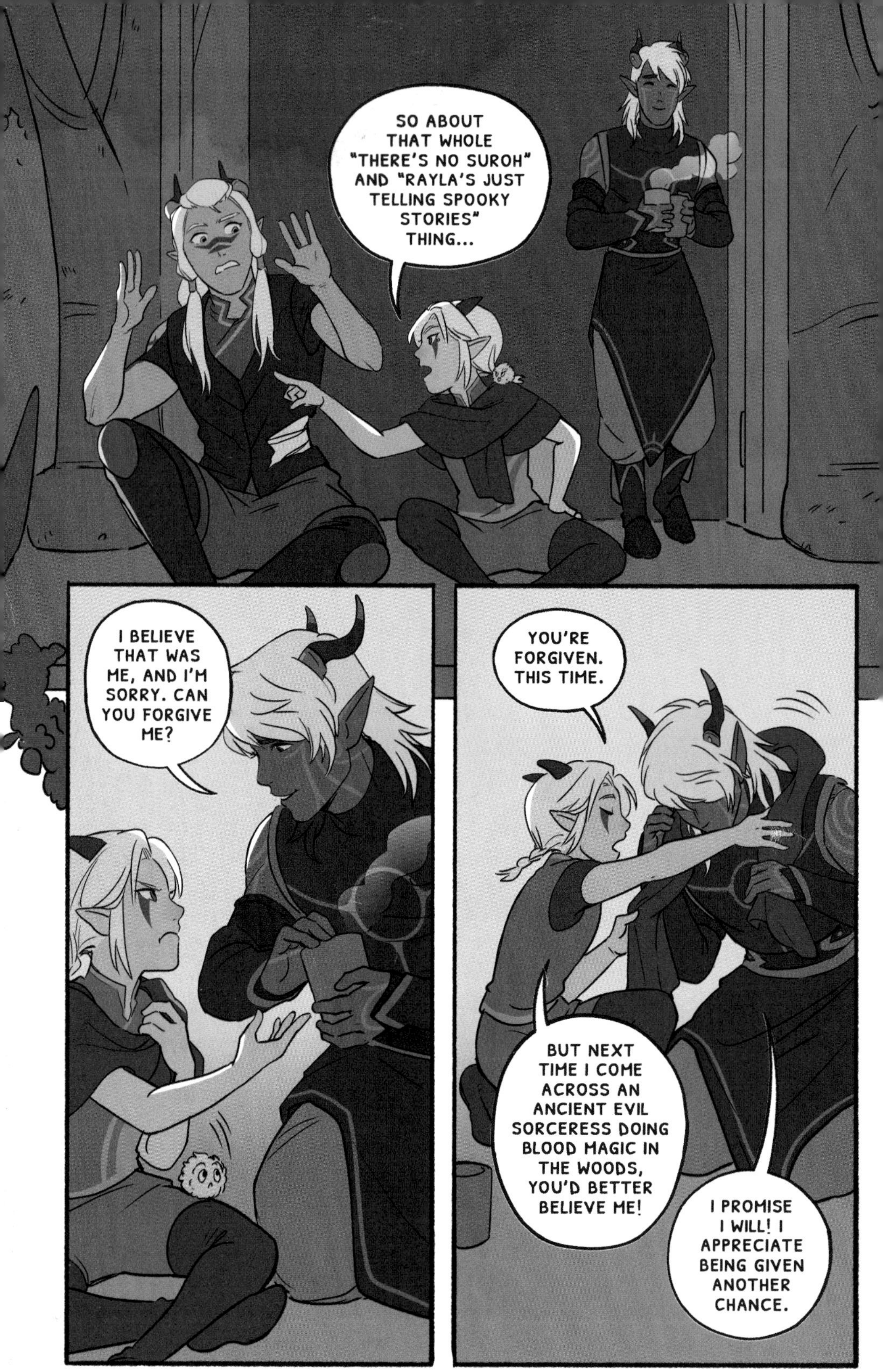
SO ABOUT THAT WHOLE "THERE'S NO SUROH" AND "RAYLA'S JUST TELLING SPOOKY STORIES" THING...
I BELIEVE THAT WAS ME, AND I'M SORRY. CAN YOU FORGIVE ME?
YOU'RE FORGIVEN. THIS TIME.
BUT NEXT TIME I COME ACROSS AN ANCIENT EVIL SORCERESS DOING BLOOD MAGIC IN THE WOODS, YOU'D BETTER BELIEVE ME!
I PROMISE I WILL! I APPRECIATE BEING GIVEN ANOTHER CHANCE.

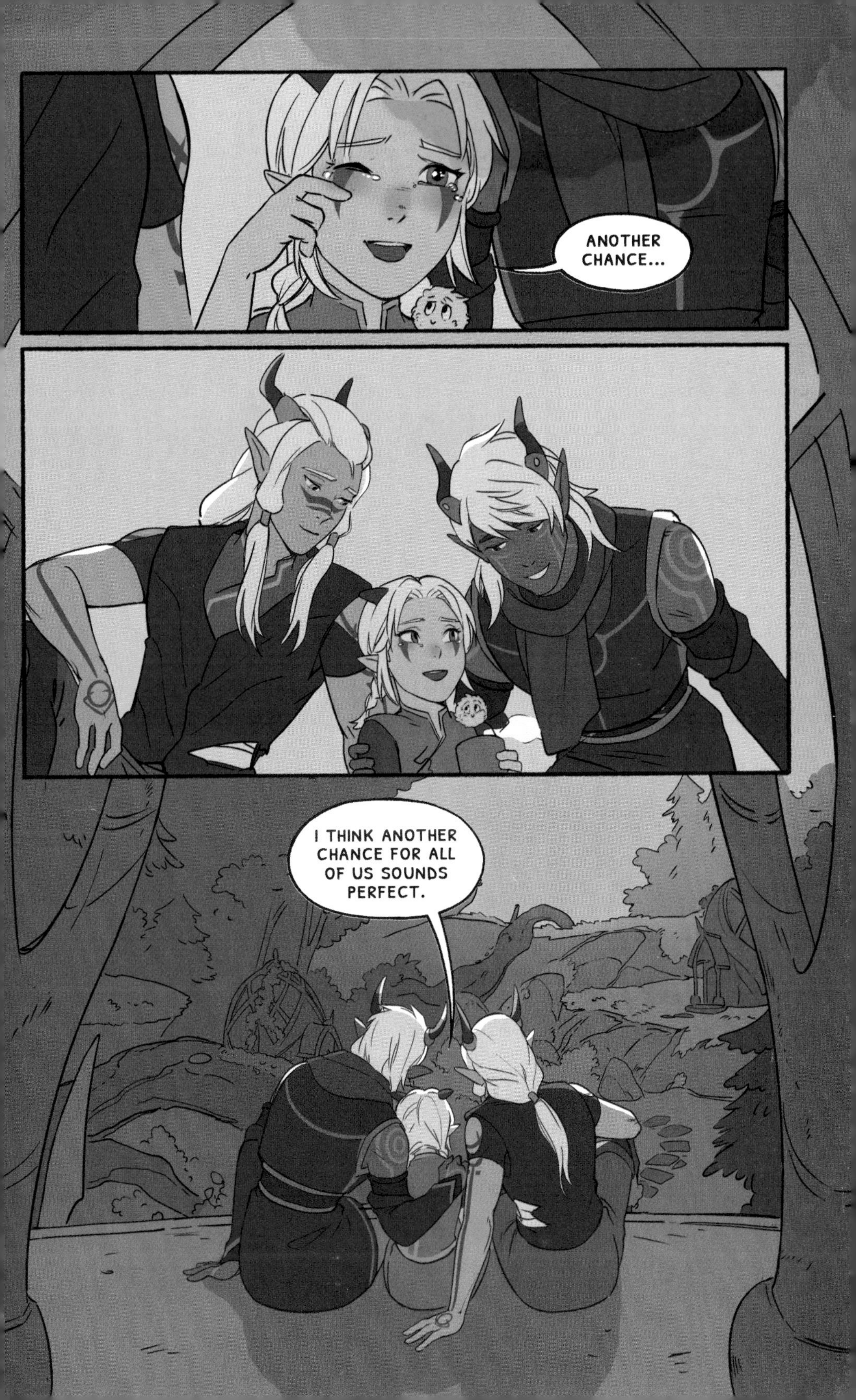
ANOTHER CHANCE...
I THINK ANOTHER CHANCE FOR ALL OF US SOUNDS PERFECT.

AARON EHASZ and **JUSTIN RICHMOND** are the creators of *The Dragon Prince* and co-founders of Wonderstorm, a media startup in Los Angeles, California. *The Dragon Prince* began as an original animated series on Netflix and is now being developed into a world-class video game by the same creative team.

Previously, Aaron was the head writer of *Avatar: The Last Airbender*, and Justin was game director on the *Uncharted* franchise.

NICOLE ANDELFINGER was crafting stories as far back as when coloring in the squiggles on your composition book was considered cool. Since then, she's only continued to dwell in the realms of magic, monsters, and myth. When not changing her hair color or writing comics for some of her favorite characters, she works a day job best described as "emails." She lives with her absolutely, most decidedly perfect cat in Los Angeles.

FELIA HANAKATA is an illustrator and comic artist based in Indonesia, where there is too much sun and rain. She believes storytelling breathes life and colors into the world. When she is not drawing, she reads, drinks lots of coffee, plays video games, and looks for inspiration in nature and her surroundings. You can find her online at feliahanakata.com.